ANIMAL STORIES

BY

PETER AND MARIA HOEY

Animal Stories © 2021 Peter Hoey and Maria Hoey

Editor-in-Chief: Chris Staros.

Published by Top Shelf Productions, an imprint of IDW Publishing, a division of Idea and Design Works, LLC. Offices: Top Shelf Productions, c/o Idea & Design Works, LLC, 2765 Truxtun Road, San Diego, CA 92106. Top Shelf Productions®, the Top Shelf logo, Idea and Design Works®, and the IDW logo are registered trademarks of Idea and Design Works, LLC. All Rights Reserved. With the exception of small excerpts of artwork used for review purposes, none of the contents of this publication may be reprinted without the permission of IDW Publishing. IDW Publishing does not read or accept unsolicited submissions of ideas, stories, or artwork.

Visit our online catalog at www.topshelfcomix.com.

ISBN 978-1-60309-502-0

Printed in Korea

25 24 23 22 21   1 2 3 4 5

ANIMAL STORIES

This book is dedicated to George, Leo, Moxie, Flynn, Nika, Laddie, Tuggo, Birdy, Devon, Zoey and Nico.

Always a part of the pack. Never forgotten.

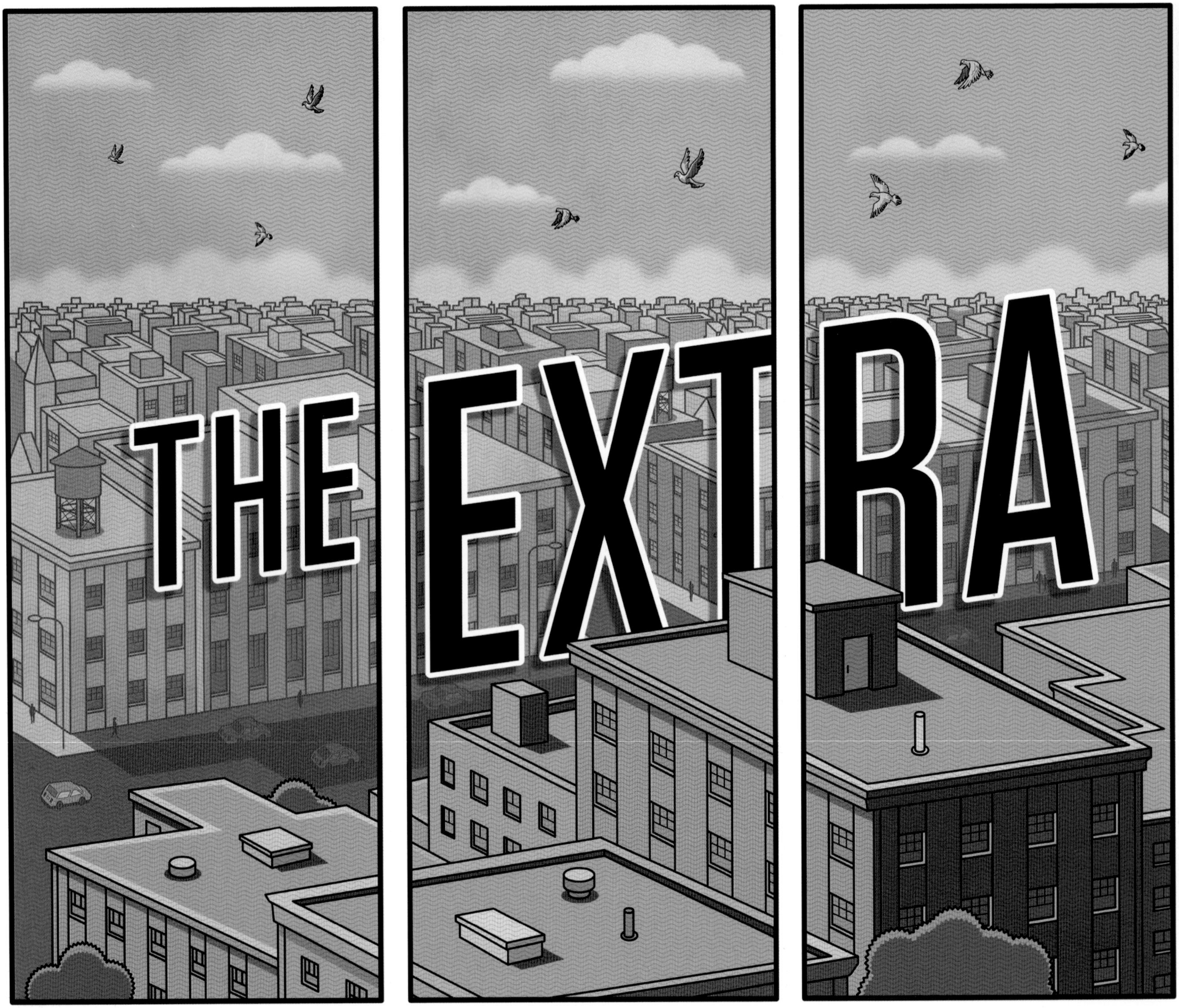
THE EXTRA

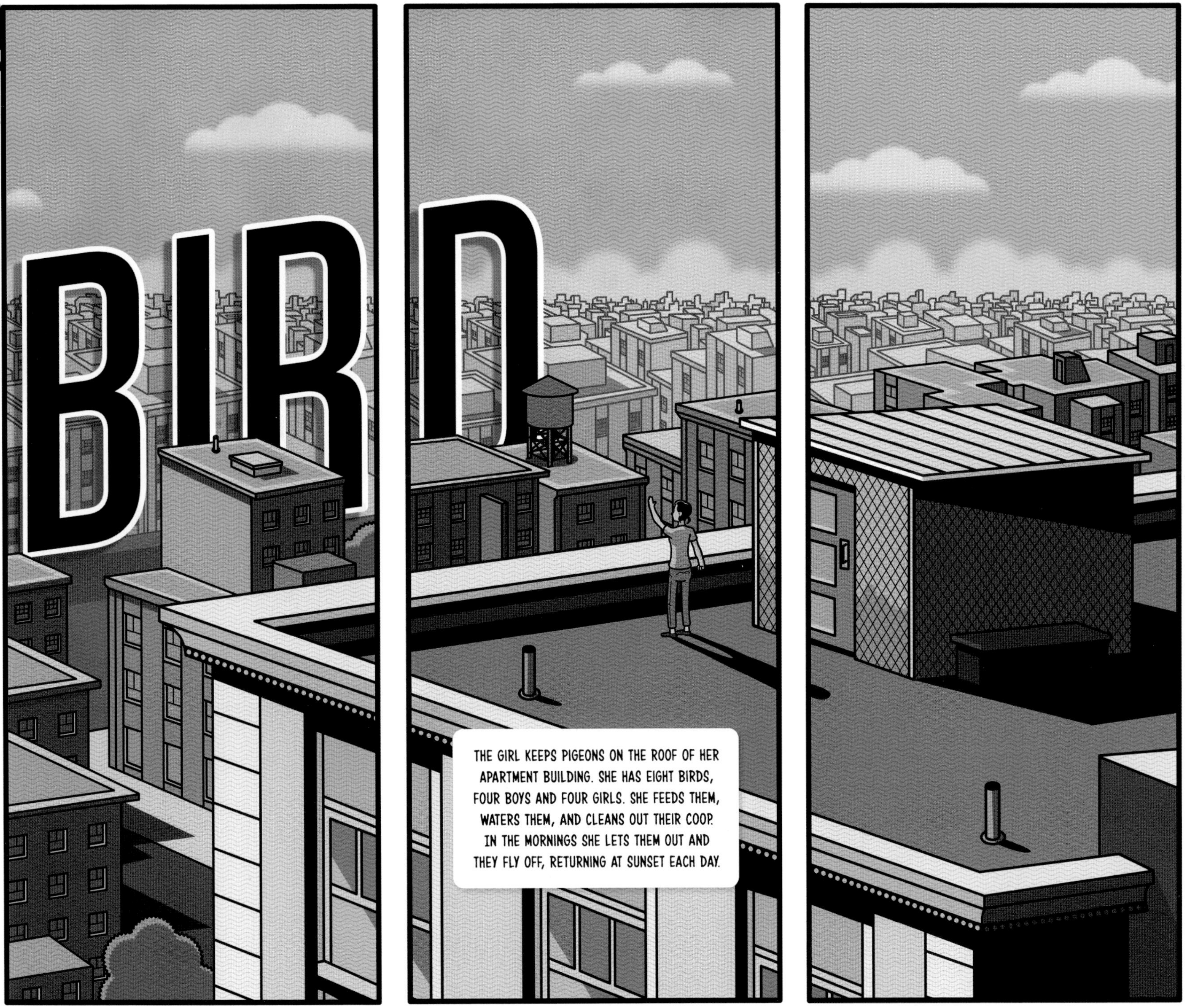
BIRD
THE GIRL KEEPS PIGEONS ON THE ROOF OF HER APARTMENT BUILDING. SHE HAS EIGHT BIRDS, FOUR BOYS AND FOUR GIRLS. SHE FEEDS THEM, WATERS THEM, AND CLEANS OUT THEIR COOP. IN THE MORNINGS SHE LETS THEM OUT AND THEY FLY OFF, RETURNING AT SUNSET EACH DAY.

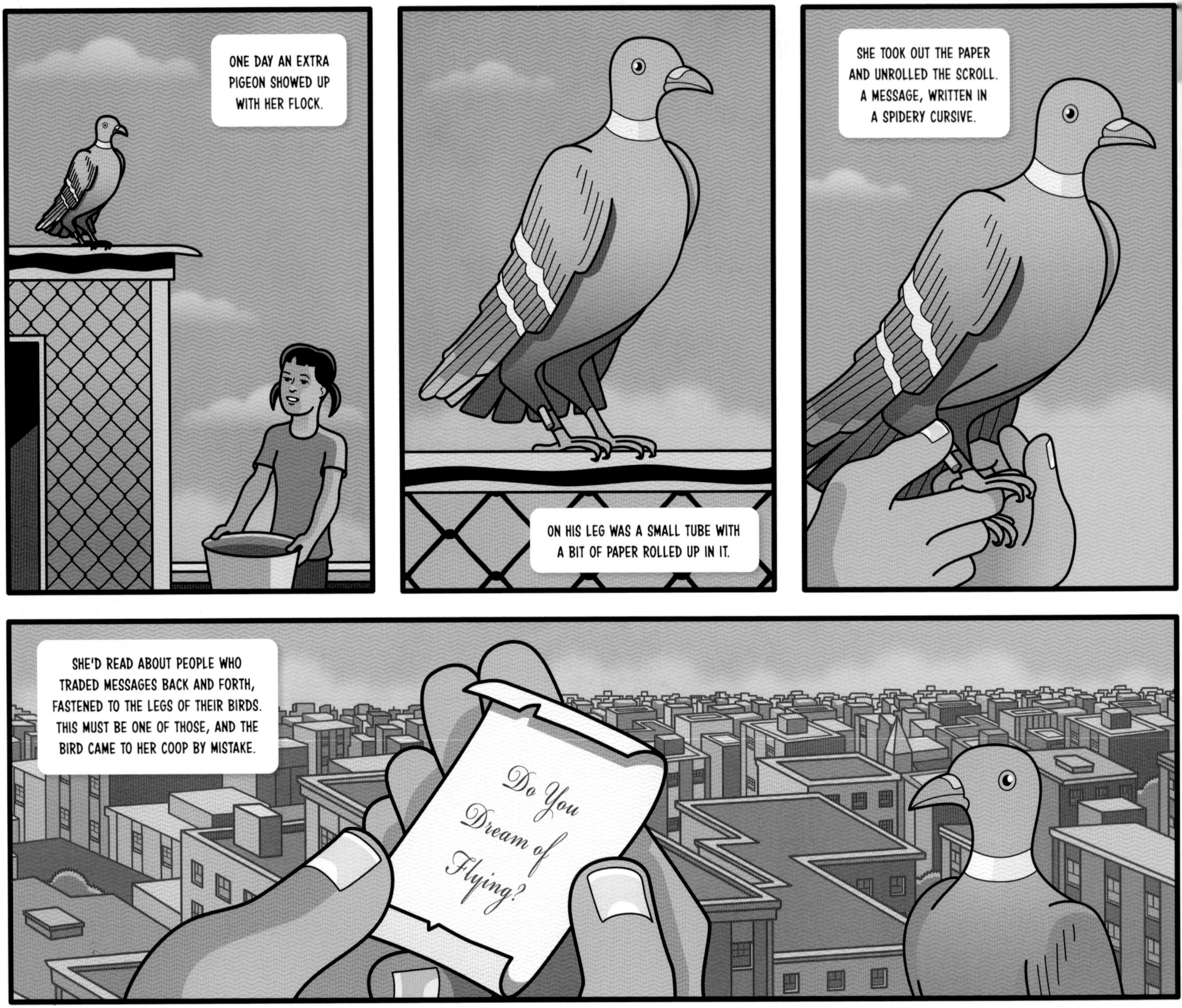
ONE DAY AN EXTRA PIGEON SHOWED UP WITH HER FLOCK.
ON HIS LEG WAS A SMALL TUBE WITH A BIT OF PAPER ROLLED UP IN IT.
SHE TOOK OUT THE PAPER AND UNROLLED THE SCROLL. A MESSAGE, WRITTEN IN A SPIDERY CURSIVE.
SHE'D READ ABOUT PEOPLE WHO TRADED MESSAGES BACK AND FORTH, FASTENED TO THE LEGS OF THEIR BIRDS. THIS MUST BE ONE OF THOSE, AND THE BIRD CAME TO HER COOP BY MISTAKE.
Do You Dream of Flying?

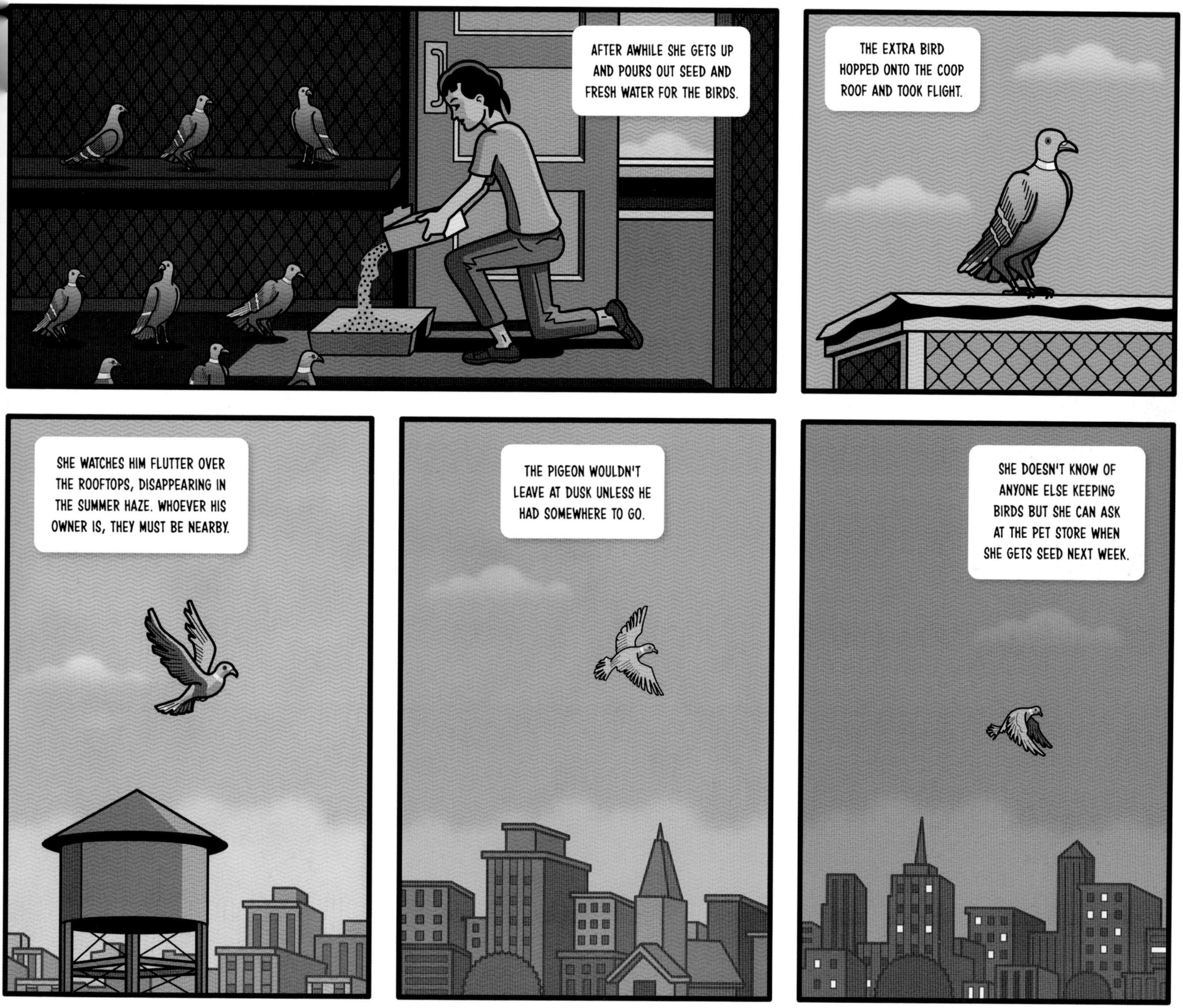
AFTER AWHILE SHE GETS UP AND POURS OUT SEED AND FRESH WATER FOR THE BIRDS.
THE EXTRA BIRD HOPPED ONTO THE COOP ROOF AND TOOK FLIGHT.
SHE WATCHES HIM FLUTTER OVER THE ROOFTOPS, DISAPPEARING IN THE SUMMER HAZE. WHOEVER HIS OWNER IS, THEY MUST BE NEARBY.
THE PIGEON WOULDN'T LEAVE AT DUSK UNLESS HE HAD SOMEWHERE TO GO.
SHE DOESN'T KNOW OF ANYONE ELSE KEEPING BIRDS BUT SHE CAN ASK AT THE PET STORE WHEN SHE GETS SEED NEXT WEEK.

AFTER PUTTING THE BIRDS IN FOR THE NIGHT SHE TOOK OUT THE PAPER AND LOOKED AT IT.

THE WORDS GLEAMING IN LIGHT PENCIL MARKS ACROSS THE PAPER.

WITH A START SHE REALIZED SHE'D FORGOTTEN TO PUT THE MESSAGE BACK ONTO THE PIGEON'S LEG BEFORE HE FLEW OFF.

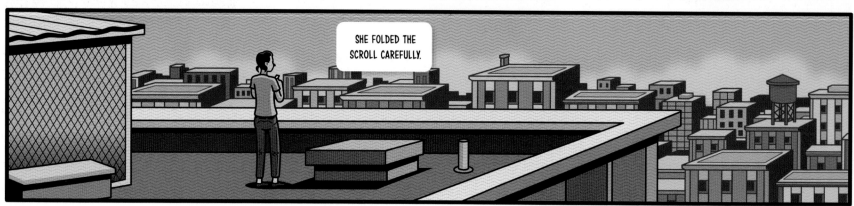

SHE FOLDED THE SCROLL CAREFULLY.

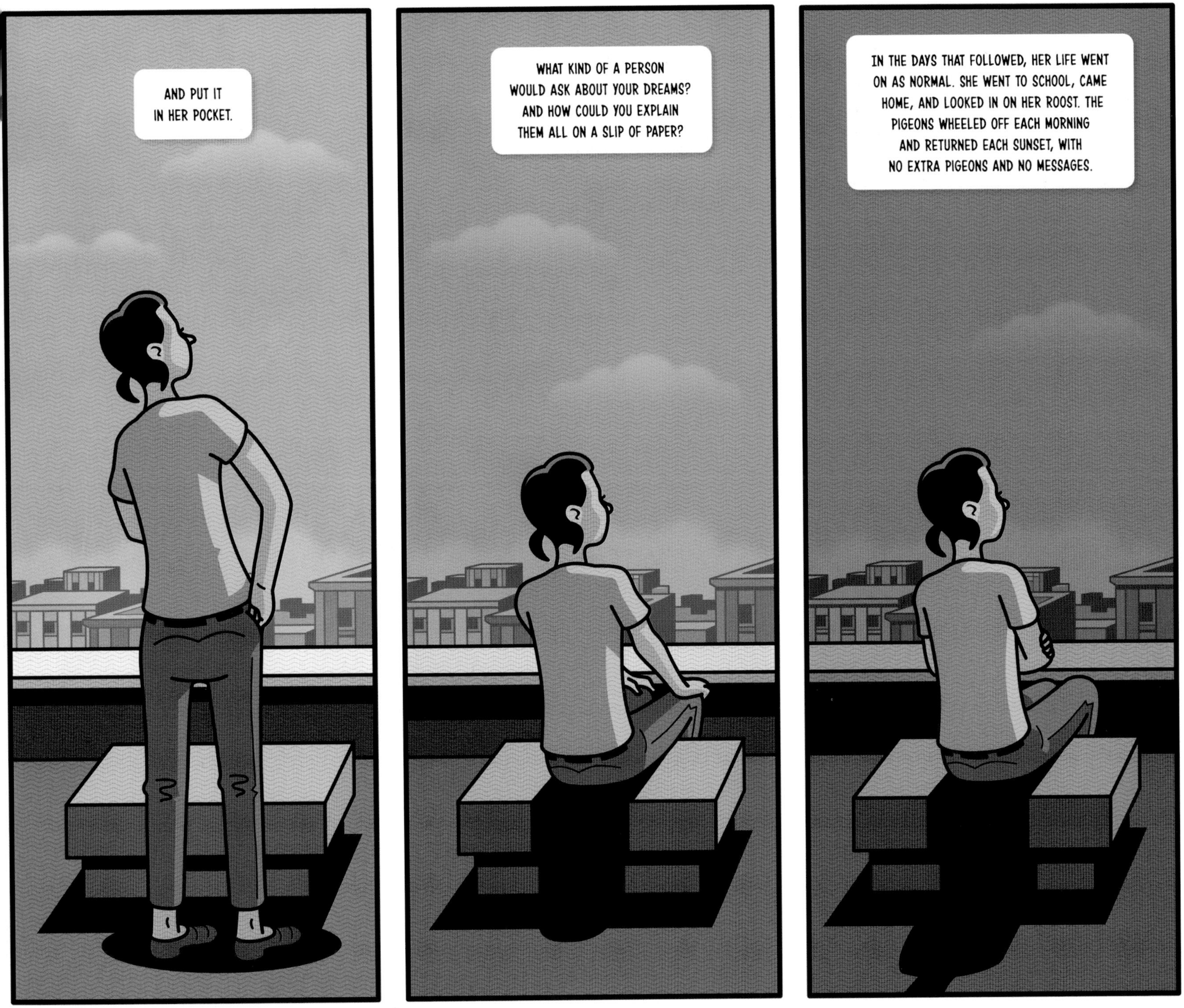
AND PUT IT IN HER POCKET.
WHAT KIND OF A PERSON WOULD ASK ABOUT YOUR DREAMS? AND HOW COULD YOU EXPLAIN THEM ALL ON A SLIP OF PAPER?
IN THE DAYS THAT FOLLOWED, HER LIFE WENT ON AS NORMAL. SHE WENT TO SCHOOL, CAME HOME, AND LOOKED IN ON HER ROOST. THE PIGEONS WHEELED OFF EACH MORNING AND RETURNED EACH SUNSET, WITH NO EXTRA PIGEONS AND NO MESSAGES.

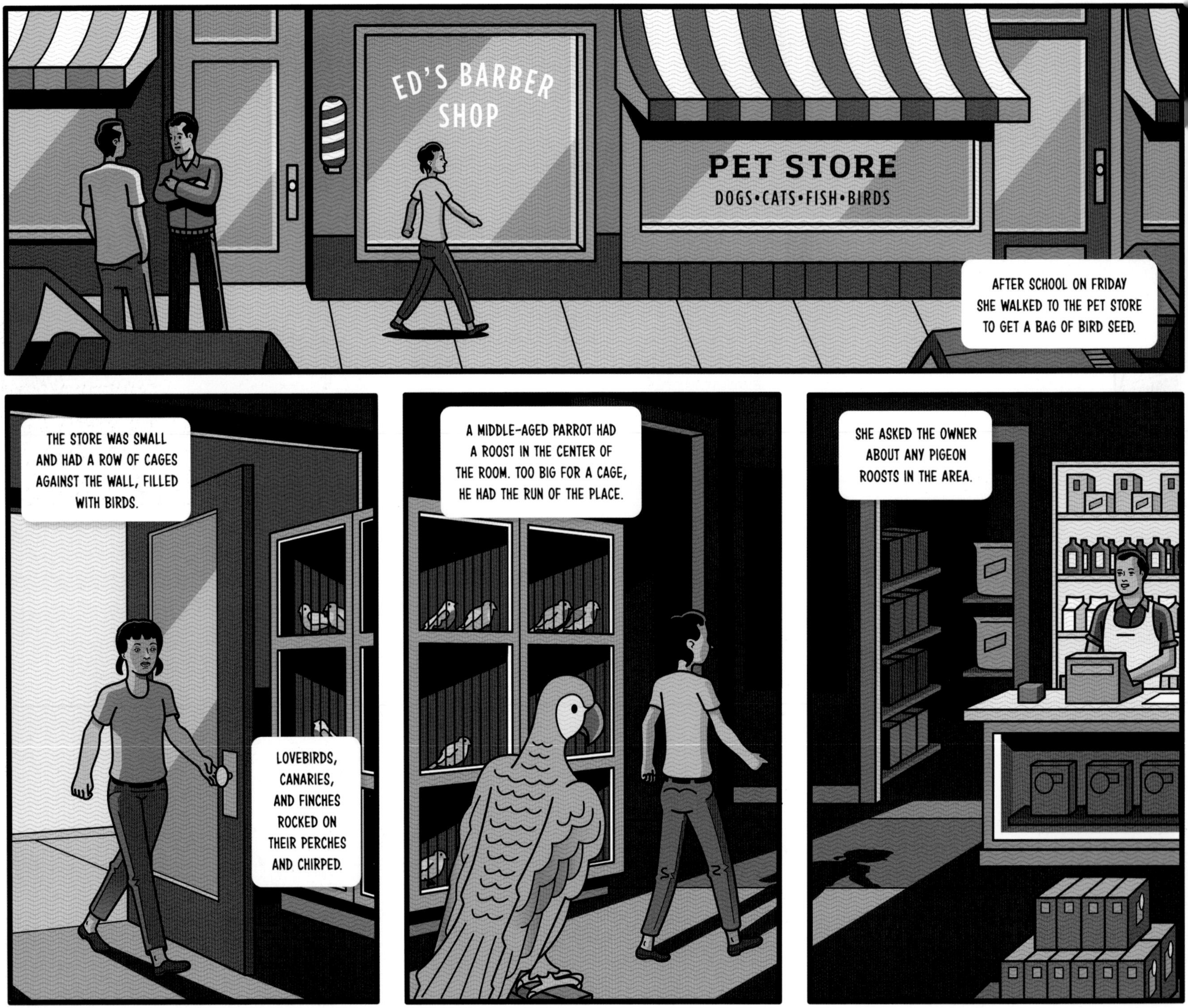
ED'S BARBER SHOP
PET STORE
DOGS•CATS•FISH•BIRDS
AFTER SCHOOL ON FRIDAY SHE WALKED TO THE PET STORE TO GET A BAG OF BIRD SEED.
THE STORE WAS SMALL AND HAD A ROW OF CAGES AGAINST THE WALL, FILLED WITH BIRDS.
LOVEBIRDS, CANARIES, AND FINCHES ROCKED ON THEIR PERCHES AND CHIRPED.
A MIDDLE-AGED PARROT HAD A ROOST IN THE CENTER OF THE ROOM. TOO BIG FOR A CAGE, HE HAD THE RUN OF THE PLACE.
SHE ASKED THE OWNER ABOUT ANY PIGEON ROOSTS IN THE AREA.

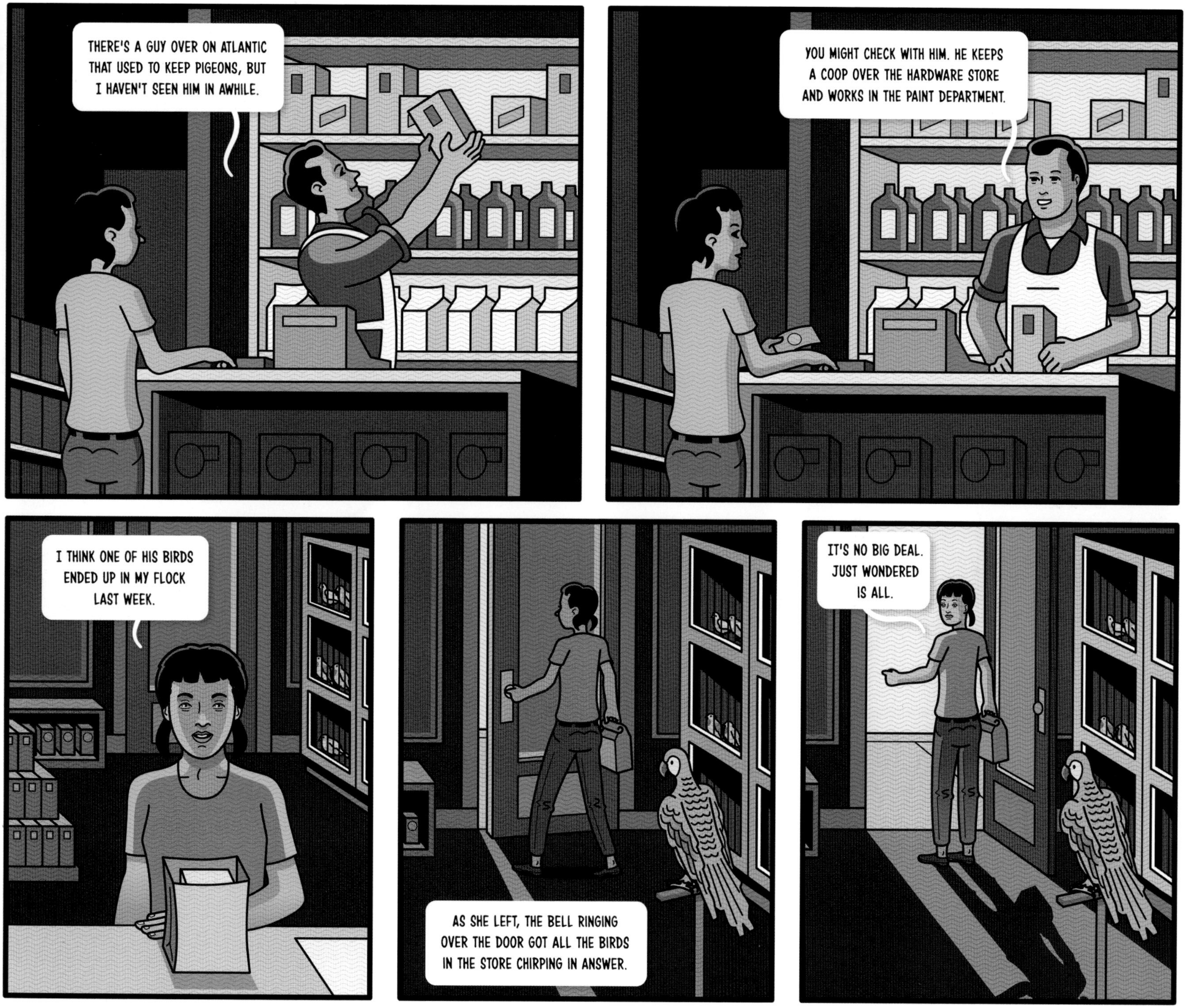
THERE'S A GUY OVER ON ATLANTIC THAT USED TO KEEP PIGEONS, BUT I HAVEN'T SEEN HIM IN AWHILE.
YOU MIGHT CHECK WITH HIM. HE KEEPS A COOP OVER THE HARDWARE STORE AND WORKS IN THE PAINT DEPARTMENT.
I THINK ONE OF HIS BIRDS ENDED UP IN MY FLOCK LAST WEEK.
AS SHE LEFT, THE BELL RINGING OVER THE DOOR GOT ALL THE BIRDS IN THE STORE CHIRPING IN ANSWER.
IT'S NO BIG DEAL. JUST WONDERED IS ALL.

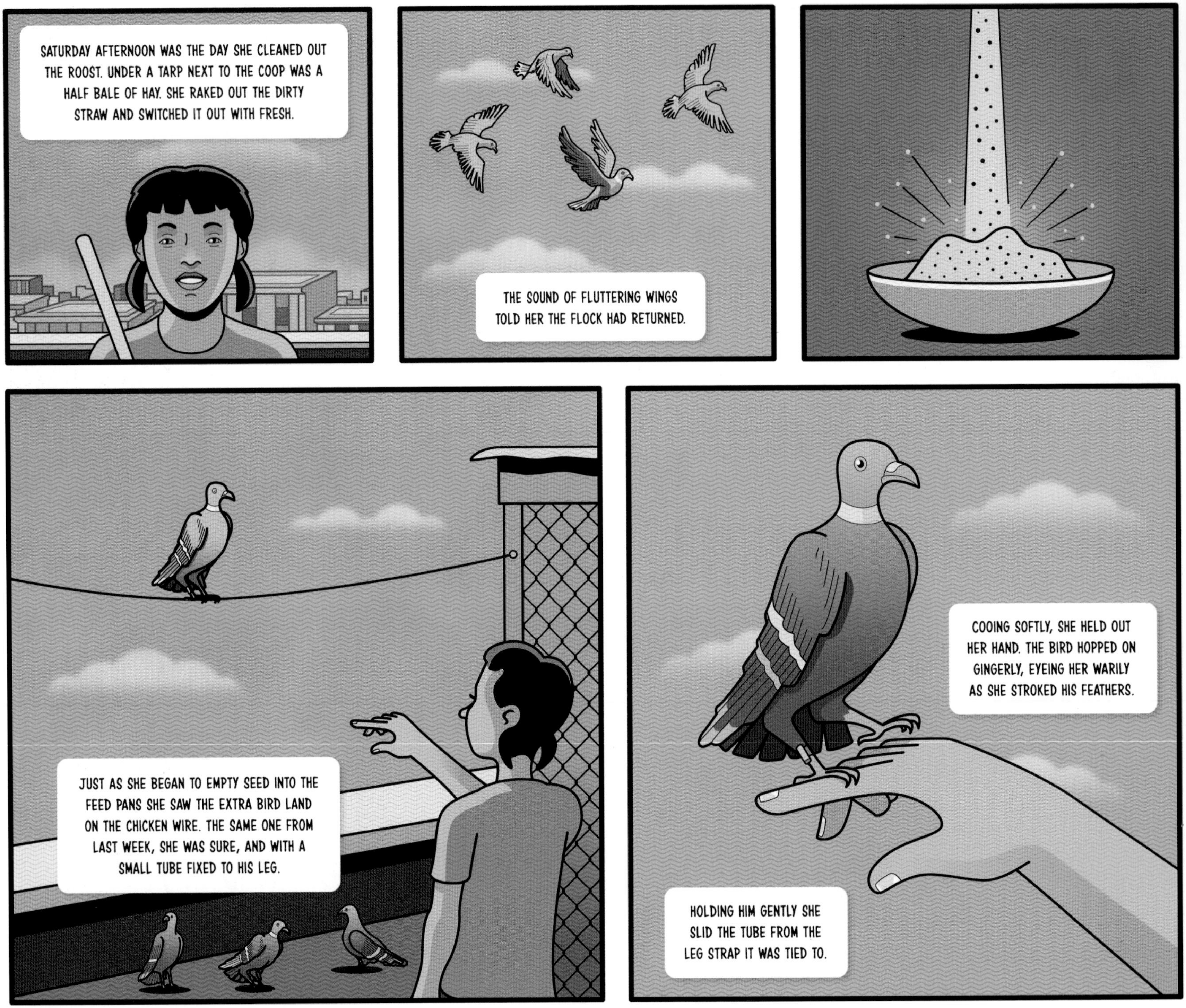
SATURDAY AFTERNOON WAS THE DAY SHE CLEANED OUT THE ROOST. UNDER A TARP NEXT TO THE COOP WAS A HALF BALE OF HAY. SHE RAKED OUT THE DIRTY STRAW AND SWITCHED IT OUT WITH FRESH.
THE SOUND OF FLUTTERING WINGS TOLD HER THE FLOCK HAD RETURNED.
JUST AS SHE BEGAN TO EMPTY SEED INTO THE FEED PANS SHE SAW THE EXTRA BIRD LAND ON THE CHICKEN WIRE. THE SAME ONE FROM LAST WEEK, SHE WAS SURE, AND WITH A SMALL TUBE FIXED TO HIS LEG.
COOING SOFTLY, SHE HELD OUT HER HAND. THE BIRD HOPPED ON GINGERLY, EYEING HER WARILY AS SHE STROKED HIS FEATHERS.
HOLDING HIM GENTLY SHE SLID THE TUBE FROM THE LEG STRAP IT WAS TIED TO.

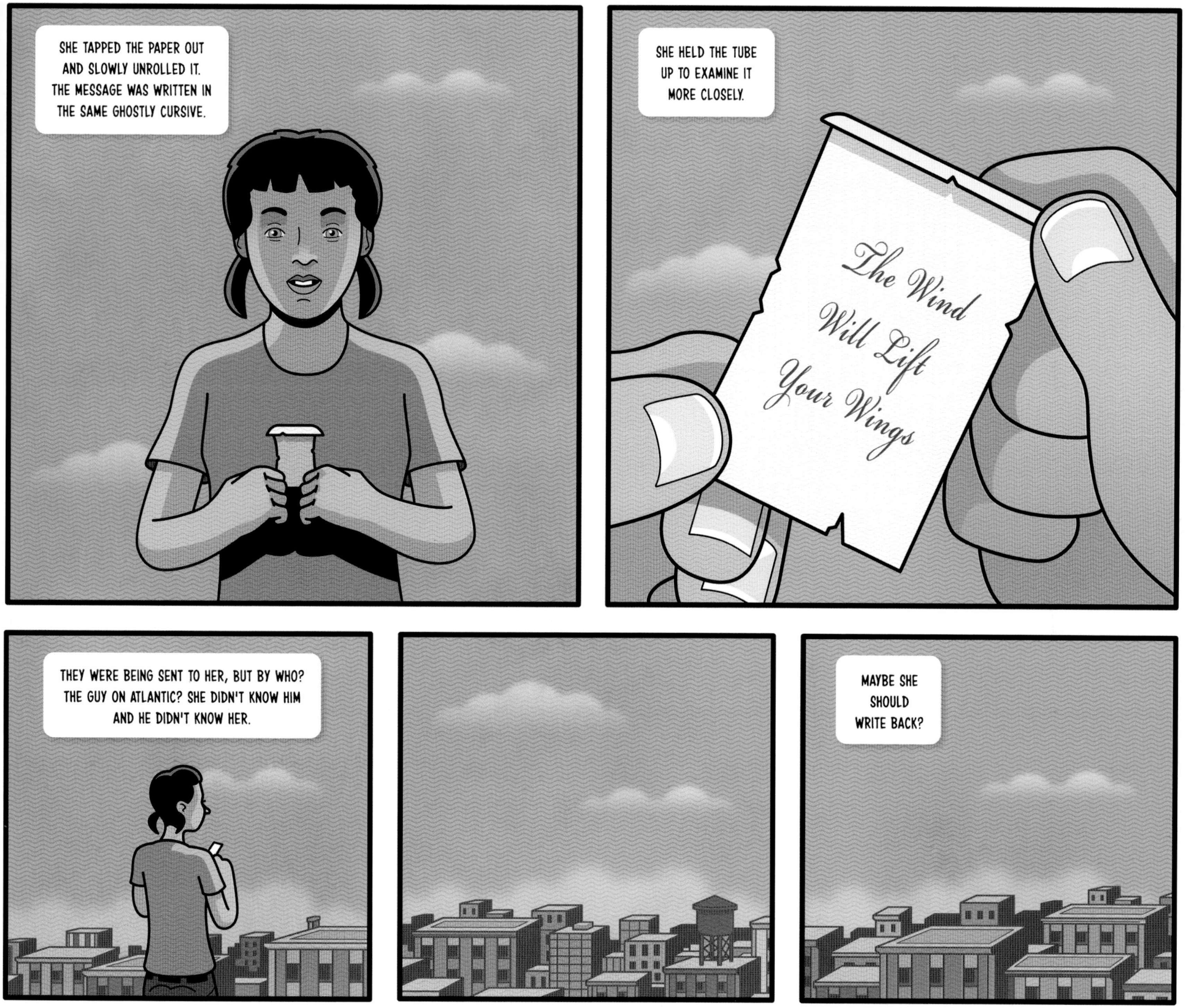
SHE TAPPED THE PAPER OUT AND SLOWLY UNROLLED IT. THE MESSAGE WAS WRITTEN IN THE SAME GHOSTLY CURSIVE.
SHE HELD THE TUBE UP TO EXAMINE IT MORE CLOSELY.
The Wind Will Lift Your Wings
THEY WERE BEING SENT TO HER, BUT BY WHO? THE GUY ON ATLANTIC? SHE DIDN'T KNOW HIM AND HE DIDN'T KNOW HER.
MAYBE SHE SHOULD WRITE BACK?

THE BIRD STOOD ON TOP OF THE DOOR, WATCHING HER.

TAKING A PENCIL FROM HER SCHOOL BAG, SHE TURNED OVER THE PAPER AND CAREFULLY BEGAN TO WRITE.

IT DIDN'T SEEM ENOUGH BUT IT WAS ALL SHE COULD THINK OF TO ASK.

Who are you?

ROLLING UP THE SLIP OF PAPER, SHE SLID IT BACK INTO THE TUBE...

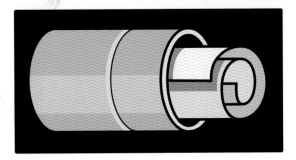

...AND FIXED IT TO THE STRAP ON THE PIGEON'S LEG.

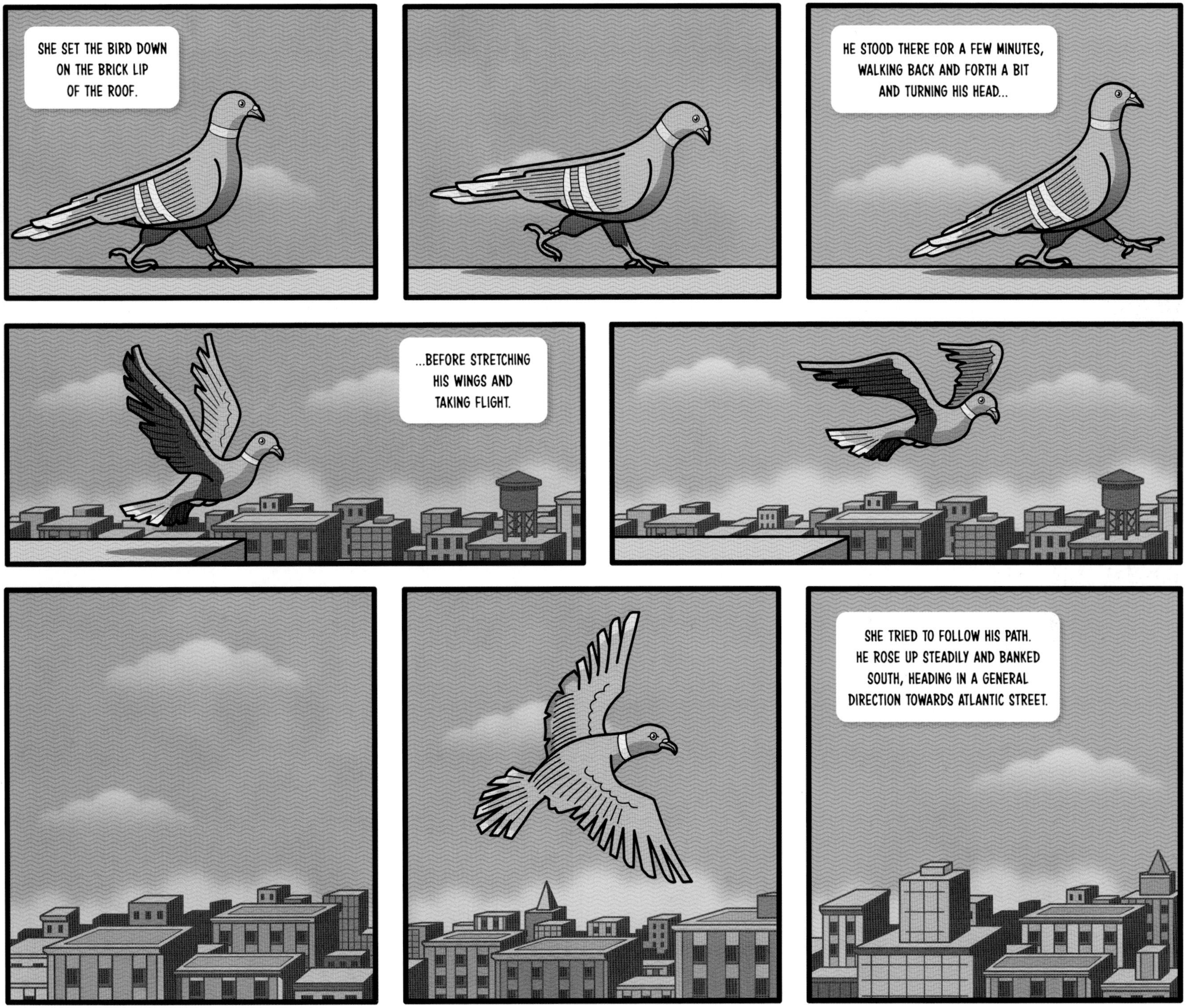
SHE SET THE BIRD DOWN ON THE BRICK LIP OF THE ROOF.
HE STOOD THERE FOR A FEW MINUTES, WALKING BACK AND FORTH A BIT AND TURNING HIS HEAD...
...BEFORE STRETCHING HIS WINGS AND TAKING FLIGHT.
SHE TRIED TO FOLLOW HIS PATH. HE ROSE UP STEADILY AND BANKED SOUTH, HEADING IN A GENERAL DIRECTION TOWARDS ATLANTIC STREET.

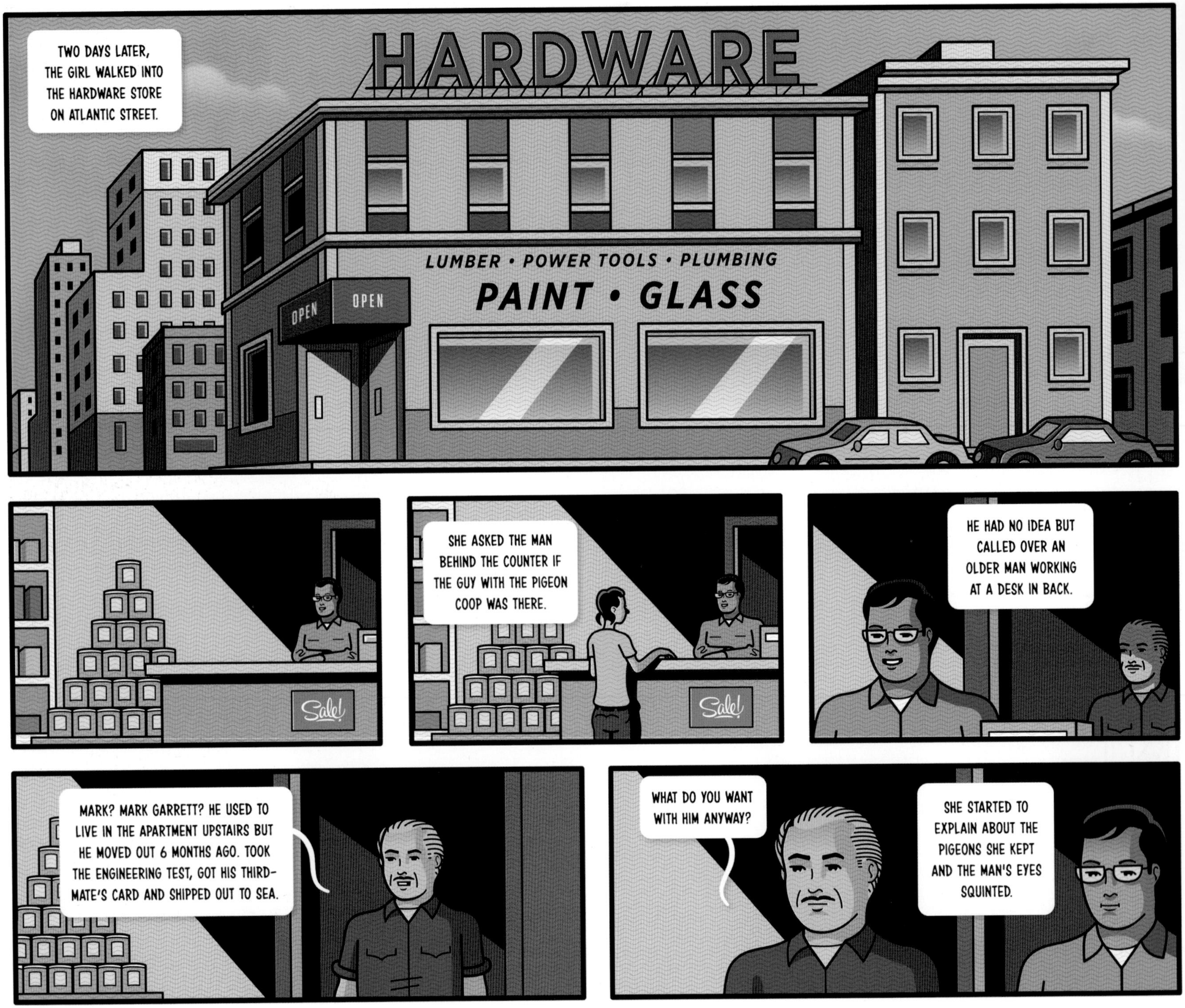
TWO DAYS LATER, THE GIRL WALKED INTO THE HARDWARE STORE ON ATLANTIC STREET.
HARDWARE
OPEN
OPEN
LUMBER • POWER TOOLS • PLUMBING
PAINT • GLASS
Sale!
SHE ASKED THE MAN BEHIND THE COUNTER IF THE GUY WITH THE PIGEON COOP WAS THERE.
Sale!
HE HAD NO IDEA BUT CALLED OVER AN OLDER MAN WORKING AT A DESK IN BACK.
MARK? MARK GARRETT? HE USED TO LIVE IN THE APARTMENT UPSTAIRS BUT HE MOVED OUT 6 MONTHS AGO. TOOK THE ENGINEERING TEST, GOT HIS THIRD-MATE'S CARD AND SHIPPED OUT TO SEA.
WHAT DO YOU WANT WITH HIM ANYWAY?
SHE STARTED TO EXPLAIN ABOUT THE PIGEONS SHE KEPT AND THE MAN'S EYES SQUINTED.

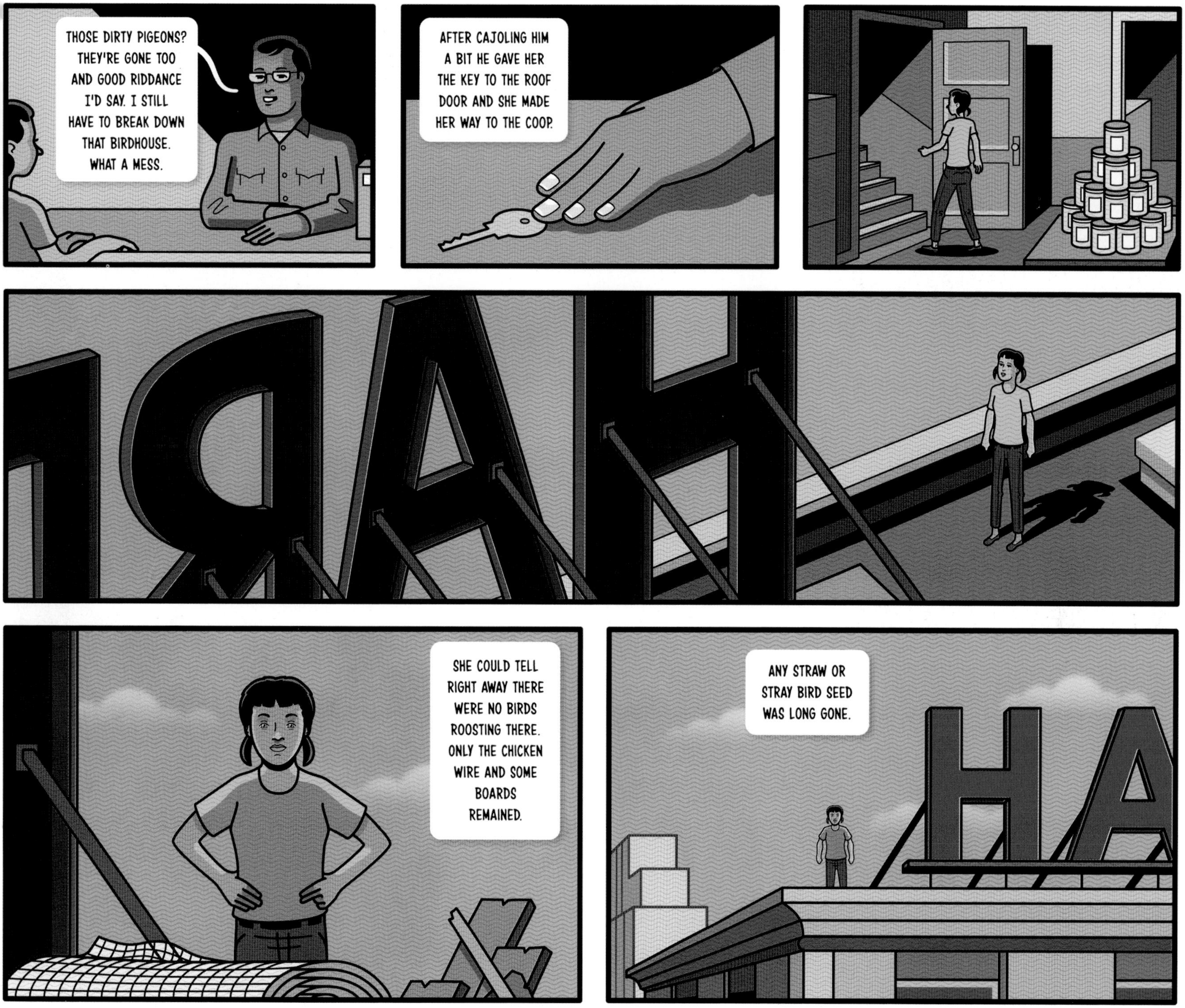
THOSE DIRTY PIGEONS? THEY'RE GONE TOO AND GOOD RIDDANCE I'D SAY. I STILL HAVE TO BREAK DOWN THAT BIRDHOUSE. WHAT A MESS.
AFTER CAJOLING HIM A BIT HE GAVE HER THE KEY TO THE ROOF DOOR AND SHE MADE HER WAY TO THE COOP.
SHE COULD TELL RIGHT AWAY THERE WERE NO BIRDS ROOSTING THERE. ONLY THE CHICKEN WIRE AND SOME BOARDS REMAINED.
ANY STRAW OR STRAY BIRD SEED WAS LONG GONE.

THANKING THE MAN FOR HIS HELP, SHE LEFT THE STORE AND TOOK THE BUS BACK HOME.

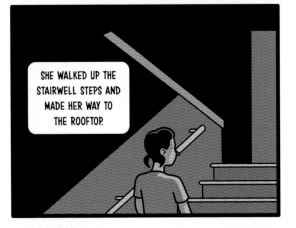

SHE WALKED UP THE STAIRWELL STEPS AND MADE HER WAY TO THE ROOFTOP.

THE BIRDS WERE WAITING FOR HER, BUT NO SIGN OF THE EXTRA BIRD.

AFTER FEEDING AND WATERING THE FLOCK SHE SAT DOWN TO THINK OVER WHAT HAD HAPPENED. IT COULDN'T BE THIS MARK GARRETT GUY, BECAUSE HE WAS GONE. SO IT MUST BE SOMEONE ELSE. BUT WHO?

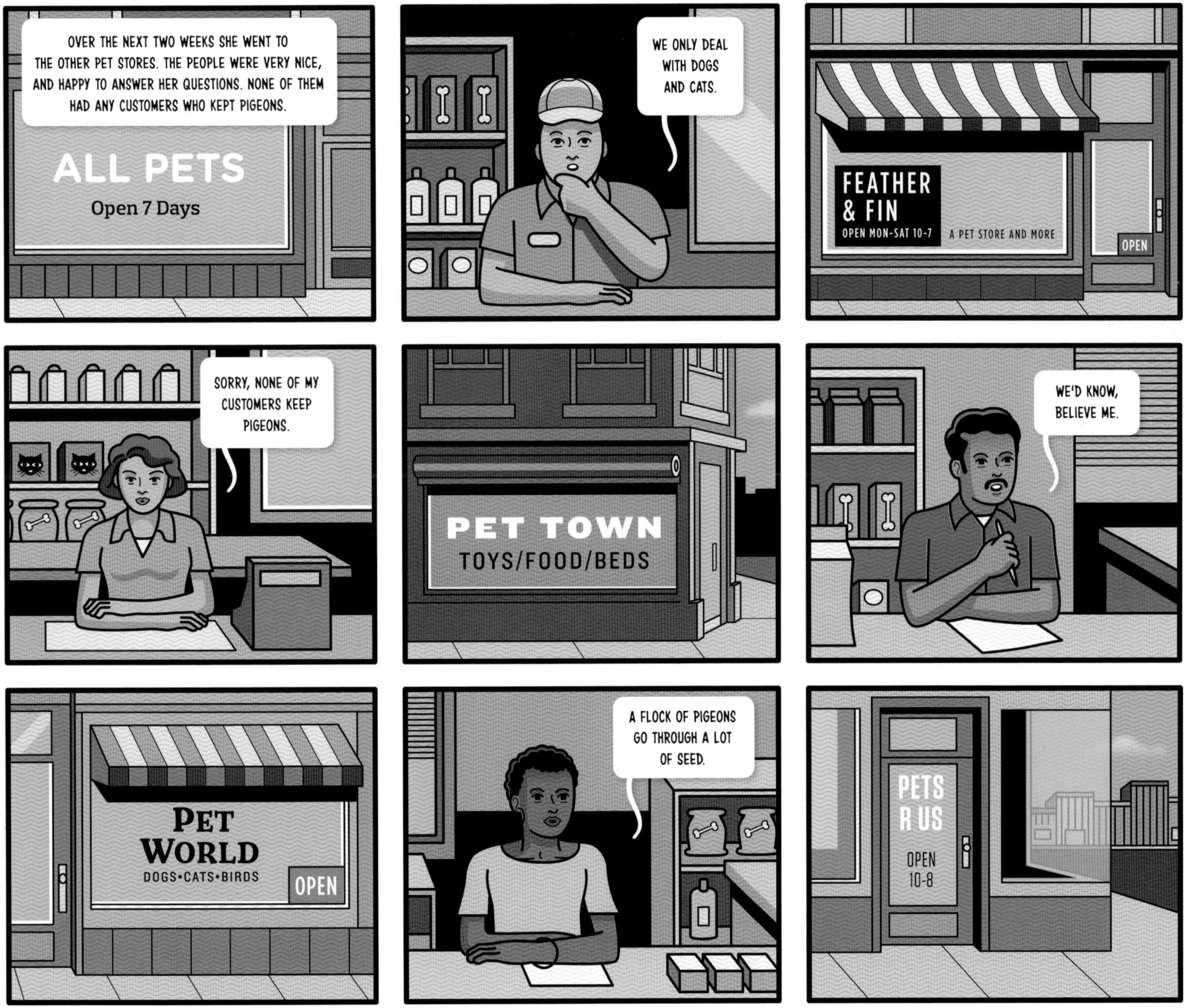
OVER THE NEXT TWO WEEKS SHE WENT TO THE OTHER PET STORES. THE PEOPLE WERE VERY NICE, AND HAPPY TO ANSWER HER QUESTIONS. NONE OF THEM HAD ANY CUSTOMERS WHO KEPT PIGEONS.
ALL PETS
Open 7 Days
WE ONLY DEAL WITH DOGS AND CATS.
FEATHER & FIN
OPEN MON-SAT 10-7
A PET STORE AND MORE
OPEN
SORRY, NONE OF MY CUSTOMERS KEEP PIGEONS.
PET TOWN
TOYS/FOOD/BEDS
WE'D KNOW, BELIEVE ME.
PET WORLD
DOGS•CATS•BIRDS
OPEN
A FLOCK OF PIGEONS GO THROUGH A LOT OF SEED.
PETS R US
OPEN 10-8

MEANWHILE, SHE BEGAN HEADING TO THE COOP A LITTLE EARLIER EACH EVENING.

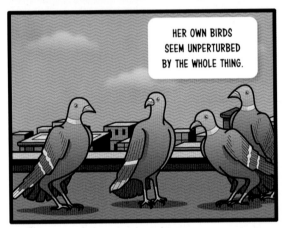

HER OWN BIRDS SEEM UNPERTURBED BY THE WHOLE THING.

THEY NEVER PAY THE NEW BIRD MUCH ATTENTION. THEY ARE MORE CONCERNED ABOUT GETTING THEIR SHARE OF BIRD SEED THAN DEALING WITH A STRANGER.

SHE WAITS FOR DUSK, WHEN HE USUALLY MAKES AN APPEARANCE.

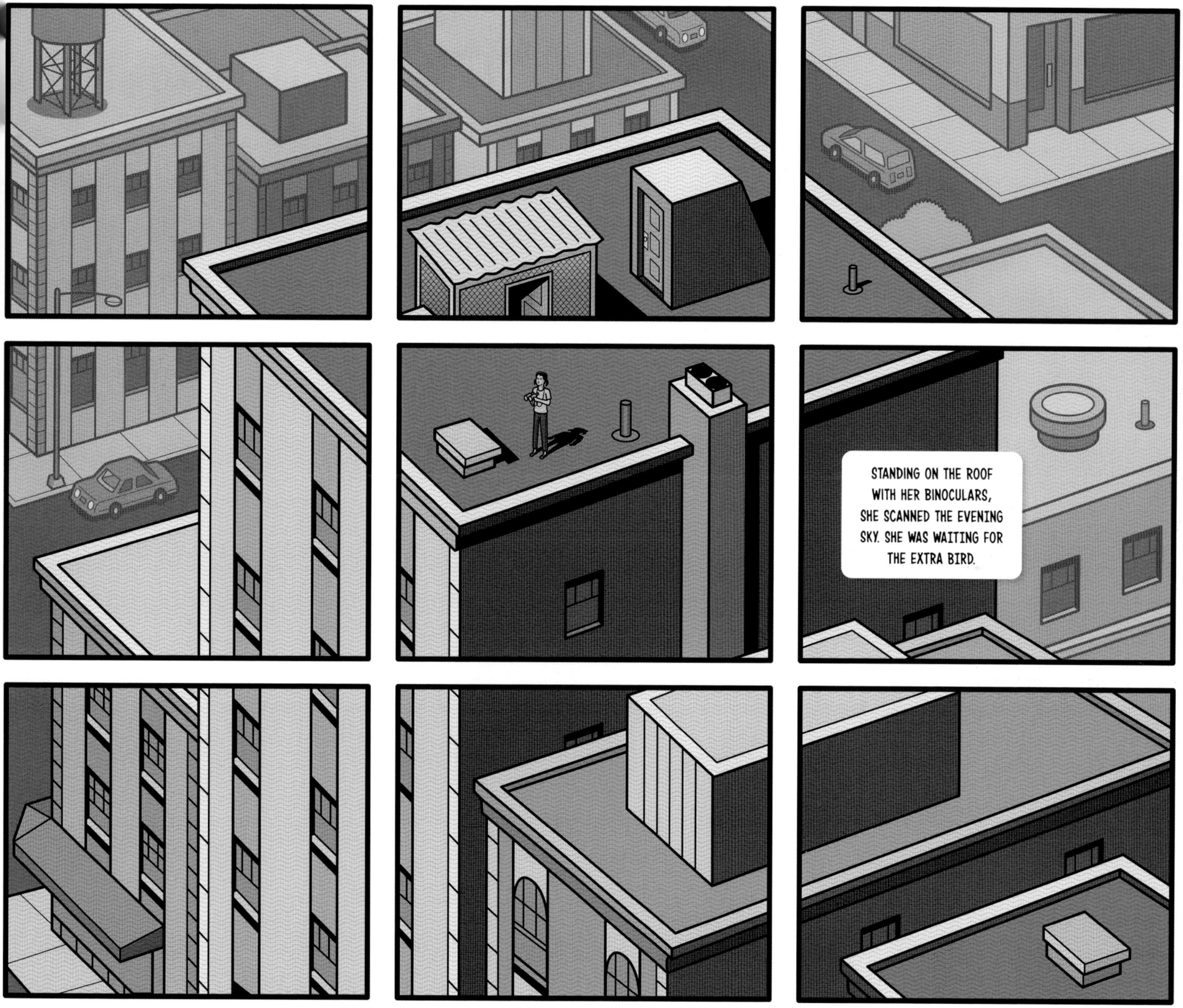
STANDING ON THE ROOF WITH HER BINOCULARS, SHE SCANNED THE EVENING SKY. SHE WAS WAITING FOR THE EXTRA BIRD.

IT WAS THE EVENING AFTER SHE HAD CHECKED ALL THE PET STORES, THAT THE EXTRA BIRD REAPPEARED. SHE NOTICED HIM FLYING SLIGHTLY BEHIND HER RETURNING FLOCK. THE BIRDS ALL CIRCLED THE COOP, AND SETTLED ONE BY ONE ON THE ROOST BARS.

THE EXTRA BIRD KEPT HIS DISTANCE AT FIRST, HOPPING FROM PLACE TO PLACE. EVENTUALLY, AS THE SEED WAS POURED OUT, HE ALLOWED HER TO GET CLOSER.

THE STRAP WAS WOUND AROUND HIS LEG, WITH THE SMALL TUBE HELD FIRMLY IN PLACE.

AFTER A BIT HE HOPPED ONTO HER OUTSTRETCHED HAND.

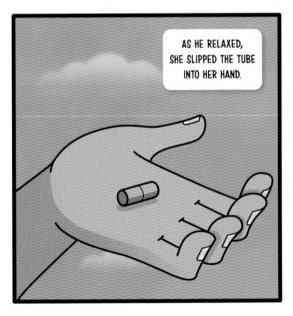

AS HE RELAXED, SHE SLIPPED THE TUBE INTO HER HAND.

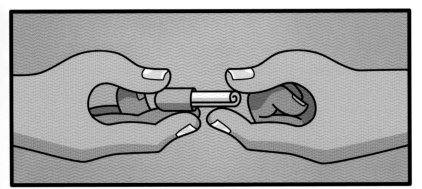

BREATHING DEEPLY, SHE POPPED THE CAP OFF AND SLID THE PAPER OUT. THE SCROLL UNROLLED IN HER HAND AND SHE COULD MAKE OUT THE FAINT WRITING.

Someone who cares about you

TURNING THE PAPER OVER, SHE WROTE HER MESSAGE ON THE BACK.

Can I meet you?

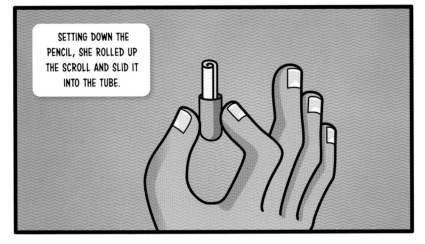

SETTING DOWN THE PENCIL, SHE ROLLED UP THE SCROLL AND SLID IT INTO THE TUBE.

THE EXTRA BIRD STAYED RIGHT AT THE SMALL STAND AND ALLOWED HER TO SLIDE THE TUBE BACK ONTO THE LEG STRAP.

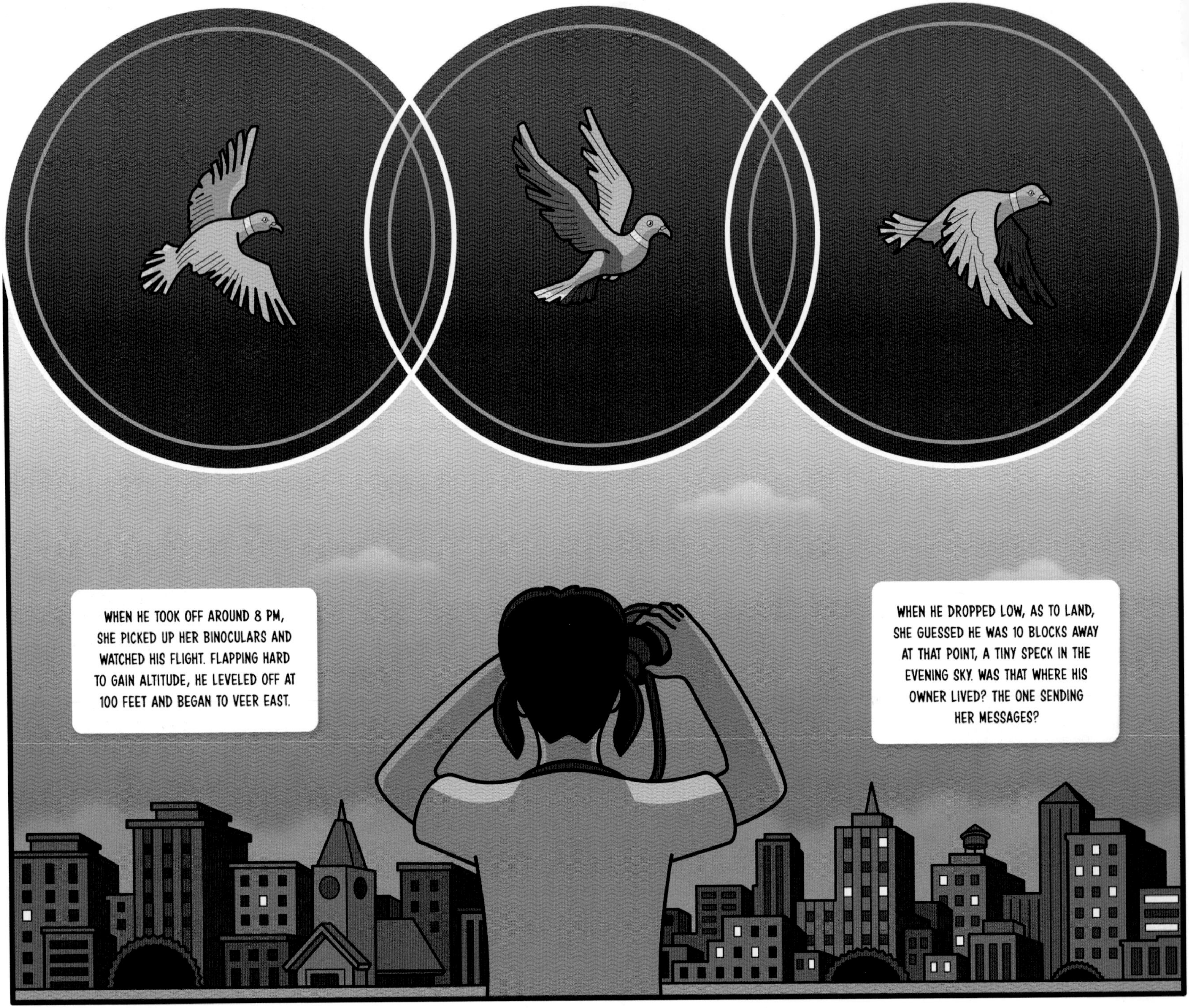
WHEN HE TOOK OFF AROUND 8 PM, SHE PICKED UP HER BINOCULARS AND WATCHED HIS FLIGHT. FLAPPING HARD TO GAIN ALTITUDE, HE LEVELED OFF AT 100 FEET AND BEGAN TO VEER EAST.
WHEN HE DROPPED LOW, AS TO LAND, SHE GUESSED HE WAS 10 BLOCKS AWAY AT THAT POINT, A TINY SPECK IN THE EVENING SKY. WAS THAT WHERE HIS OWNER LIVED? THE ONE SENDING HER MESSAGES?

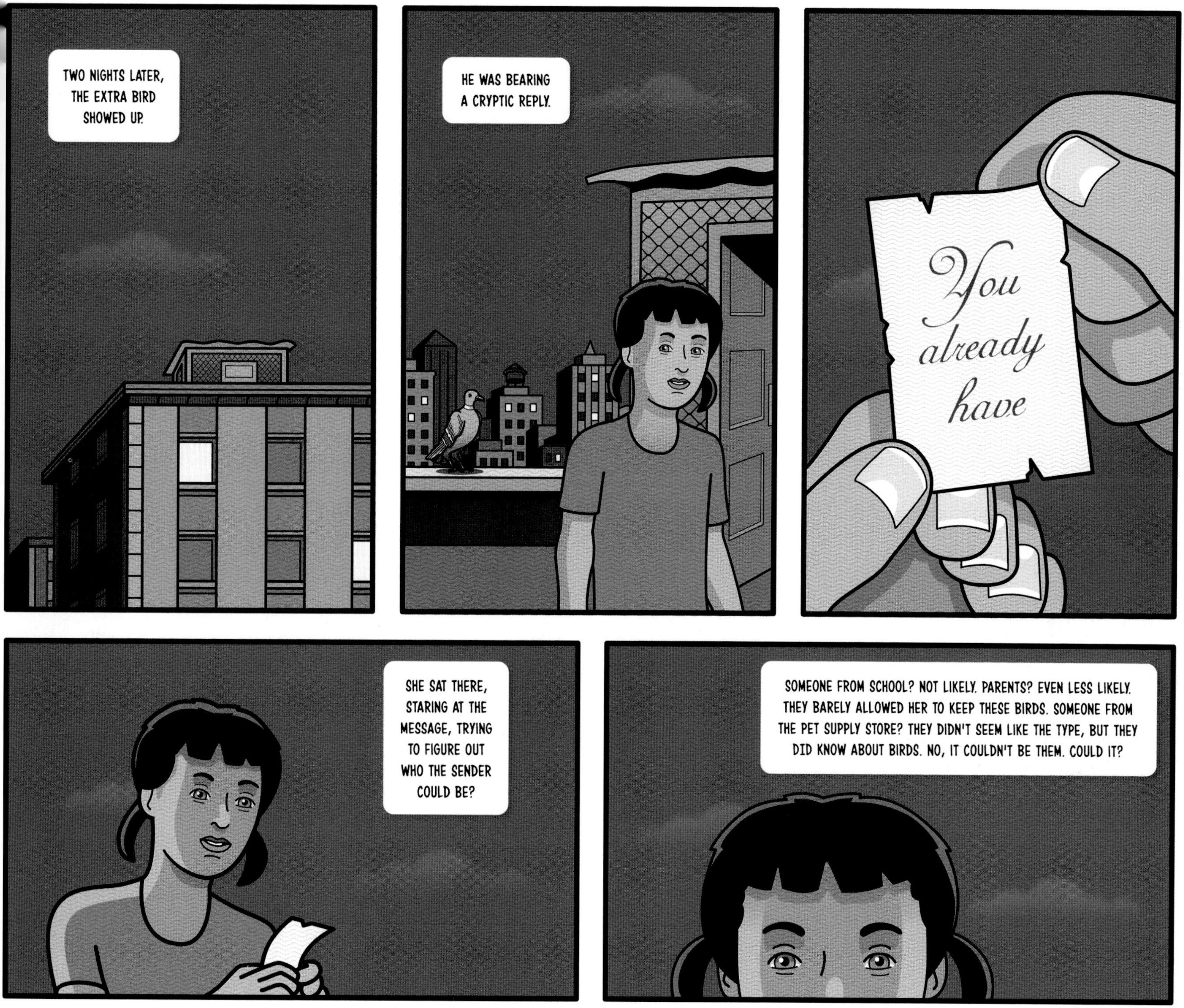
TWO NIGHTS LATER, THE EXTRA BIRD SHOWED UP.
HE WAS BEARING A CRYPTIC REPLY.
You already have
SHE SAT THERE, STARING AT THE MESSAGE, TRYING TO FIGURE OUT WHO THE SENDER COULD BE?
SOMEONE FROM SCHOOL? NOT LIKELY. PARENTS? EVEN LESS LIKELY. THEY BARELY ALLOWED HER TO KEEP THESE BIRDS. SOMEONE FROM THE PET SUPPLY STORE? THEY DIDN'T SEEM LIKE THE TYPE, BUT THEY DID KNOW ABOUT BIRDS. NO, IT COULDN'T BE THEM. COULD IT?

TAKING OUT HER PENCIL, SHE QUICKLY WROTE ON BACK.

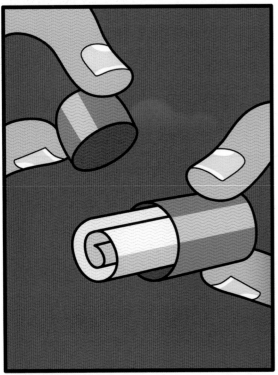

SHE COAXED THE BIRD CLOSER AND HE ALLOWED HER TO ATTACH THE NOTE TO HIS LEG.

HE FLEW UP INTO THE SKY.

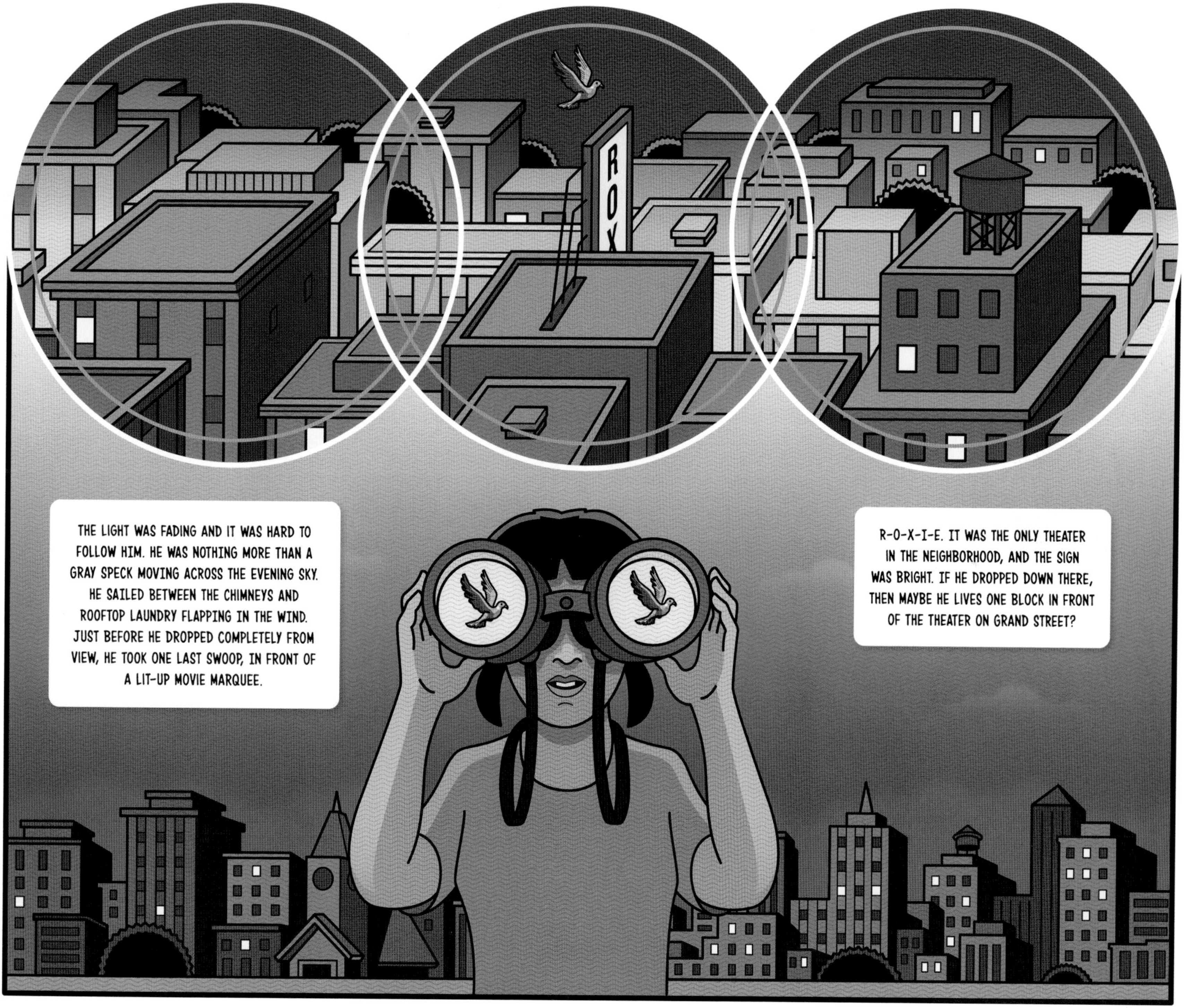
ROX
THE LIGHT WAS FADING AND IT WAS HARD TO FOLLOW HIM. HE WAS NOTHING MORE THAN A GRAY SPECK MOVING ACROSS THE EVENING SKY. HE SAILED BETWEEN THE CHIMNEYS AND ROOFTOP LAUNDRY FLAPPING IN THE WIND. JUST BEFORE HE DROPPED COMPLETELY FROM VIEW, HE TOOK ONE LAST SWOOP, IN FRONT OF A LIT-UP MOVIE MARQUEE.
R-O-X-I-E. IT WAS THE ONLY THEATER IN THE NEIGHBORHOOD, AND THE SIGN WAS BRIGHT. IF HE DROPPED DOWN THERE, THEN MAYBE HE LIVES ONE BLOCK IN FRONT OF THE THEATER ON GRAND STREET?

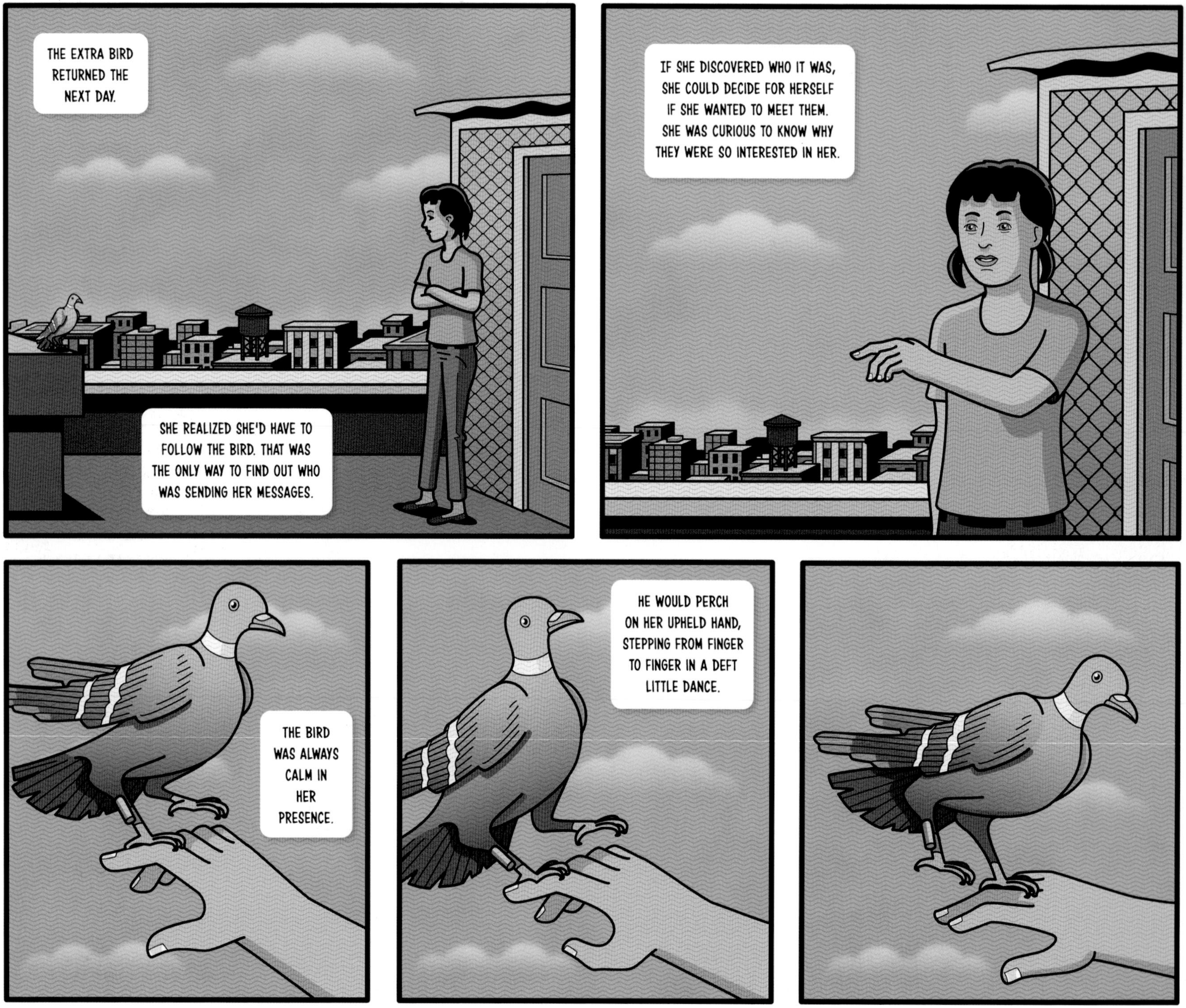

THE EXTRA BIRD RETURNED THE NEXT DAY.
SHE REALIZED SHE'D HAVE TO FOLLOW THE BIRD. THAT WAS THE ONLY WAY TO FIND OUT WHO WAS SENDING HER MESSAGES.
IF SHE DISCOVERED WHO IT WAS, SHE COULD DECIDE FOR HERSELF IF SHE WANTED TO MEET THEM. SHE WAS CURIOUS TO KNOW WHY THEY WERE SO INTERESTED IN HER.
THE BIRD WAS ALWAYS CALM IN HER PRESENCE.
HE WOULD PERCH ON HER UPHELD HAND, STEPPING FROM FINGER TO FINGER IN A DEFT LITTLE DANCE.

You'll Find It

ASKING THE PERSON TO DESCRIBE THEIR APPEARANCE WOULD BE A CLUE TO THEIR IDENTITY.

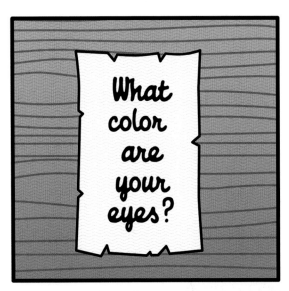

What color are your eyes?

ROLLING UP THE SCROLL AND TUCKING IT INTO THE NARROW TUBE HAD GOTTEN TO BE SECOND NATURE TO HER.

WHEN HE TOOK OFF THAT EVENING HE CIRCLED THE COOP TWICE, LIKE HE WAS UNWILLING TO LEAVE.

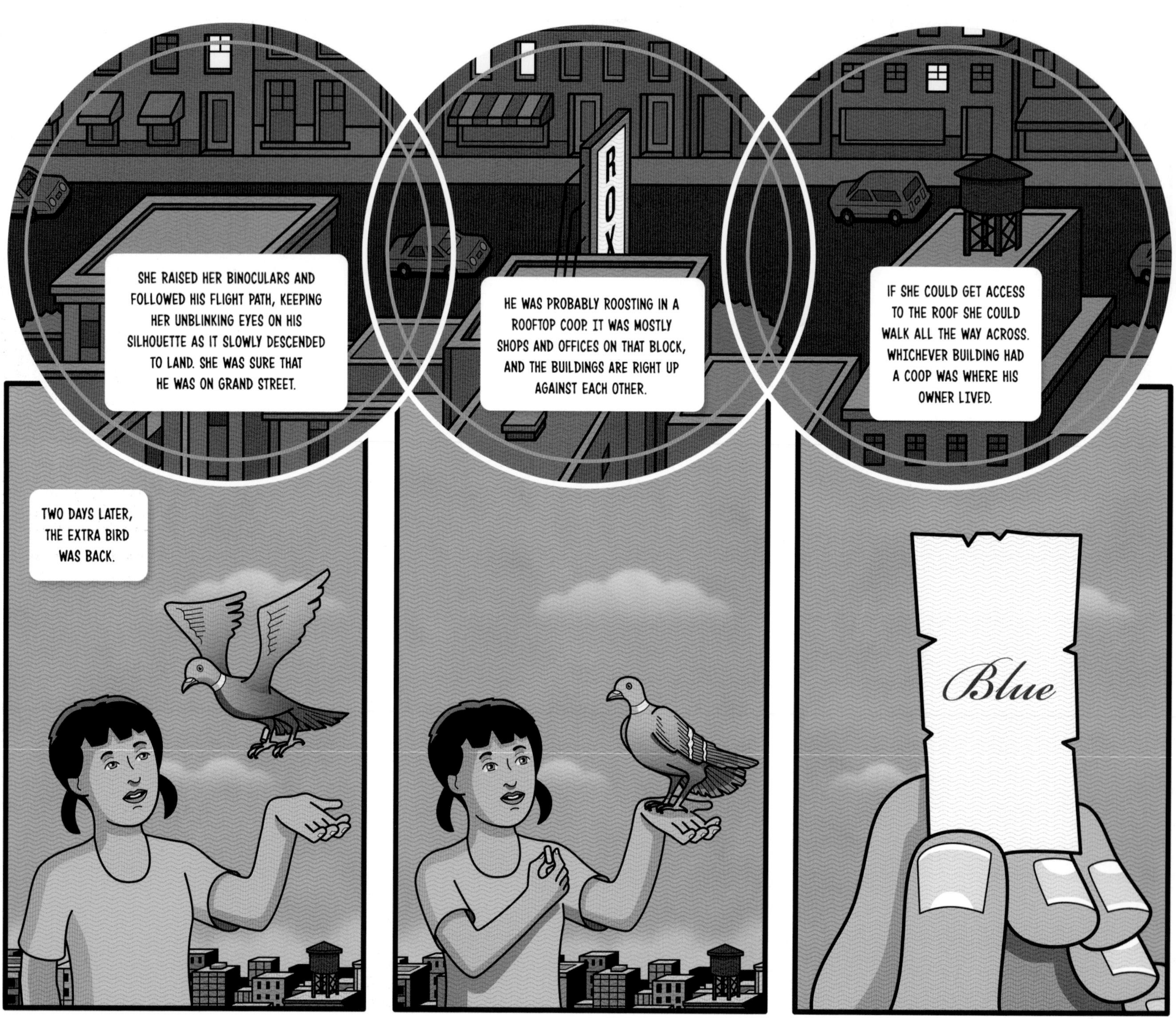
SHE RAISED HER BINOCULARS AND FOLLOWED HIS FLIGHT PATH, KEEPING HER UNBLINKING EYES ON HIS SILHOUETTE AS IT SLOWLY DESCENDED TO LAND. SHE WAS SURE THAT HE WAS ON GRAND STREET.
ROX
HE WAS PROBABLY ROOSTING IN A ROOFTOP COOP. IT WAS MOSTLY SHOPS AND OFFICES ON THAT BLOCK, AND THE BUILDINGS ARE RIGHT UP AGAINST EACH OTHER.
IF SHE COULD GET ACCESS TO THE ROOF SHE COULD WALK ALL THE WAY ACROSS. WHICHEVER BUILDING HAD A COOP WAS WHERE HIS OWNER LIVED.
TWO DAYS LATER, THE EXTRA BIRD WAS BACK.
Blue

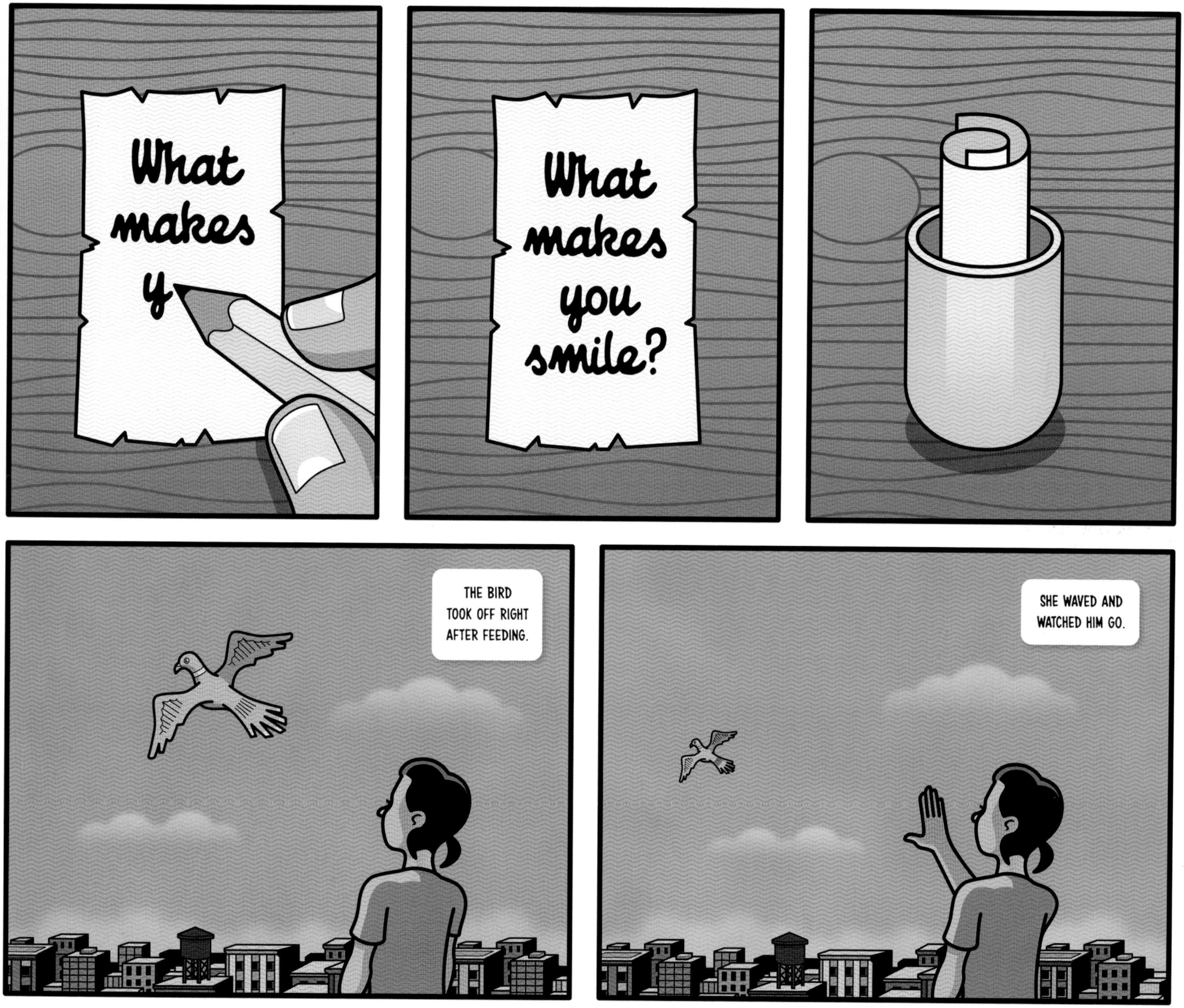
What makes y
What makes you smile?
THE BIRD TOOK OFF RIGHT AFTER FEEDING.
SHE WAVED AND WATCHED HIM GO.

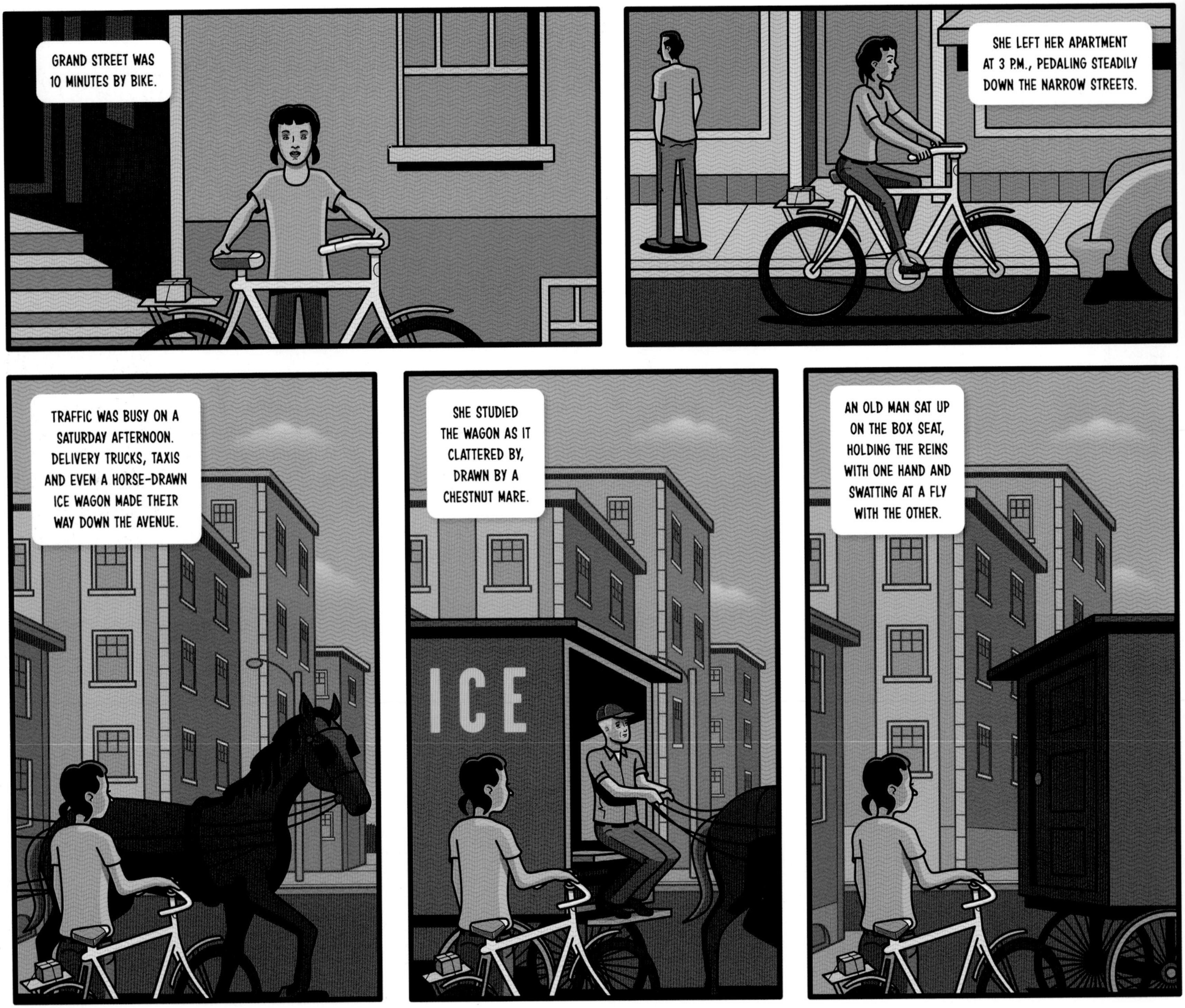
GRAND STREET WAS 10 MINUTES BY BIKE.
SHE LEFT HER APARTMENT AT 3 P.M., PEDALING STEADILY DOWN THE NARROW STREETS.
TRAFFIC WAS BUSY ON A SATURDAY AFTERNOON. DELIVERY TRUCKS, TAXIS AND EVEN A HORSE-DRAWN ICE WAGON MADE THEIR WAY DOWN THE AVENUE.
SHE STUDIED THE WAGON AS IT CLATTERED BY, DRAWN BY A CHESTNUT MARE.
ICE
AN OLD MAN SAT UP ON THE BOX SEAT, HOLDING THE REINS WITH ONE HAND AND SWATTING AT A FLY WITH THE OTHER.

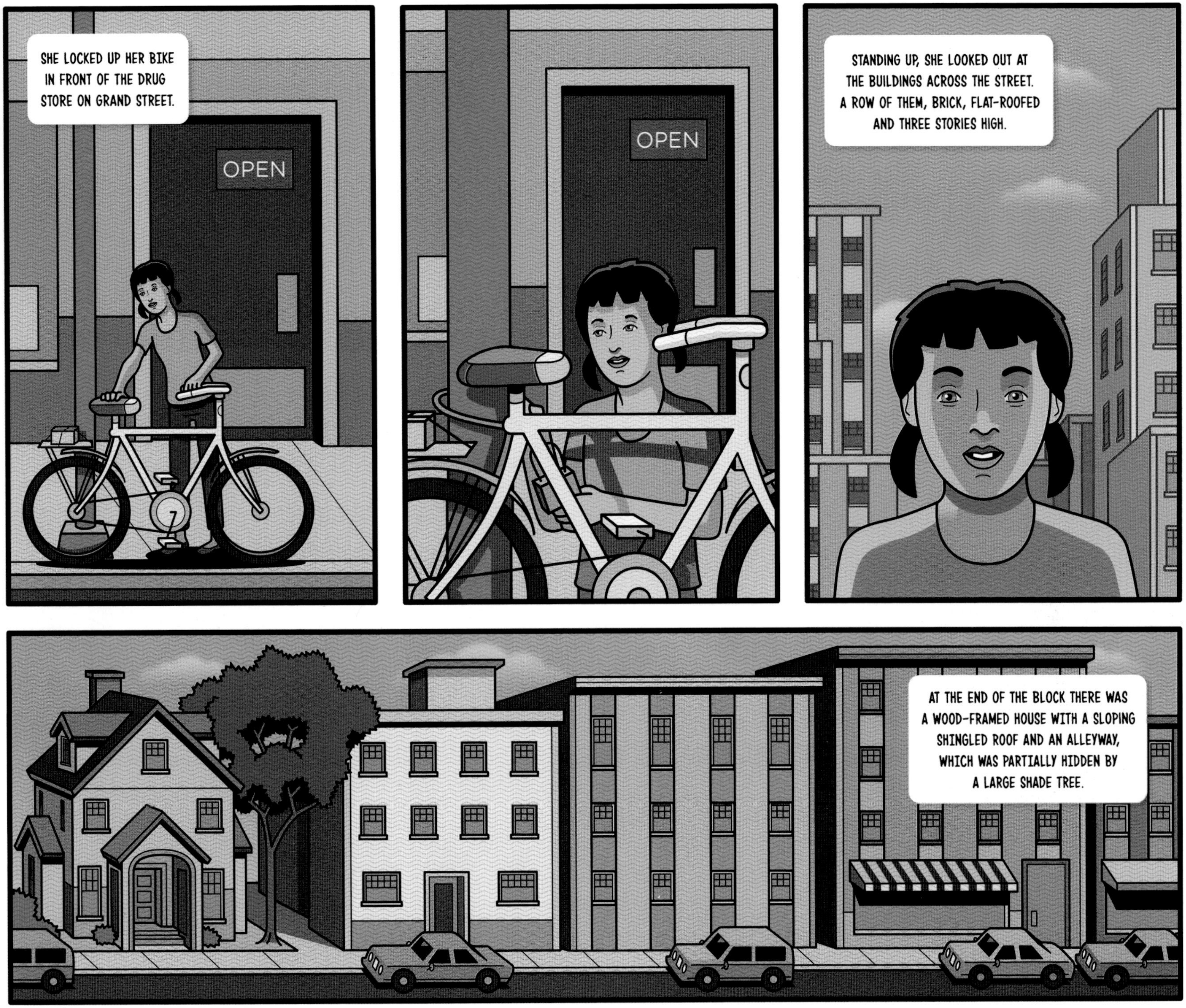
SHE LOCKED UP HER BIKE IN FRONT OF THE DRUG STORE ON GRAND STREET.
OPEN
OPEN
STANDING UP, SHE LOOKED OUT AT THE BUILDINGS ACROSS THE STREET. A ROW OF THEM, BRICK, FLAT-ROOFED AND THREE STORIES HIGH.
AT THE END OF THE BLOCK THERE WAS A WOOD-FRAMED HOUSE WITH A SLOPING SHINGLED ROOF AND AN ALLEYWAY, WHICH WAS PARTIALLY HIDDEN BY A LARGE SHADE TREE.

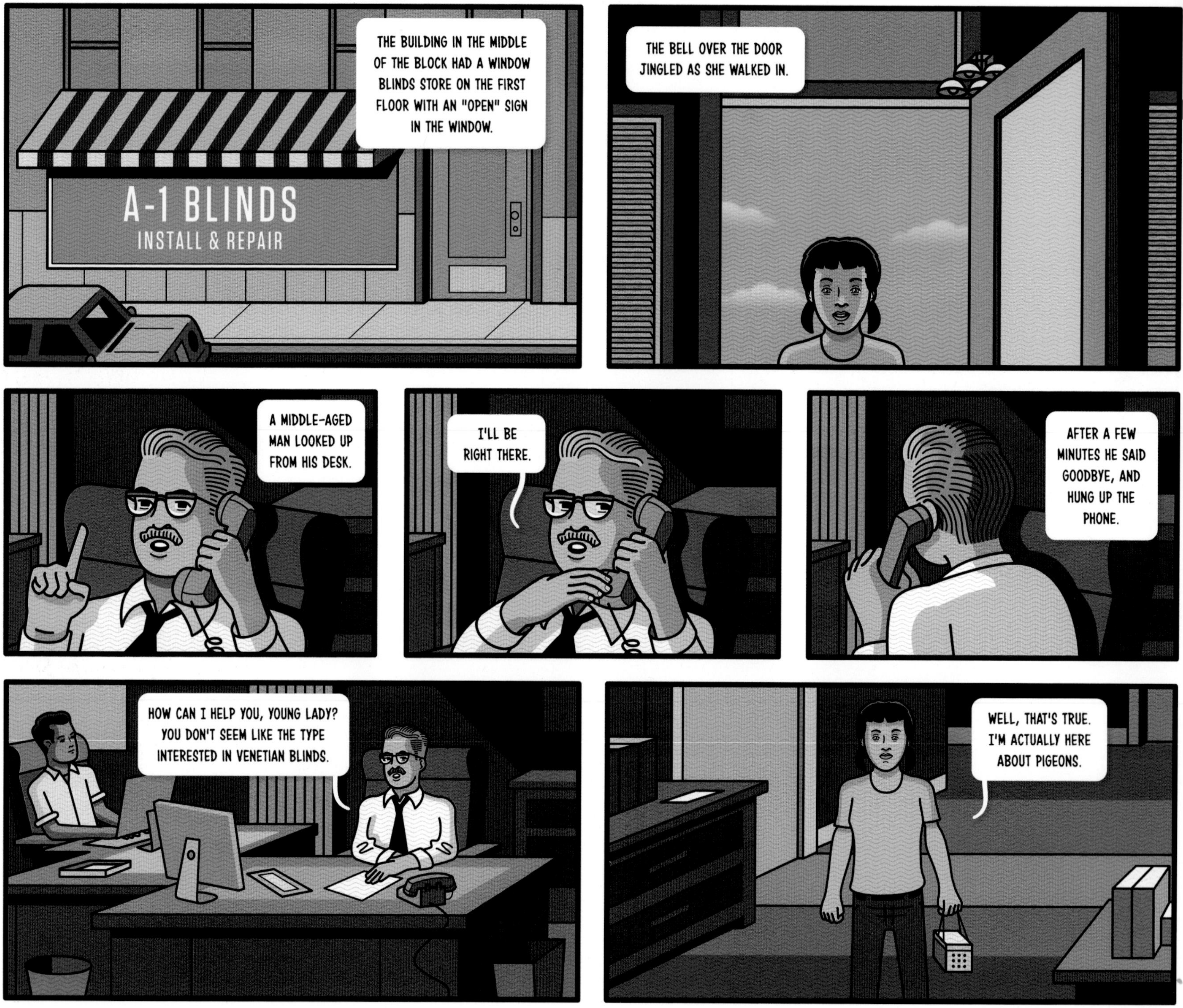
THE BUILDING IN THE MIDDLE OF THE BLOCK HAD A WINDOW BLINDS STORE ON THE FIRST FLOOR WITH AN "OPEN" SIGN IN THE WINDOW.
A-1 BLINDS
INSTALL & REPAIR
THE BELL OVER THE DOOR JINGLED AS SHE WALKED IN.
A MIDDLE-AGED MAN LOOKED UP FROM HIS DESK.
I'LL BE RIGHT THERE.
AFTER A FEW MINUTES HE SAID GOODBYE, AND HUNG UP THE PHONE.
HOW CAN I HELP YOU, YOUNG LADY? YOU DON'T SEEM LIKE THE TYPE INTERESTED IN VENETIAN BLINDS.
WELL, THAT'S TRUE. I'M ACTUALLY HERE ABOUT PIGEONS.

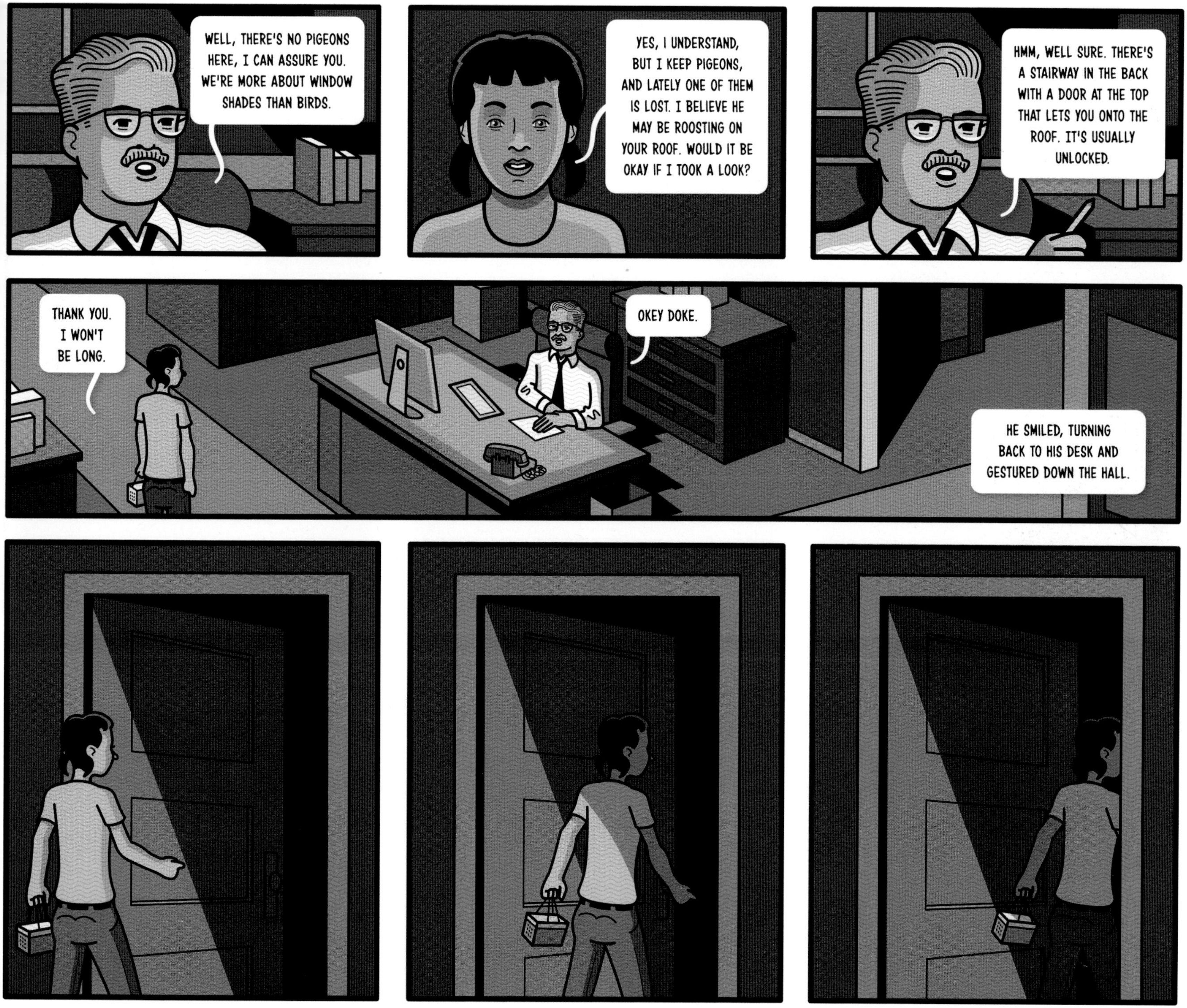
WELL, THERE'S NO PIGEONS HERE, I CAN ASSURE YOU. WE'RE MORE ABOUT WINDOW SHADES THAN BIRDS.
YES, I UNDERSTAND, BUT I KEEP PIGEONS, AND LATELY ONE OF THEM IS LOST. I BELIEVE HE MAY BE ROOSTING ON YOUR ROOF. WOULD IT BE OKAY IF I TOOK A LOOK?
HMM, WELL SURE. THERE'S A STAIRWAY IN THE BACK WITH A DOOR AT THE TOP THAT LETS YOU ONTO THE ROOF. IT'S USUALLY UNLOCKED.
THANK YOU. I WON'T BE LONG.
OKEY DOKE.
HE SMILED, TURNING BACK TO HIS DESK AND GESTURED DOWN THE HALL.

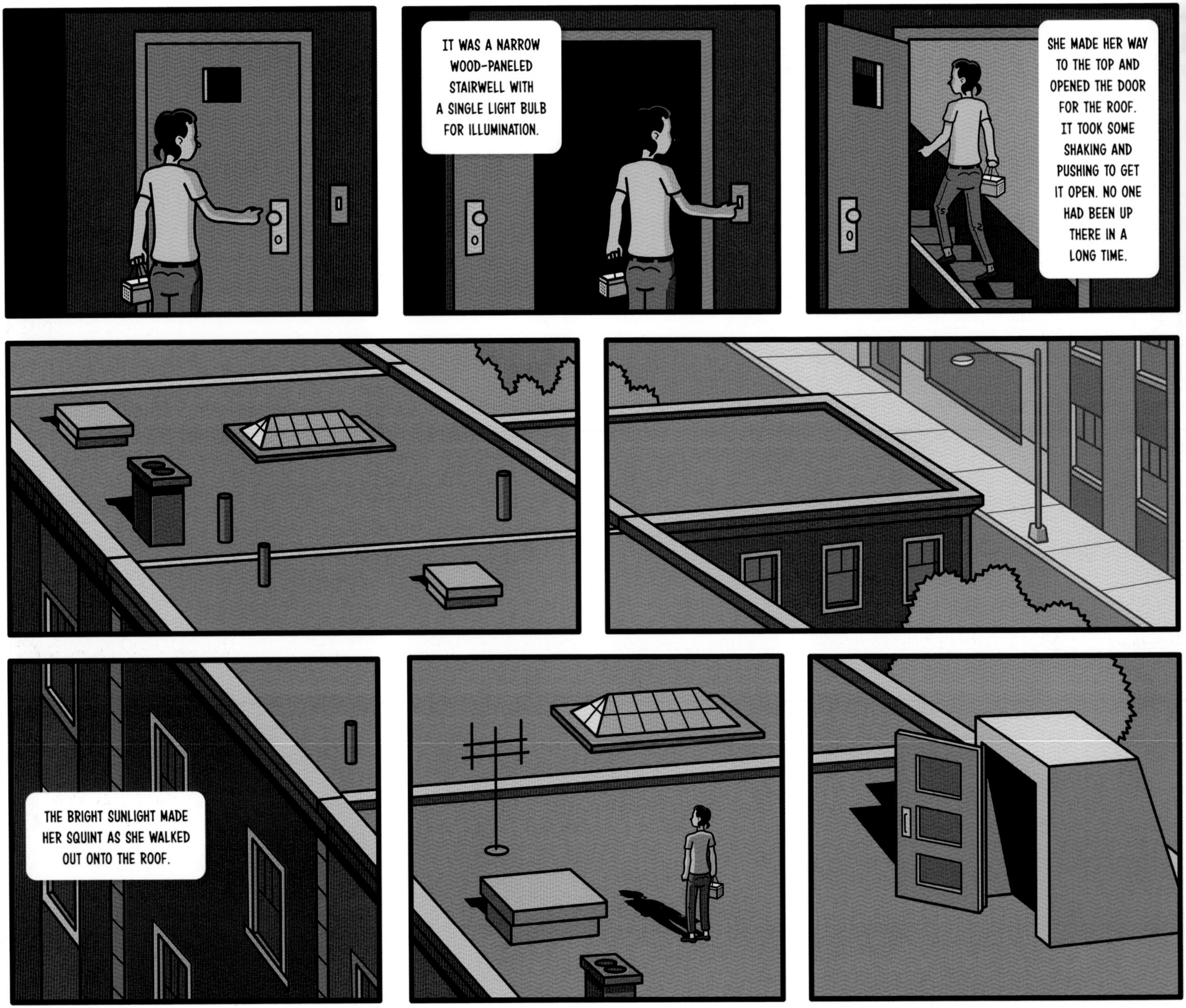
IT WAS A NARROW WOOD-PANELED STAIRWELL WITH A SINGLE LIGHT BULB FOR ILLUMINATION.
SHE MADE HER WAY TO THE TOP AND OPENED THE DOOR FOR THE ROOF. IT TOOK SOME SHAKING AND PUSHING TO GET IT OPEN. NO ONE HAD BEEN UP THERE IN A LONG TIME.
THE BRIGHT SUNLIGHT MADE HER SQUINT AS SHE WALKED OUT ONTO THE ROOF.

AT THE SIDE OF EACH ROOF WAS A LOW WALL SEPARATING ONE BUILDING FROM ANOTHER.

WITHIN A FEW SECONDS SHE COULD SEE THERE WAS NO COOP ON ANY OF THE ROOFS.

DISAPPOINTED, SHE MADE HER WAY DOWN THE ENTIRE ROW.

NOTHING BUT A FEW EMPTY BOTTLES AND SOME AIR DUCTS.

WHEN SHE GOT TO THE END SHE LOOKED OUT AT THE MASSIVE TREE IN FRONT OF HER. THE WOOD-SHINGLED HOUSE WAS NEARLY HIDDEN AWAY BEHIND ITS LEAVES.

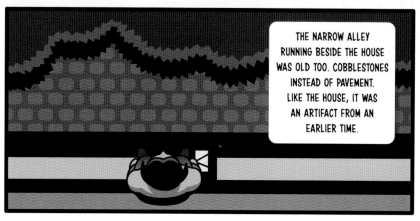

THE NARROW ALLEY RUNNING BESIDE THE HOUSE WAS OLD TOO. COBBLESTONES INSTEAD OF PAVEMENT. LIKE THE HOUSE, IT WAS AN ARTIFACT FROM AN EARLIER TIME.

IT WAS THEN, WHEN SHE WAS LOOKING DOWN AT THE COBBLESTONES THAT SHE HEARD A DISTANT COOING SOUND.

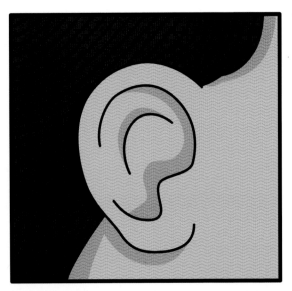

SHE STUDIED THE TREE, LOOKING FOR THE BIRD.

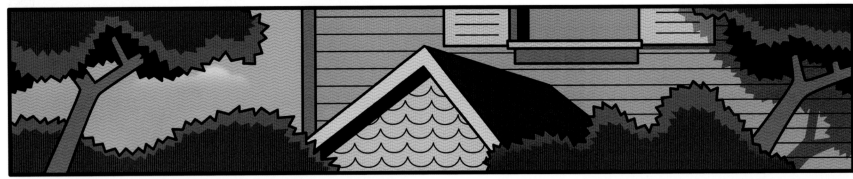

IT WAS A PIGEON'S CALL, SHE WAS SURE OF IT. WAS IT SITTING ON ONE OF THE BRANCHES?

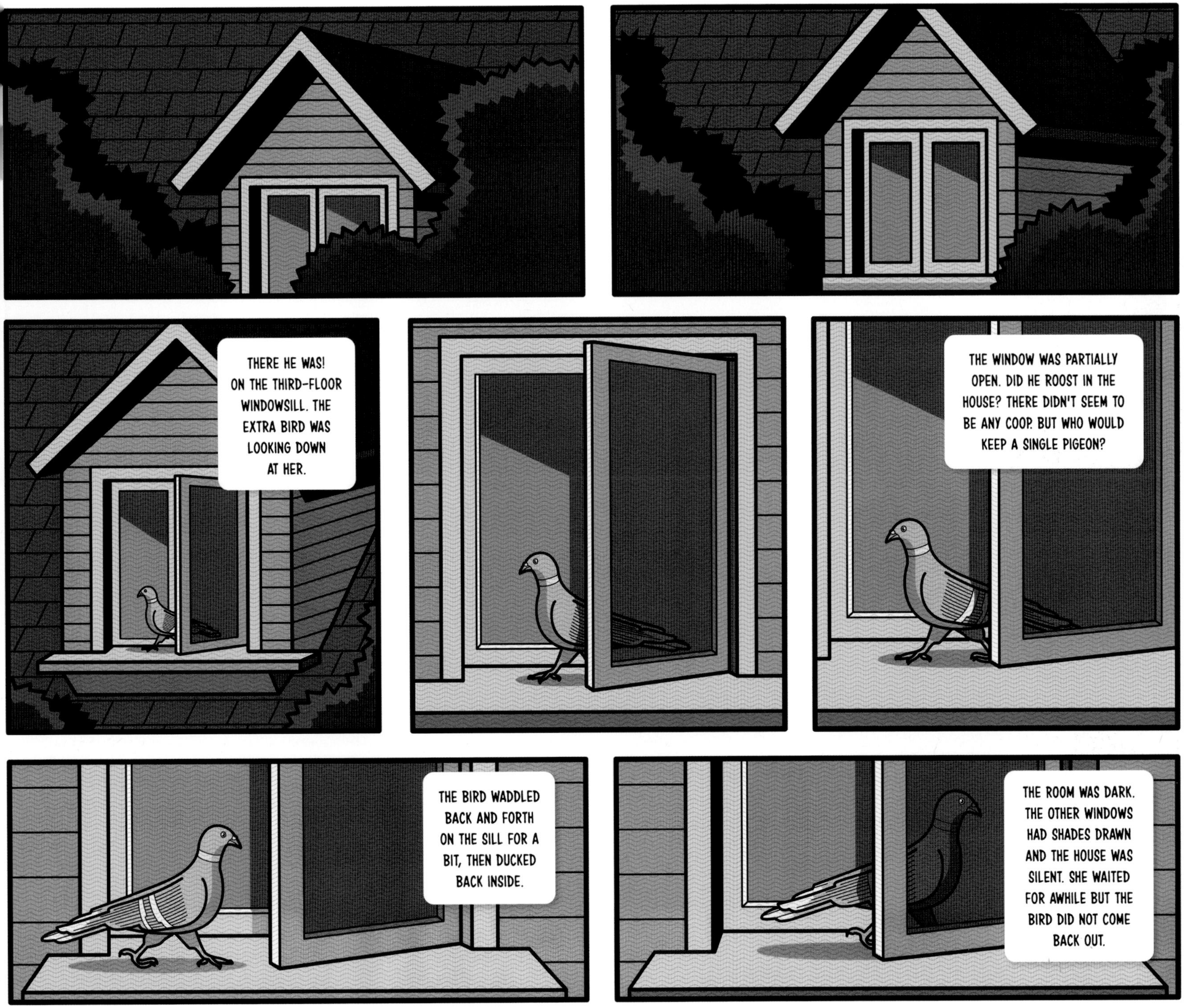
THERE HE WAS! ON THE THIRD-FLOOR WINDOWSILL. THE EXTRA BIRD WAS LOOKING DOWN AT HER.
THE WINDOW WAS PARTIALLY OPEN. DID HE ROOST IN THE HOUSE? THERE DIDN'T SEEM TO BE ANY COOP. BUT WHO WOULD KEEP A SINGLE PIGEON?
THE BIRD WADDLED BACK AND FORTH ON THE SILL FOR A BIT, THEN DUCKED BACK INSIDE.
THE ROOM WAS DARK. THE OTHER WINDOWS HAD SHADES DRAWN AND THE HOUSE WAS SILENT. SHE WAITED FOR AWHILE BUT THE BIRD DID NOT COME BACK OUT.

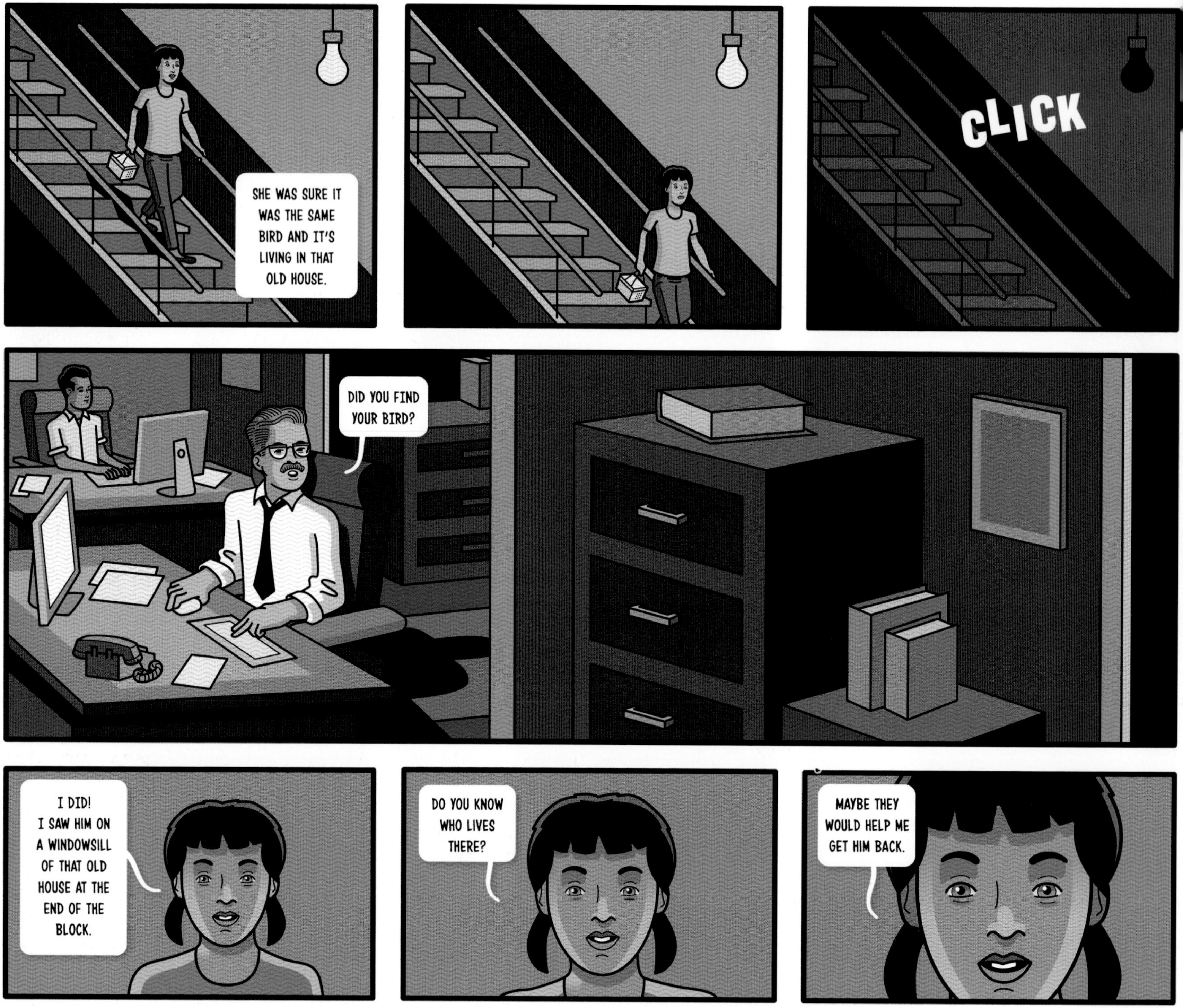
SHE WAS SURE IT WAS THE SAME BIRD AND IT'S LIVING IN THAT OLD HOUSE.
CLICK
DID YOU FIND YOUR BIRD?
I DID! I SAW HIM ON A WINDOWSILL OF THAT OLD HOUSE AT THE END OF THE BLOCK.
DO YOU KNOW WHO LIVES THERE?
MAYBE THEY WOULD HELP ME GET HIM BACK.

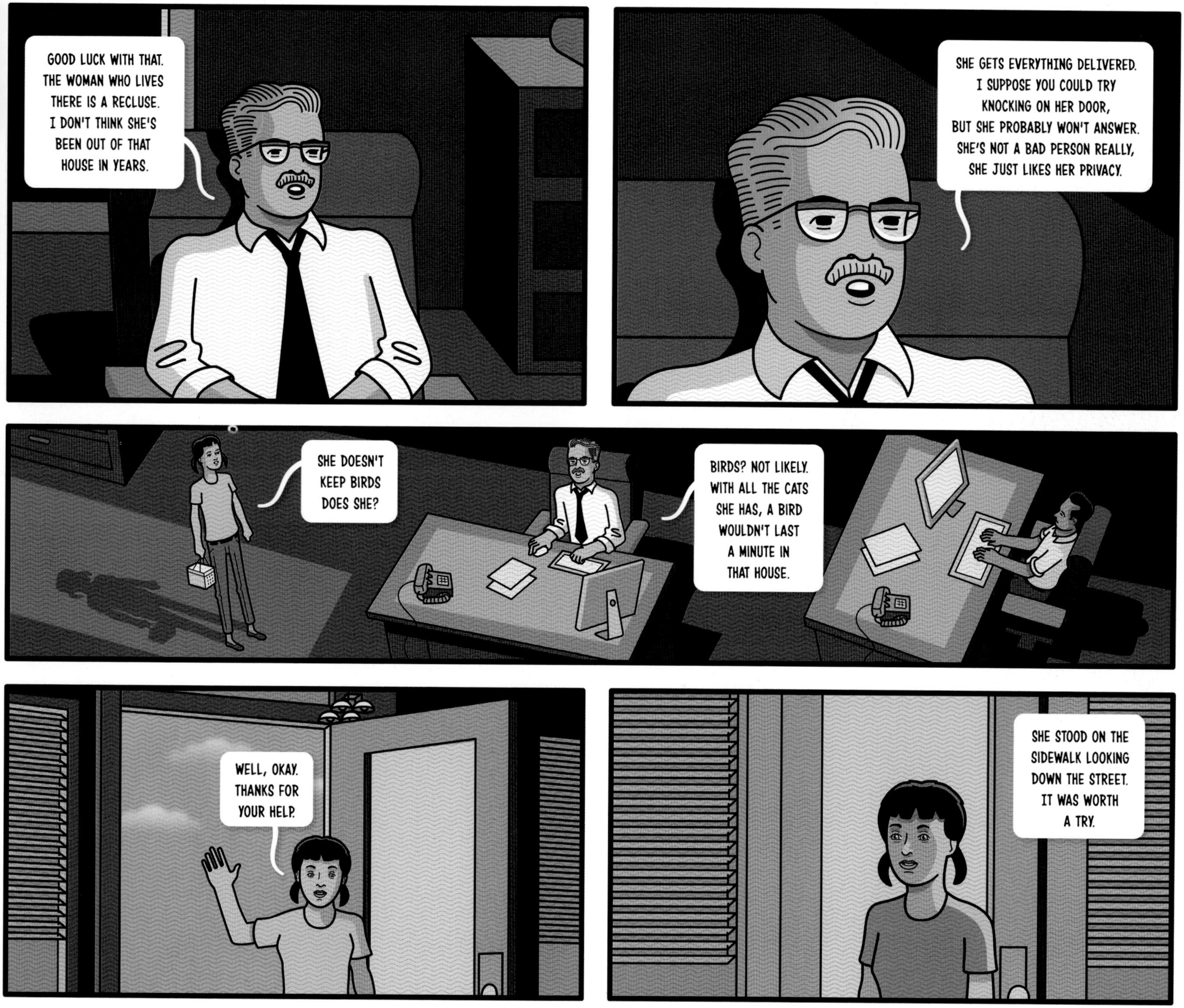
GOOD LUCK WITH THAT. THE WOMAN WHO LIVES THERE IS A RECLUSE. I DON'T THINK SHE'S BEEN OUT OF THAT HOUSE IN YEARS.
SHE GETS EVERYTHING DELIVERED. I SUPPOSE YOU COULD TRY KNOCKING ON HER DOOR, BUT SHE PROBABLY WON'T ANSWER. SHE'S NOT A BAD PERSON REALLY, SHE JUST LIKES HER PRIVACY.
SHE DOESN'T KEEP BIRDS DOES SHE?
BIRDS? NOT LIKELY. WITH ALL THE CATS SHE HAS, A BIRD WOULDN'T LAST A MINUTE IN THAT HOUSE.
WELL, OKAY. THANKS FOR YOUR HELP.
SHE STOOD ON THE SIDEWALK LOOKING DOWN THE STREET. IT WAS WORTH A TRY.

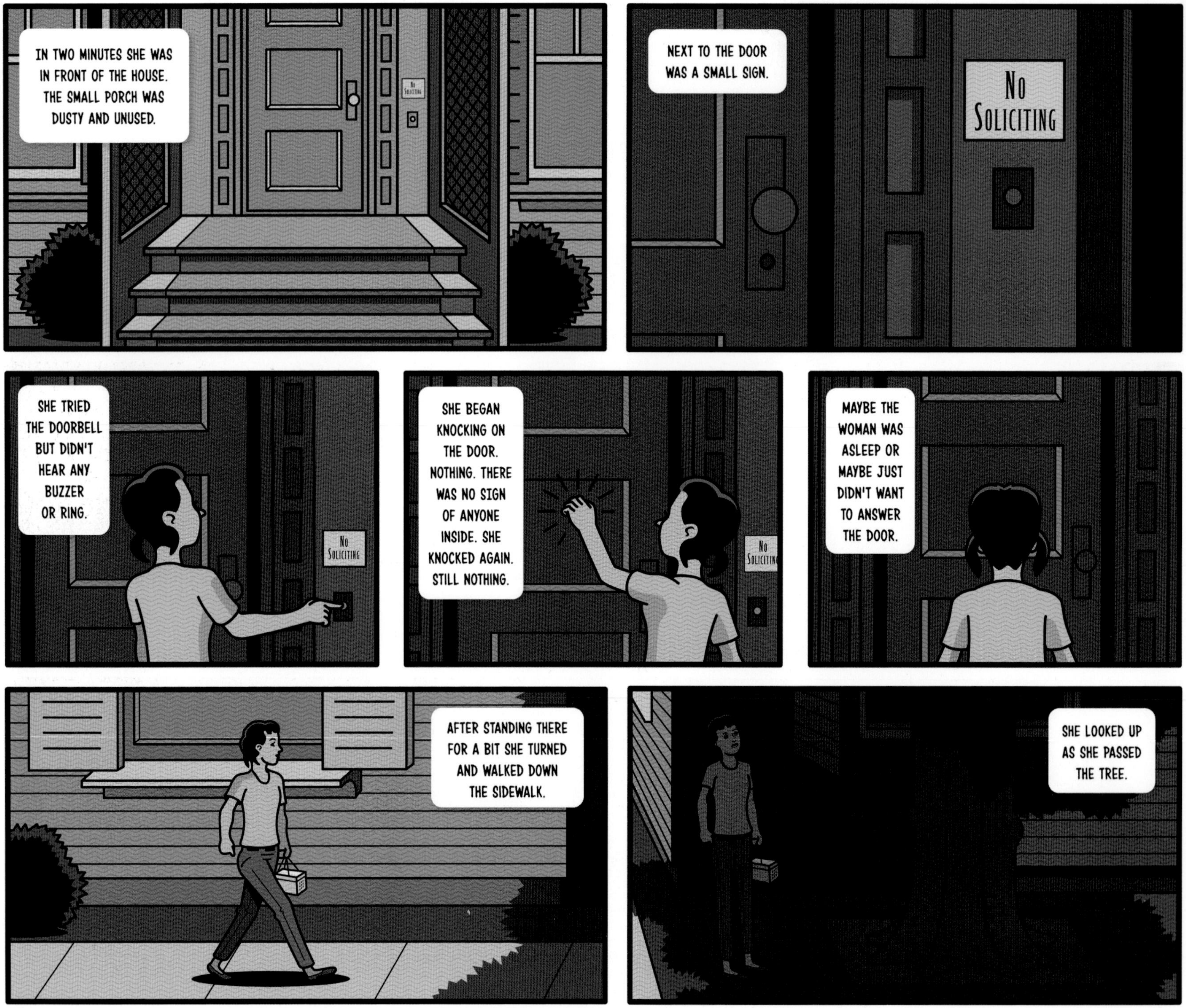
IN TWO MINUTES SHE WAS IN FRONT OF THE HOUSE. THE SMALL PORCH WAS DUSTY AND UNUSED.
NEXT TO THE DOOR WAS A SMALL SIGN.
NO SOLICITING
SHE TRIED THE DOORBELL BUT DIDN'T HEAR ANY BUZZER OR RING.
NO SOLICITING
SHE BEGAN KNOCKING ON THE DOOR. NOTHING. THERE WAS NO SIGN OF ANYONE INSIDE. SHE KNOCKED AGAIN. STILL NOTHING.
MAYBE THE WOMAN WAS ASLEEP OR MAYBE JUST DIDN'T WANT TO ANSWER THE DOOR.
AFTER STANDING THERE FOR A BIT SHE TURNED AND WALKED DOWN THE SIDEWALK.
SHE LOOKED UP AS SHE PASSED THE TREE.

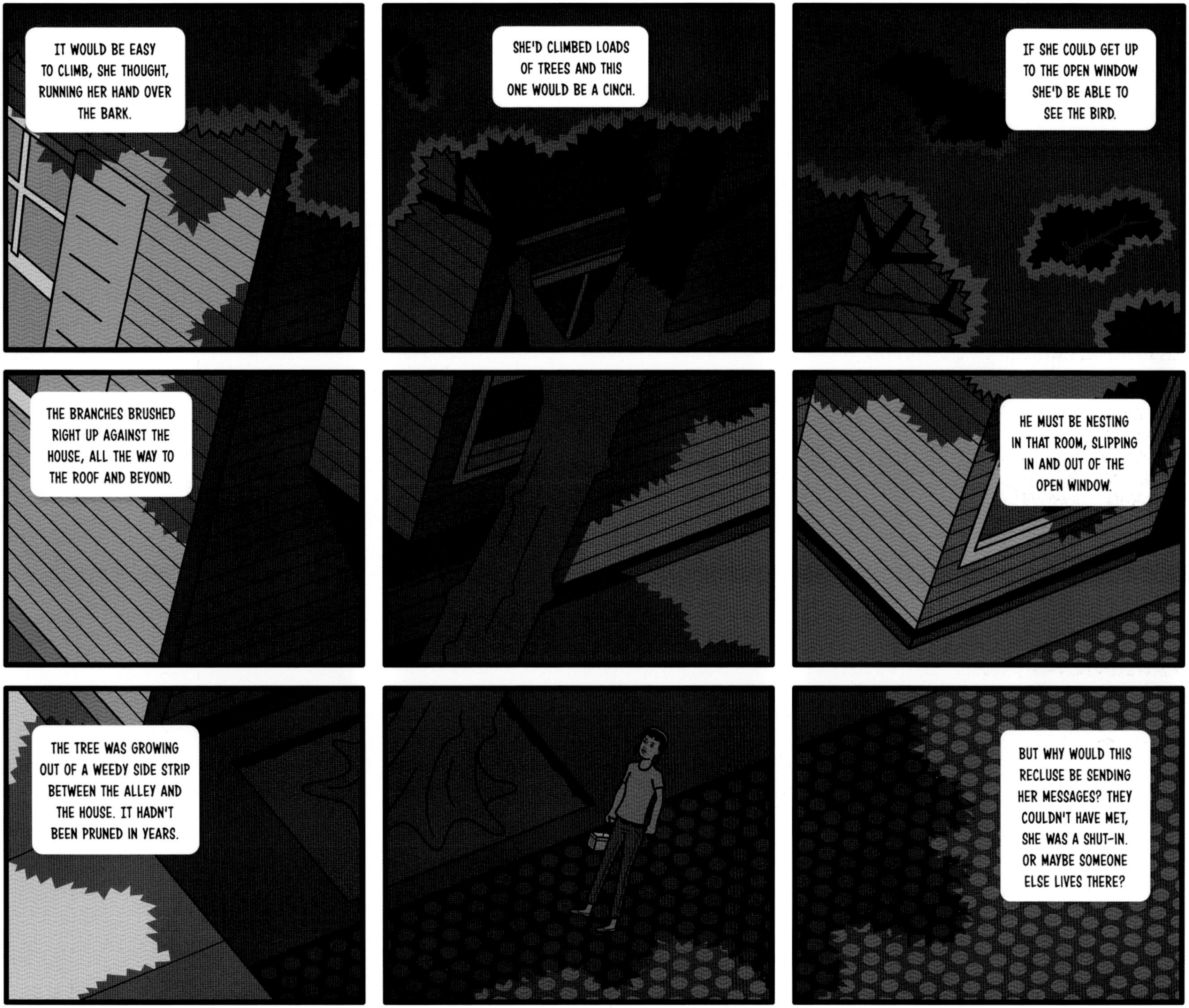
IT WOULD BE EASY TO CLIMB, SHE THOUGHT, RUNNING HER HAND OVER THE BARK.
SHE'D CLIMBED LOADS OF TREES AND THIS ONE WOULD BE A CINCH.
IF SHE COULD GET UP TO THE OPEN WINDOW SHE'D BE ABLE TO SEE THE BIRD.
THE BRANCHES BRUSHED RIGHT UP AGAINST THE HOUSE, ALL THE WAY TO THE ROOF AND BEYOND.
HE MUST BE NESTING IN THAT ROOM, SLIPPING IN AND OUT OF THE OPEN WINDOW.
THE TREE WAS GROWING OUT OF A WEEDY SIDE STRIP BETWEEN THE ALLEY AND THE HOUSE. IT HADN'T BEEN PRUNED IN YEARS.
BUT WHY WOULD THIS RECLUSE BE SENDING HER MESSAGES? THEY COULDN'T HAVE MET, SHE WAS A SHUT-IN. OR MAYBE SOMEONE ELSE LIVES THERE?

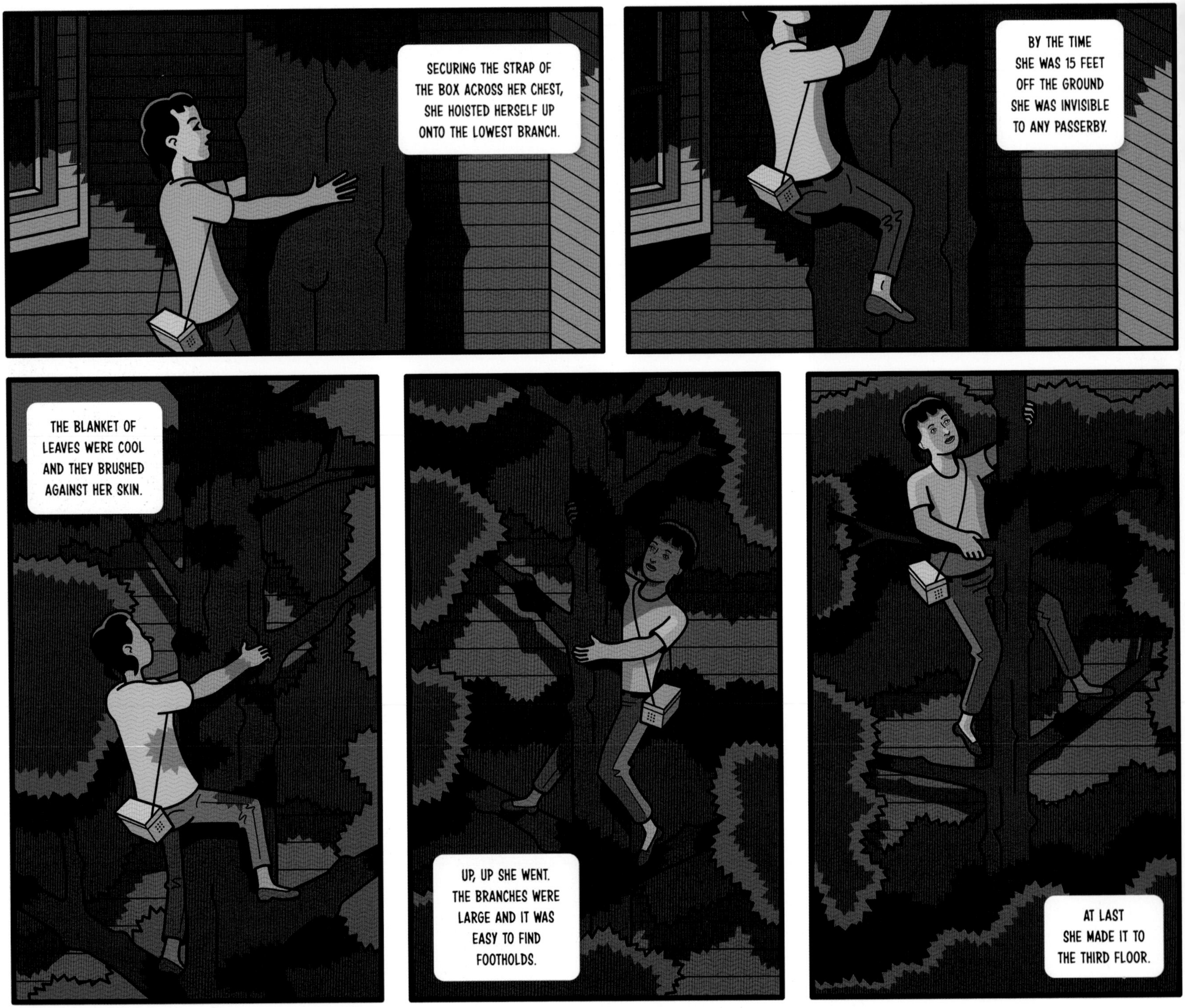
SECURING THE STRAP OF THE BOX ACROSS HER CHEST, SHE HOISTED HERSELF UP ONTO THE LOWEST BRANCH.
BY THE TIME SHE WAS 15 FEET OFF THE GROUND SHE WAS INVISIBLE TO ANY PASSERBY.
THE BLANKET OF LEAVES WERE COOL AND THEY BRUSHED AGAINST HER SKIN.
UP, UP SHE WENT. THE BRANCHES WERE LARGE AND IT WAS EASY TO FIND FOOTHOLDS.
AT LAST SHE MADE IT TO THE THIRD FLOOR.

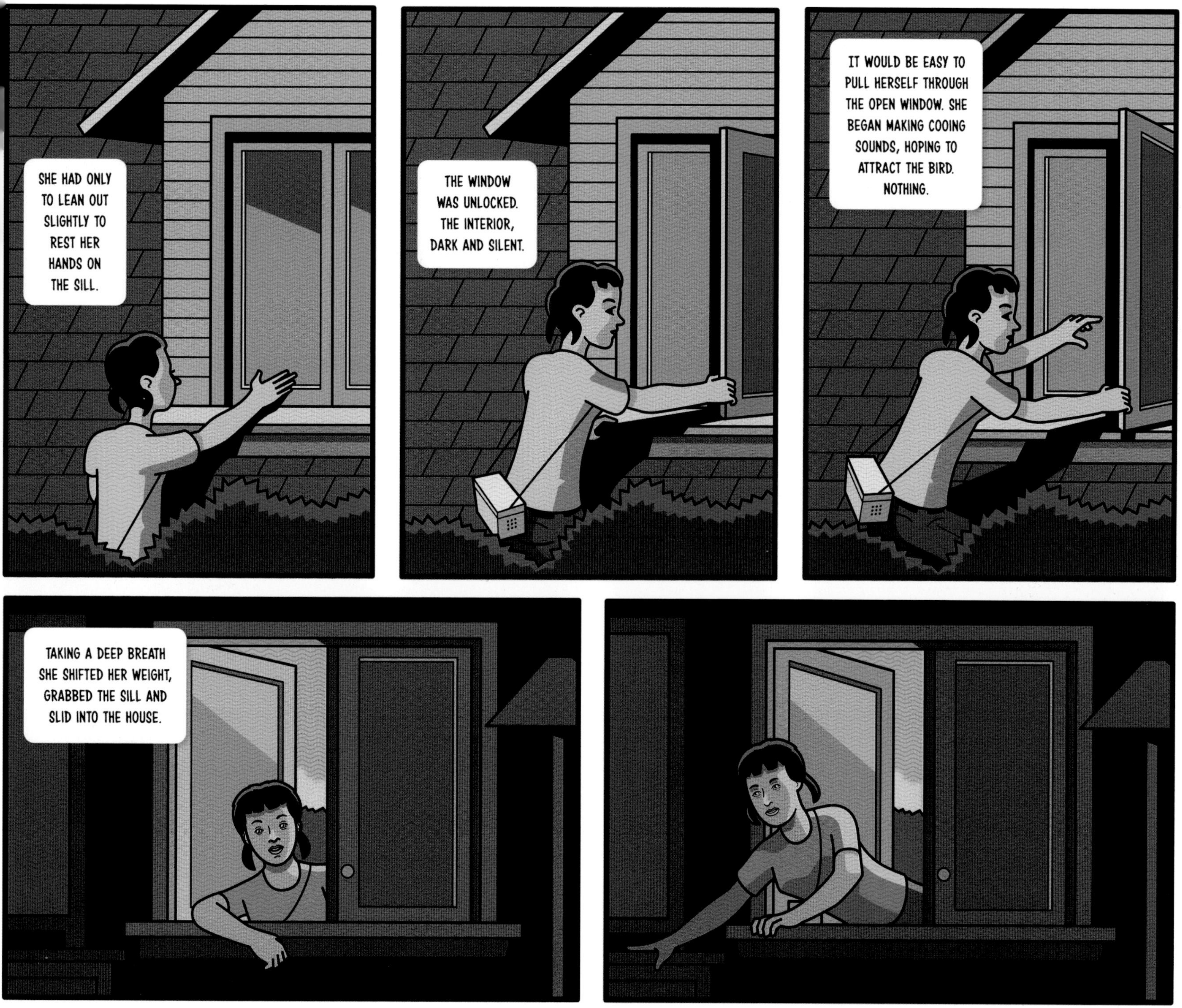
SHE HAD ONLY TO LEAN OUT SLIGHTLY TO REST HER HANDS ON THE SILL.
THE WINDOW WAS UNLOCKED. THE INTERIOR, DARK AND SILENT.
IT WOULD BE EASY TO PULL HERSELF THROUGH THE OPEN WINDOW. SHE BEGAN MAKING COOING SOUNDS, HOPING TO ATTRACT THE BIRD. NOTHING.
TAKING A DEEP BREATH SHE SHIFTED HER WEIGHT, GRABBED THE SILL AND SLID INTO THE HOUSE.

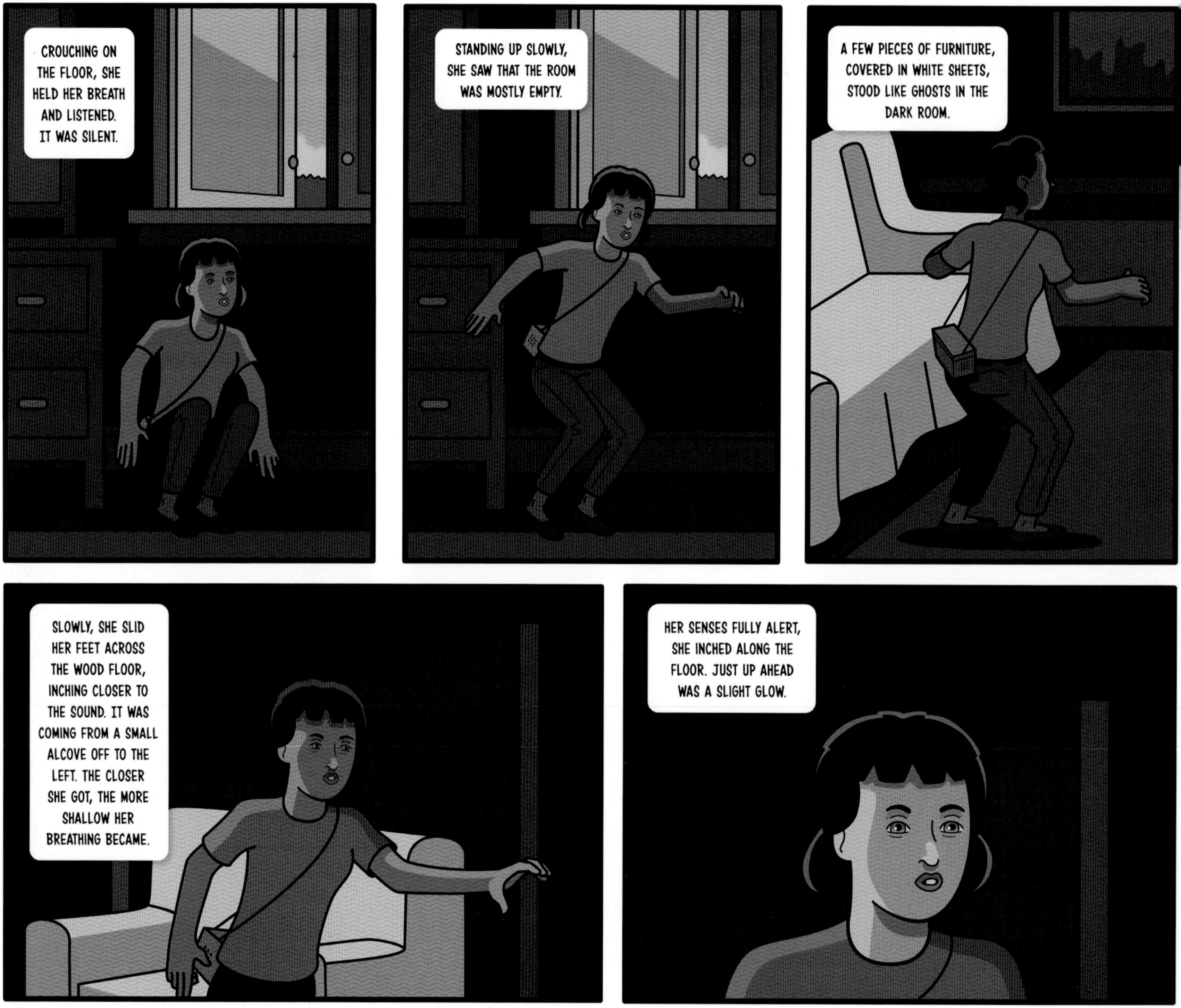
CROUCHING ON THE FLOOR, SHE HELD HER BREATH AND LISTENED. IT WAS SILENT.
STANDING UP SLOWLY, SHE SAW THAT THE ROOM WAS MOSTLY EMPTY.
A FEW PIECES OF FURNITURE, COVERED IN WHITE SHEETS, STOOD LIKE GHOSTS IN THE DARK ROOM.
SLOWLY, SHE SLID HER FEET ACROSS THE WOOD FLOOR, INCHING CLOSER TO THE SOUND. IT WAS COMING FROM A SMALL ALCOVE OFF TO THE LEFT. THE CLOSER SHE GOT, THE MORE SHALLOW HER BREATHING BECAME.
HER SENSES FULLY ALERT, SHE INCHED ALONG THE FLOOR. JUST UP AHEAD WAS A SLIGHT GLOW.

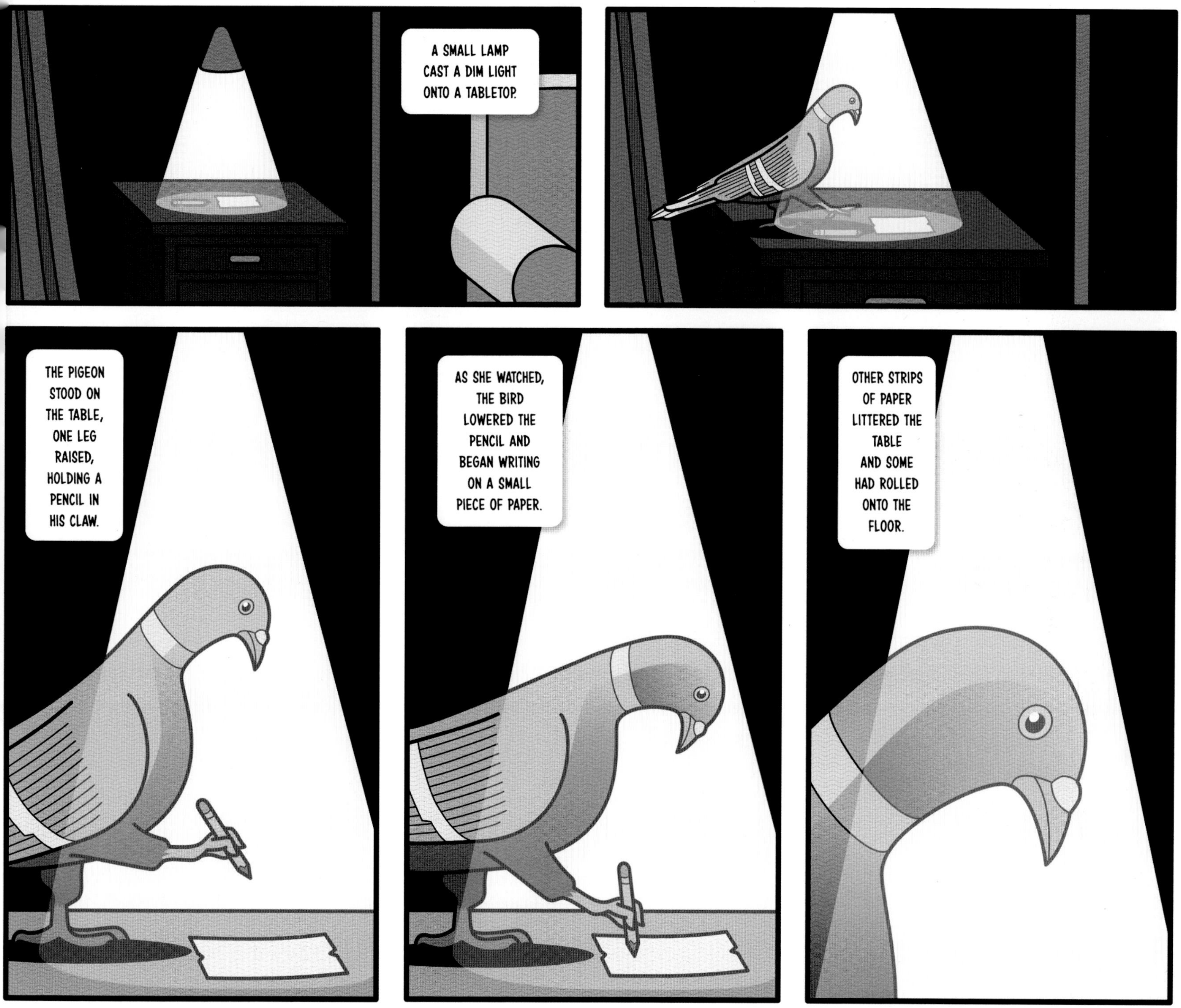
A SMALL LAMP CAST A DIM LIGHT ONTO A TABLETOP.
THE PIGEON STOOD ON THE TABLE, ONE LEG RAISED, HOLDING A PENCIL IN HIS CLAW.
AS SHE WATCHED, THE BIRD LOWERED THE PENCIL AND BEGAN WRITING ON A SMALL PIECE OF PAPER.
OTHER STRIPS OF PAPER LITTERED THE TABLE AND SOME HAD ROLLED ONTO THE FLOOR.

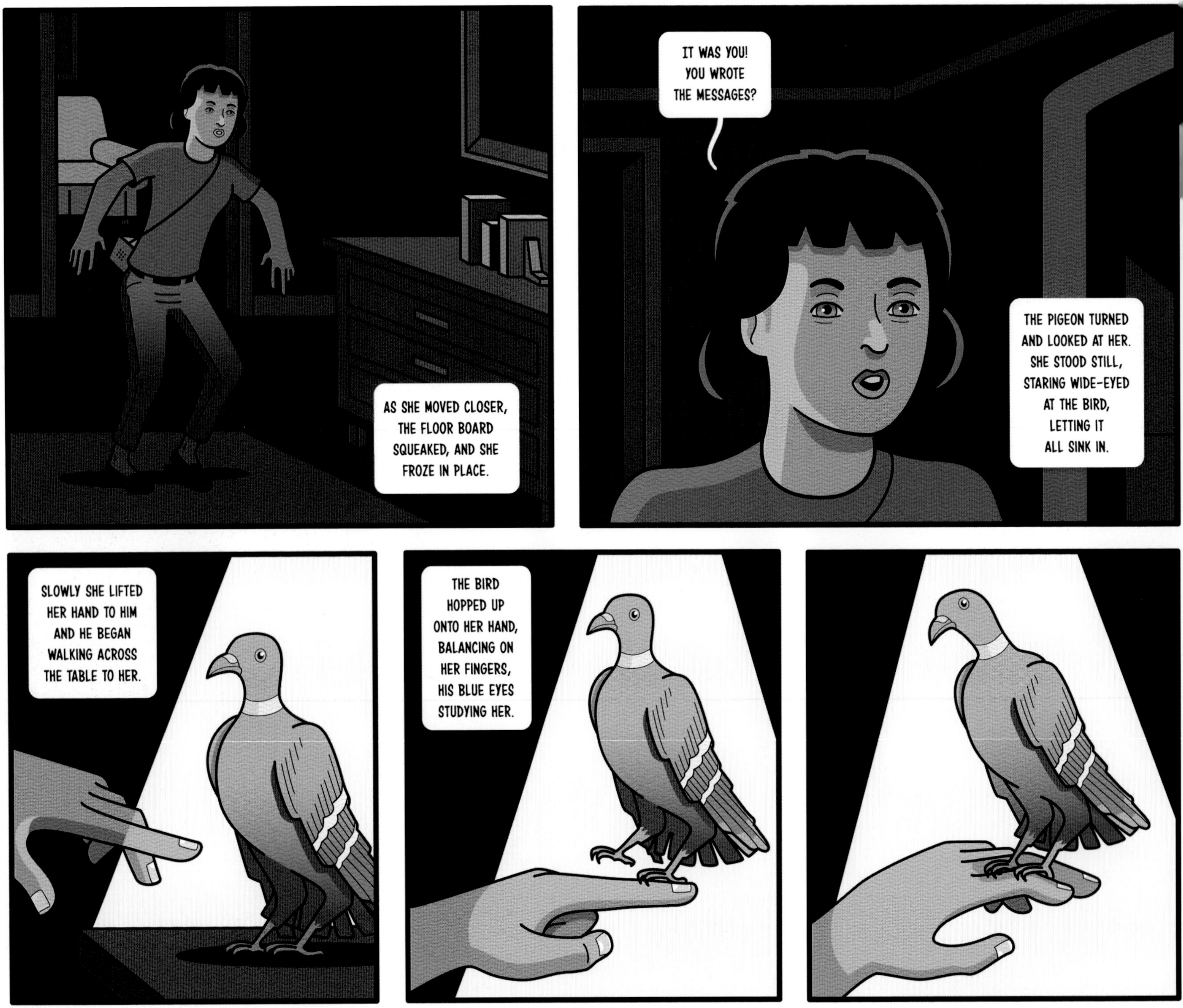
AS SHE MOVED CLOSER, THE FLOOR BOARD SQUEAKED, AND SHE FROZE IN PLACE.
IT WAS YOU! YOU WROTE THE MESSAGES?
THE PIGEON TURNED AND LOOKED AT HER. SHE STOOD STILL, STARING WIDE-EYED AT THE BIRD, LETTING IT ALL SINK IN.
SLOWLY SHE LIFTED HER HAND TO HIM AND HE BEGAN WALKING ACROSS THE TABLE TO HER.
THE BIRD HOPPED UP ONTO HER HAND, BALANCING ON HER FINGERS, HIS BLUE EYES STUDYING HER.

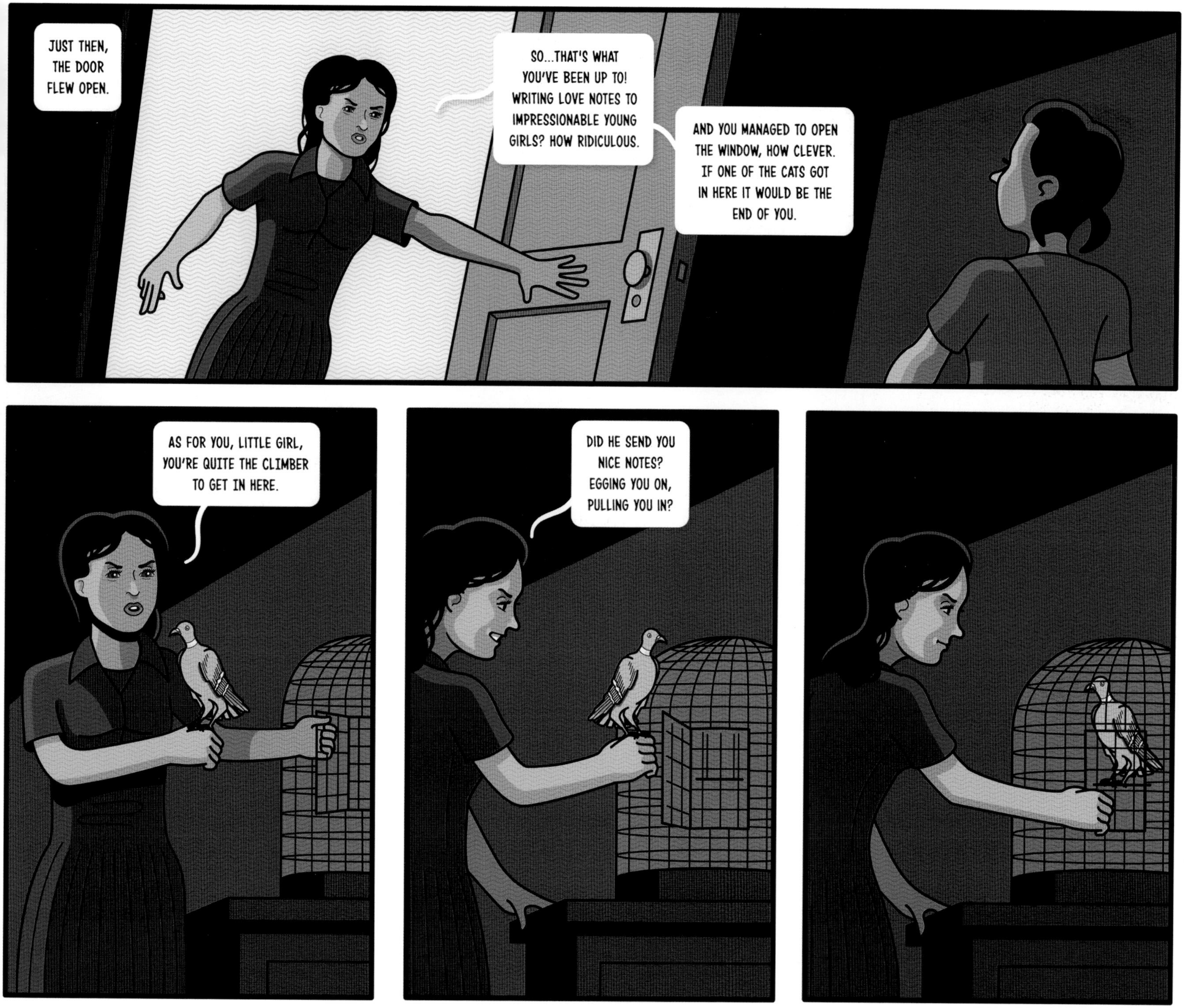
JUST THEN, THE DOOR FLEW OPEN.
SO...THAT'S WHAT YOU'VE BEEN UP TO! WRITING LOVE NOTES TO IMPRESSIONABLE YOUNG GIRLS? HOW RIDICULOUS.
AND YOU MANAGED TO OPEN THE WINDOW, HOW CLEVER. IF ONE OF THE CATS GOT IN HERE IT WOULD BE THE END OF YOU.
AS FOR YOU, LITTLE GIRL, YOU'RE QUITE THE CLIMBER TO GET IN HERE.
DID HE SEND YOU NICE NOTES? EGGING YOU ON, PULLING YOU IN?

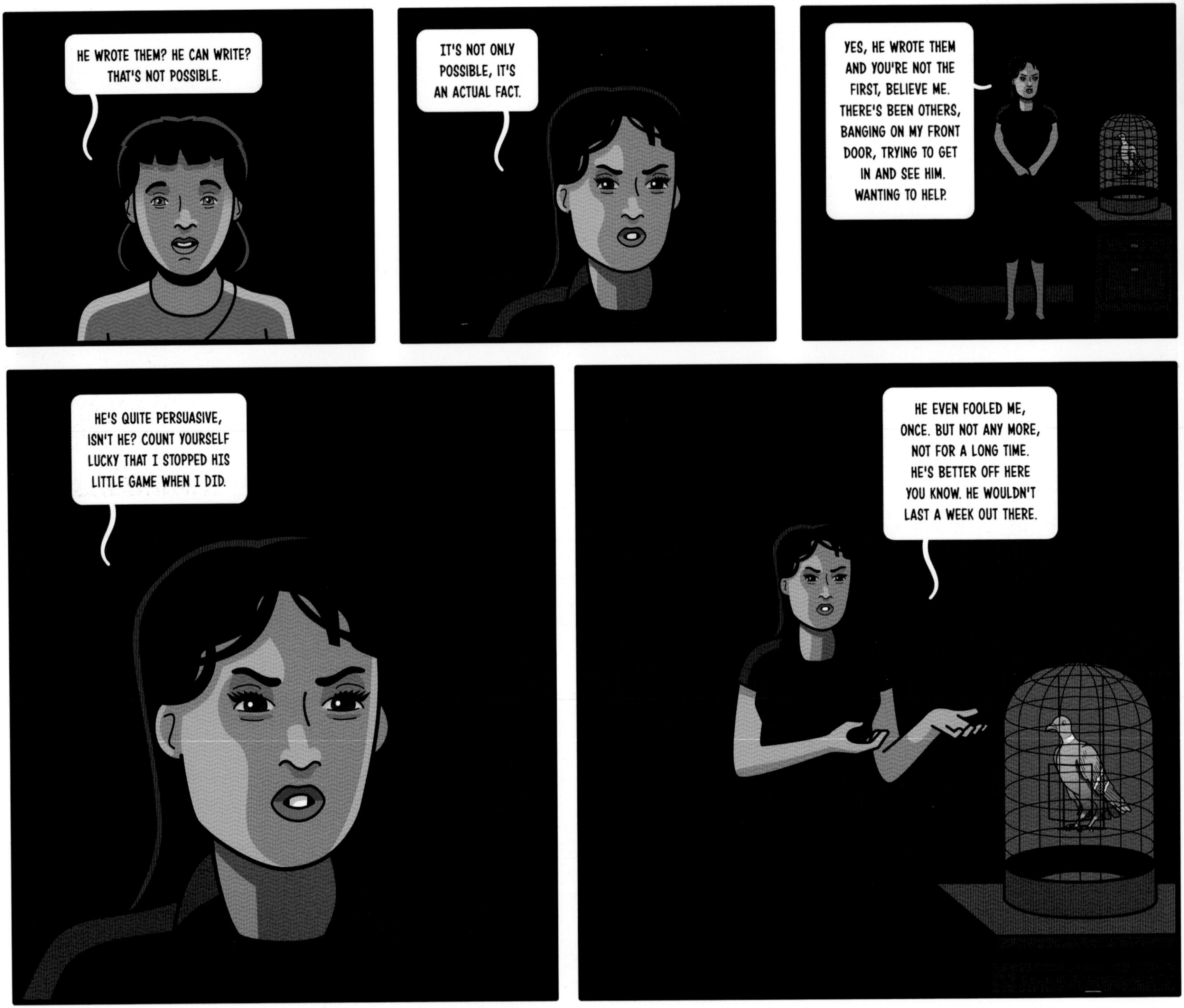
HE WROTE THEM? HE CAN WRITE? THAT'S NOT POSSIBLE.
IT'S NOT ONLY POSSIBLE, IT'S AN ACTUAL FACT.
YES, HE WROTE THEM AND YOU'RE NOT THE FIRST, BELIEVE ME. THERE'S BEEN OTHERS, BANGING ON MY FRONT DOOR, TRYING TO GET IN AND SEE HIM. WANTING TO HELP.
HE'S QUITE PERSUASIVE, ISN'T HE? COUNT YOURSELF LUCKY THAT I STOPPED HIS LITTLE GAME WHEN I DID.
HE EVEN FOOLED ME, ONCE. BUT NOT ANY MORE, NOT FOR A LONG TIME. HE'S BETTER OFF HERE YOU KNOW. HE WOULDN'T LAST A WEEK OUT THERE.

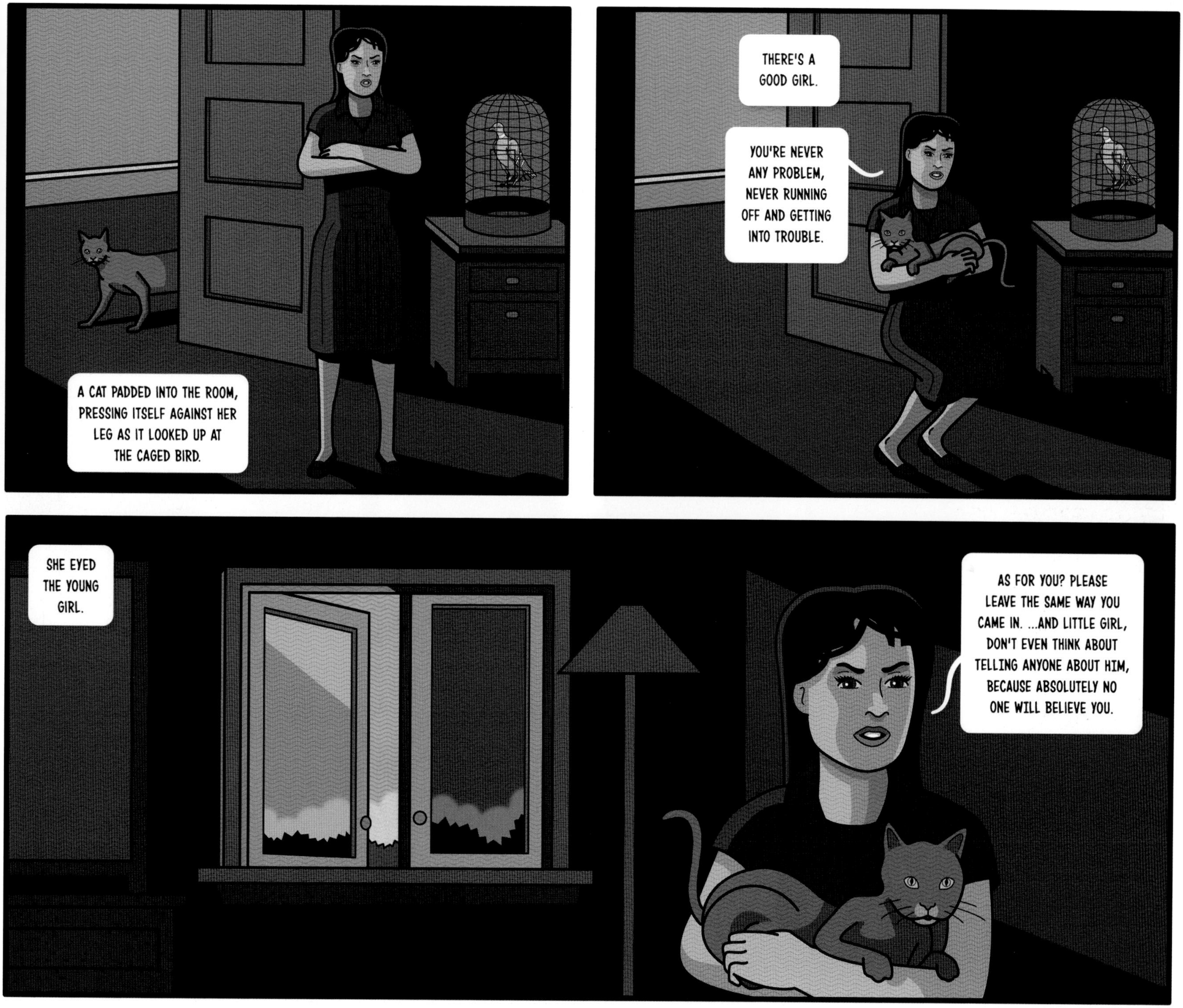
A CAT PADDED INTO THE ROOM, PRESSING ITSELF AGAINST HER LEG AS IT LOOKED UP AT THE CAGED BIRD.
THERE'S A GOOD GIRL.
YOU'RE NEVER ANY PROBLEM, NEVER RUNNING OFF AND GETTING INTO TROUBLE.
SHE EYED THE YOUNG GIRL.
AS FOR YOU? PLEASE LEAVE THE SAME WAY YOU CAME IN. ...AND LITTLE GIRL, DON'T EVEN THINK ABOUT TELLING ANYONE ABOUT HIM, BECAUSE ABSOLUTELY NO ONE WILL BELIEVE YOU.

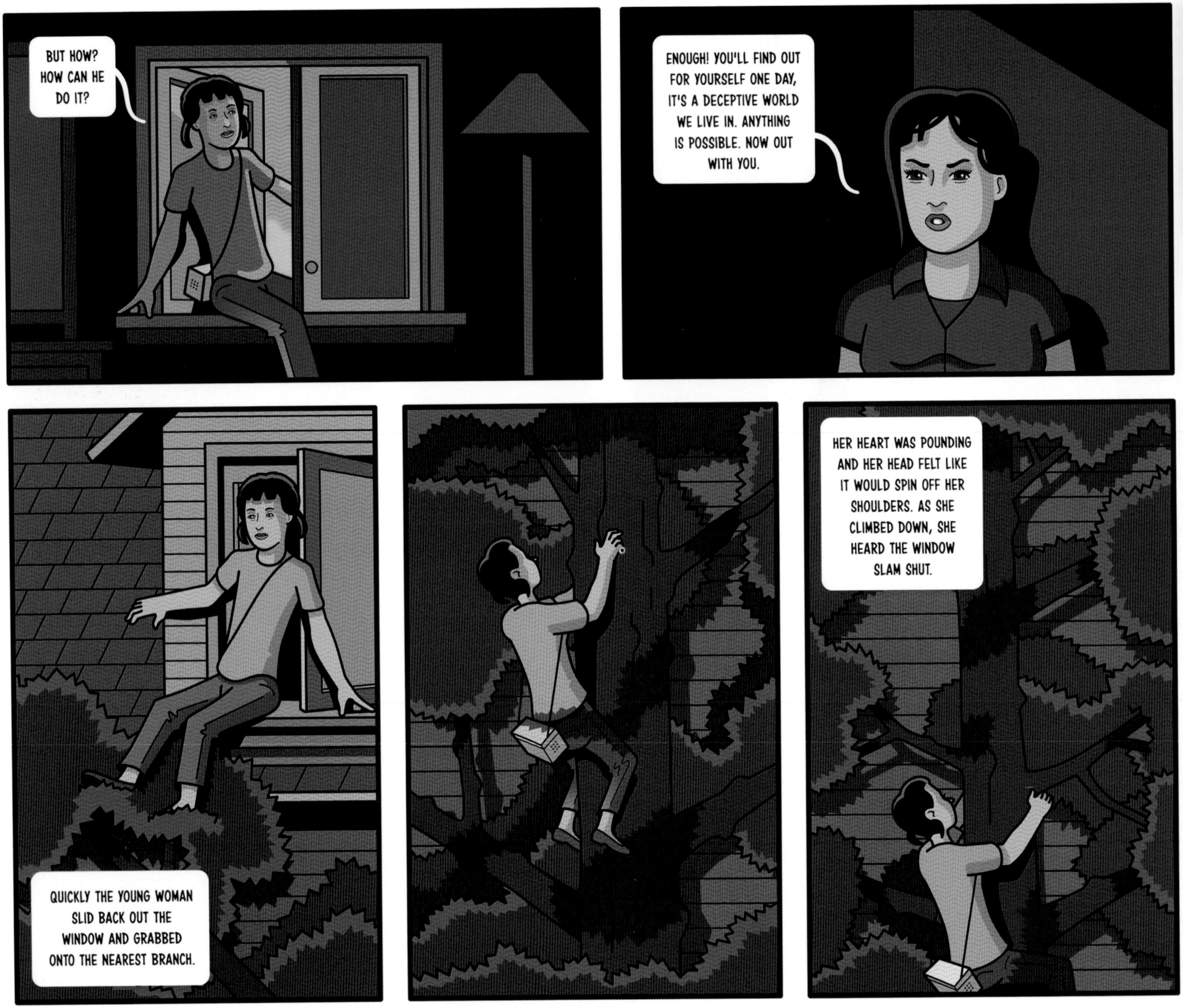
BUT HOW? HOW CAN HE DO IT?
ENOUGH! YOU'LL FIND OUT FOR YOURSELF ONE DAY, IT'S A DECEPTIVE WORLD WE LIVE IN. ANYTHING IS POSSIBLE. NOW OUT WITH YOU.
QUICKLY THE YOUNG WOMAN SLID BACK OUT THE WINDOW AND GRABBED ONTO THE NEAREST BRANCH.
HER HEART WAS POUNDING AND HER HEAD FELT LIKE IT WOULD SPIN OFF HER SHOULDERS. AS SHE CLIMBED DOWN, SHE HEARD THE WINDOW SLAM SHUT.

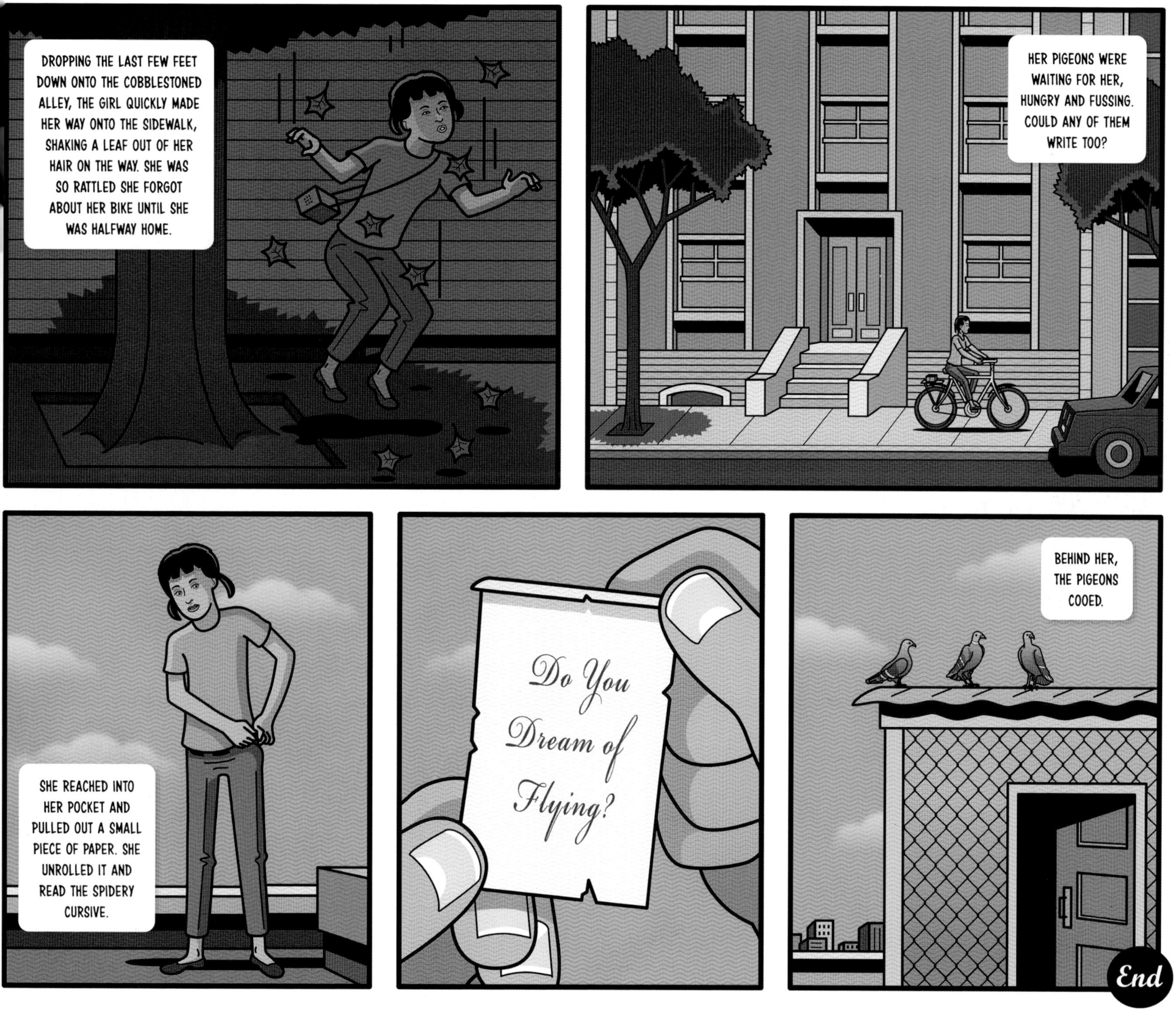
DROPPING THE LAST FEW FEET DOWN ONTO THE COBBLESTONED ALLEY, THE GIRL QUICKLY MADE HER WAY ONTO THE SIDEWALK, SHAKING A LEAF OUT OF HER HAIR ON THE WAY. SHE WAS SO RATTLED SHE FORGOT ABOUT HER BIKE UNTIL SHE WAS HALFWAY HOME.
HER PIGEONS WERE WAITING FOR HER, HUNGRY AND FUSSING. COULD ANY OF THEM WRITE TOO?
SHE REACHED INTO HER POCKET AND PULLED OUT A SMALL PIECE OF PAPER. SHE UNROLLED IT AND READ THE SPIDERY CURSIVE.
Do You Dream of Flying?
BEHIND HER, THE PIGEONS COOED.
End

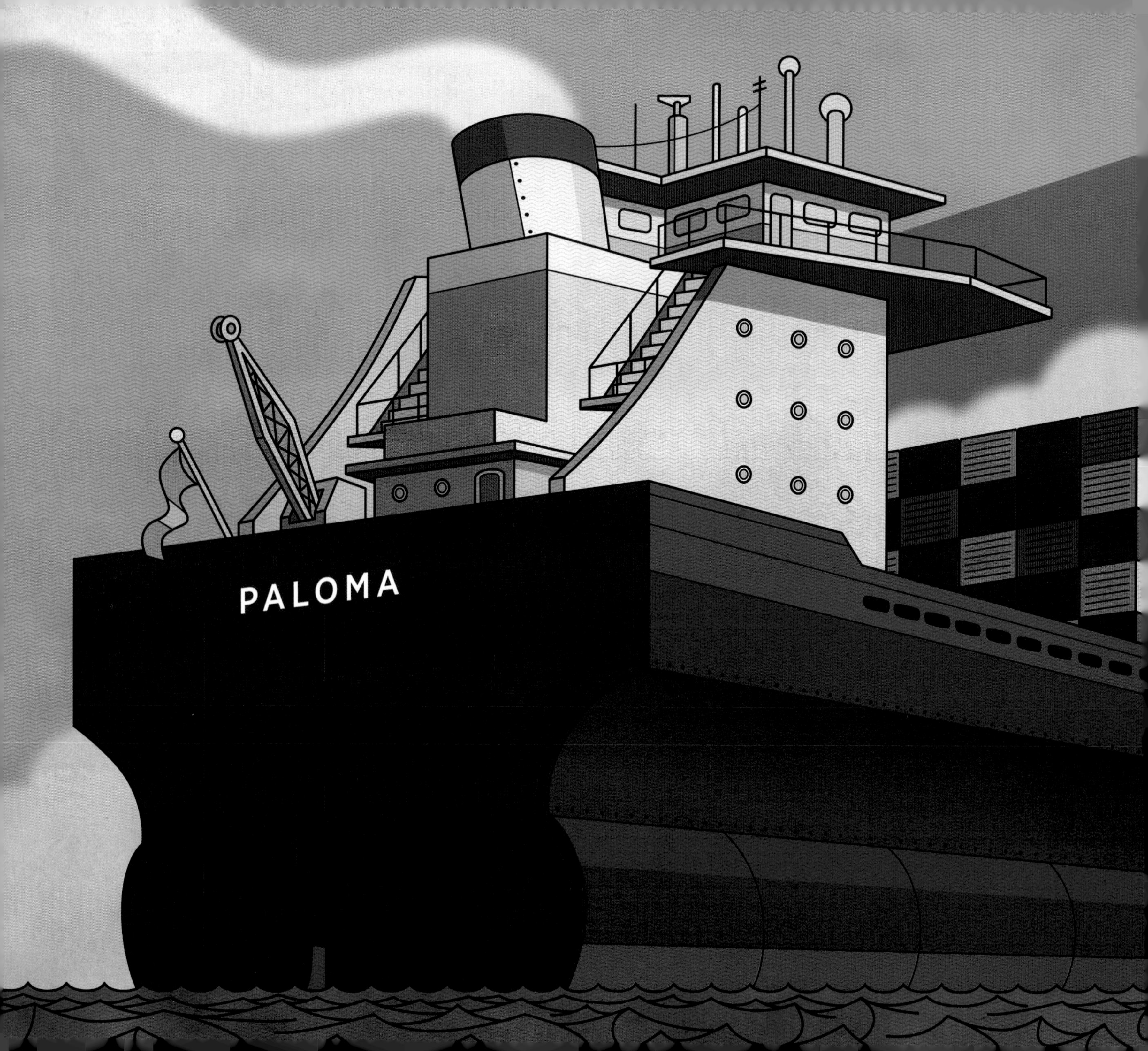
PALOMA

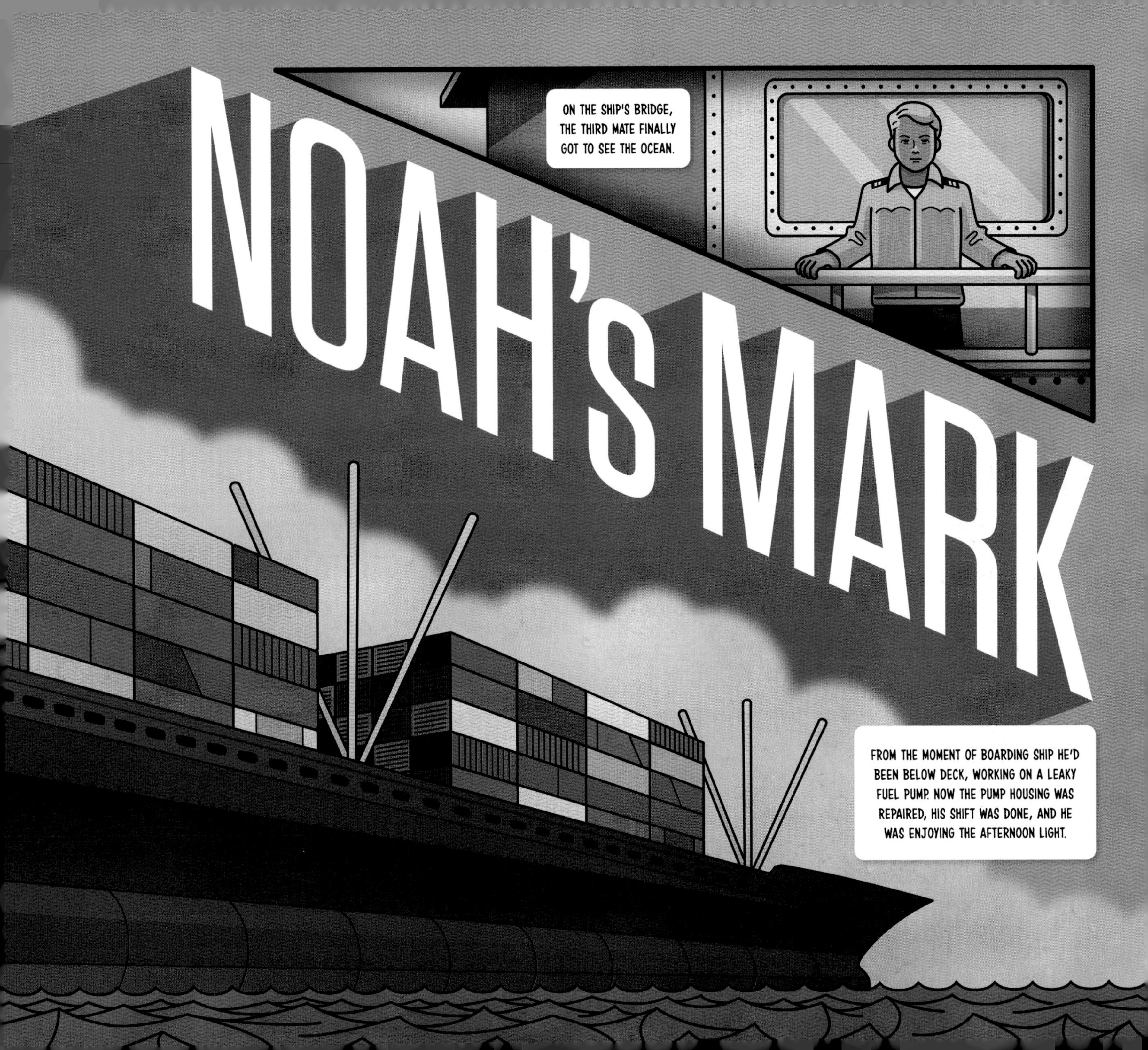
NOAH'S MARK
ON THE SHIP'S BRIDGE, THE THIRD MATE FINALLY GOT TO SEE THE OCEAN.
FROM THE MOMENT OF BOARDING SHIP HE'D BEEN BELOW DECK, WORKING ON A LEAKY FUEL PUMP. NOW THE PUMP HOUSING WAS REPAIRED, HIS SHIFT WAS DONE, AND HE WAS ENJOYING THE AFTERNOON LIGHT.

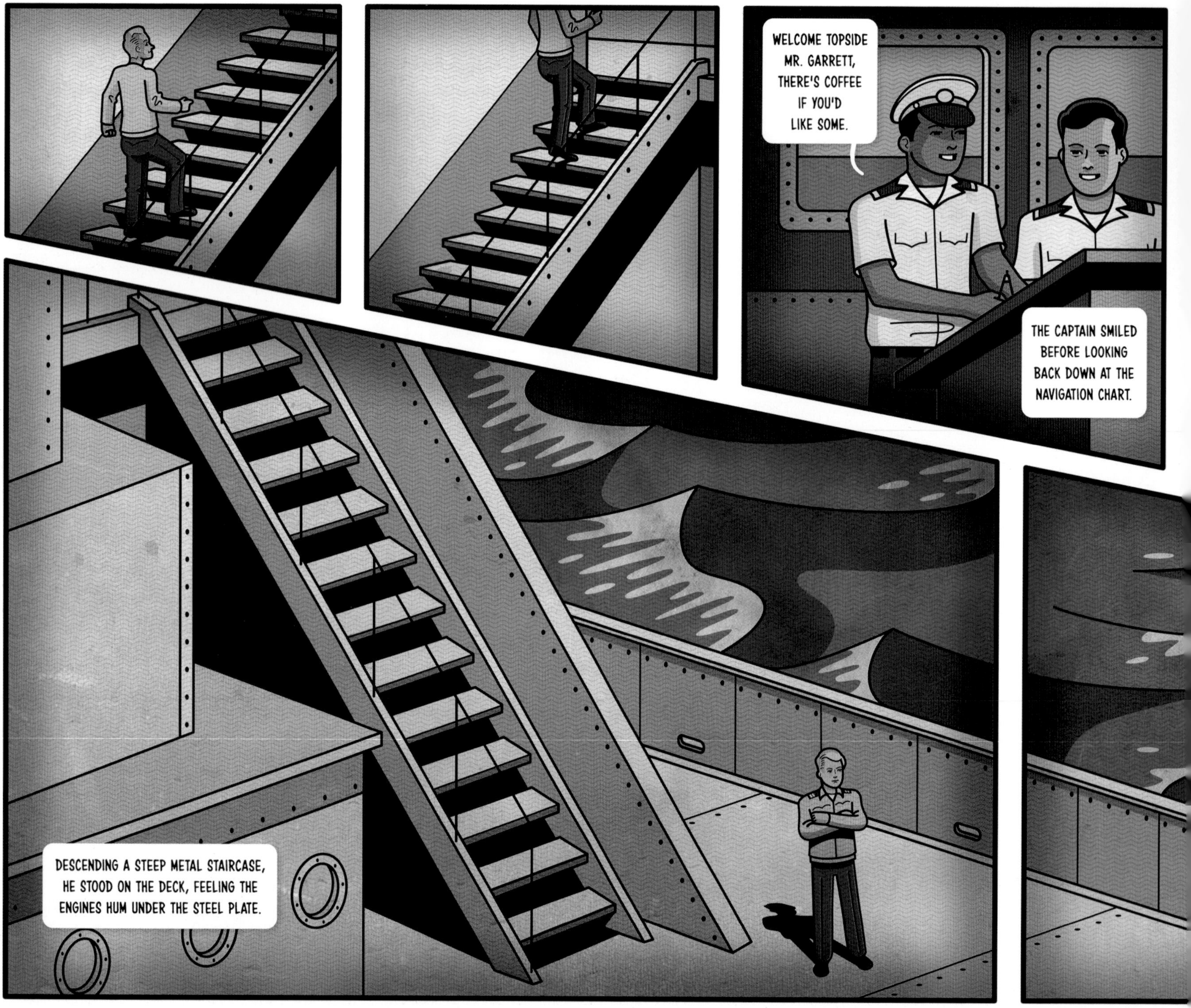
WELCOME TOPSIDE MR. GARRETT, THERE'S COFFEE IF YOU'D LIKE SOME.
THE CAPTAIN SMILED BEFORE LOOKING BACK DOWN AT THE NAVIGATION CHART.
DESCENDING A STEEP METAL STAIRCASE, HE STOOD ON THE DECK, FEELING THE ENGINES HUM UNDER THE STEEL PLATE.

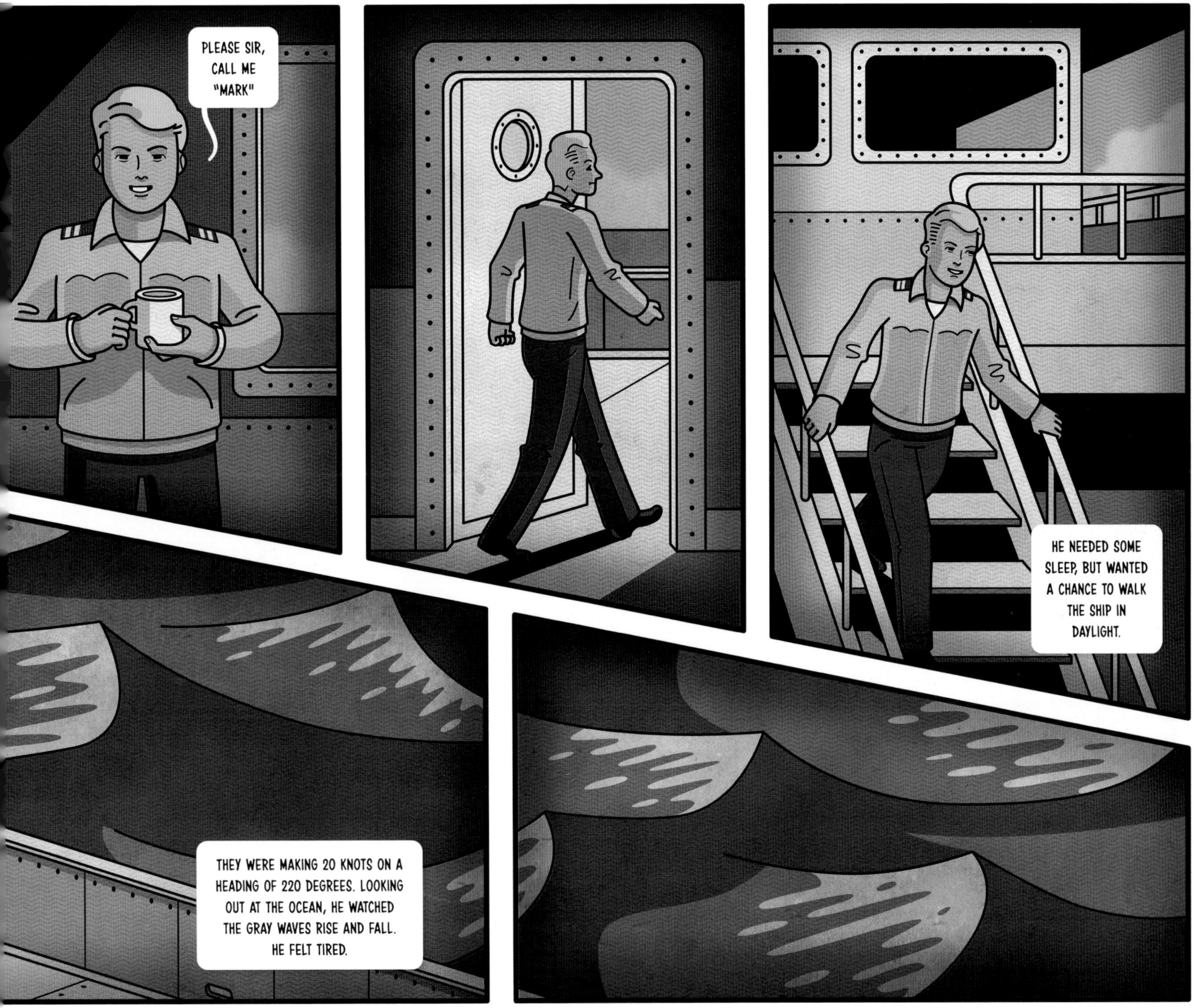
PLEASE SIR, CALL ME "MARK"
HE NEEDED SOME SLEEP, BUT WANTED A CHANCE TO WALK THE SHIP IN DAYLIGHT.
THEY WERE MAKING 20 KNOTS ON A HEADING OF 220 DEGREES. LOOKING OUT AT THE OCEAN, HE WATCHED THE GRAY WAVES RISE AND FALL. HE FELT TIRED.

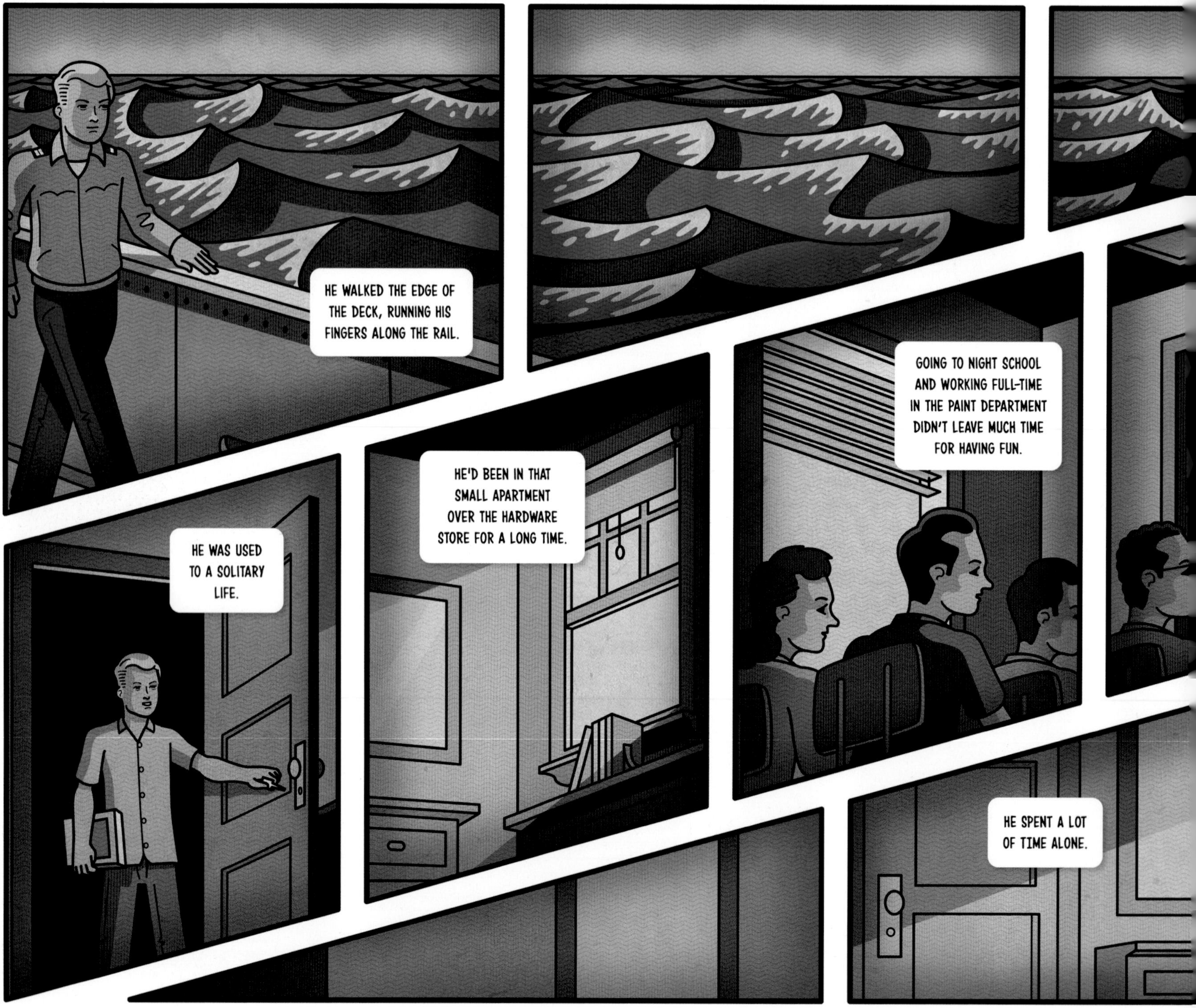
HE WALKED THE EDGE OF THE DECK, RUNNING HIS FINGERS ALONG THE RAIL.
HE WAS USED TO A SOLITARY LIFE.
HE'D BEEN IN THAT SMALL APARTMENT OVER THE HARDWARE STORE FOR A LONG TIME.
GOING TO NIGHT SCHOOL AND WORKING FULL-TIME IN THE PAINT DEPARTMENT DIDN'T LEAVE MUCH TIME FOR HAVING FUN.
HE SPENT A LOT OF TIME ALONE.

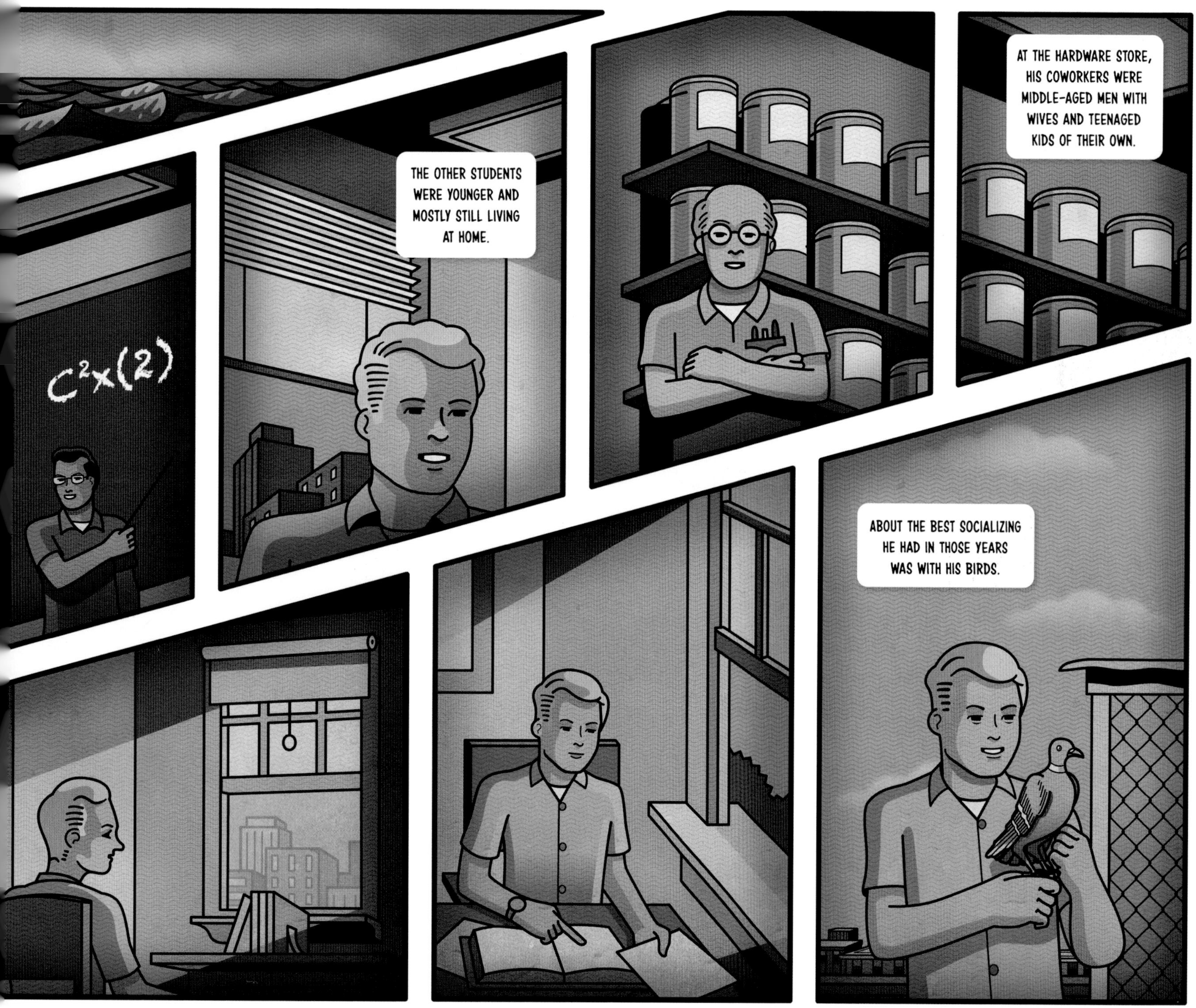
THE OTHER STUDENTS WERE YOUNGER AND MOSTLY STILL LIVING AT HOME.
AT THE HARDWARE STORE, HIS COWORKERS WERE MIDDLE-AGED MEN WITH WIVES AND TEENAGED KIDS OF THEIR OWN.
ABOUT THE BEST SOCIALIZING HE HAD IN THOSE YEARS WAS WITH HIS BIRDS.

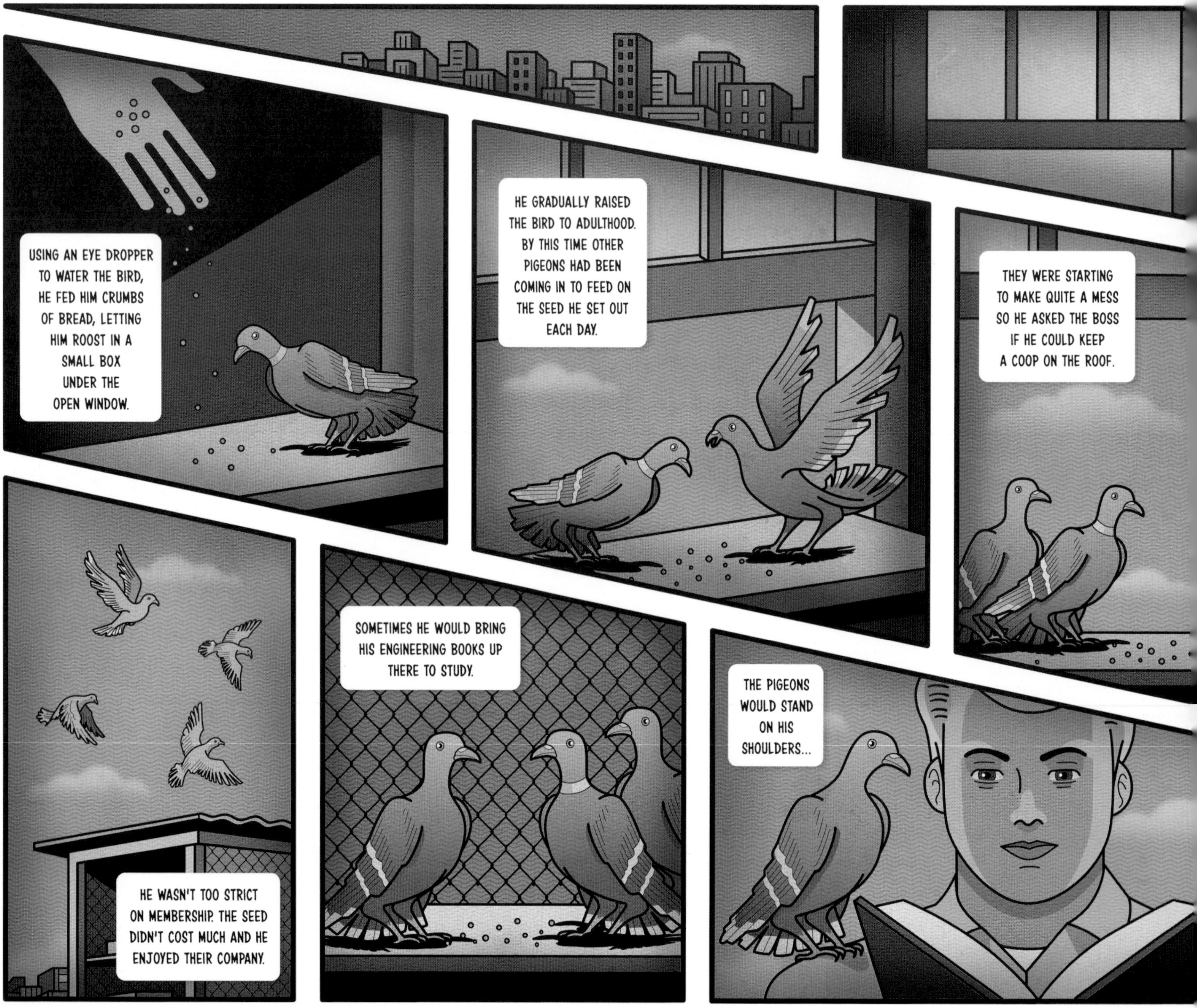
USING AN EYE DROPPER TO WATER THE BIRD, HE FED HIM CRUMBS OF BREAD, LETTING HIM ROOST IN A SMALL BOX UNDER THE OPEN WINDOW.
HE GRADUALLY RAISED THE BIRD TO ADULTHOOD. BY THIS TIME OTHER PIGEONS HAD BEEN COMING IN TO FEED ON THE SEED HE SET OUT EACH DAY.
THEY WERE STARTING TO MAKE QUITE A MESS SO HE ASKED THE BOSS IF HE COULD KEEP A COOP ON THE ROOF.
HE WASN'T TOO STRICT ON MEMBERSHIP. THE SEED DIDN'T COST MUCH AND HE ENJOYED THEIR COMPANY.
SOMETIMES HE WOULD BRING HIS ENGINEERING BOOKS UP THERE TO STUDY.
THE PIGEONS WOULD STAND ON HIS SHOULDERS...

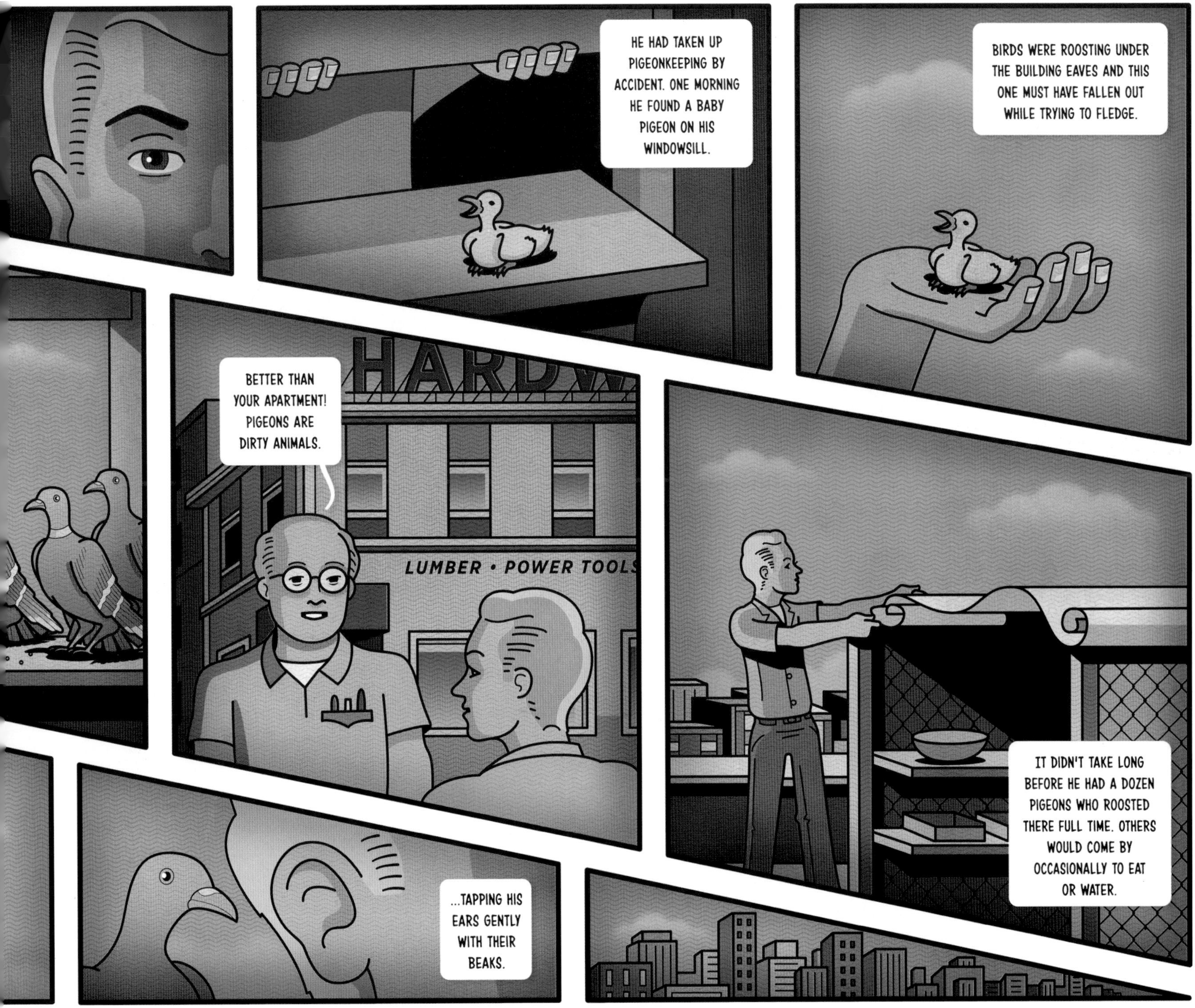
HE HAD TAKEN UP PIGEONKEEPING BY ACCIDENT. ONE MORNING HE FOUND A BABY PIGEON ON HIS WINDOWSILL.
BIRDS WERE ROOSTING UNDER THE BUILDING EAVES AND THIS ONE MUST HAVE FALLEN OUT WHILE TRYING TO FLEDGE.
HARD
BETTER THAN YOUR APARTMENT! PIGEONS ARE DIRTY ANIMALS.
LUMBER • POWER TOOLS
IT DIDN'T TAKE LONG BEFORE HE HAD A DOZEN PIGEONS WHO ROOSTED THERE FULL TIME. OTHERS WOULD COME BY OCCASIONALLY TO EAT OR WATER.
...TAPPING HIS EARS GENTLY WITH THEIR BEAKS.

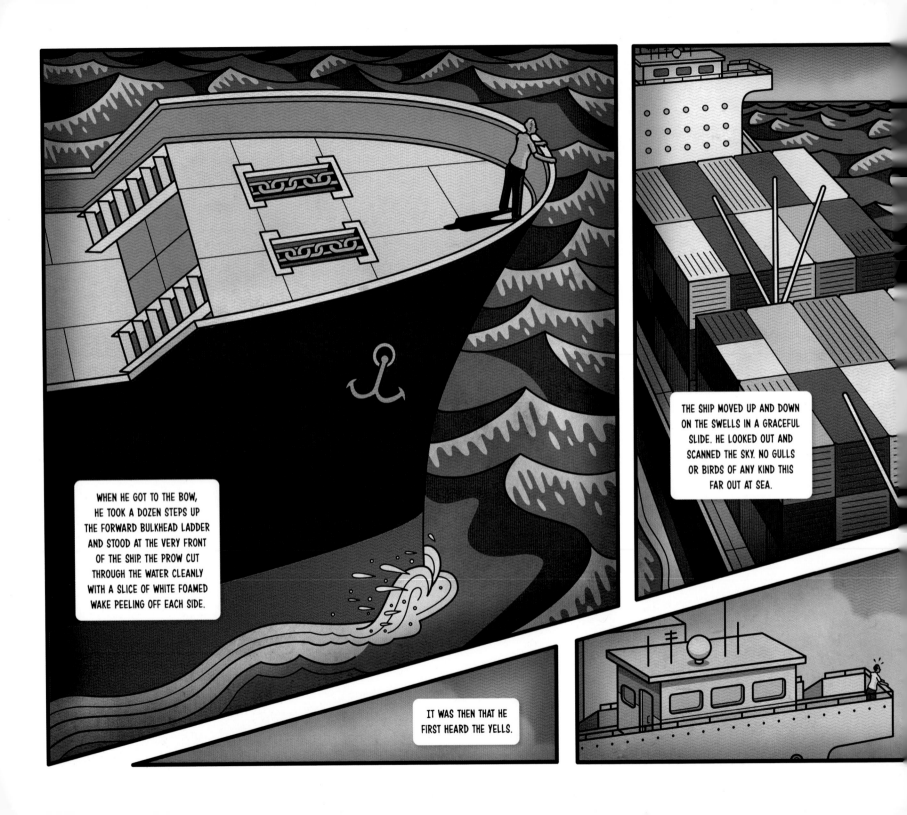

WHEN HE GOT TO THE BOW, HE TOOK A DOZEN STEPS UP THE FORWARD BULKHEAD LADDER AND STOOD AT THE VERY FRONT OF THE SHIP. THE PROW CUT THROUGH THE WATER CLEANLY WITH A SLICE OF WHITE FOAMED WAKE PEELING OFF EACH SIDE.

THE SHIP MOVED UP AND DOWN ON THE SWELLS IN A GRACEFUL SLIDE. HE LOOKED OUT AND SCANNED THE SKY. NO GULLS OR BIRDS OF ANY KIND THIS FAR OUT AT SEA.

IT WAS THEN THAT HE FIRST HEARD THE YELLS.

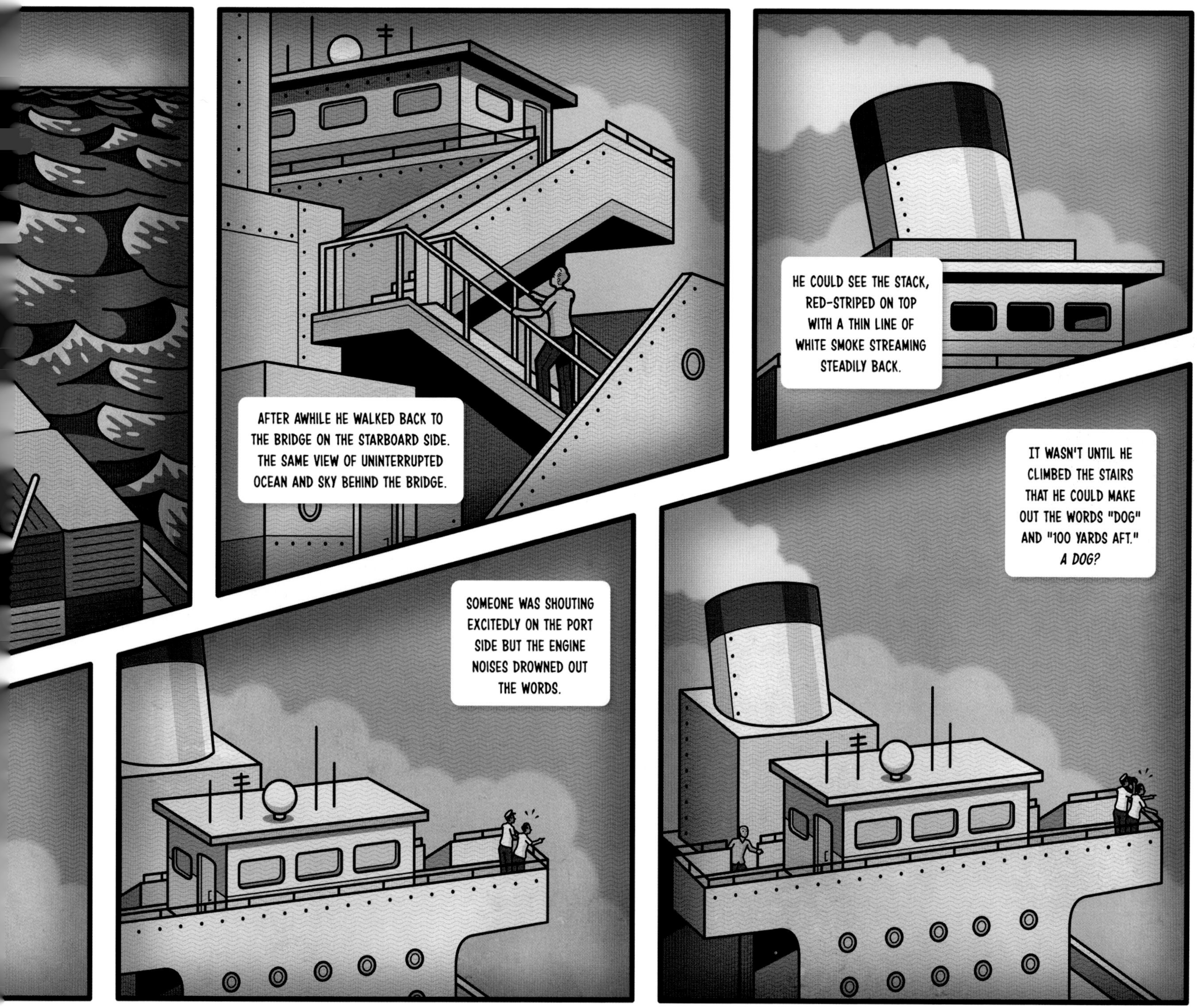
AFTER AWHILE HE WALKED BACK TO THE BRIDGE ON THE STARBOARD SIDE. THE SAME VIEW OF UNINTERRUPTED OCEAN AND SKY BEHIND THE BRIDGE.
HE COULD SEE THE STACK, RED-STRIPED ON TOP WITH A THIN LINE OF WHITE SMOKE STREAMING STEADILY BACK.
SOMEONE WAS SHOUTING EXCITEDLY ON THE PORT SIDE BUT THE ENGINE NOISES DROWNED OUT THE WORDS.
IT WASN'T UNTIL HE CLIMBED THE STAIRS THAT HE COULD MAKE OUT THE WORDS "DOG" AND "100 YARDS AFT." *A DOG?*

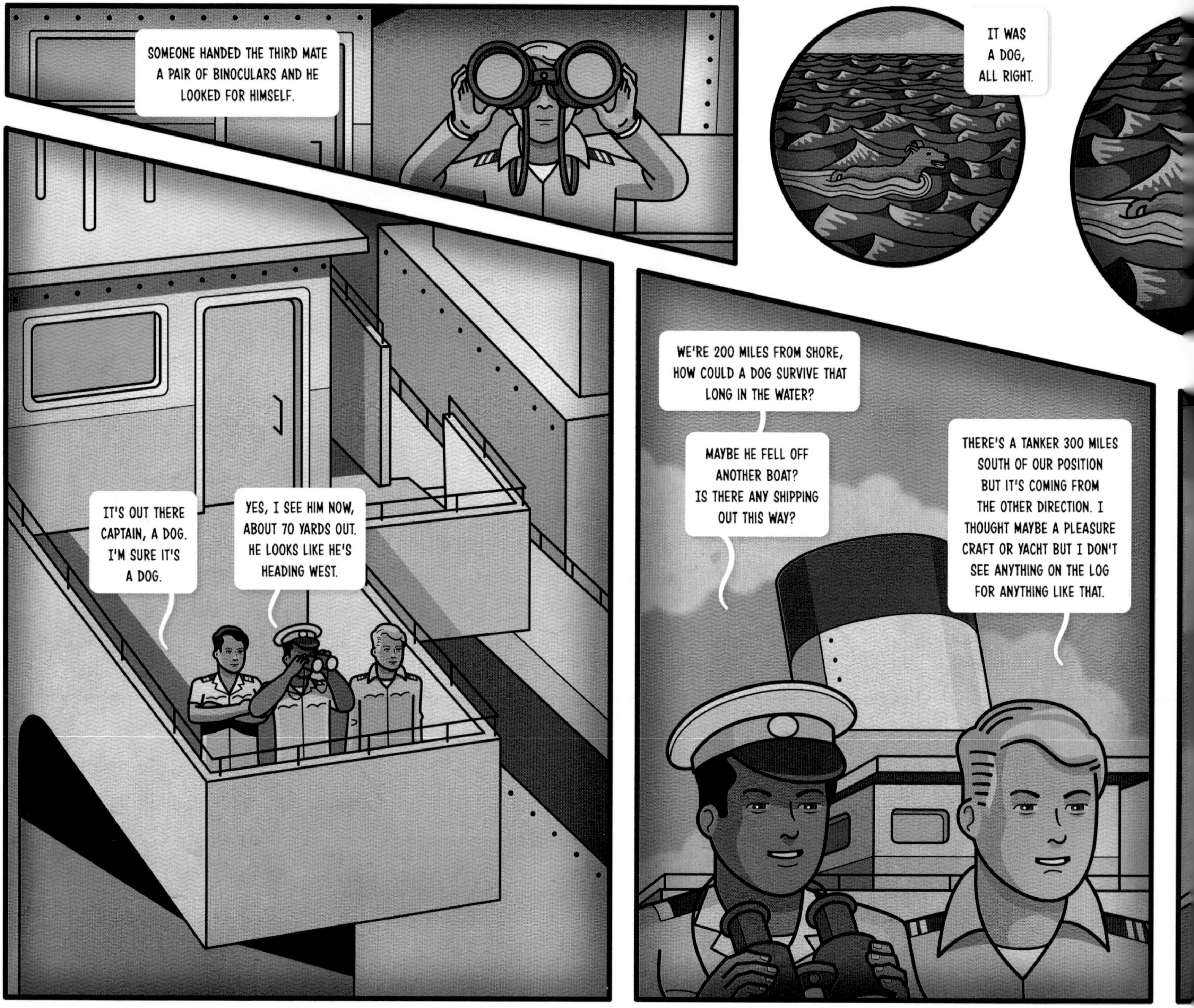
SOMEONE HANDED THE THIRD MATE A PAIR OF BINOCULARS AND HE LOOKED FOR HIMSELF.
IT WAS A DOG, ALL RIGHT.
IT'S OUT THERE CAPTAIN, A DOG. I'M SURE IT'S A DOG.
YES, I SEE HIM NOW, ABOUT 70 YARDS OUT. HE LOOKS LIKE HE'S HEADING WEST.
WE'RE 200 MILES FROM SHORE, HOW COULD A DOG SURVIVE THAT LONG IN THE WATER?
MAYBE HE FELL OFF ANOTHER BOAT? IS THERE ANY SHIPPING OUT THIS WAY?
THERE'S A TANKER 300 MILES SOUTH OF OUR POSITION BUT IT'S COMING FROM THE OTHER DIRECTION. I THOUGHT MAYBE A PLEASURE CRAFT OR YACHT BUT I DON'T SEE ANYTHING ON THE LOG FOR ANYTHING LIKE THAT.

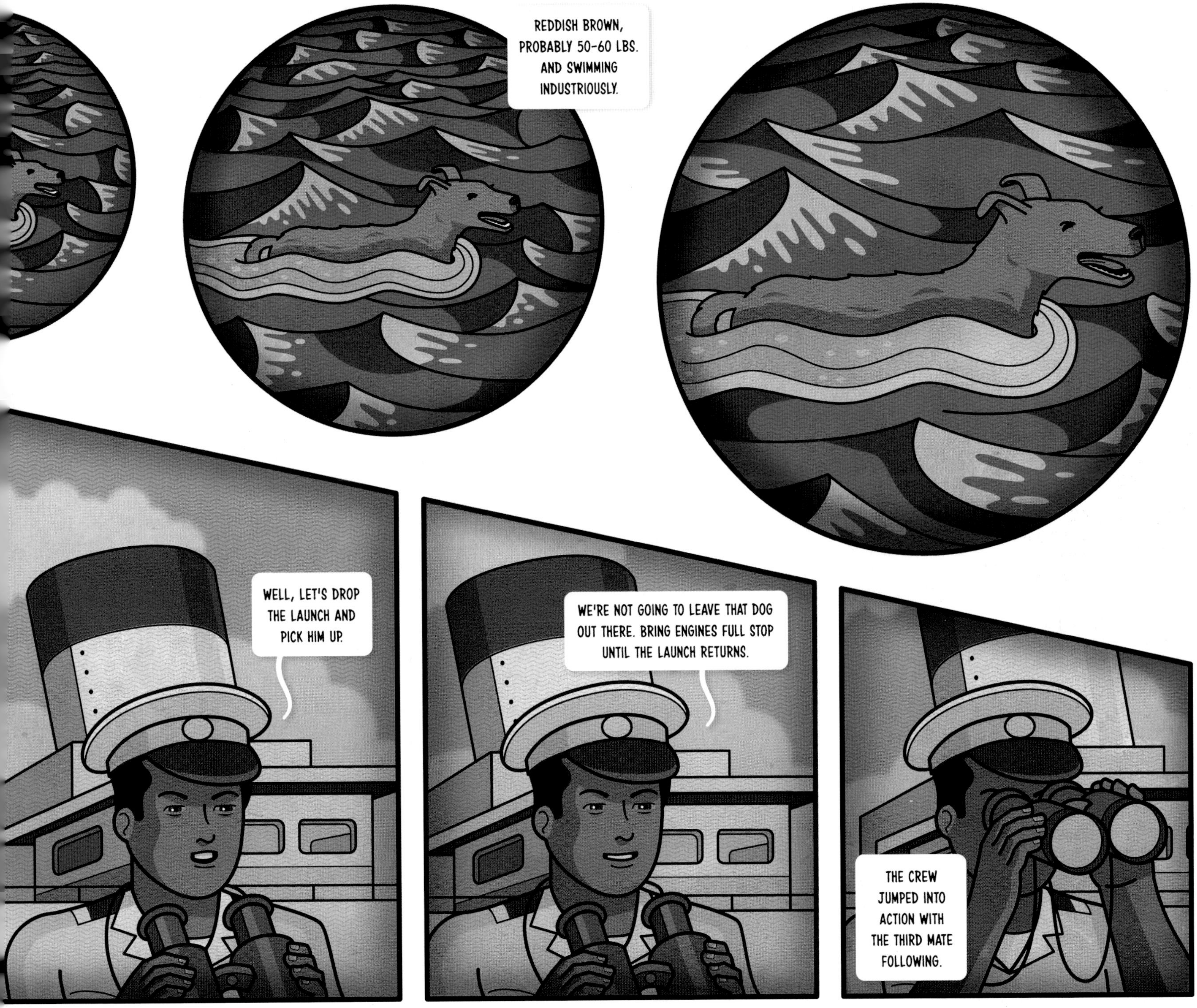
REDDISH BROWN, PROBABLY 50-60 LBS. AND SWIMMING INDUSTRIOUSLY.
WELL, LET'S DROP THE LAUNCH AND PICK HIM UP.
WE'RE NOT GOING TO LEAVE THAT DOG OUT THERE. BRING ENGINES FULL STOP UNTIL THE LAUNCH RETURNS.
THE CREW JUMPED INTO ACTION WITH THE THIRD MATE FOLLOWING.

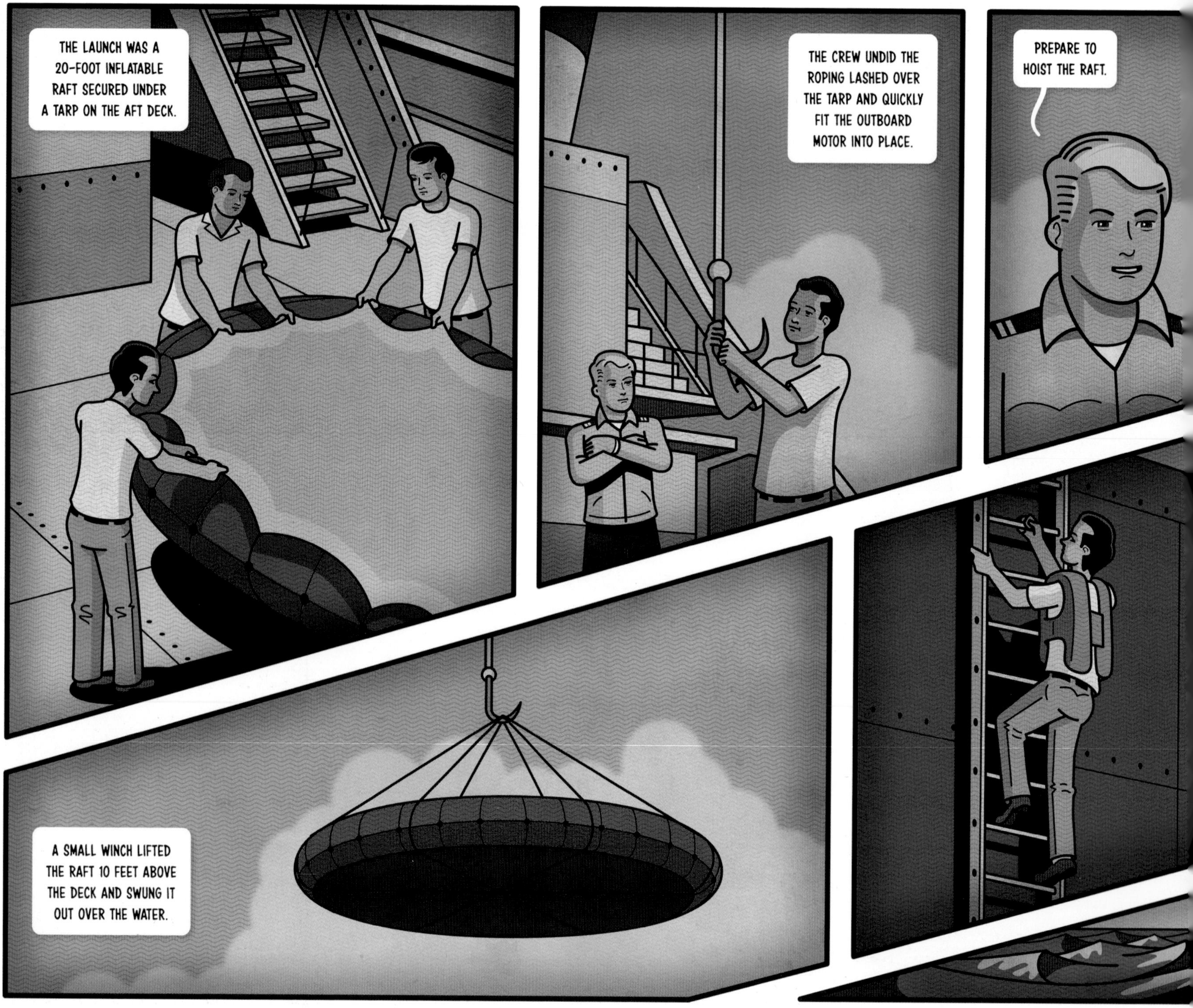
THE LAUNCH WAS A 20-FOOT INFLATABLE RAFT SECURED UNDER A TARP ON THE AFT DECK.
THE CREW UNDID THE ROPING LASHED OVER THE TARP AND QUICKLY FIT THE OUTBOARD MOTOR INTO PLACE.
PREPARE TO HOIST THE RAFT.
A SMALL WINCH LIFTED THE RAFT 10 FEET ABOVE THE DECK AND SWUNG IT OUT OVER THE WATER.

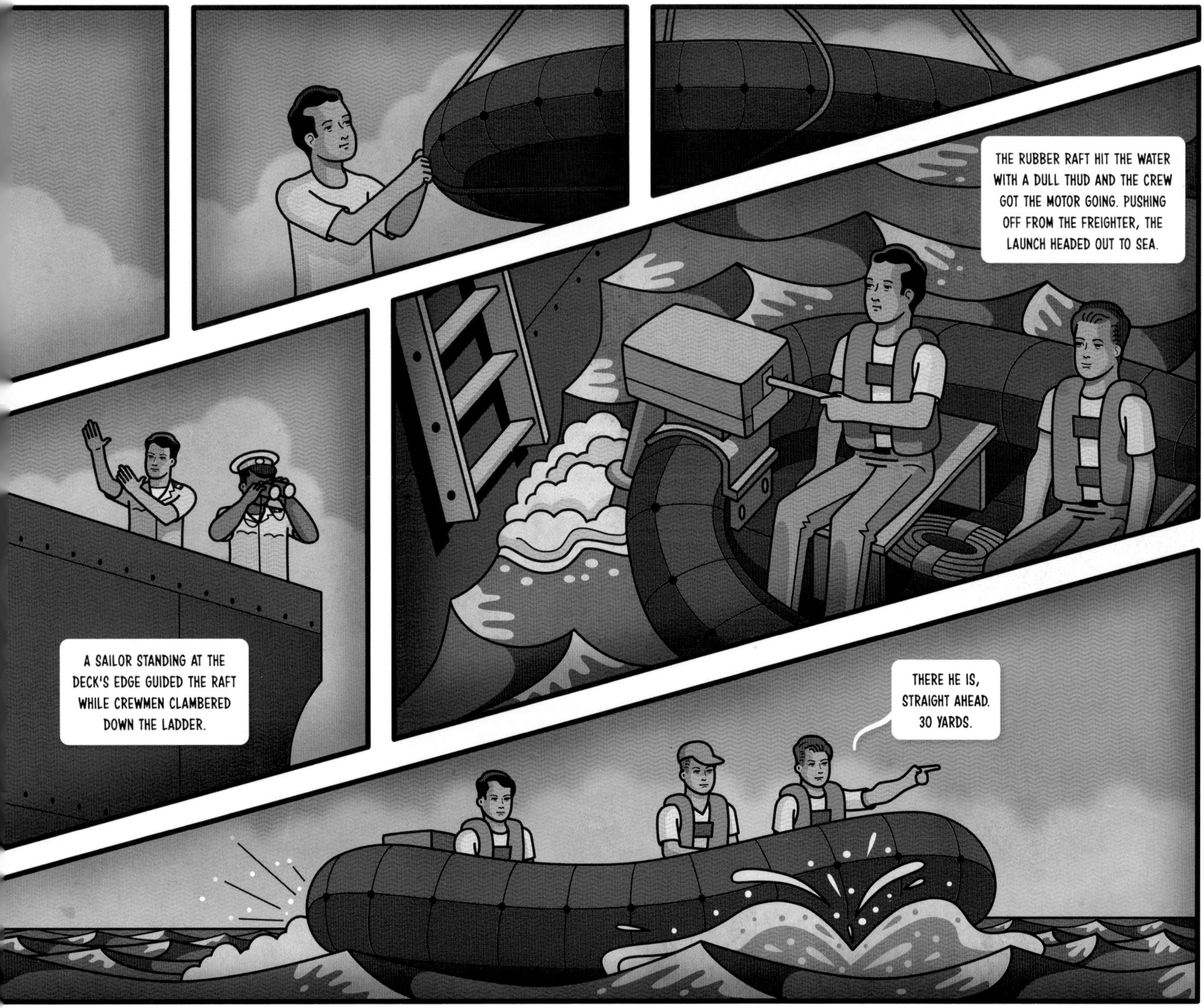
THE RUBBER RAFT HIT THE WATER WITH A DULL THUD AND THE CREW GOT THE MOTOR GOING. PUSHING OFF FROM THE FREIGHTER, THE LAUNCH HEADED OUT TO SEA.
A SAILOR STANDING AT THE DECK'S EDGE GUIDED THE RAFT WHILE CREWMEN CLAMBERED DOWN THE LADDER.
THERE HE IS, STRAIGHT AHEAD. 30 YARDS.

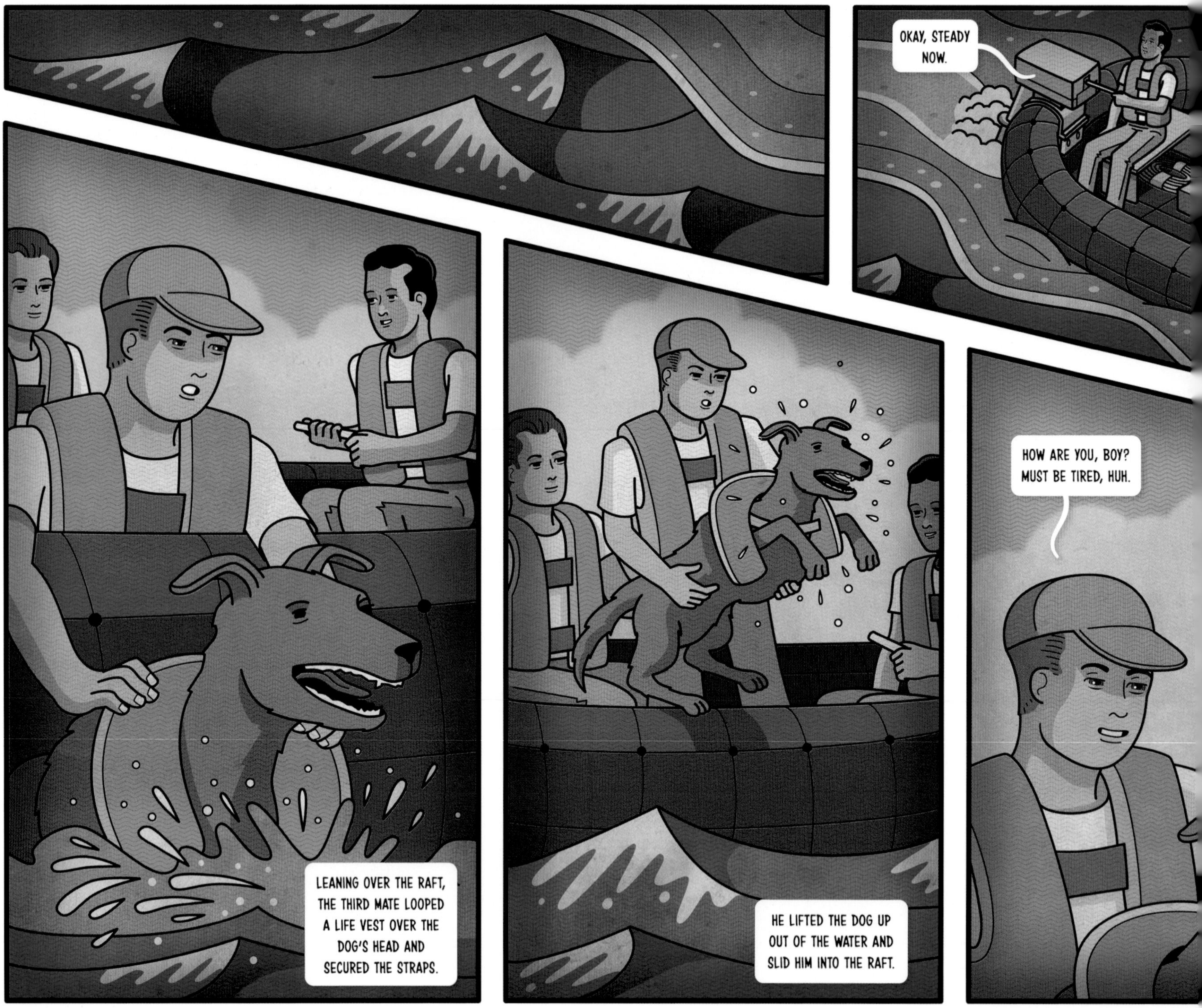
OKAY, STEADY NOW.
LEANING OVER THE RAFT, THE THIRD MATE LOOPED A LIFE VEST OVER THE DOG'S HEAD AND SECURED THE STRAPS.
HE LIFTED THE DOG UP OUT OF THE WATER AND SLID HIM INTO THE RAFT.
HOW ARE YOU, BOY? MUST BE TIRED, HUH.

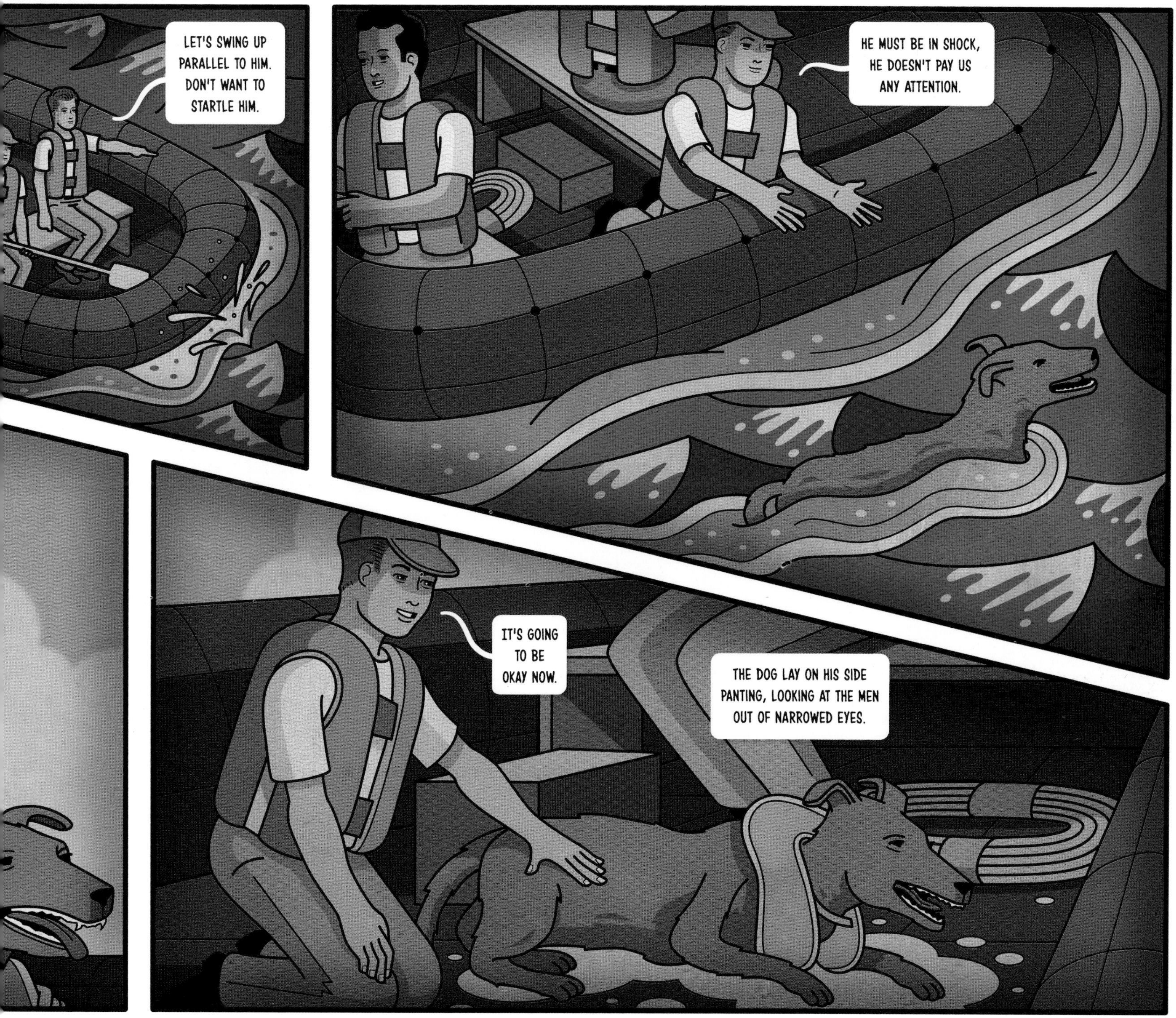
LET'S SWING UP PARALLEL TO HIM. DON'T WANT TO STARTLE HIM.
HE MUST BE IN SHOCK, HE DOESN'T PAY US ANY ATTENTION.
IT'S GOING TO BE OKAY NOW.
THE DOG LAY ON HIS SIDE PANTING, LOOKING AT THE MEN OUT OF NARROWED EYES.

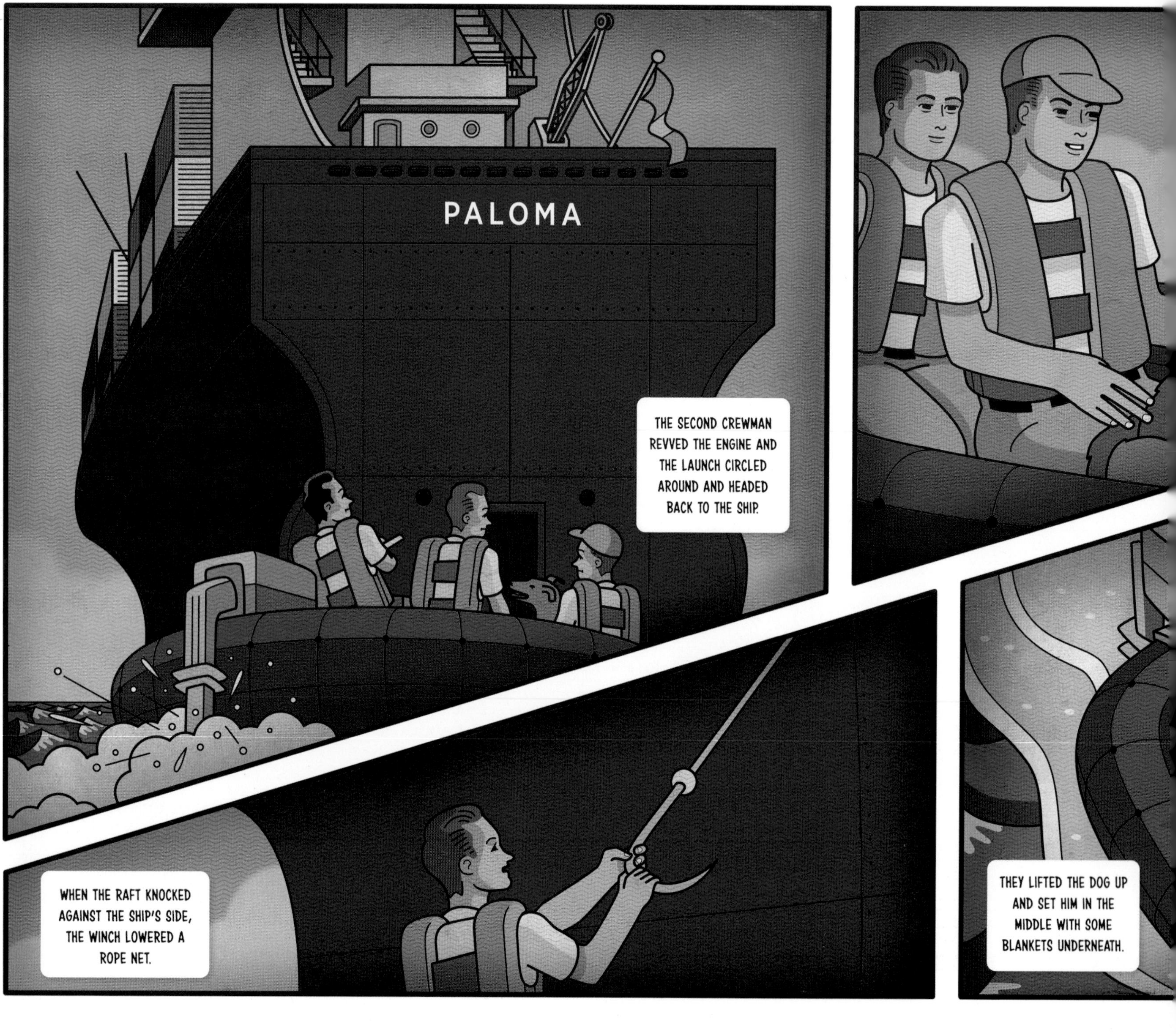
PALOMA
THE SECOND CREWMAN REVVED THE ENGINE AND THE LAUNCH CIRCLED AROUND AND HEADED BACK TO THE SHIP.
WHEN THE RAFT KNOCKED AGAINST THE SHIP'S SIDE, THE WINCH LOWERED A ROPE NET.
THEY LIFTED THE DOG UP AND SET HIM IN THE MIDDLE WITH SOME BLANKETS UNDERNEATH.

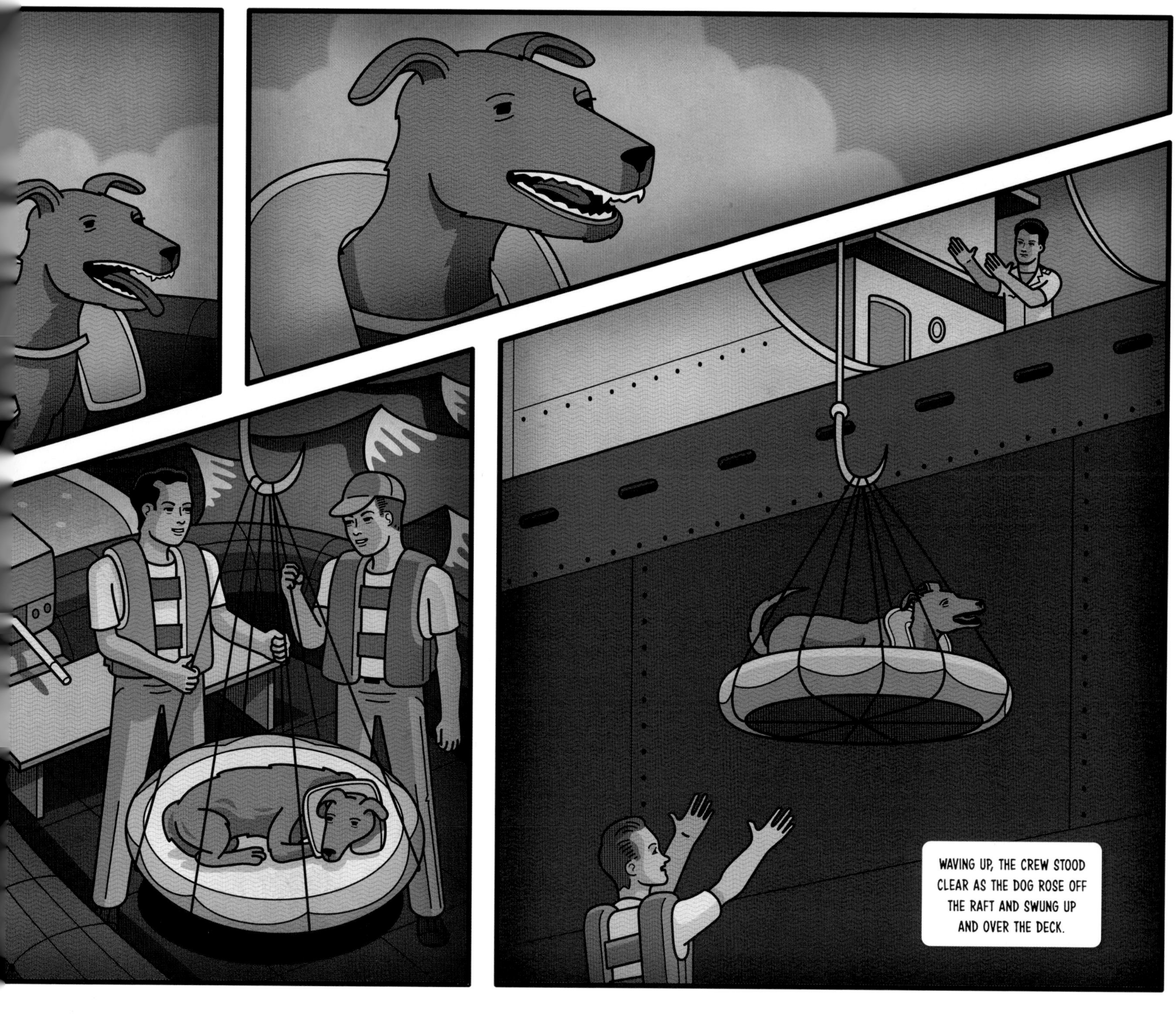
WAVING UP, THE CREW STOOD CLEAR AS THE DOG ROSE OFF THE RAFT AND SWUNG UP AND OVER THE DECK.

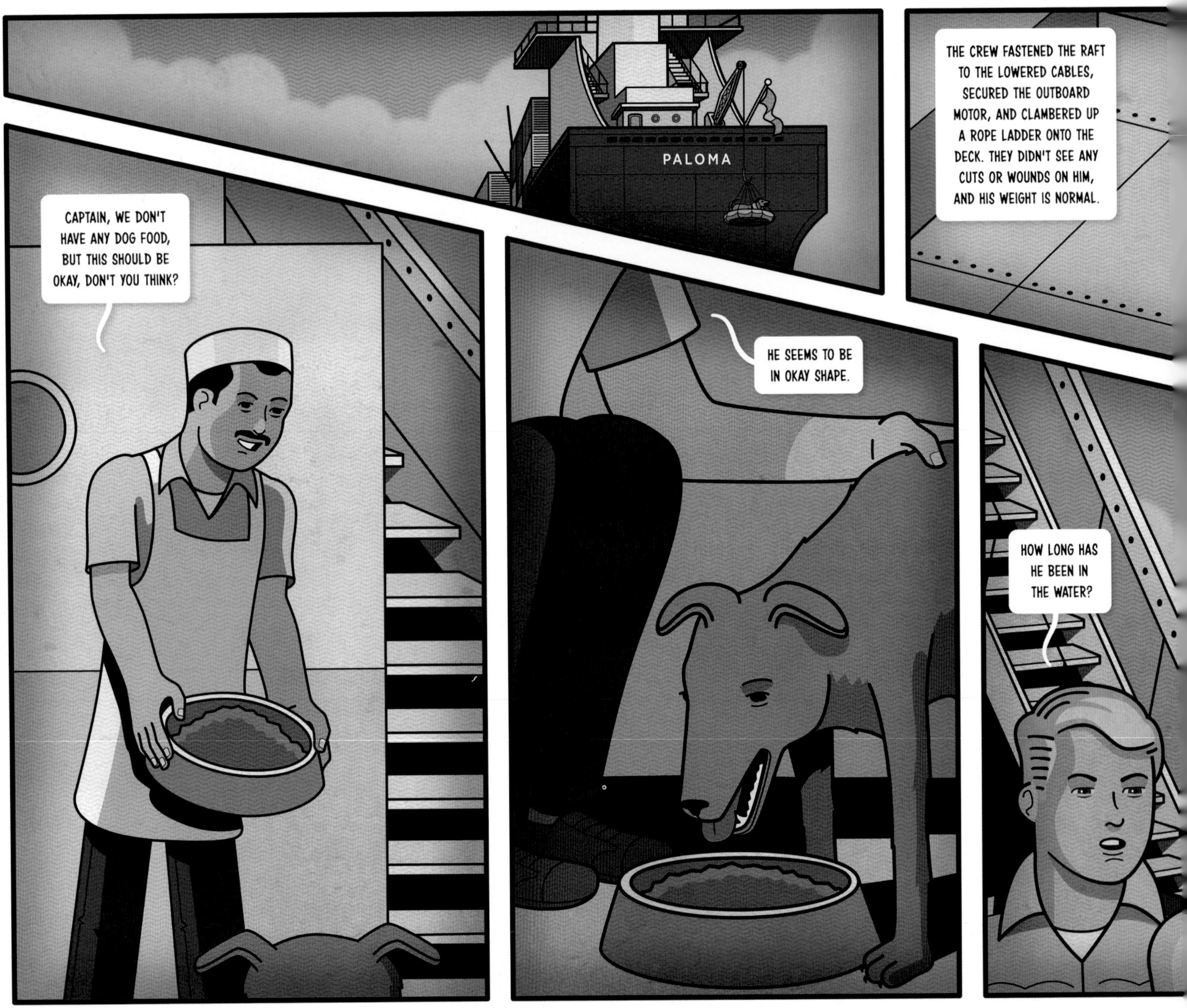
PALOMA
THE CREW FASTENED THE RAFT TO THE LOWERED CABLES, SECURED THE OUTBOARD MOTOR, AND CLAMBERED UP A ROPE LADDER ONTO THE DECK. THEY DIDN'T SEE ANY CUTS OR WOUNDS ON HIM, AND HIS WEIGHT IS NORMAL.
CAPTAIN, WE DON'T HAVE ANY DOG FOOD, BUT THIS SHOULD BE OKAY, DON'T YOU THINK?
HE SEEMS TO BE IN OKAY SHAPE.
HOW LONG HAS HE BEEN IN THE WATER?

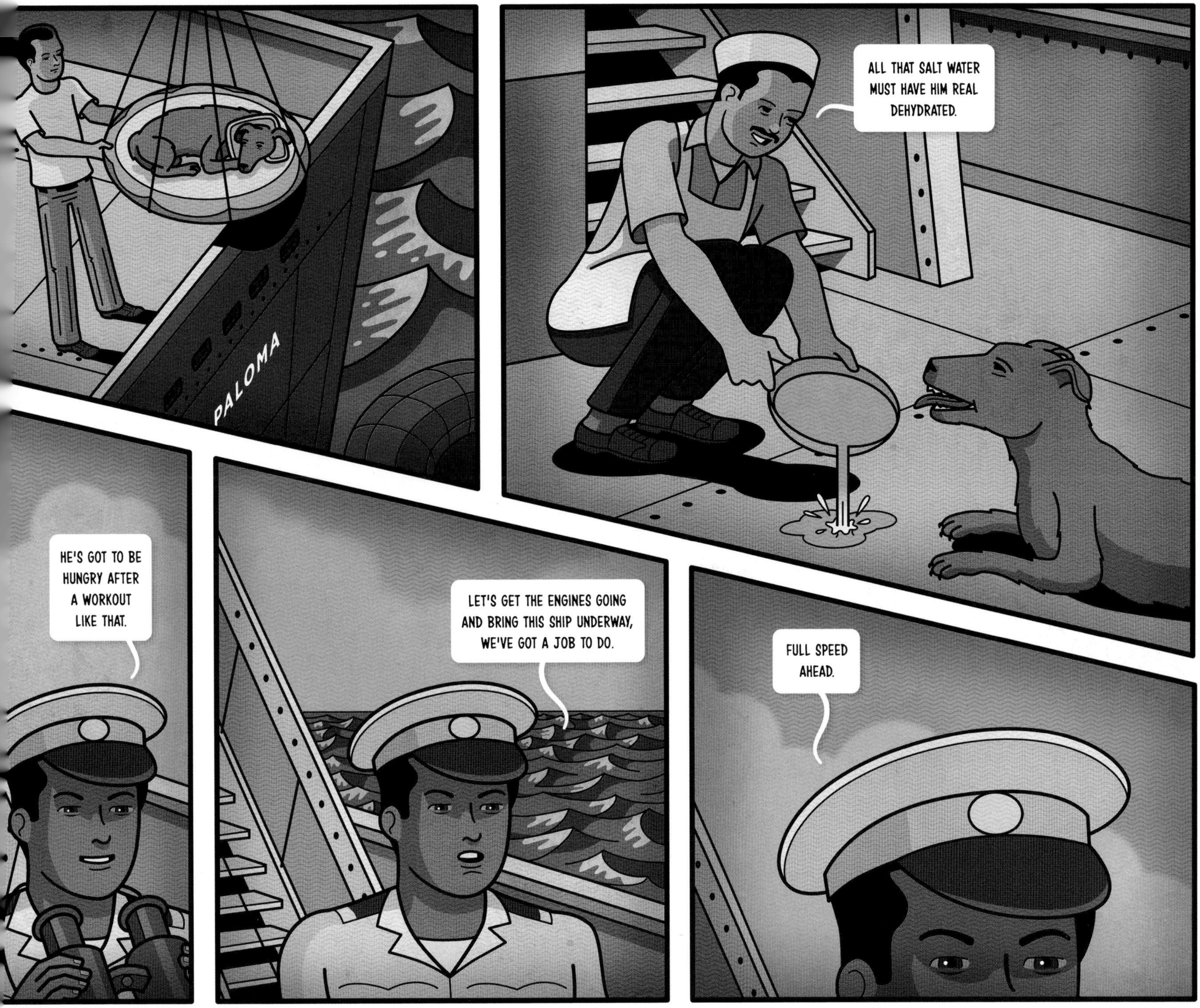
ALL THAT SALT WATER MUST HAVE HIM REAL DEHYDRATED.
HE'S GOT TO BE HUNGRY AFTER A WORKOUT LIKE THAT.
LET'S GET THE ENGINES GOING AND BRING THIS SHIP UNDERWAY, WE'VE GOT A JOB TO DO.
FULL SPEED AHEAD.

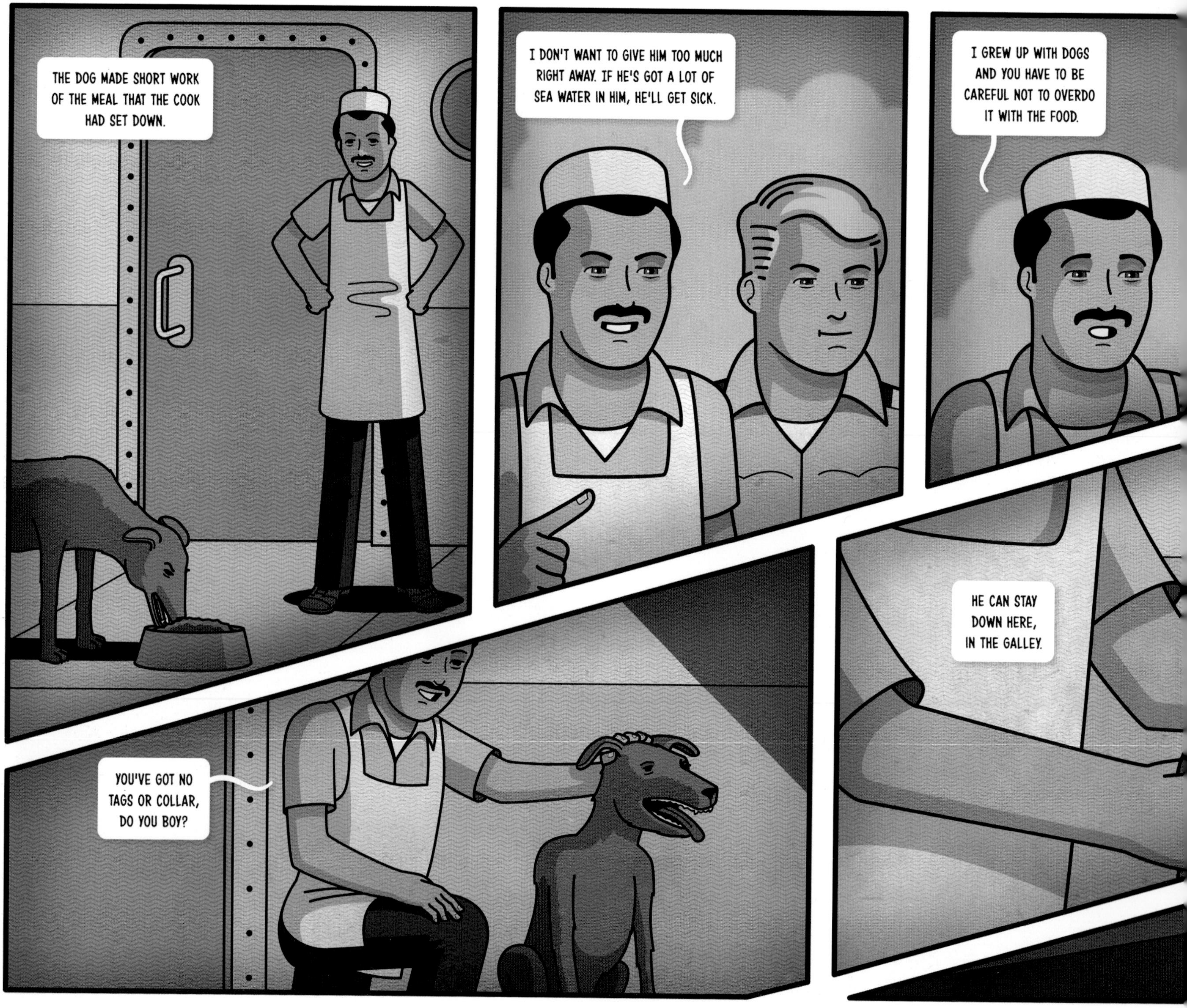
THE DOG MADE SHORT WORK OF THE MEAL THAT THE COOK HAD SET DOWN.
I DON'T WANT TO GIVE HIM TOO MUCH RIGHT AWAY. IF HE'S GOT A LOT OF SEA WATER IN HIM, HE'LL GET SICK.
I GREW UP WITH DOGS AND YOU HAVE TO BE CAREFUL NOT TO OVERDO IT WITH THE FOOD.
YOU'VE GOT NO TAGS OR COLLAR, DO YOU BOY?
HE CAN STAY DOWN HERE, IN THE GALLEY.

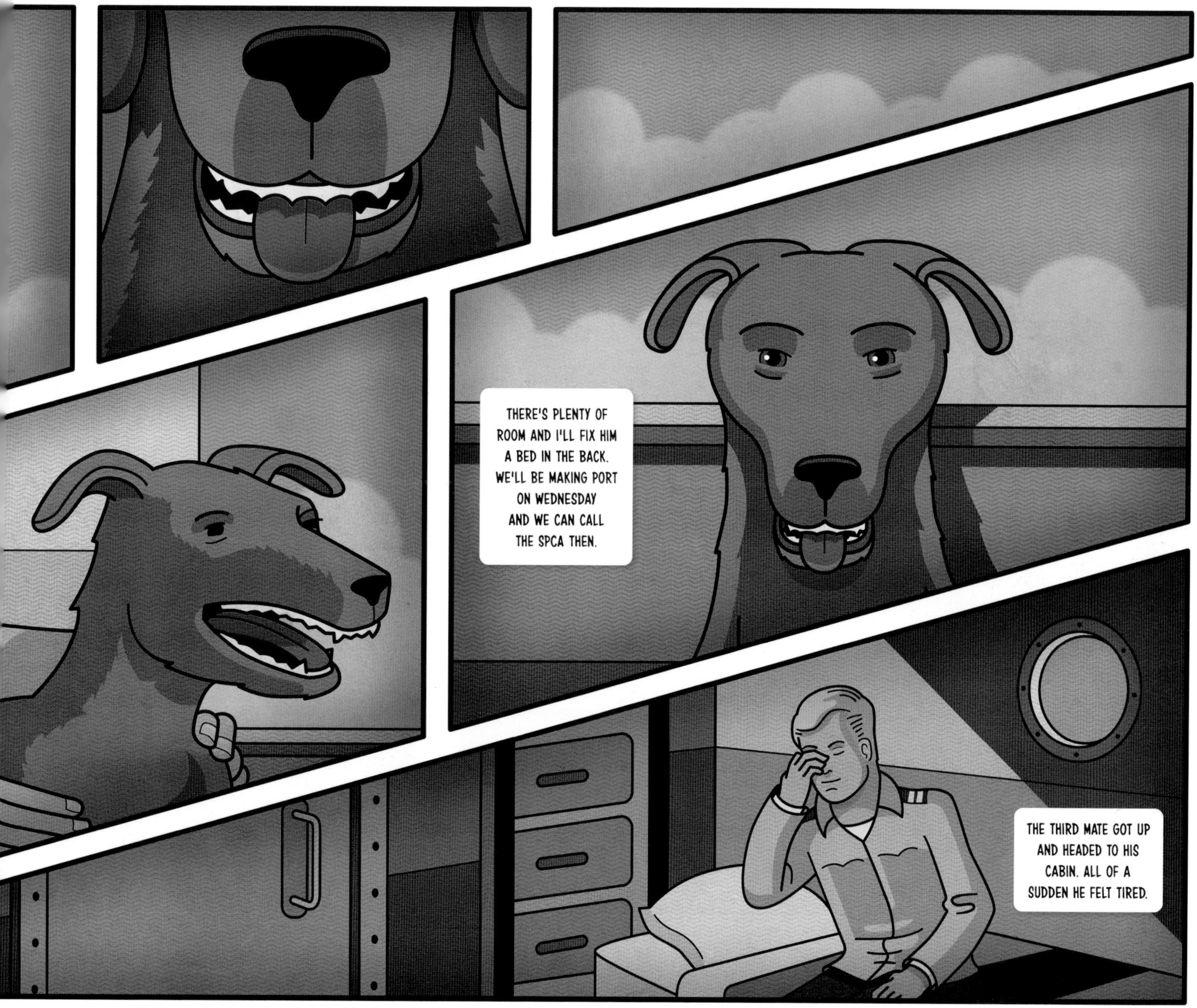
THERE'S PLENTY OF ROOM AND I'LL FIX HIM A BED IN THE BACK. WE'LL BE MAKING PORT ON WEDNESDAY AND WE CAN CALL THE SPCA THEN.
THE THIRD MATE GOT UP AND HEADED TO HIS CABIN. ALL OF A SUDDEN HE FELT TIRED.

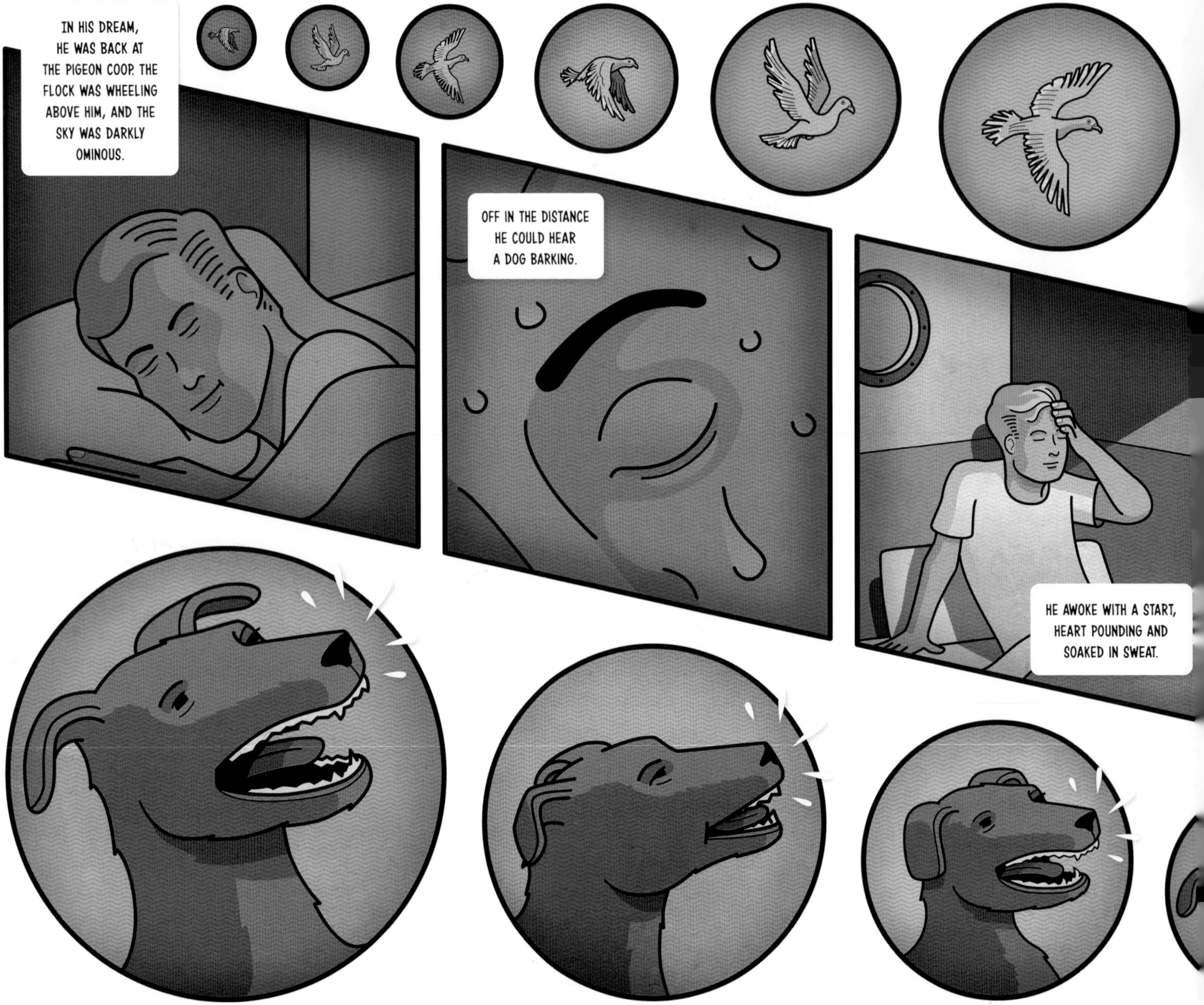
IN HIS DREAM, HE WAS BACK AT THE PIGEON COOP. THE FLOCK WAS WHEELING ABOVE HIM, AND THE SKY WAS DARKLY OMINOUS.
OFF IN THE DISTANCE HE COULD HEAR A DOG BARKING.
HE AWOKE WITH A START, HEART POUNDING AND SOAKED IN SWEAT.

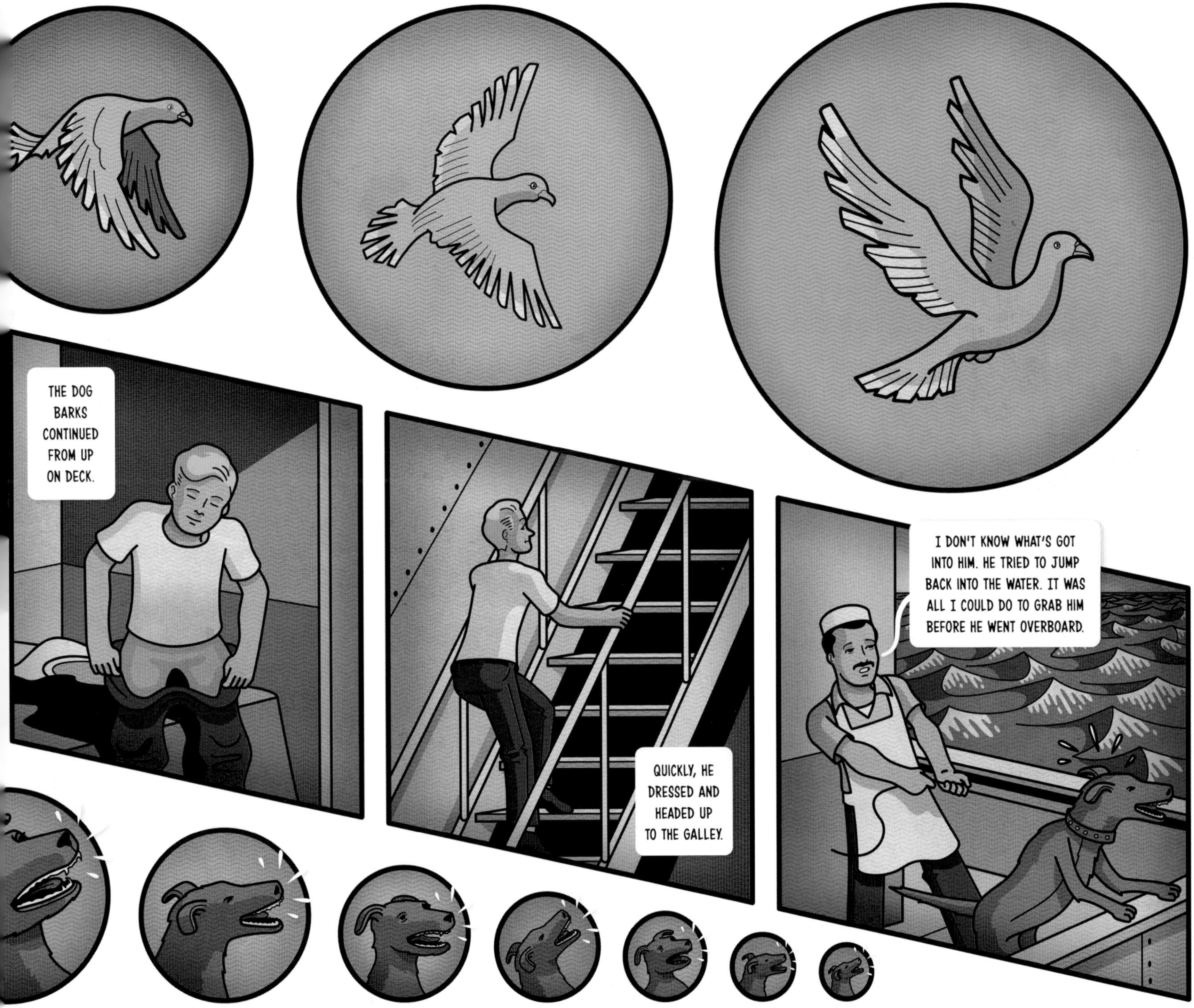
THE DOG BARKS CONTINUED FROM UP ON DECK.
QUICKLY, HE DRESSED AND HEADED UP TO THE GALLEY.
I DON'T KNOW WHAT'S GOT INTO HIM. HE TRIED TO JUMP BACK INTO THE WATER. IT WAS ALL I COULD DO TO GRAB HIM BEFORE HE WENT OVERBOARD.

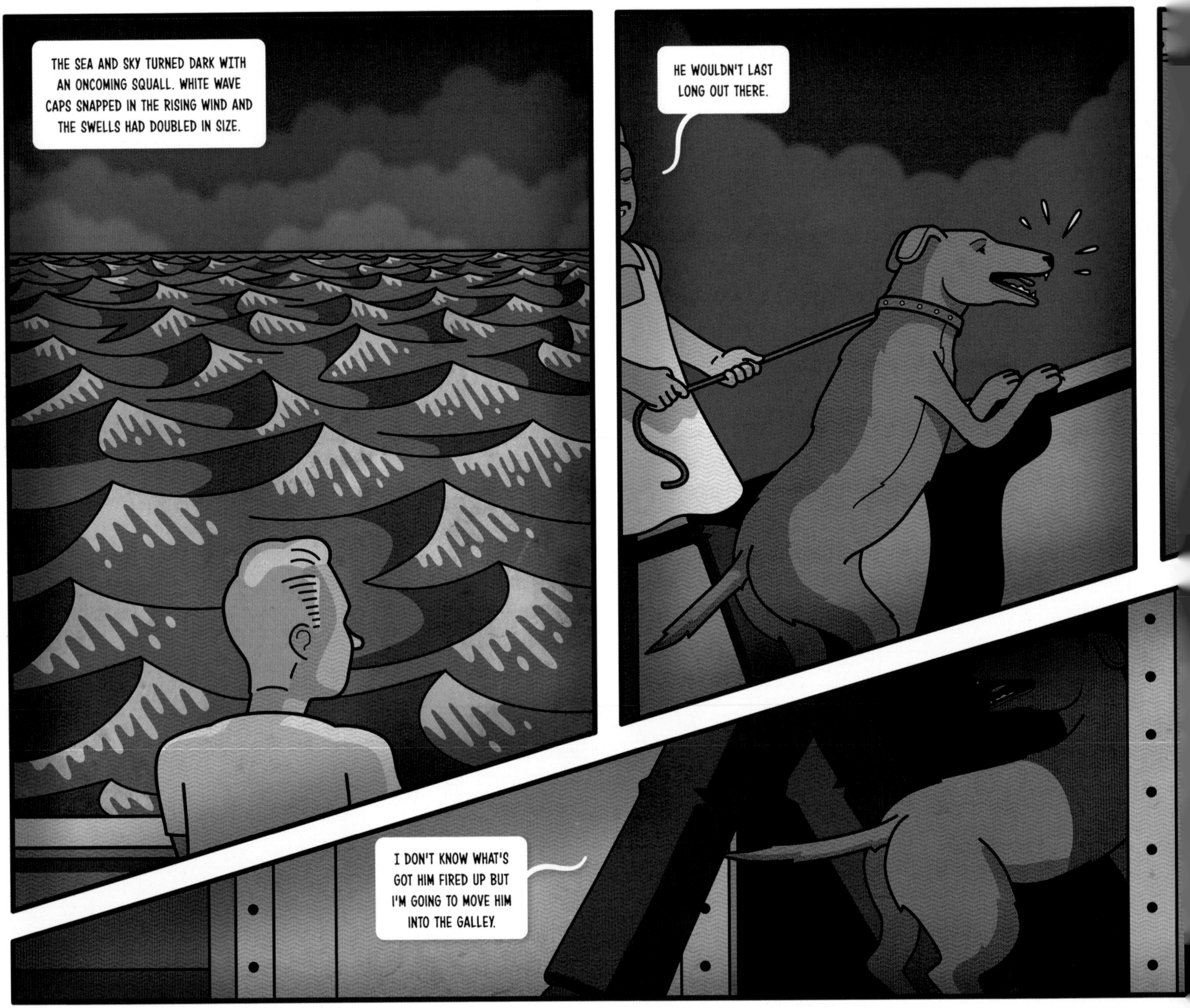
THE SEA AND SKY TURNED DARK WITH AN ONCOMING SQUALL. WHITE WAVE CAPS SNAPPED IN THE RISING WIND AND THE SWELLS HAD DOUBLED IN SIZE.
HE WOULDN'T LAST LONG OUT THERE.
I DON'T KNOW WHAT'S GOT HIM FIRED UP BUT I'M GOING TO MOVE HIM INTO THE GALLEY.

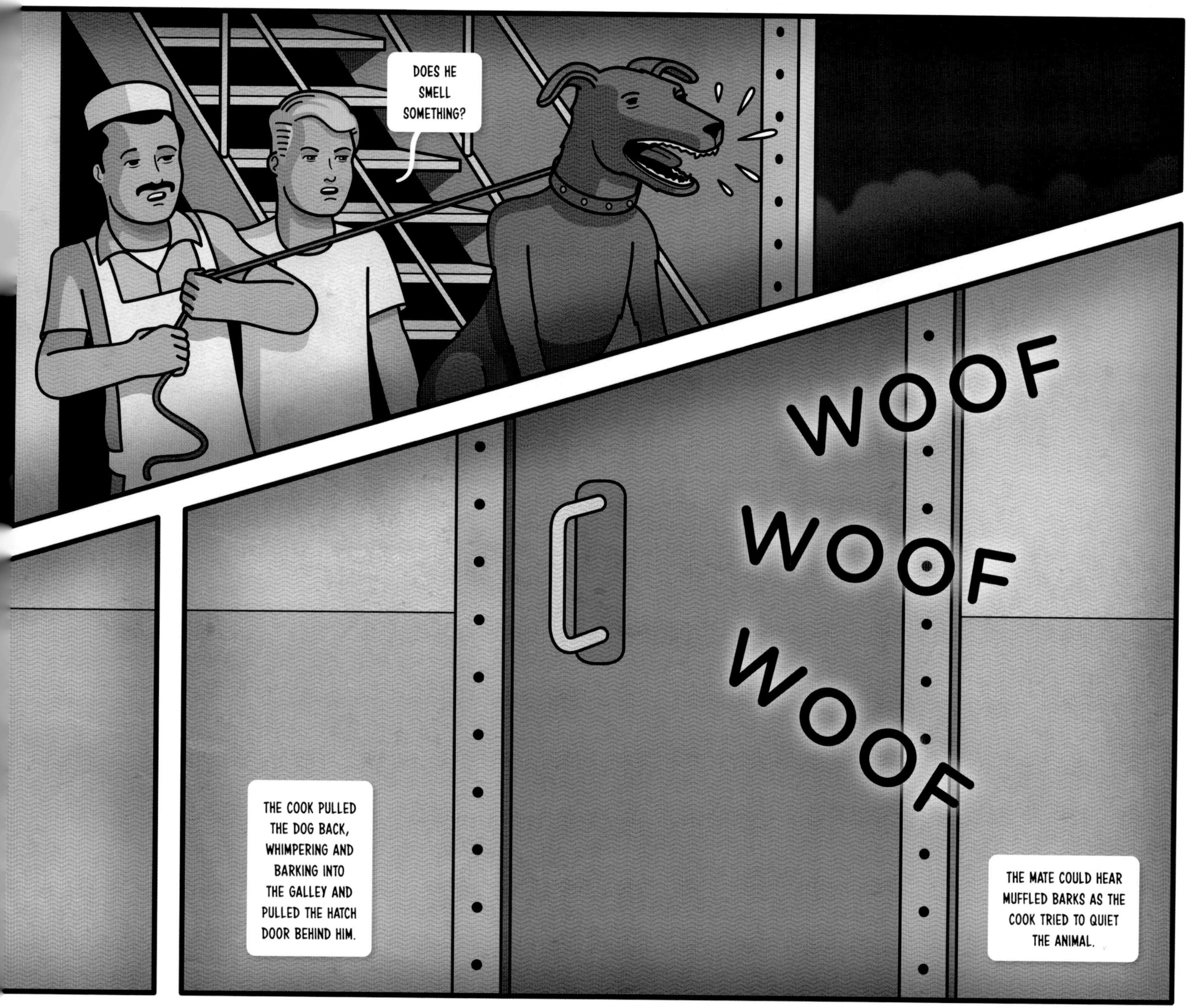

DOES HE SMELL SOMETHING?
WOOF WOOF WOOF
THE COOK PULLED THE DOG BACK, WHIMPERING AND BARKING INTO THE GALLEY AND PULLED THE HATCH DOOR BEHIND HIM.
THE MATE COULD HEAR MUFFLED BARKS AS THE COOK TRIED TO QUIET THE ANIMAL.

HE MADE HIS WAY TO THE BRIDGE.

SOMETHING'S OUT THERE, SEE FOR YOURSELF.

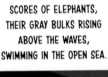

SCORES OF ELEPHANTS, THEIR GRAY BULKS RISING ABOVE THE WAVES, SWIMMING IN THE OPEN SEA.

THE TUSKS ON THE BULL GLEAMED WHITE IN THE SPRAY.

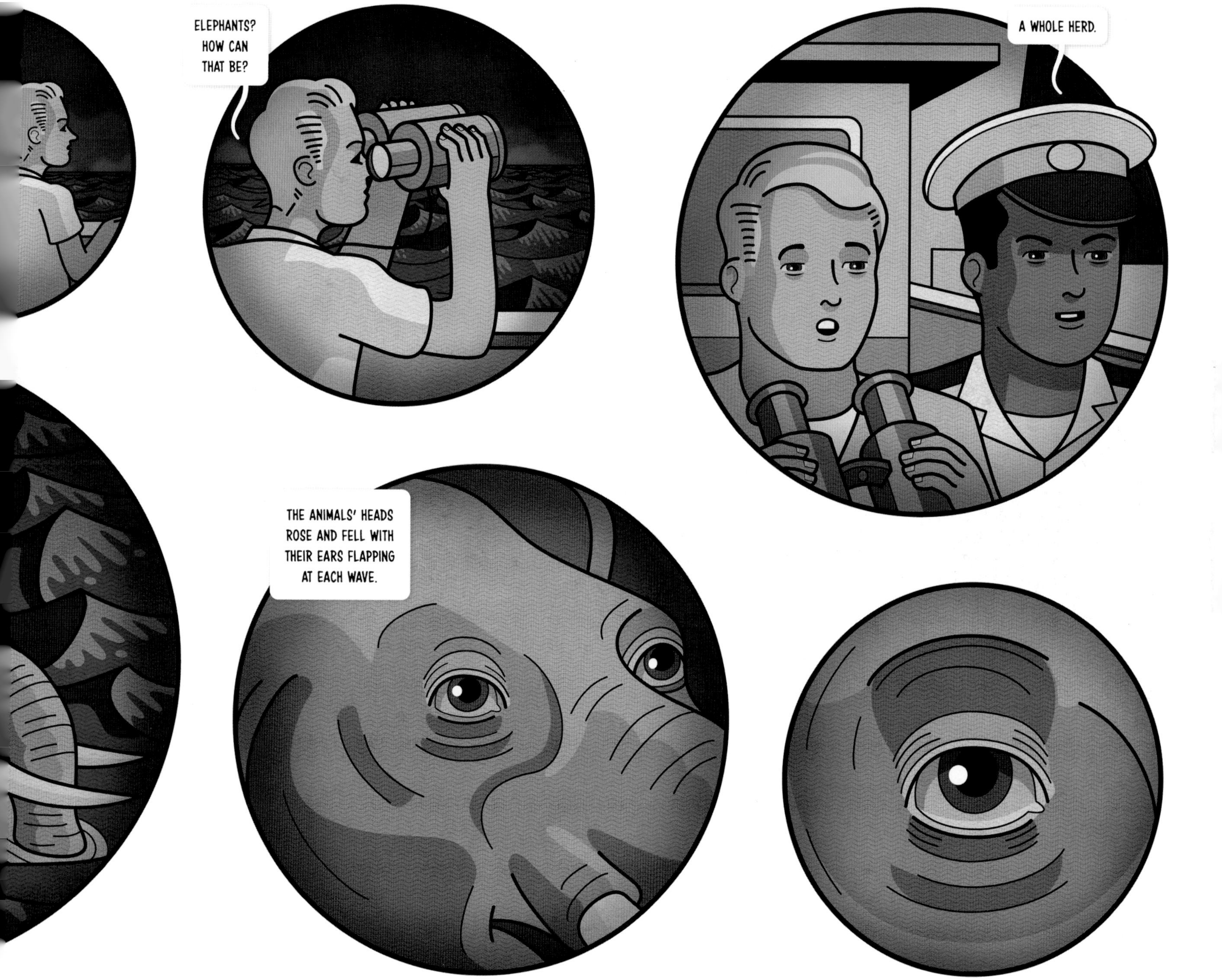
ELEPHANTS? HOW CAN THAT BE?
A WHOLE HERD.
THE ANIMALS' HEADS ROSE AND FELL WITH THEIR EARS FLAPPING AT EACH WAVE.

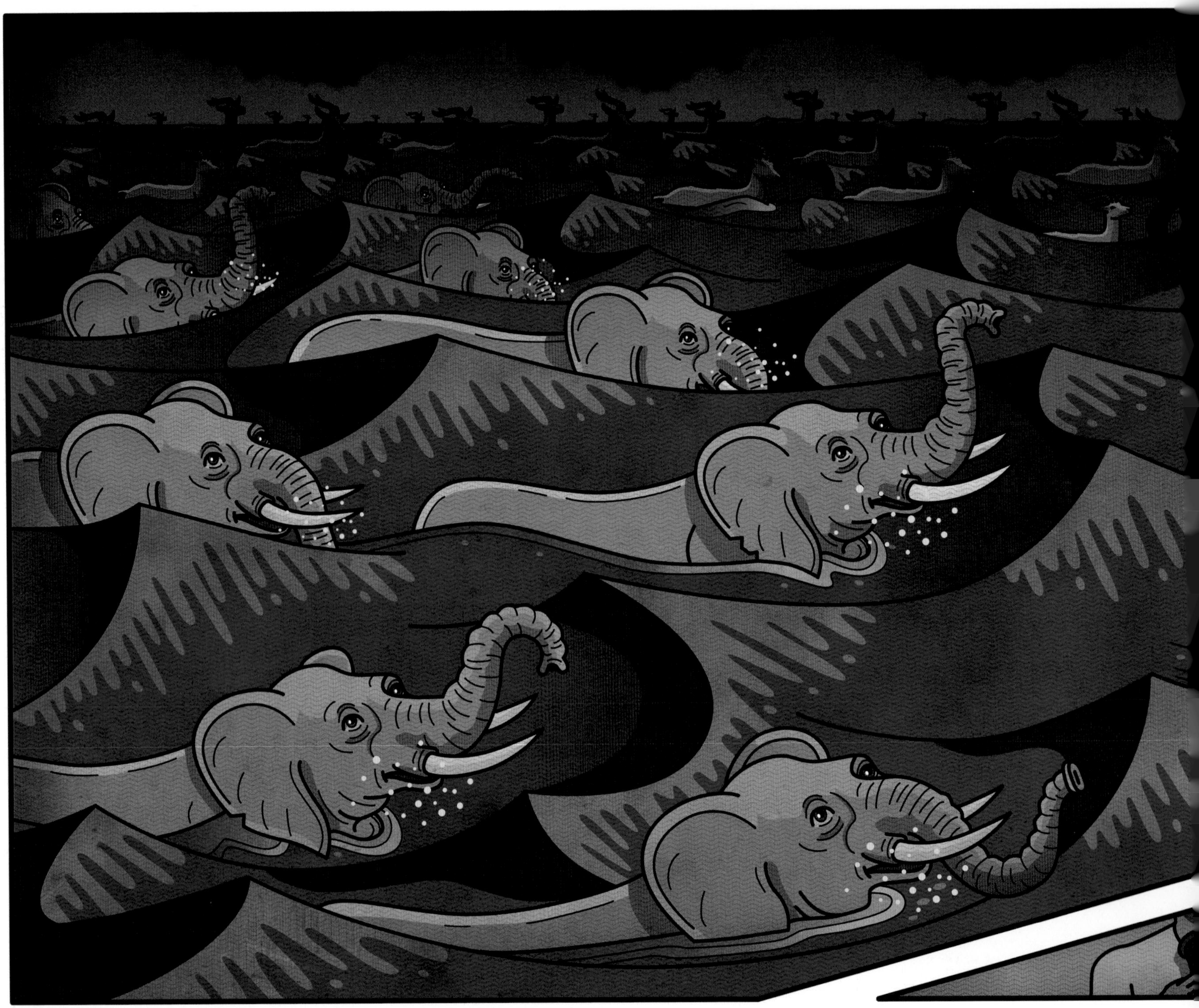

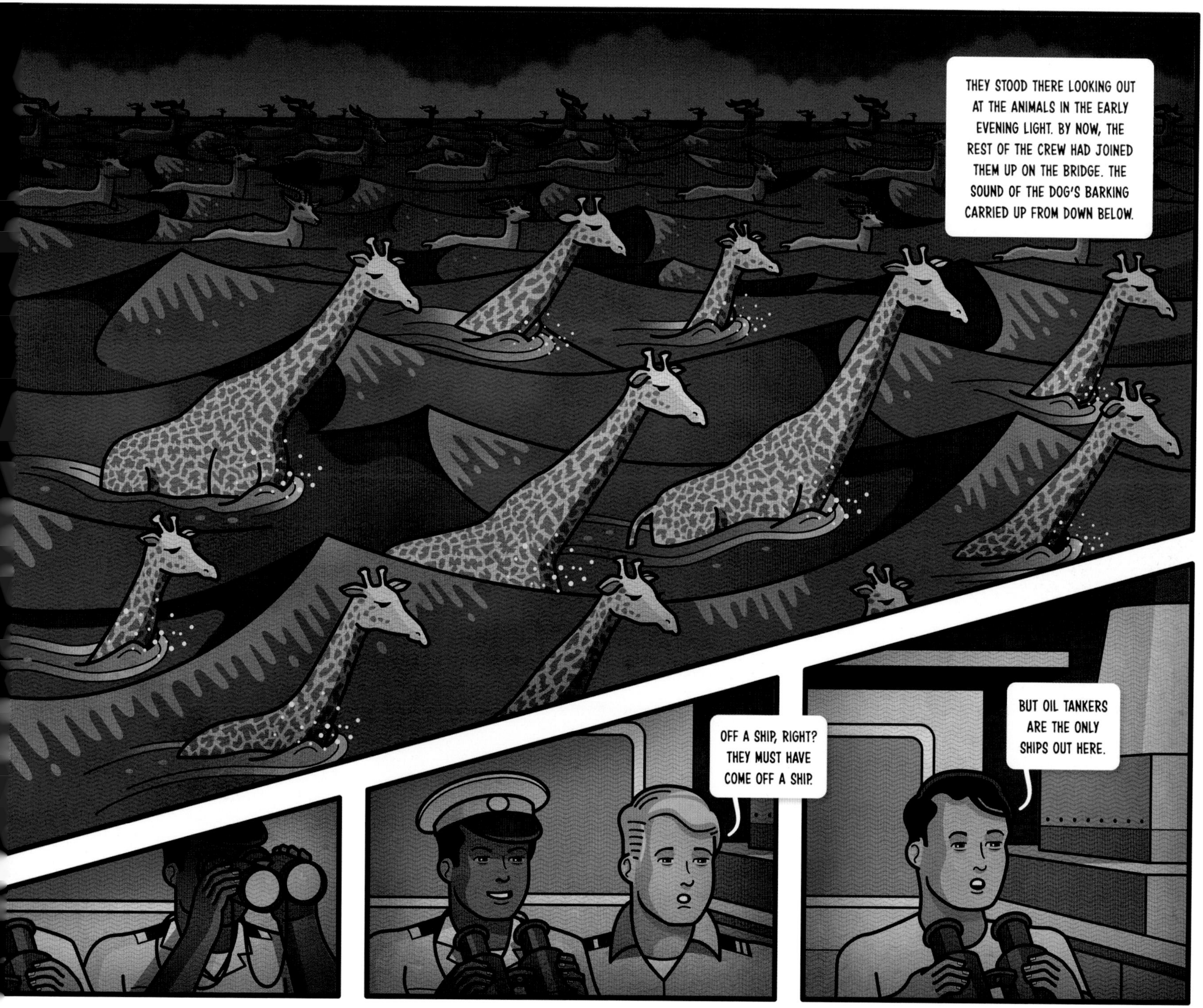
THEY STOOD THERE LOOKING OUT AT THE ANIMALS IN THE EARLY EVENING LIGHT. BY NOW, THE REST OF THE CREW HAD JOINED THEM UP ON THE BRIDGE. THE SOUND OF THE DOG'S BARKING CARRIED UP FROM DOWN BELOW.
OFF A SHIP, RIGHT? THEY MUST HAVE COME OFF A SHIP.
BUT OIL TANKERS ARE THE ONLY SHIPS OUT HERE.

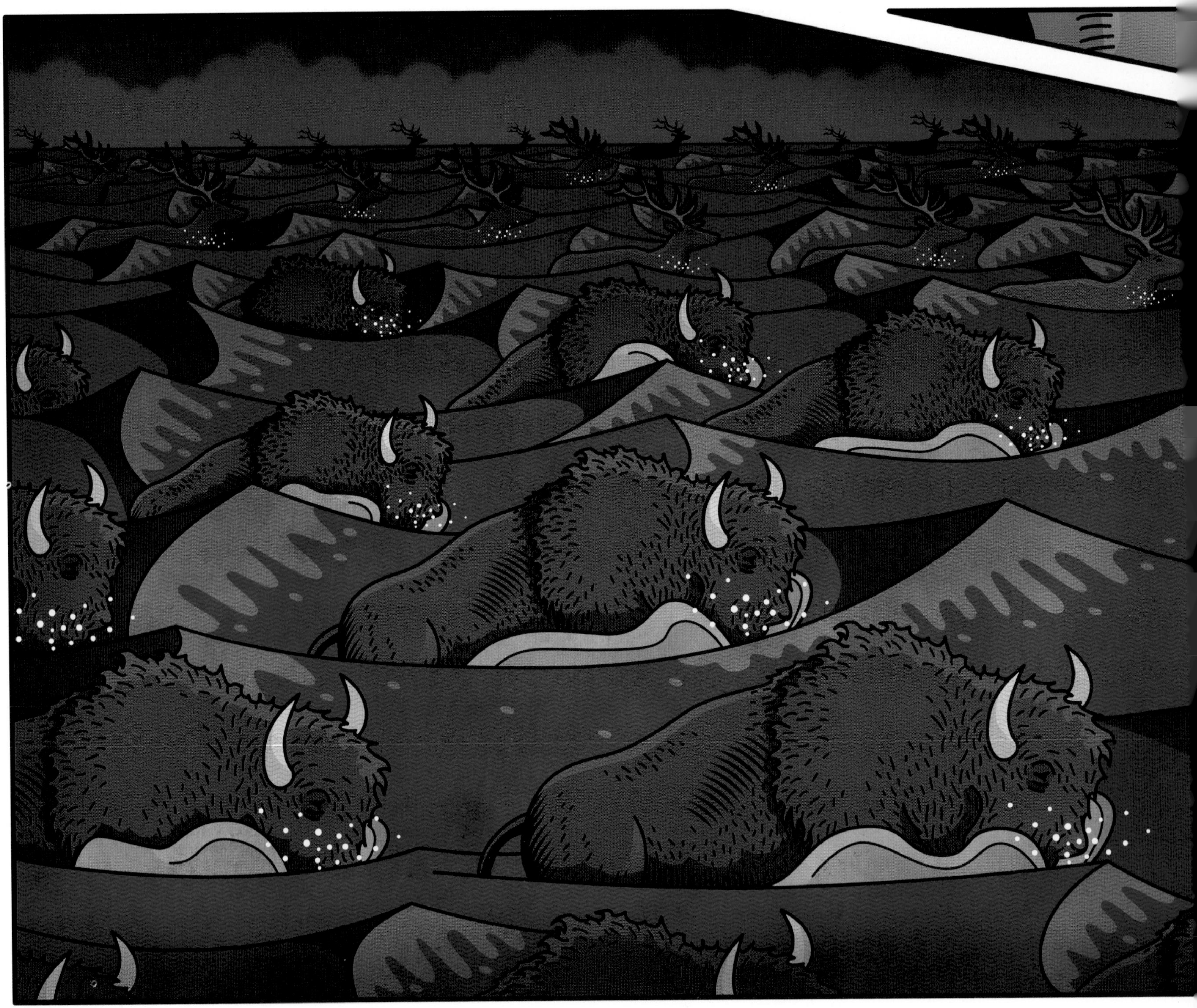

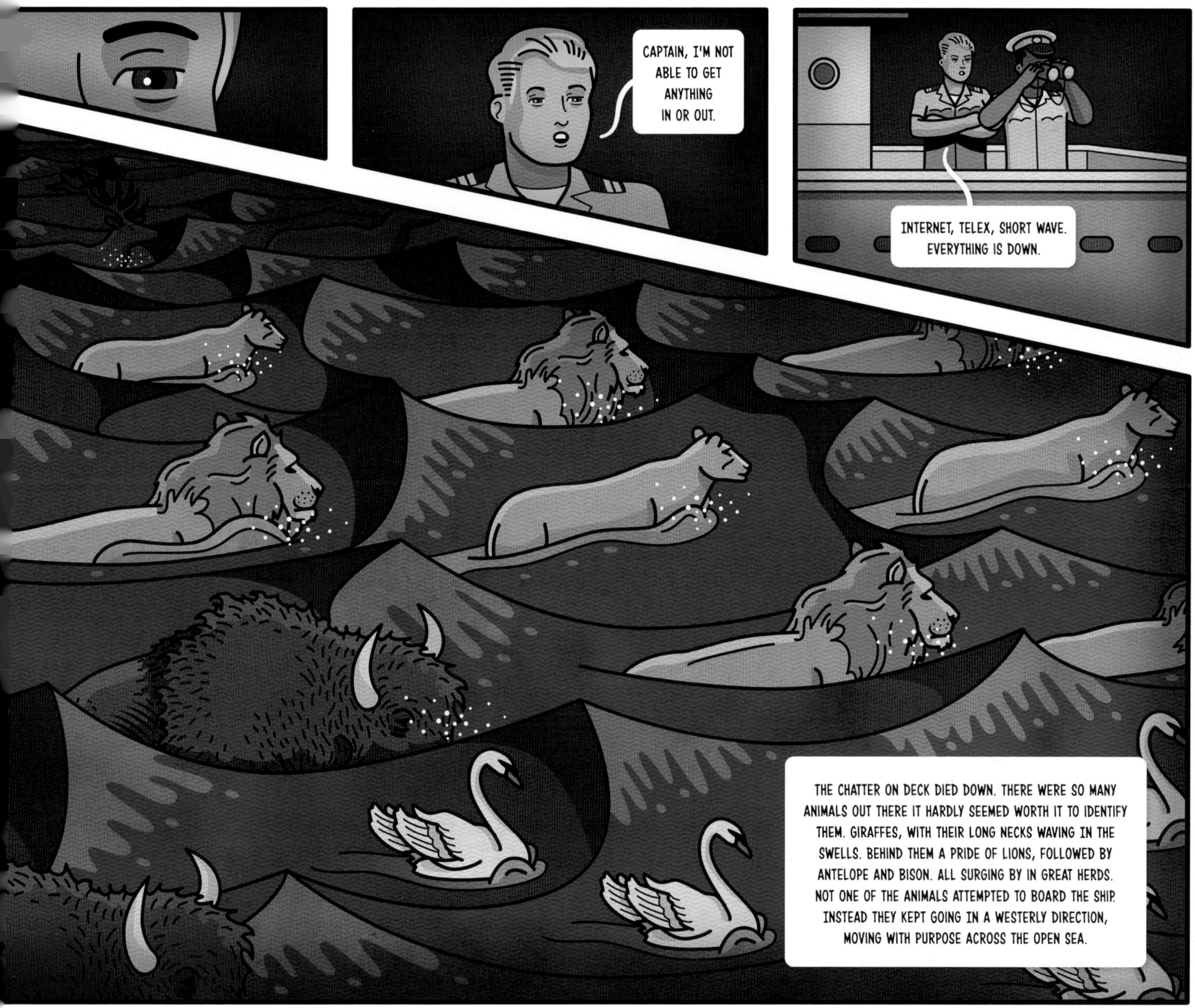
CAPTAIN, I'M NOT ABLE TO GET ANYTHING IN OR OUT.
INTERNET, TELEX, SHORT WAVE. EVERYTHING IS DOWN.
THE CHATTER ON DECK DIED DOWN. THERE WERE SO MANY ANIMALS OUT THERE IT HARDLY SEEMED WORTH IT TO IDENTIFY THEM. GIRAFFES, WITH THEIR LONG NECKS WAVING IN THE SWELLS. BEHIND THEM A PRIDE OF LIONS, FOLLOWED BY ANTELOPE AND BISON. ALL SURGING BY IN GREAT HERDS. NOT ONE OF THE ANIMALS ATTEMPTED TO BOARD THE SHIP. INSTEAD THEY KEPT GOING IN A WESTERLY DIRECTION, MOVING WITH PURPOSE ACROSS THE OPEN SEA.

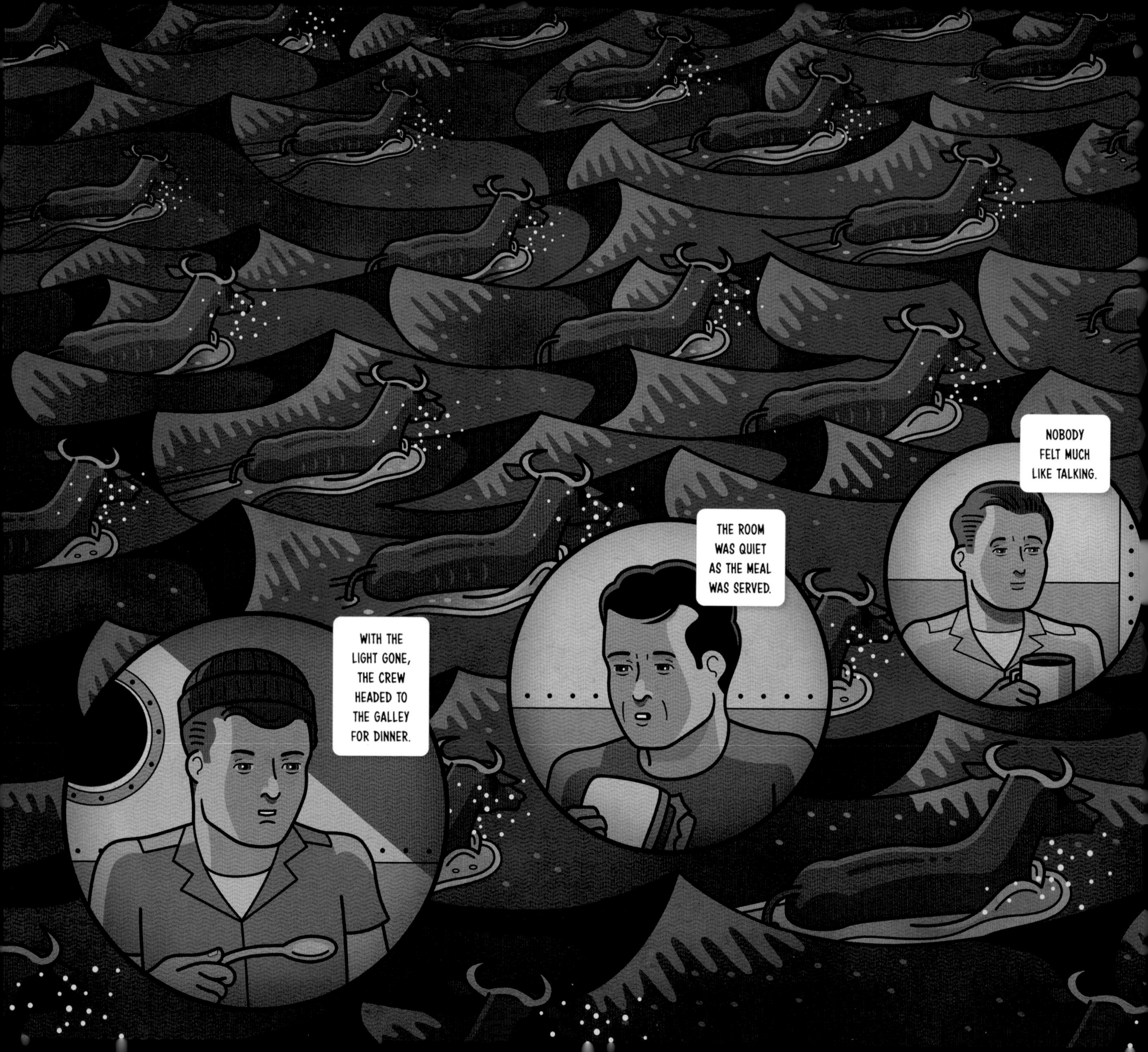
WITH THE LIGHT GONE, THE CREW HEADED TO THE GALLEY FOR DINNER.
THE ROOM WAS QUIET AS THE MEAL WAS SERVED.
NOBODY FELT MUCH LIKE TALKING.

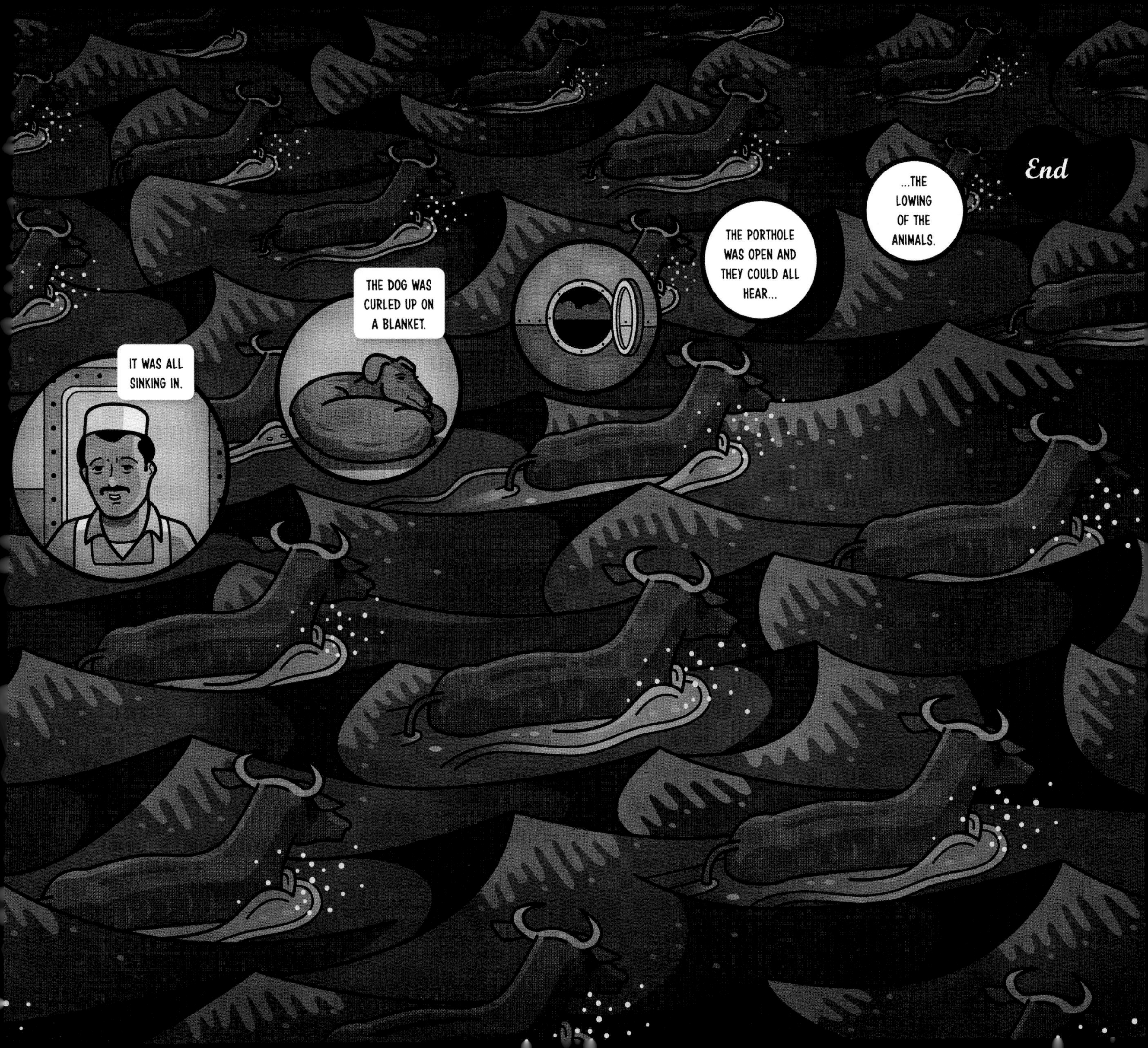
IT WAS ALL SINKING IN.
THE DOG WAS CURLED UP ON A BLANKET.
THE PORTHOLE WAS OPEN AND THEY COULD ALL HEAR...
...THE LOWING OF THE ANIMALS.
End

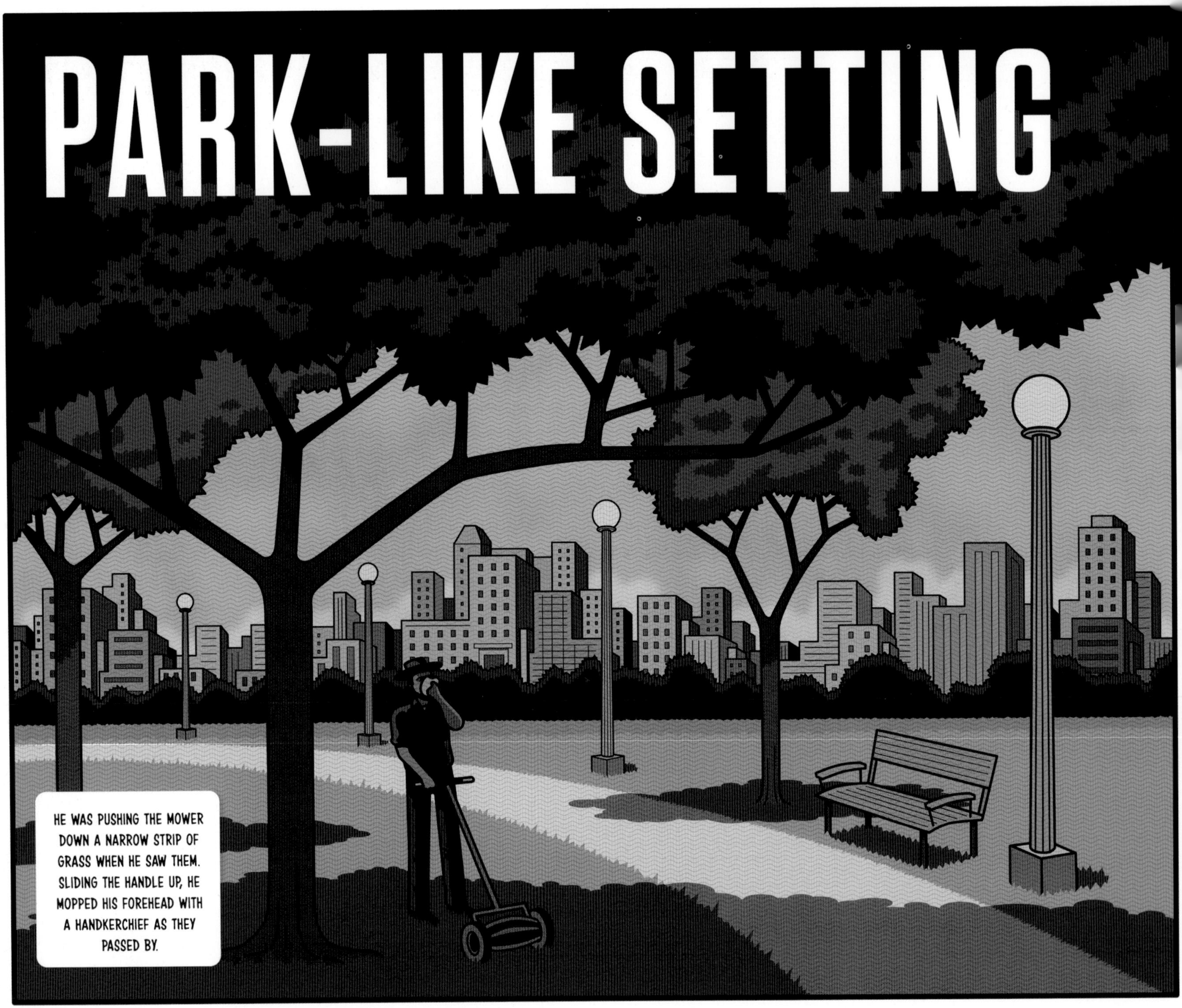
PARK-LIKE SETTING
HE WAS PUSHING THE MOWER DOWN A NARROW STRIP OF GRASS WHEN HE SAW THEM. SLIDING THE HANDLE UP, HE MOPPED HIS FOREHEAD WITH A HANDKERCHIEF AS THEY PASSED BY.

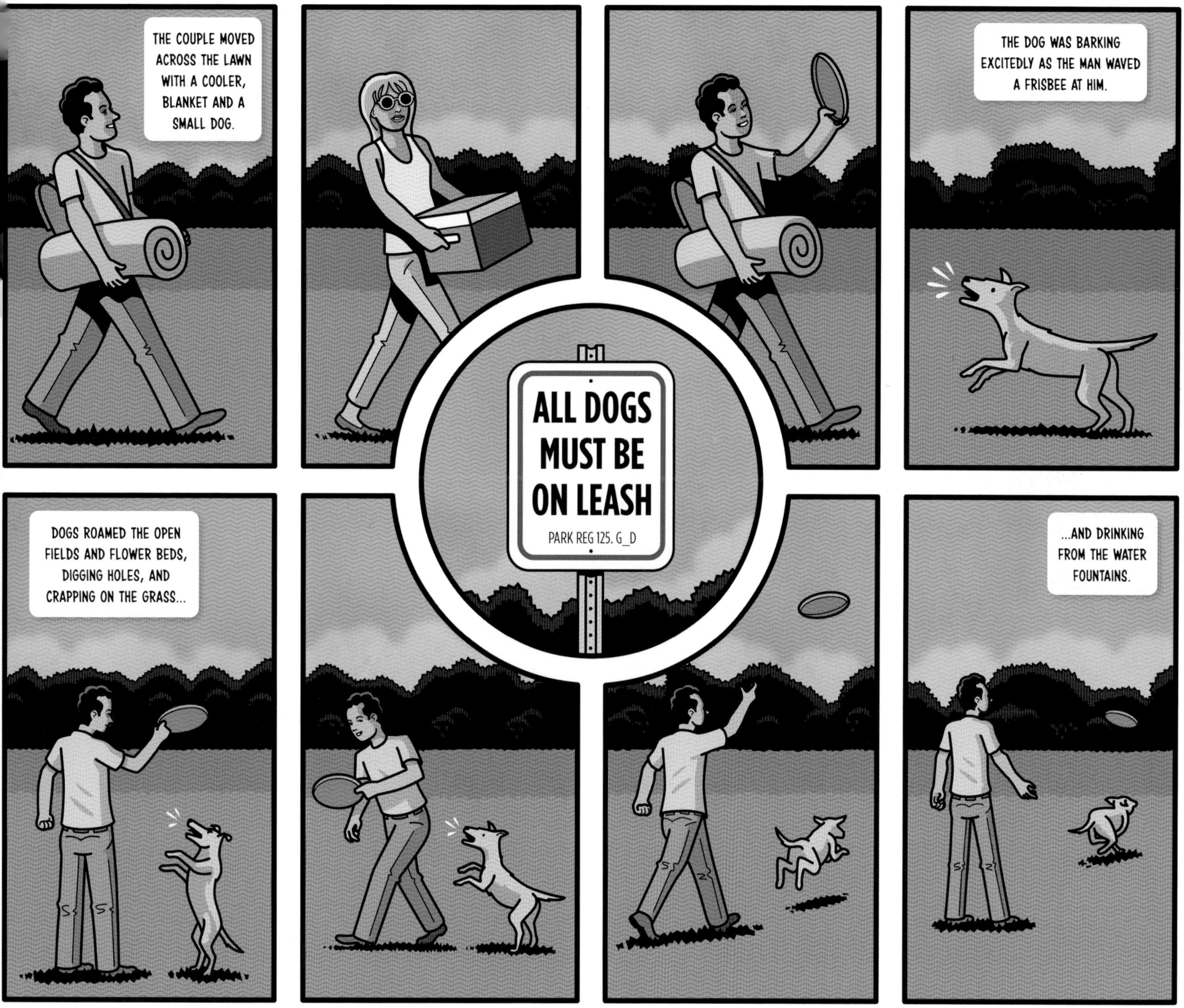
THE COUPLE MOVED ACROSS THE LAWN WITH A COOLER, BLANKET AND A SMALL DOG.
THE DOG WAS BARKING EXCITEDLY AS THE MAN WAVED A FRISBEE AT HIM.
ALL DOGS MUST BE ON LEASH
PARK REG 125. G_D
DOGS ROAMED THE OPEN FIELDS AND FLOWER BEDS, DIGGING HOLES, AND CRAPPING ON THE GRASS...
...AND DRINKING FROM THE WATER FOUNTAINS.

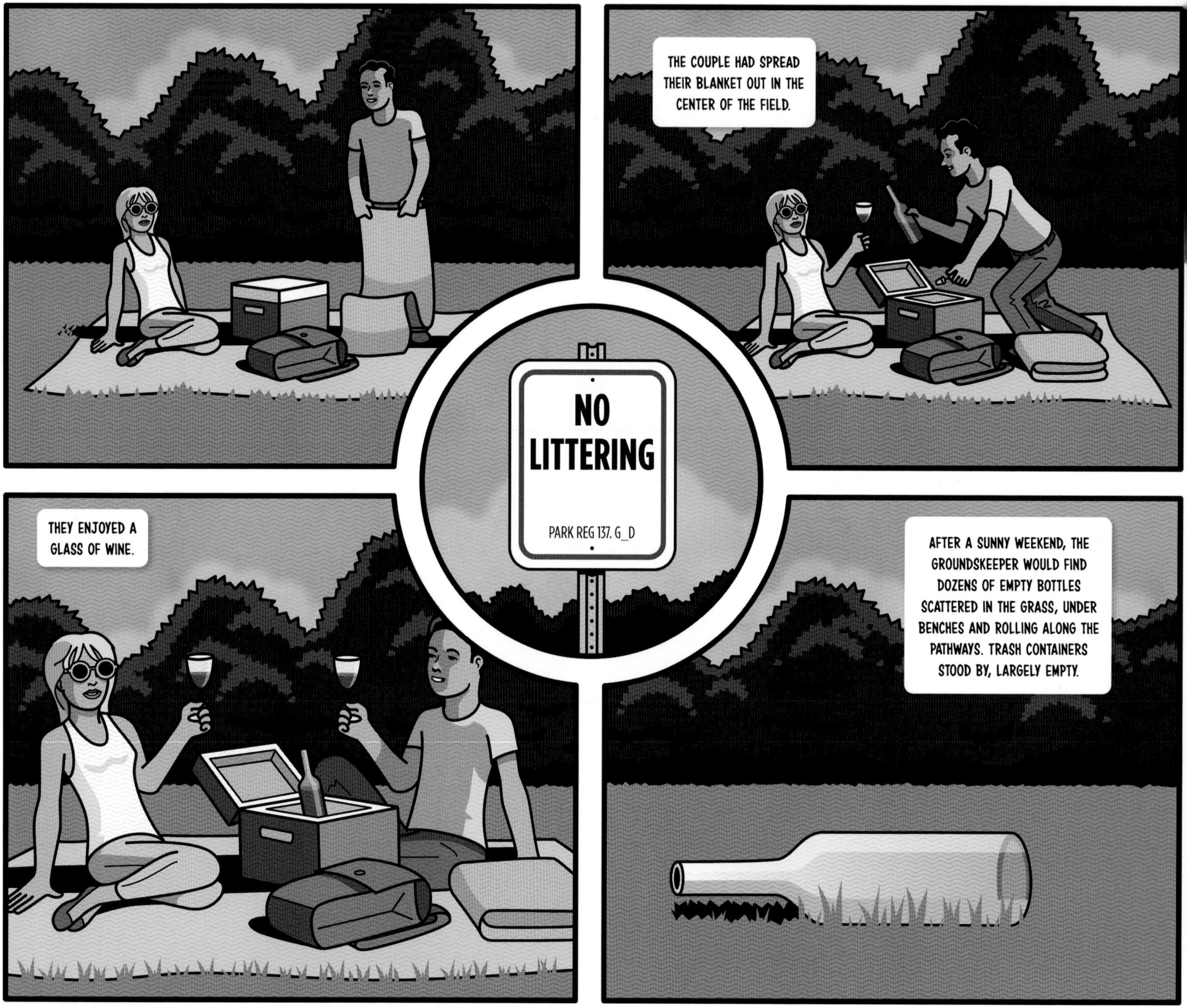
THE COUPLE HAD SPREAD THEIR BLANKET OUT IN THE CENTER OF THE FIELD.
NO LITTERING
PARK REG 137. G_D
THEY ENJOYED A GLASS OF WINE.
AFTER A SUNNY WEEKEND, THE GROUNDSKEEPER WOULD FIND DOZENS OF EMPTY BOTTLES SCATTERED IN THE GRASS, UNDER BENCHES AND ROLLING ALONG THE PATHWAYS. TRASH CONTAINERS STOOD BY, LARGELY EMPTY.

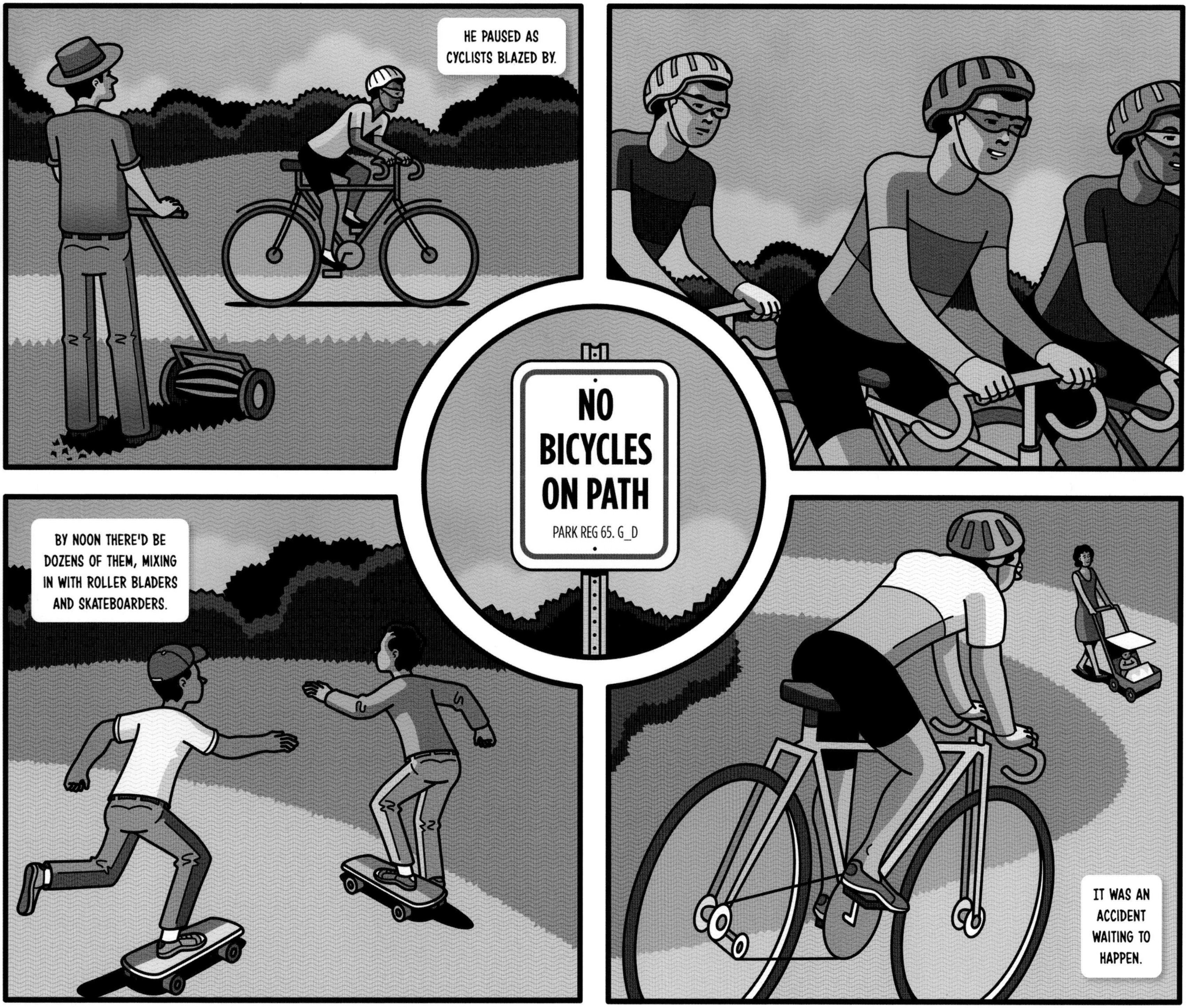
HE PAUSED AS CYCLISTS BLAZED BY.
NO BICYCLES ON PATH
PARK REG 65. G_D
BY NOON THERE'D BE DOZENS OF THEM, MIXING IN WITH ROLLER BLADERS AND SKATEBOARDERS.
IT WAS AN ACCIDENT WAITING TO HAPPEN.

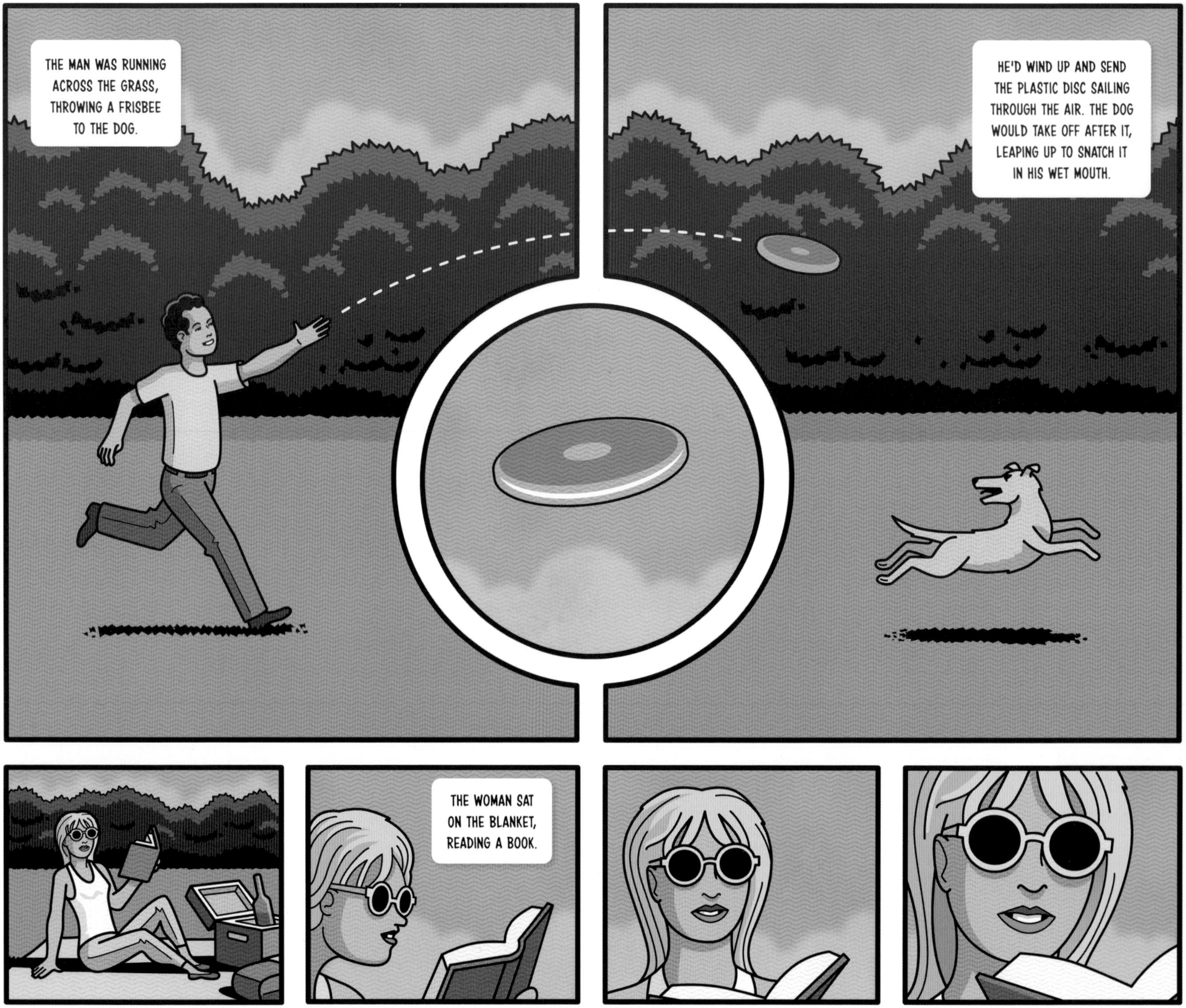
THE MAN WAS RUNNING ACROSS THE GRASS, THROWING A FRISBEE TO THE DOG.
HE'D WIND UP AND SEND THE PLASTIC DISC SAILING THROUGH THE AIR. THE DOG WOULD TAKE OFF AFTER IT, LEAPING UP TO SNATCH IT IN HIS WET MOUTH.
THE WOMAN SAT ON THE BLANKET, READING A BOOK.

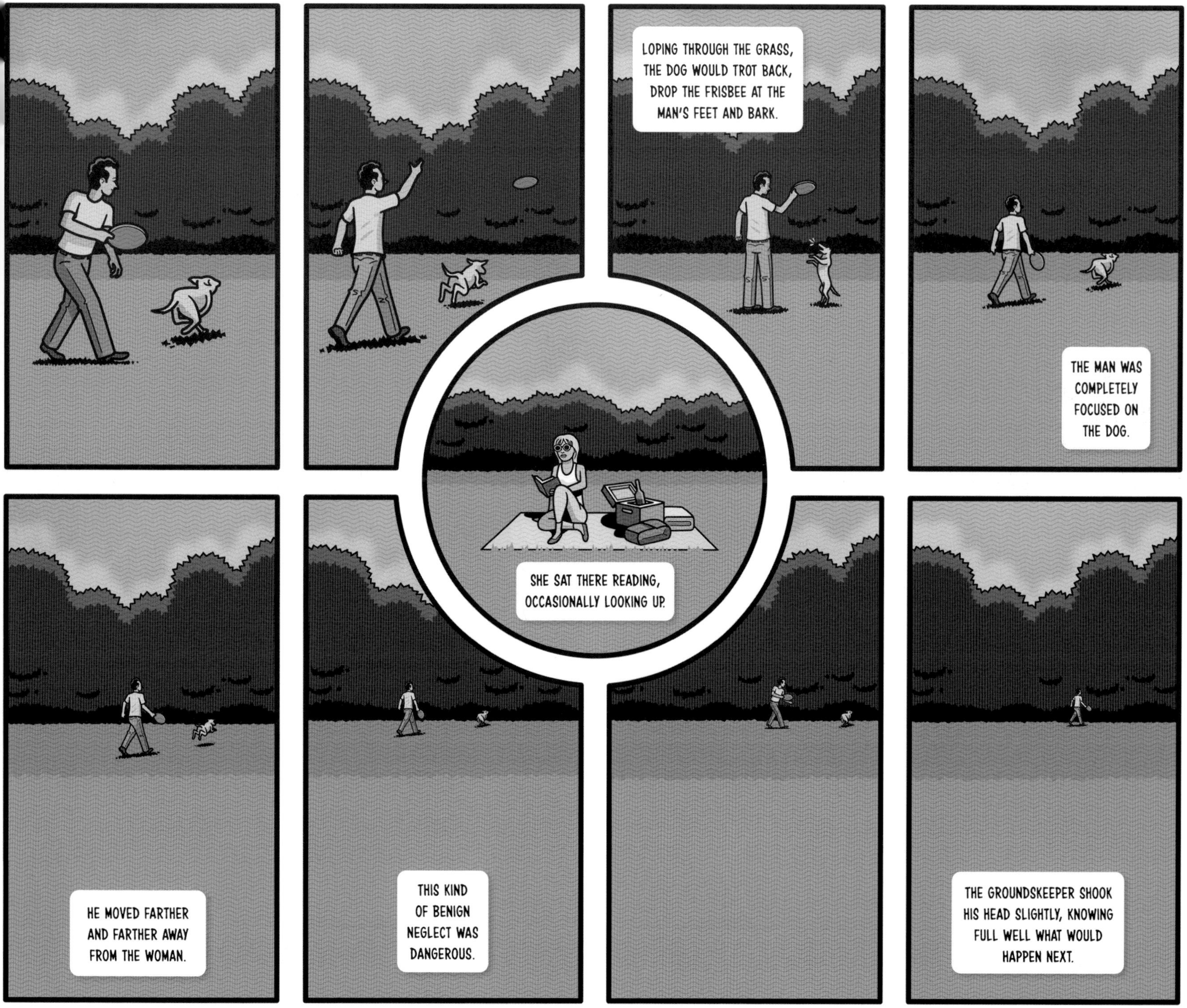
LOPING THROUGH THE GRASS, THE DOG WOULD TROT BACK, DROP THE FRISBEE AT THE MAN'S FEET AND BARK.
THE MAN WAS COMPLETELY FOCUSED ON THE DOG.
SHE SAT THERE READING, OCCASIONALLY LOOKING UP.
HE MOVED FARTHER AND FARTHER AWAY FROM THE WOMAN.
THIS KIND OF BENIGN NEGLECT WAS DANGEROUS.
THE GROUNDSKEEPER SHOOK HIS HEAD SLIGHTLY, KNOWING FULL WELL WHAT WOULD HAPPEN NEXT.

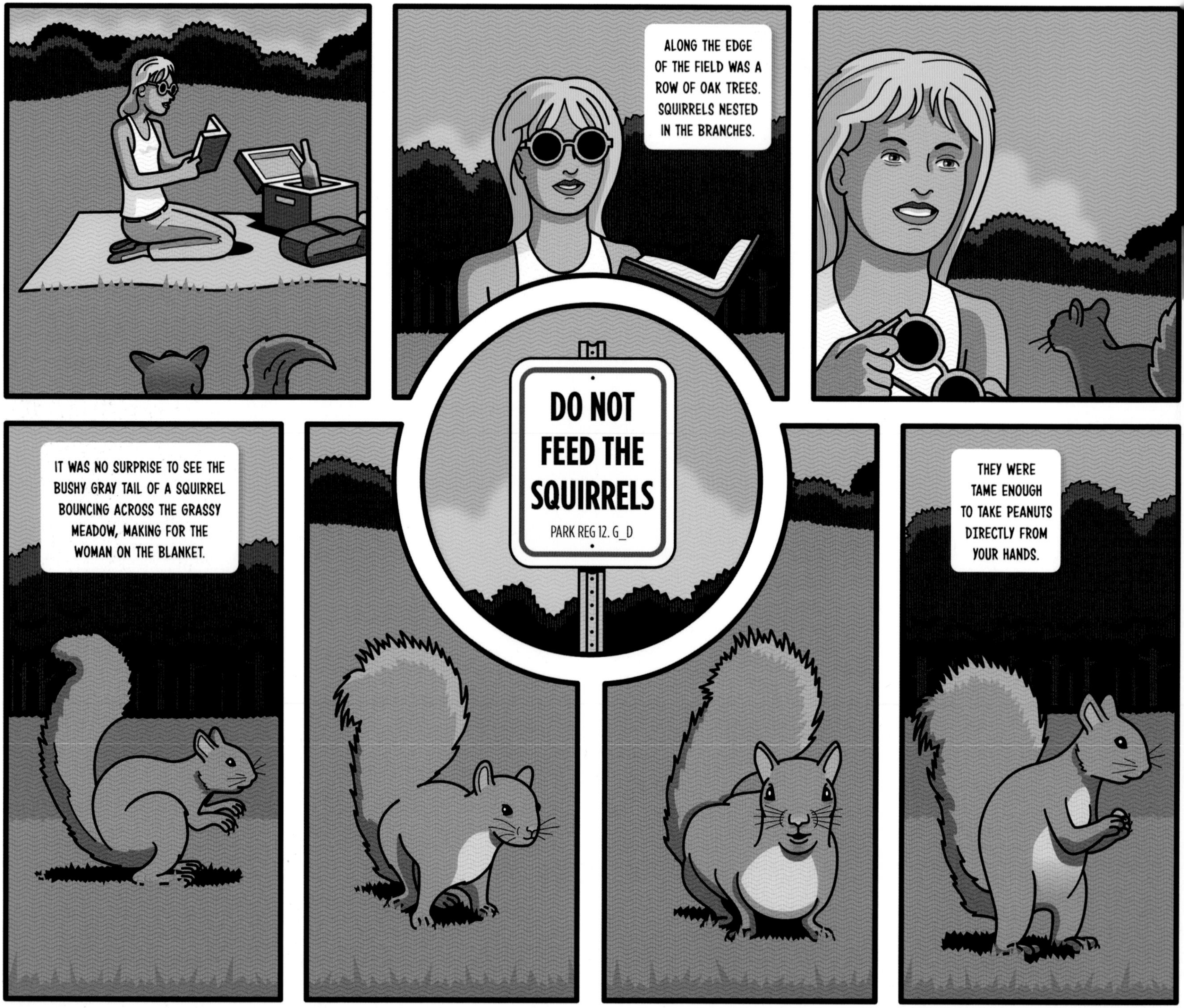
ALONG THE EDGE OF THE FIELD WAS A ROW OF OAK TREES. SQUIRRELS NESTED IN THE BRANCHES.
DO NOT FEED THE SQUIRRELS
PARK REG 12. G_D
IT WAS NO SURPRISE TO SEE THE BUSHY GRAY TAIL OF A SQUIRREL BOUNCING ACROSS THE GRASSY MEADOW, MAKING FOR THE WOMAN ON THE BLANKET.
THEY WERE TAME ENOUGH TO TAKE PEANUTS DIRECTLY FROM YOUR HANDS.

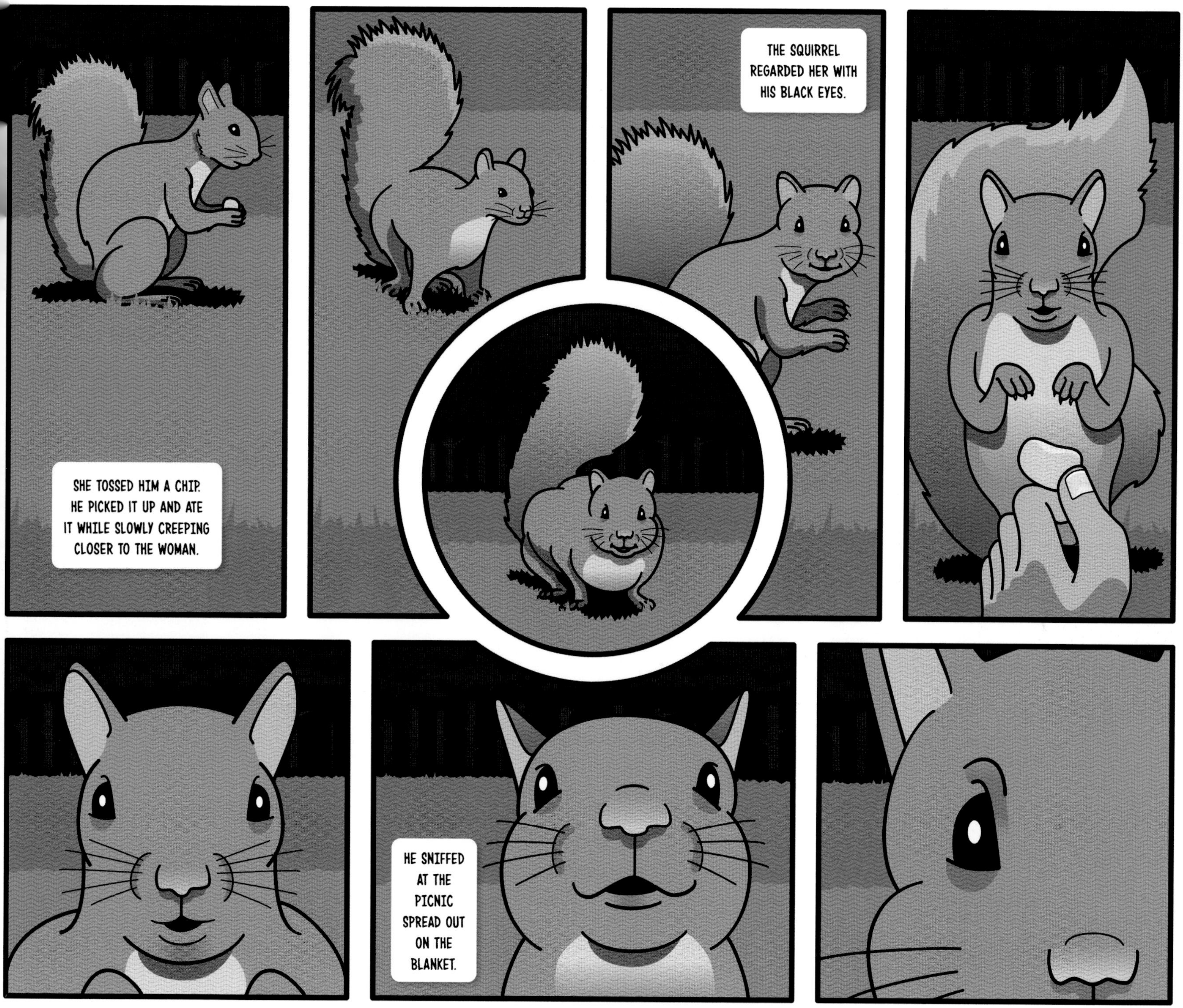
SHE TOSSED HIM A CHIP. HE PICKED IT UP AND ATE IT WHILE SLOWLY CREEPING CLOSER TO THE WOMAN.
THE SQUIRREL REGARDED HER WITH HIS BLACK EYES.
HE SNIFFED AT THE PICNIC SPREAD OUT ON THE BLANKET.

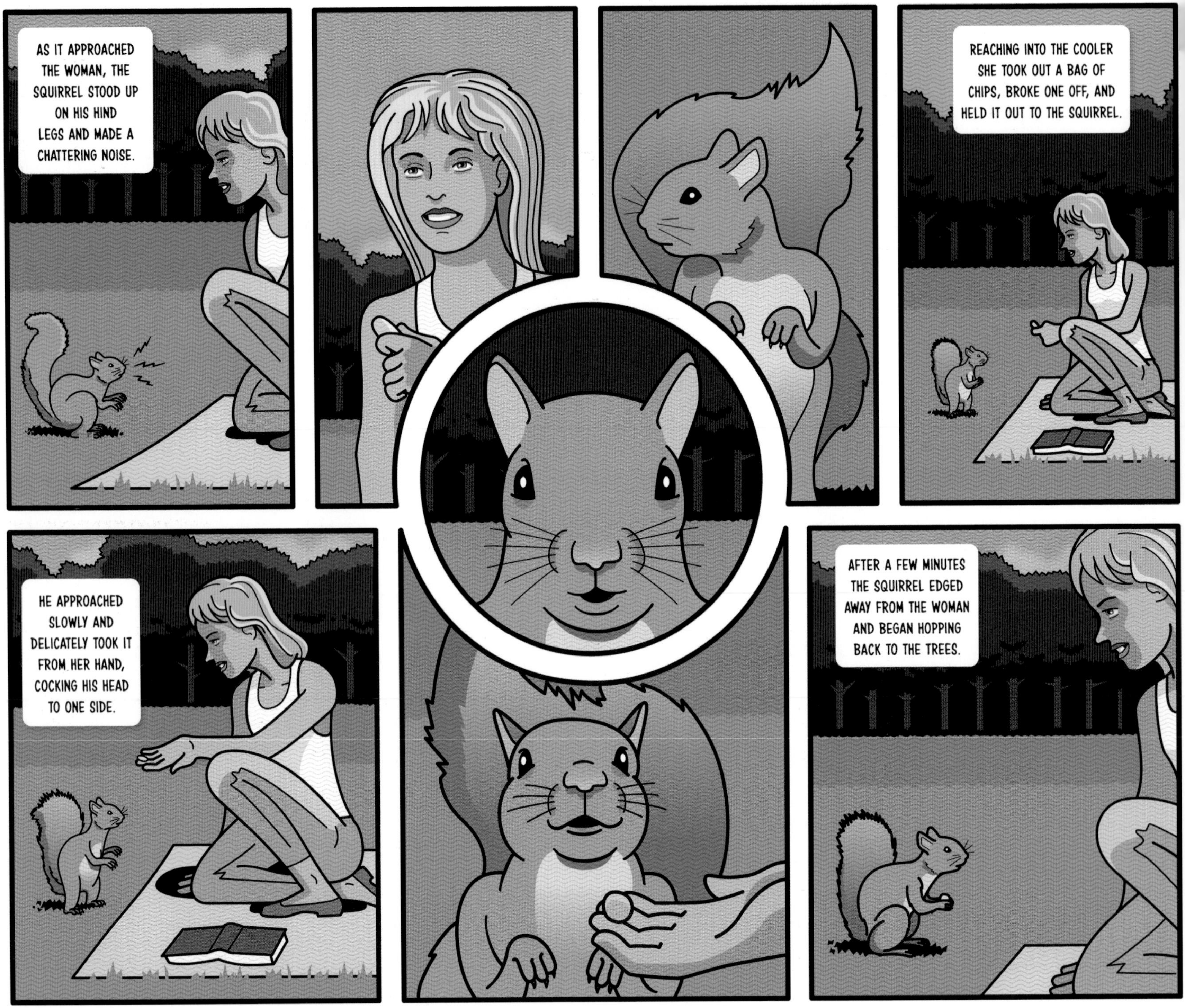
AS IT APPROACHED THE WOMAN, THE SQUIRREL STOOD UP ON HIS HIND LEGS AND MADE A CHATTERING NOISE.
REACHING INTO THE COOLER SHE TOOK OUT A BAG OF CHIPS, BROKE ONE OFF, AND HELD IT OUT TO THE SQUIRREL.
HE APPROACHED SLOWLY AND DELICATELY TOOK IT FROM HER HAND, COCKING HIS HEAD TO ONE SIDE.
AFTER A FEW MINUTES THE SQUIRREL EDGED AWAY FROM THE WOMAN AND BEGAN HOPPING BACK TO THE TREES.

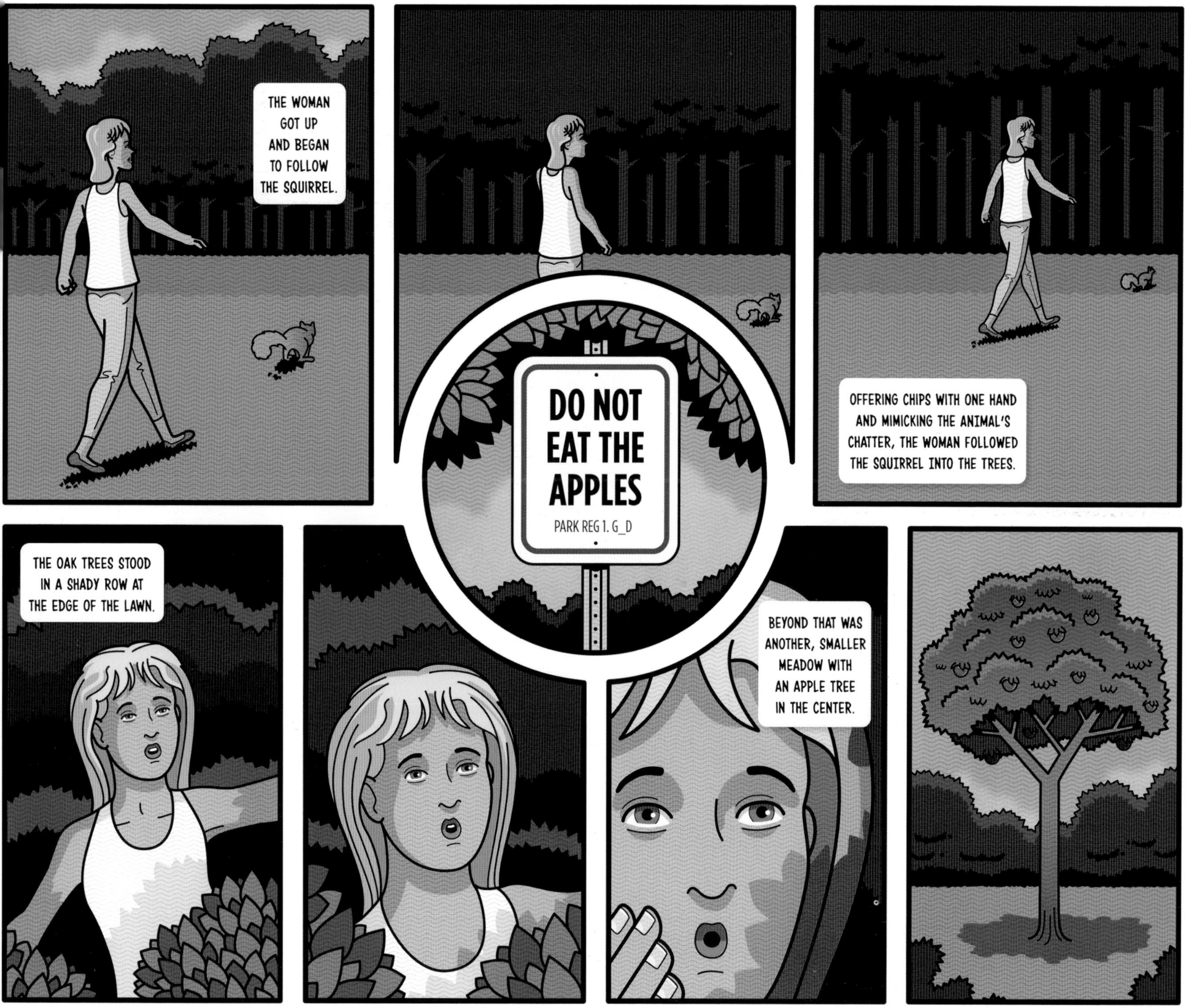
THE WOMAN GOT UP AND BEGAN TO FOLLOW THE SQUIRREL.
OFFERING CHIPS WITH ONE HAND AND MIMICKING THE ANIMAL'S CHATTER, THE WOMAN FOLLOWED THE SQUIRREL INTO THE TREES.
DO NOT EAT THE APPLES
PARK REG 1. G_D
THE OAK TREES STOOD IN A SHADY ROW AT THE EDGE OF THE LAWN.
BEYOND THAT WAS ANOTHER, SMALLER MEADOW WITH AN APPLE TREE IN THE CENTER.

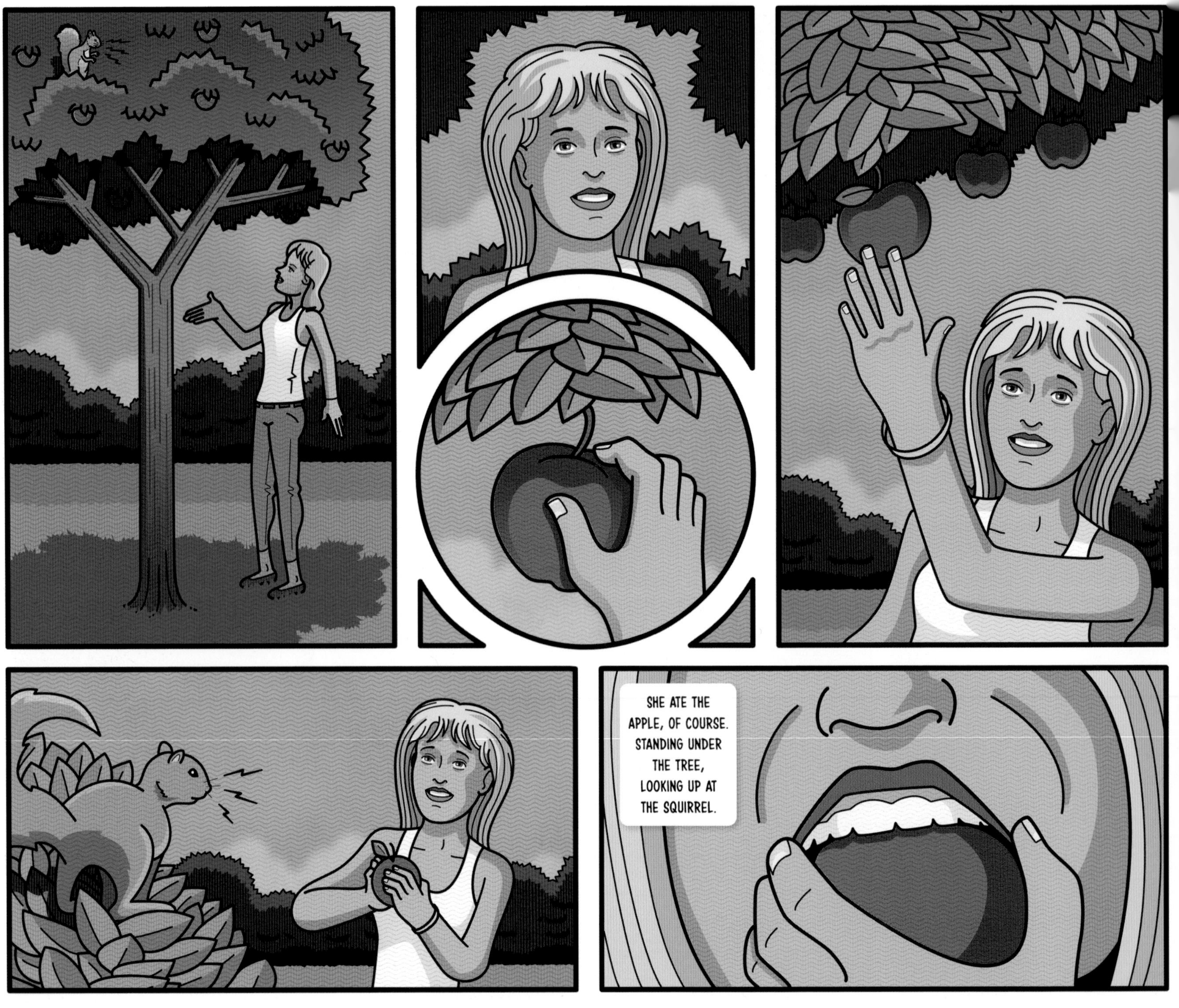
SHE ATE THE APPLE, OF COURSE. STANDING UNDER THE TREE, LOOKING UP AT THE SQUIRREL.

SOME WOMEN WOULD LOOK AROUND TO SEE IF ANYONE WAS WATCHING BEFORE SNAPPING AN APPLE OFF THE TREE. NOT THIS ONE.

SHE DIDN'T HESITATE FOR A MOMENT.

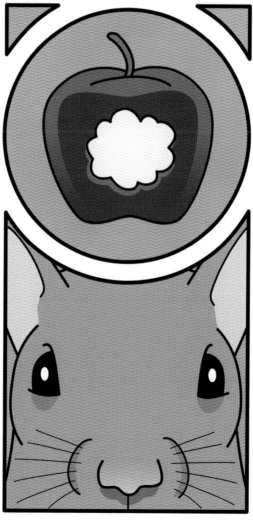

TOOK A BIG BITE, THEN ANOTHER.

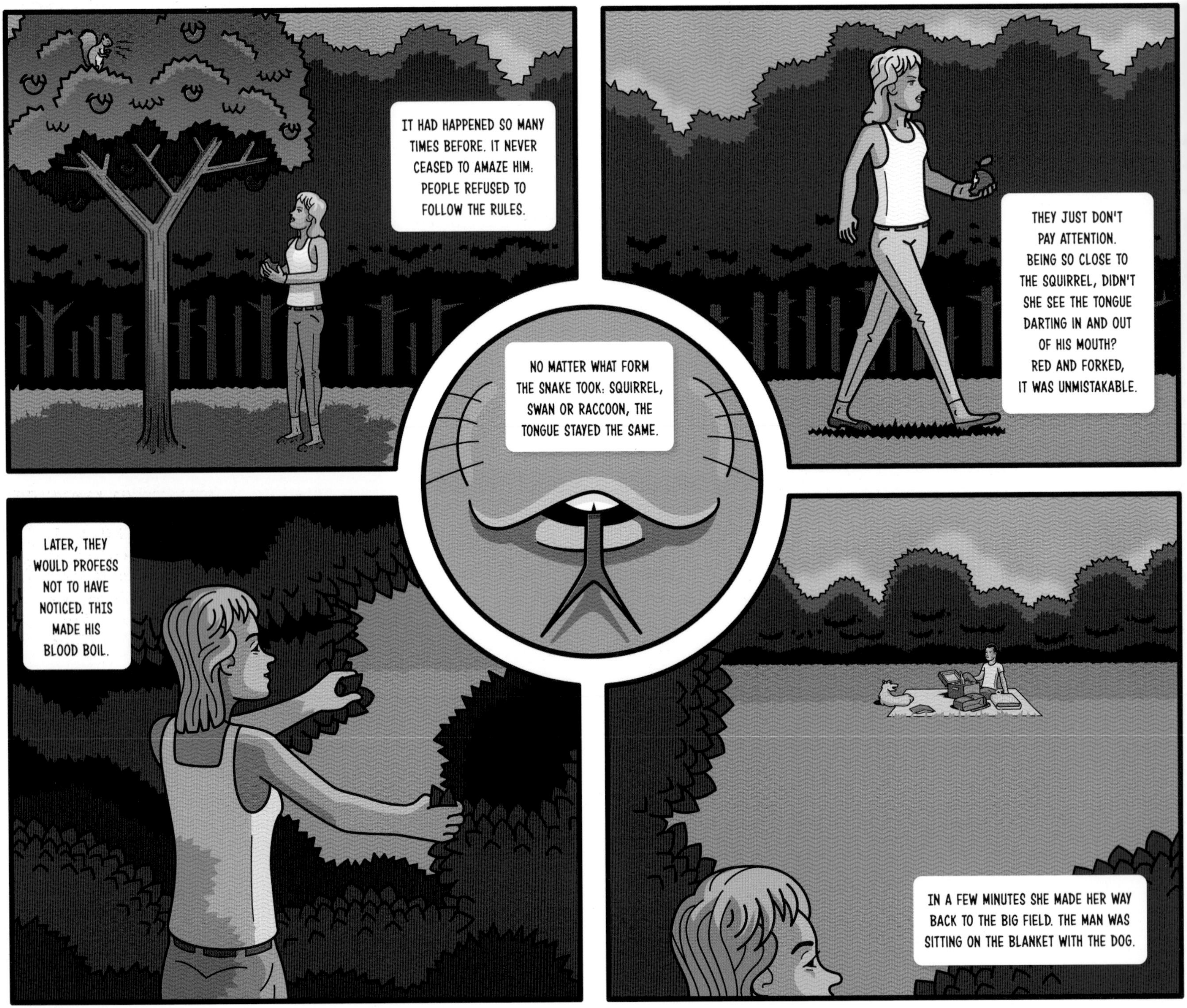
IT HAD HAPPENED SO MANY TIMES BEFORE. IT NEVER CEASED TO AMAZE HIM: PEOPLE REFUSED TO FOLLOW THE RULES.
THEY JUST DON'T PAY ATTENTION. BEING SO CLOSE TO THE SQUIRREL, DIDN'T SHE SEE THE TONGUE DARTING IN AND OUT OF HIS MOUTH? RED AND FORKED, IT WAS UNMISTAKABLE.
NO MATTER WHAT FORM THE SNAKE TOOK: SQUIRREL, SWAN OR RACCOON, THE TONGUE STAYED THE SAME.
LATER, THEY WOULD PROFESS NOT TO HAVE NOTICED. THIS MADE HIS BLOOD BOIL.
IN A FEW MINUTES SHE MADE HER WAY BACK TO THE BIG FIELD. THE MAN WAS SITTING ON THE BLANKET WITH THE DOG.

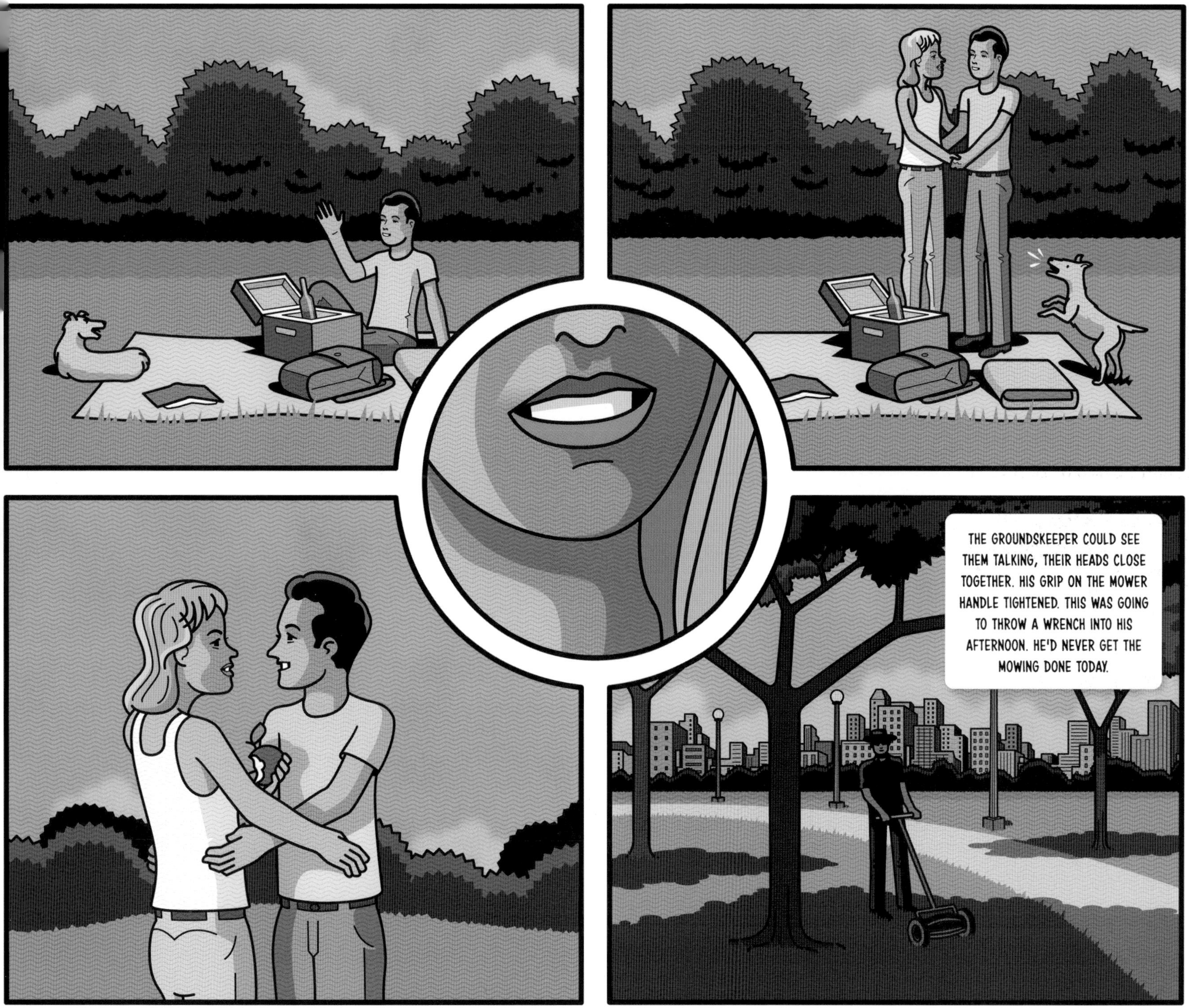
THE GROUNDSKEEPER COULD SEE THEM TALKING, THEIR HEADS CLOSE TOGETHER. HIS GRIP ON THE MOWER HANDLE TIGHTENED. THIS WAS GOING TO THROW A WRENCH INTO HIS AFTERNOON. HE'D NEVER GET THE MOWING DONE TODAY.

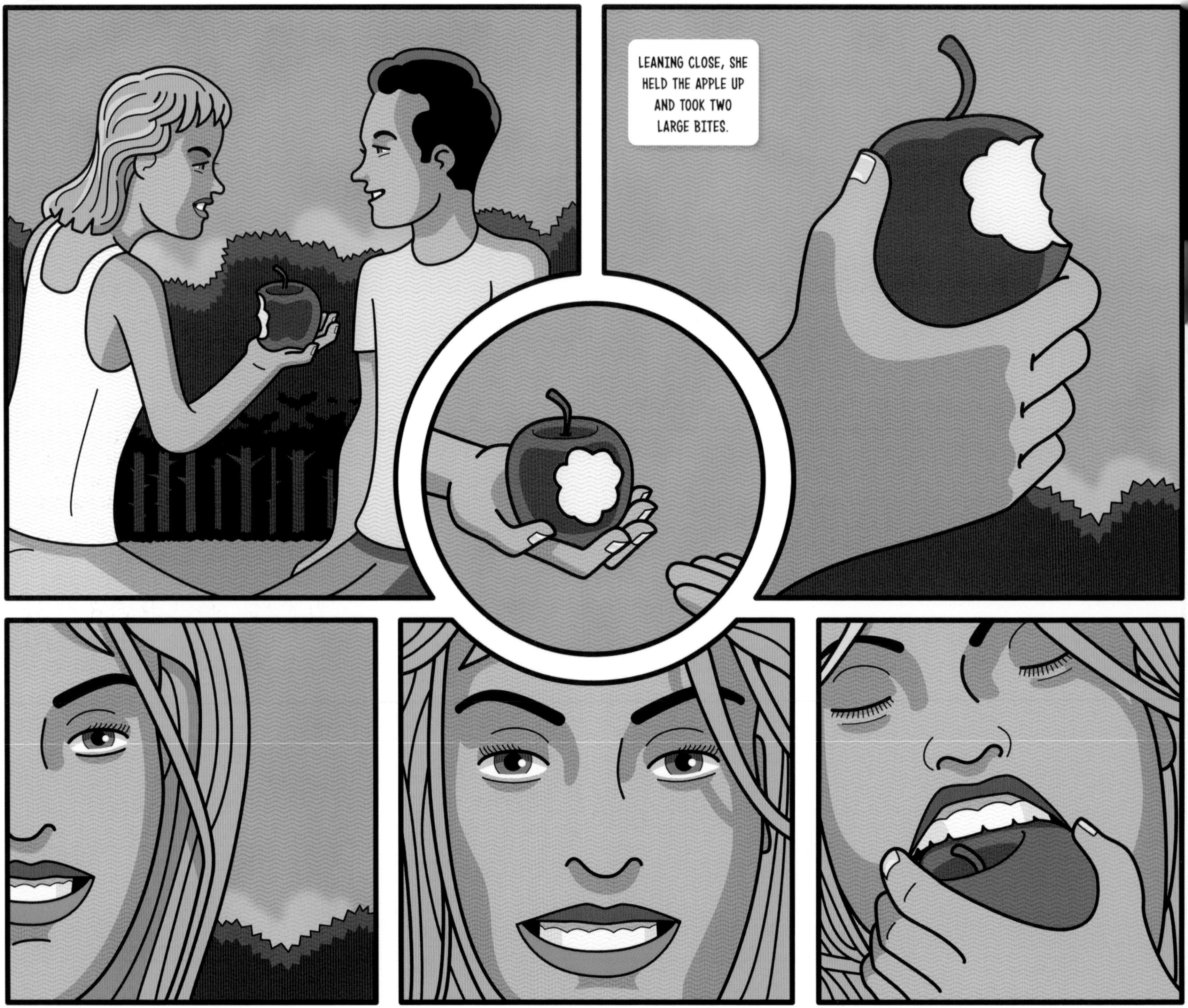
LEANING CLOSE, SHE HELD THE APPLE UP AND TOOK TWO LARGE BITES.

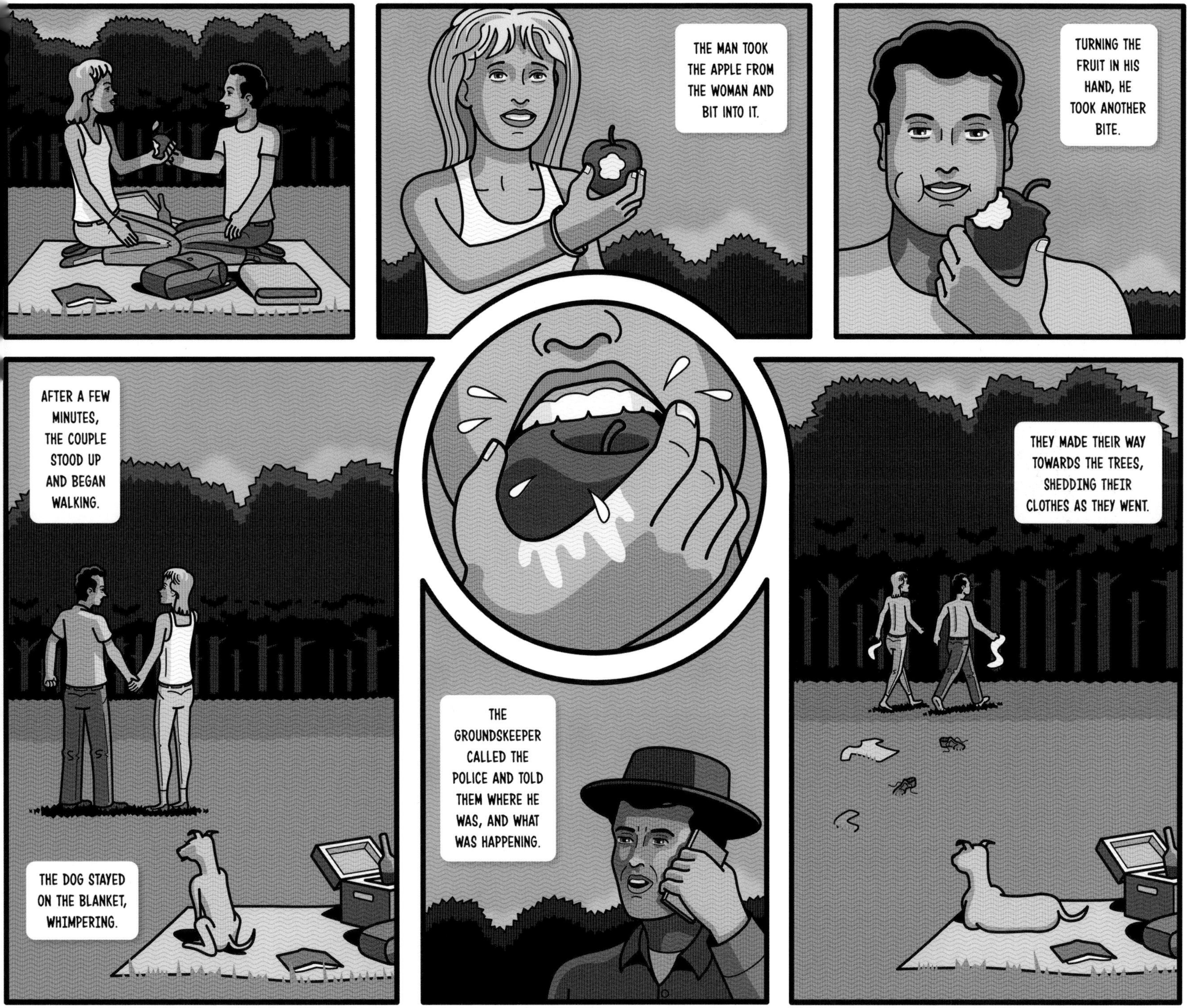
THE MAN TOOK THE APPLE FROM THE WOMAN AND BIT INTO IT.
TURNING THE FRUIT IN HIS HAND, HE TOOK ANOTHER BITE.
AFTER A FEW MINUTES, THE COUPLE STOOD UP AND BEGAN WALKING.
THE DOG STAYED ON THE BLANKET, WHIMPERING.
THE GROUNDSKEEPER CALLED THE POLICE AND TOLD THEM WHERE HE WAS, AND WHAT WAS HAPPENING.
THEY MADE THEIR WAY TOWARDS THE TREES, SHEDDING THEIR CLOTHES AS THEY WENT.

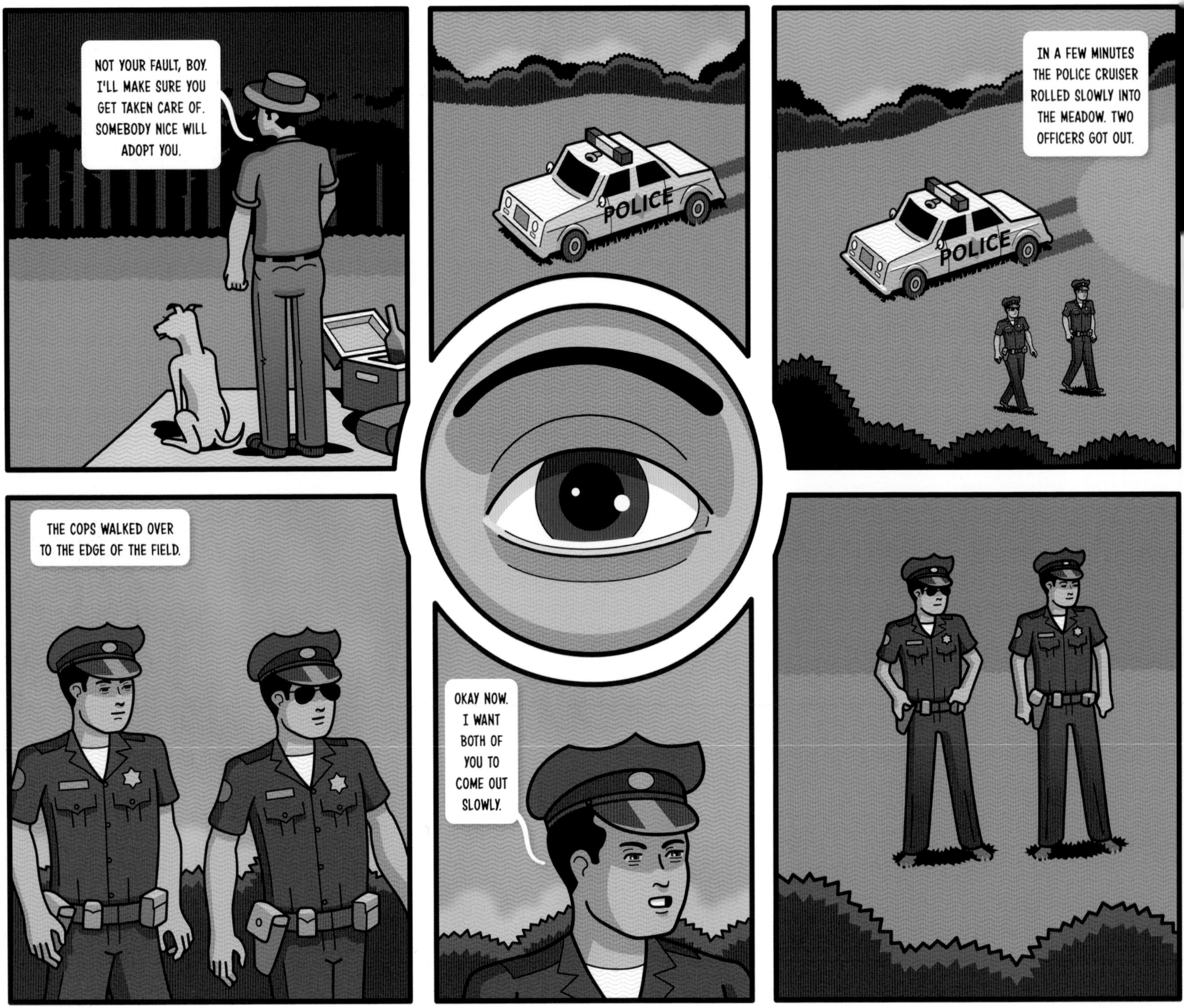
NOT YOUR FAULT, BOY. I'LL MAKE SURE YOU GET TAKEN CARE OF. SOMEBODY NICE WILL ADOPT YOU.
POLICE
IN A FEW MINUTES THE POLICE CRUISER ROLLED SLOWLY INTO THE MEADOW. TWO OFFICERS GOT OUT.
POLICE
THE COPS WALKED OVER TO THE EDGE OF THE FIELD.
OKAY NOW. I WANT BOTH OF YOU TO COME OUT SLOWLY.

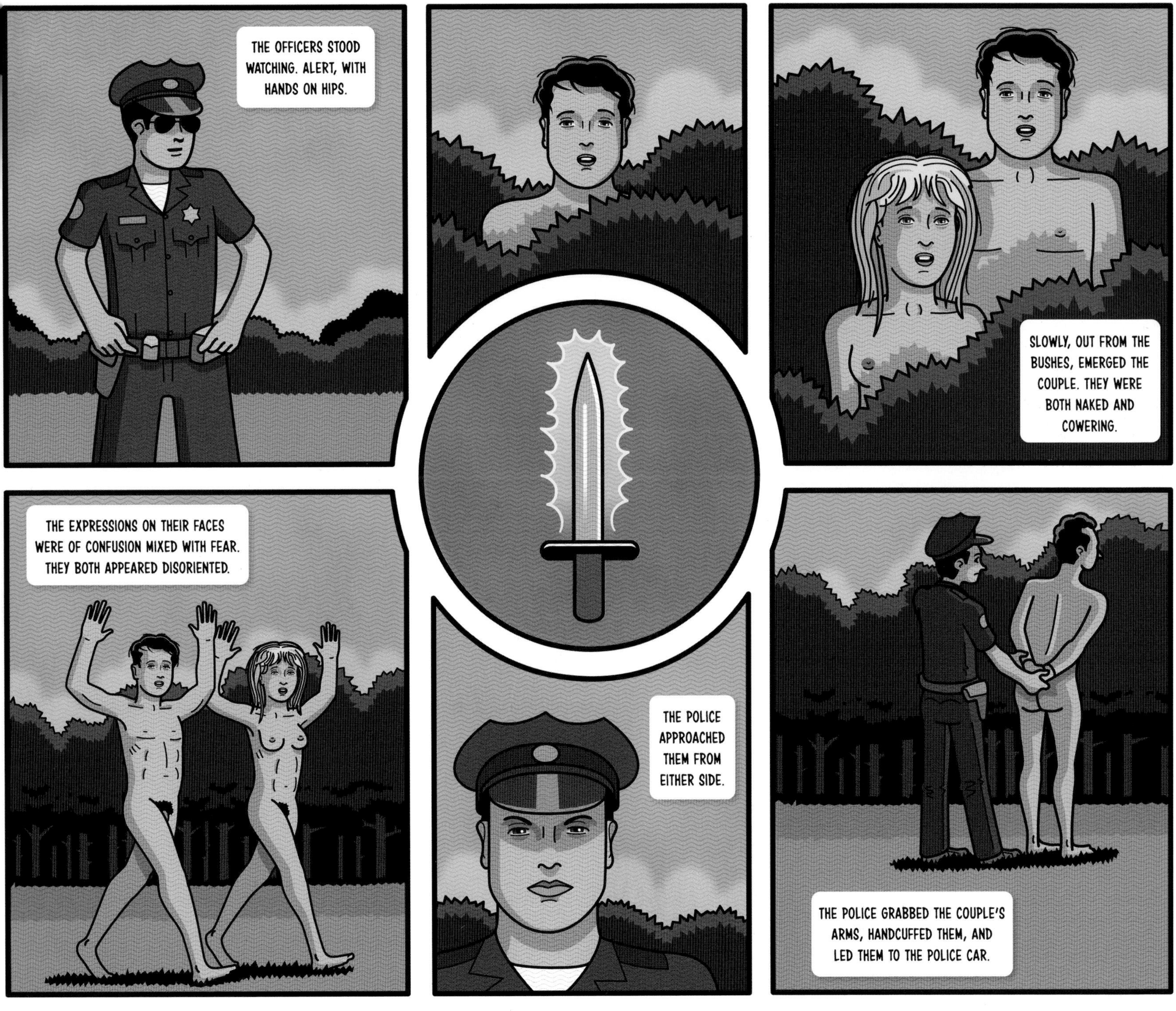
THE OFFICERS STOOD WATCHING. ALERT, WITH HANDS ON HIPS.
SLOWLY, OUT FROM THE BUSHES, EMERGED THE COUPLE. THEY WERE BOTH NAKED AND COWERING.
THE EXPRESSIONS ON THEIR FACES WERE OF CONFUSION MIXED WITH FEAR. THEY BOTH APPEARED DISORIENTED.
THE POLICE APPROACHED THEM FROM EITHER SIDE.
THE POLICE GRABBED THE COUPLE'S ARMS, HANDCUFFED THEM, AND LED THEM TO THE POLICE CAR.

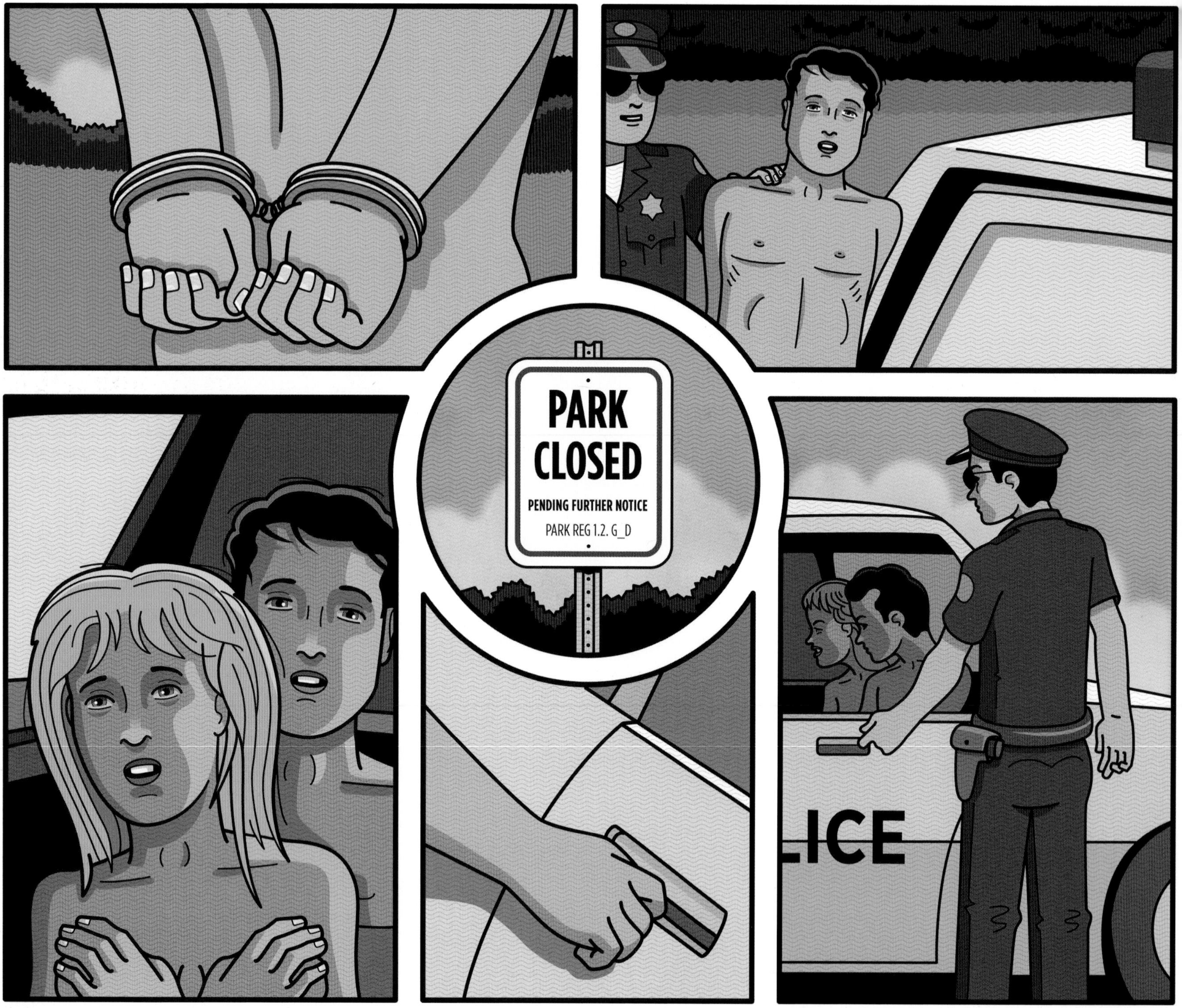
PARK
CLOSED
PENDING FURTHER NOTICE
PARK REG 1.2. G_D
LICE

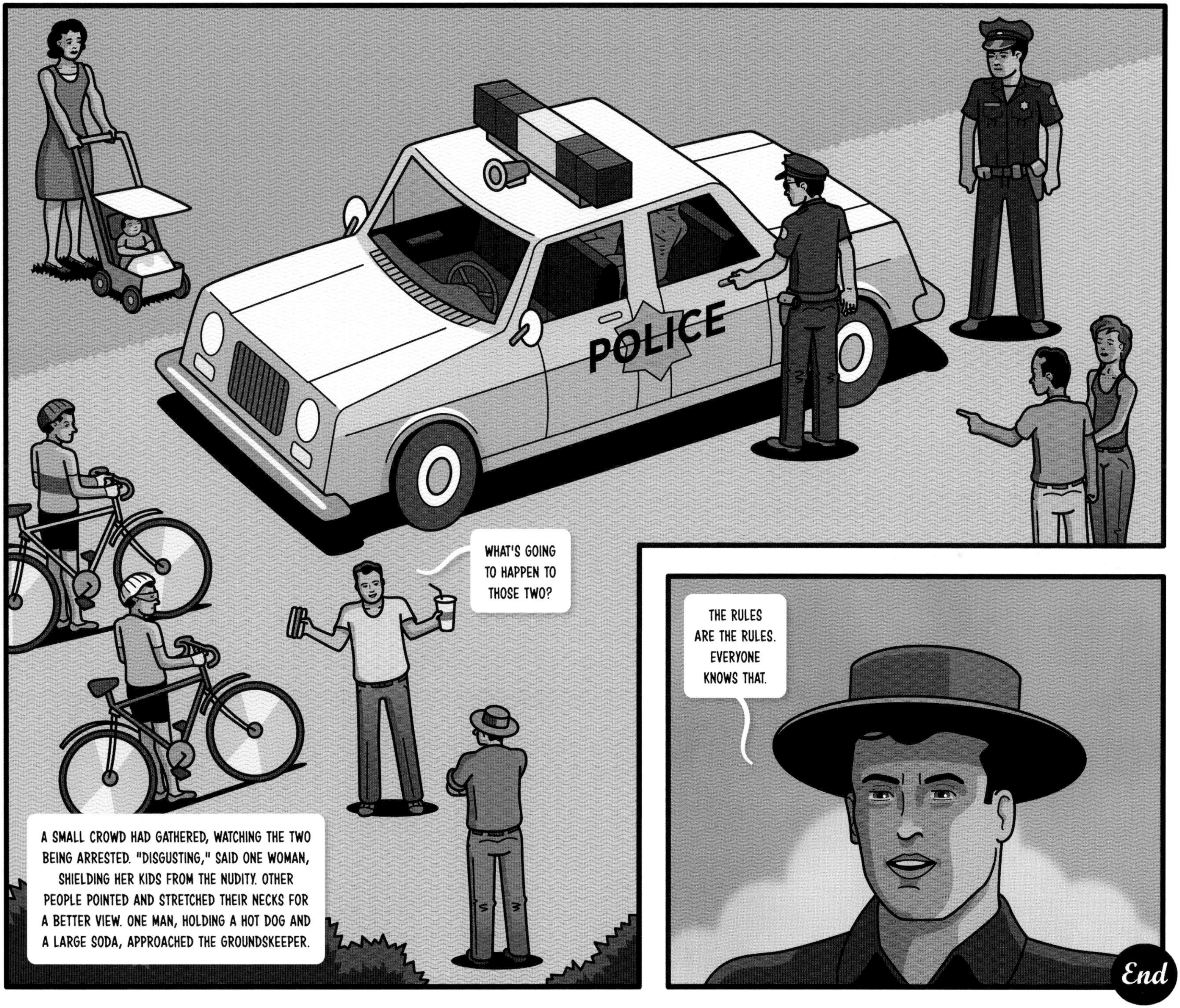
WHAT'S GOING TO HAPPEN TO THOSE TWO?
A SMALL CROWD HAD GATHERED, WATCHING THE TWO BEING ARRESTED. "DISGUSTING," SAID ONE WOMAN, SHIELDING HER KIDS FROM THE NUDITY. OTHER PEOPLE POINTED AND STRETCHED THEIR NECKS FOR A BETTER VIEW. ONE MAN, HOLDING A HOT DOG AND A LARGE SODA, APPROACHED THE GROUNDSKEEPER.
THE RULES ARE THE RULES. EVERYONE KNOWS THAT.
End

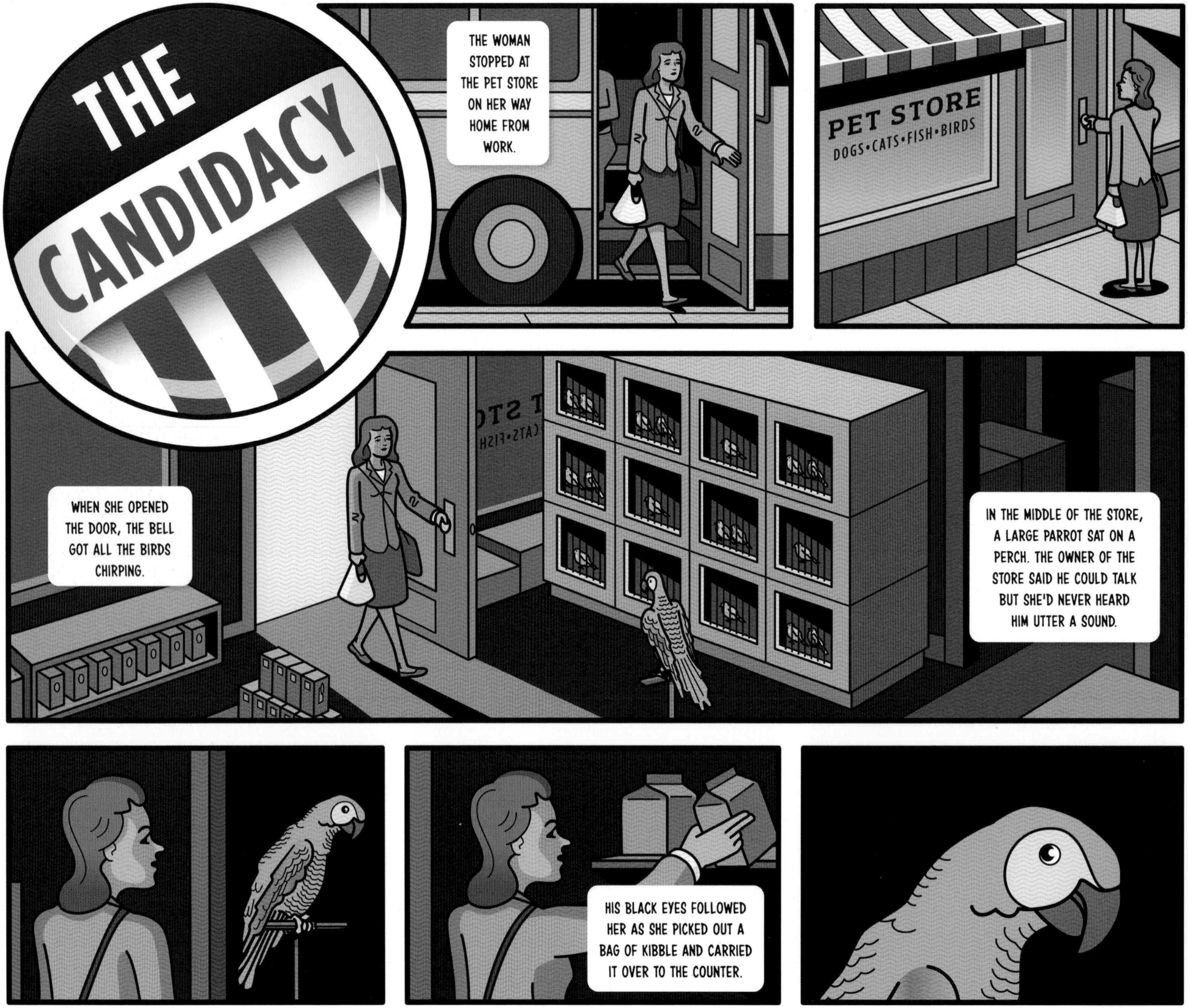
THE CANDIDACY
THE WOMAN STOPPED AT THE PET STORE ON HER WAY HOME FROM WORK.
PET STORE
DOGS•CATS•FISH•BIRDS
WHEN SHE OPENED THE DOOR, THE BELL GOT ALL THE BIRDS CHIRPING.
IN THE MIDDLE OF THE STORE, A LARGE PARROT SAT ON A PERCH. THE OWNER OF THE STORE SAID HE COULD TALK BUT SHE'D NEVER HEARD HIM UTTER A SOUND.
HIS BLACK EYES FOLLOWED HER AS SHE PICKED OUT A BAG OF KIBBLE AND CARRIED IT OVER TO THE COUNTER.

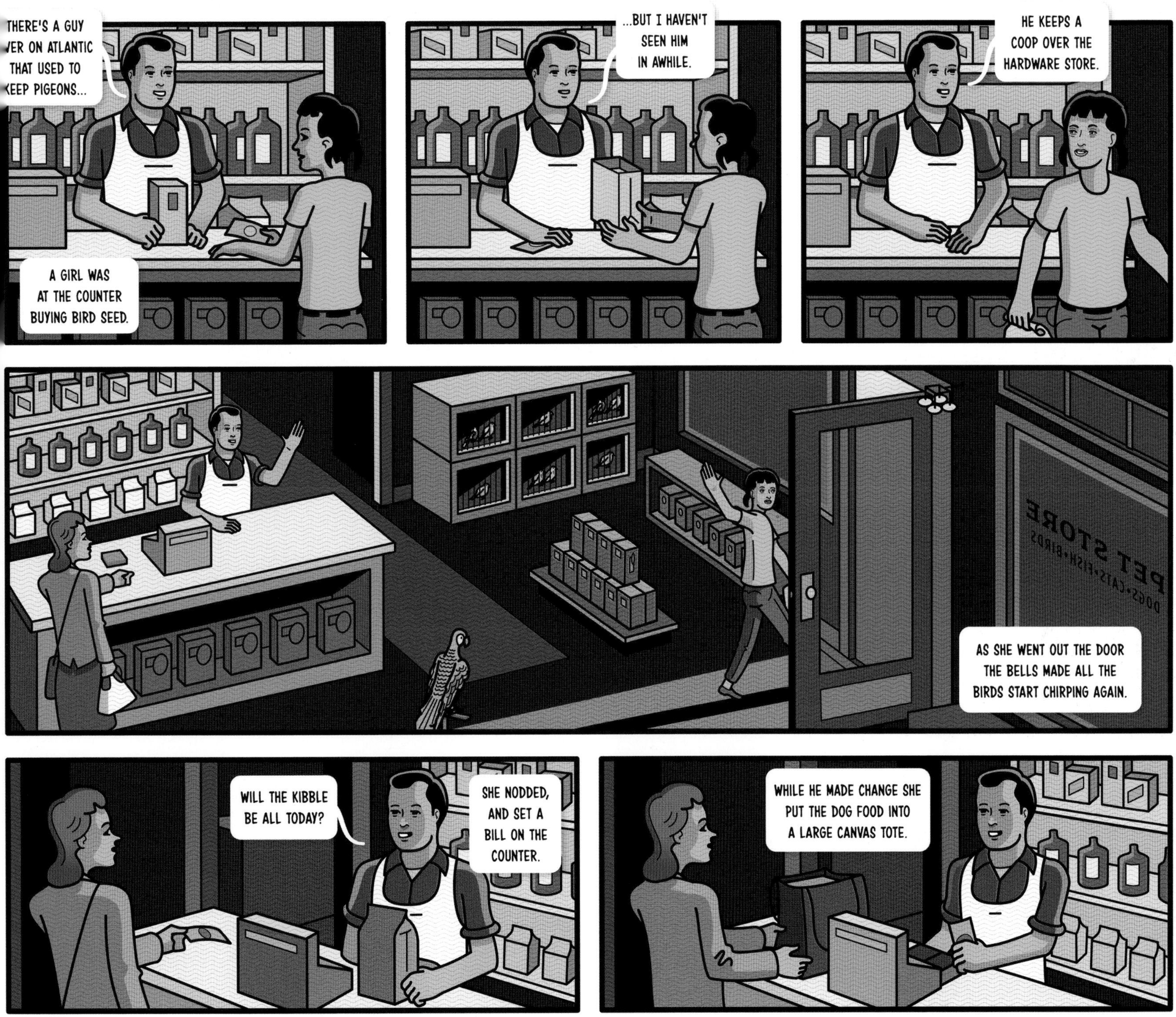
THERE'S A GUY VER ON ATLANTIC THAT USED TO EEP PIGEONS...
A GIRL WAS AT THE COUNTER BUYING BIRD SEED.
...BUT I HAVEN'T SEEN HIM IN AWHILE.
HE KEEPS A COOP OVER THE HARDWARE STORE.
PET STORE
DOGS•CATS•FISH•BIRDS
AS SHE WENT OUT THE DOOR THE BELLS MADE ALL THE BIRDS START CHIRPING AGAIN.
WILL THE KIBBLE BE ALL TODAY?
SHE NODDED, AND SET A BILL ON THE COUNTER.
WHILE HE MADE CHANGE SHE PUT THE DOG FOOD INTO A LARGE CANVAS TOTE.

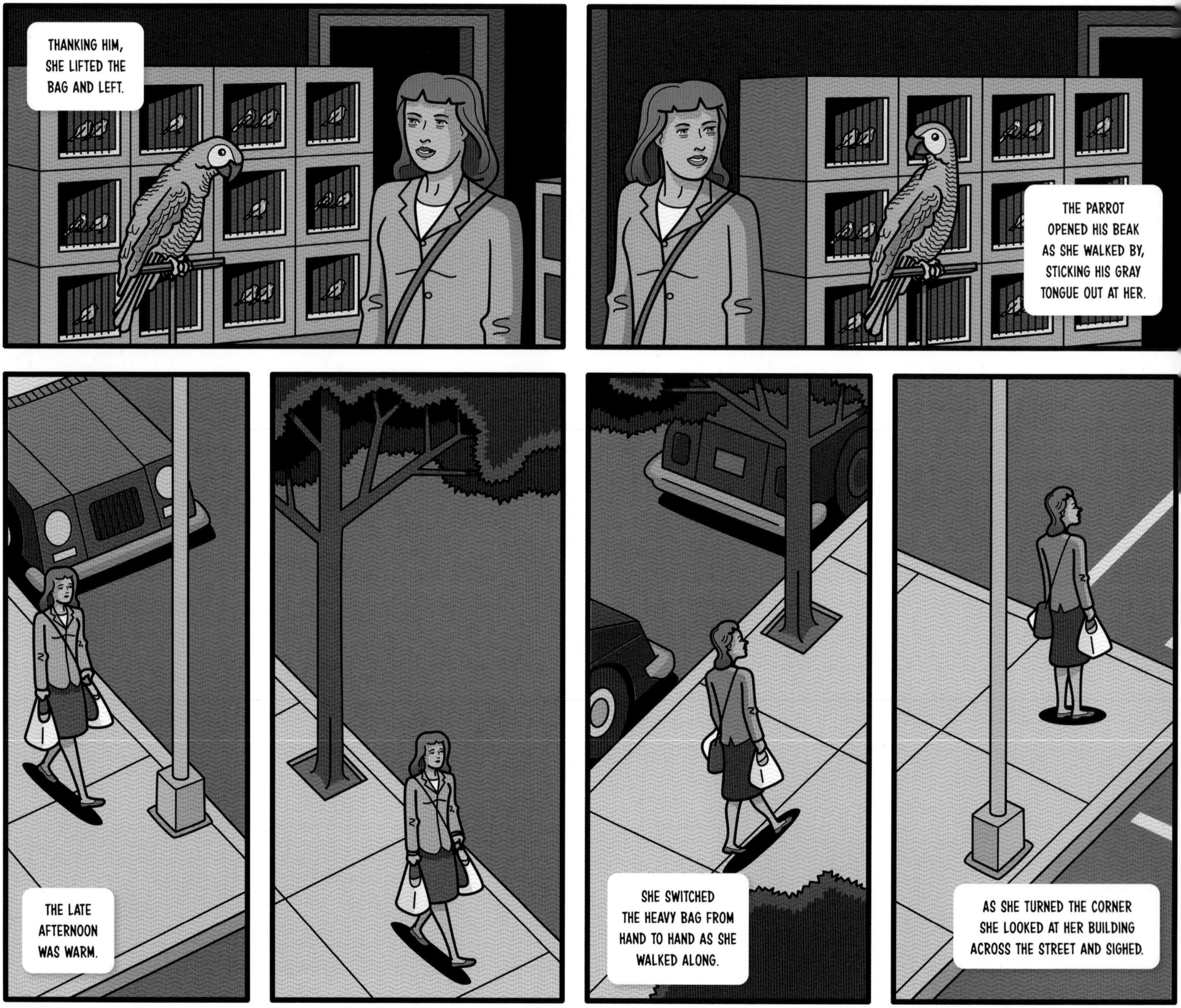
THANKING HIM, SHE LIFTED THE BAG AND LEFT.
THE PARROT OPENED HIS BEAK AS SHE WALKED BY, STICKING HIS GRAY TONGUE OUT AT HER.
THE LATE AFTERNOON WAS WARM.
SHE SWITCHED THE HEAVY BAG FROM HAND TO HAND AS SHE WALKED ALONG.
AS SHE TURNED THE CORNER SHE LOOKED AT HER BUILDING ACROSS THE STREET AND SIGHED.

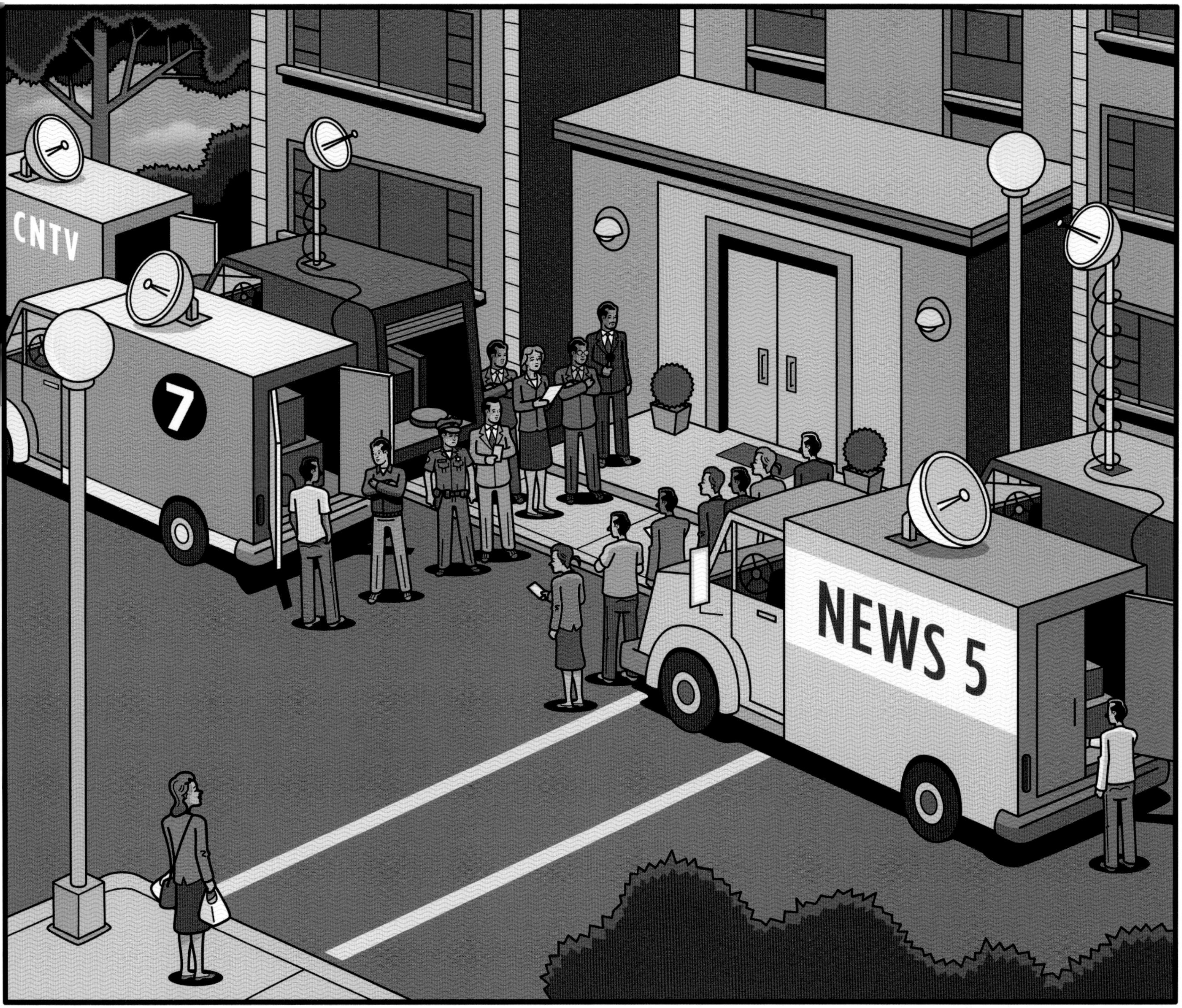
CNTV
7
NEWS 5

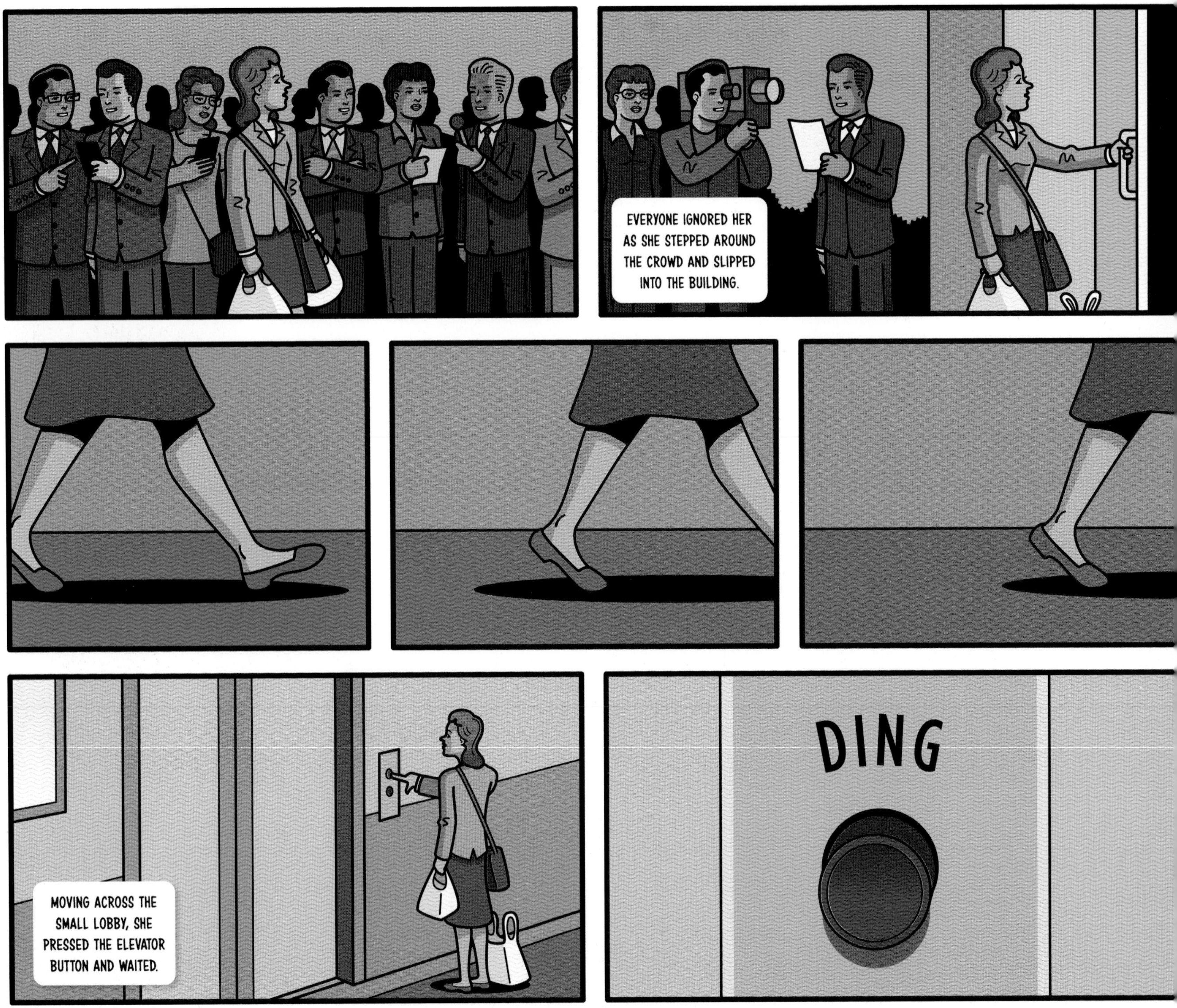
EVERYONE IGNORED HER AS SHE STEPPED AROUND THE CROWD AND SLIPPED INTO THE BUILDING.
MOVING ACROSS THE SMALL LOBBY, SHE PRESSED THE ELEVATOR BUTTON AND WAITED.
DING

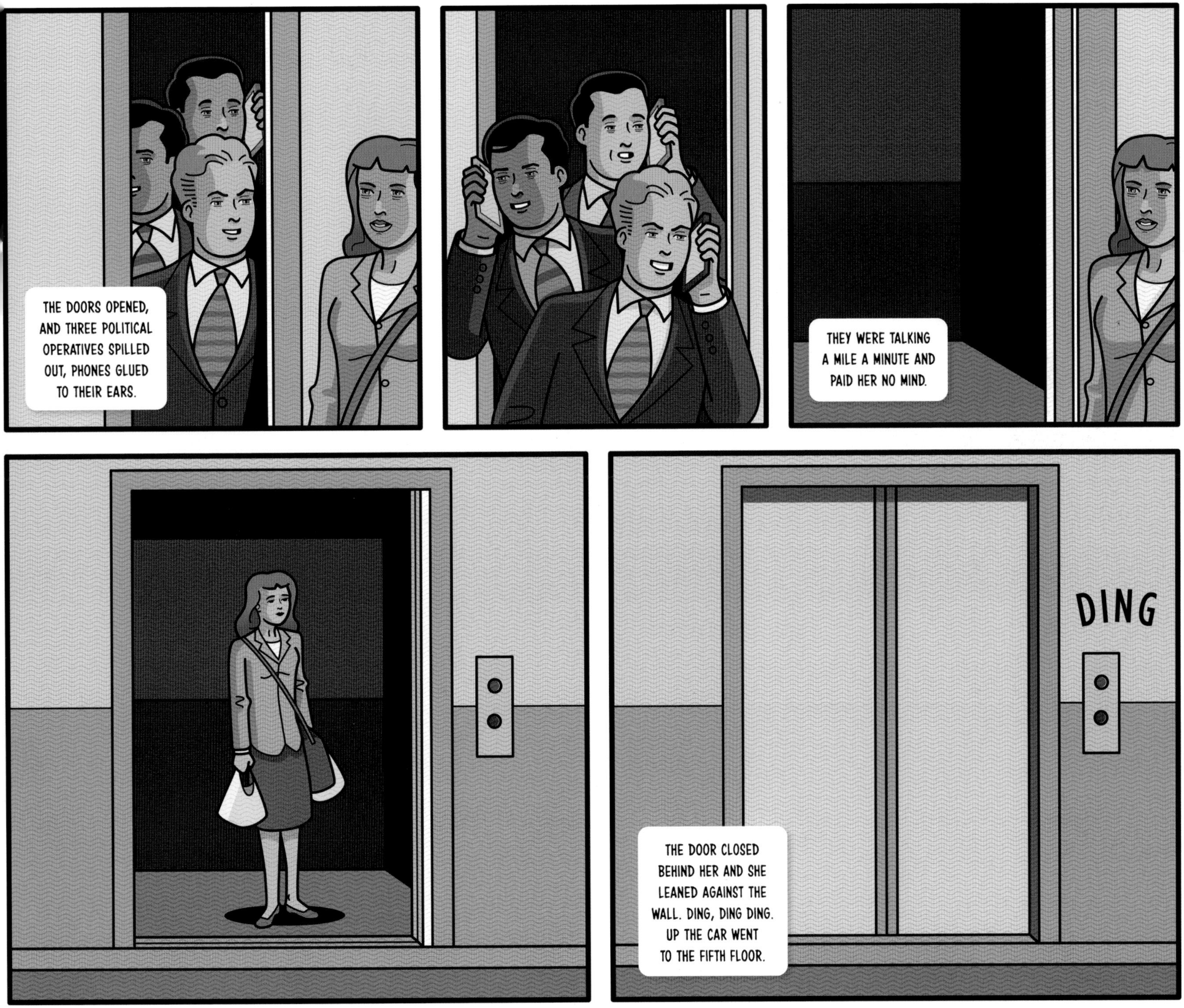
THE DOORS OPENED, AND THREE POLITICAL OPERATIVES SPILLED OUT, PHONES GLUED TO THEIR EARS.
THEY WERE TALKING A MILE A MINUTE AND PAID HER NO MIND.
DING
THE DOOR CLOSED BEHIND HER AND SHE LEANED AGAINST THE WALL. DING, DING DING. UP THE CAR WENT TO THE FIFTH FLOOR.

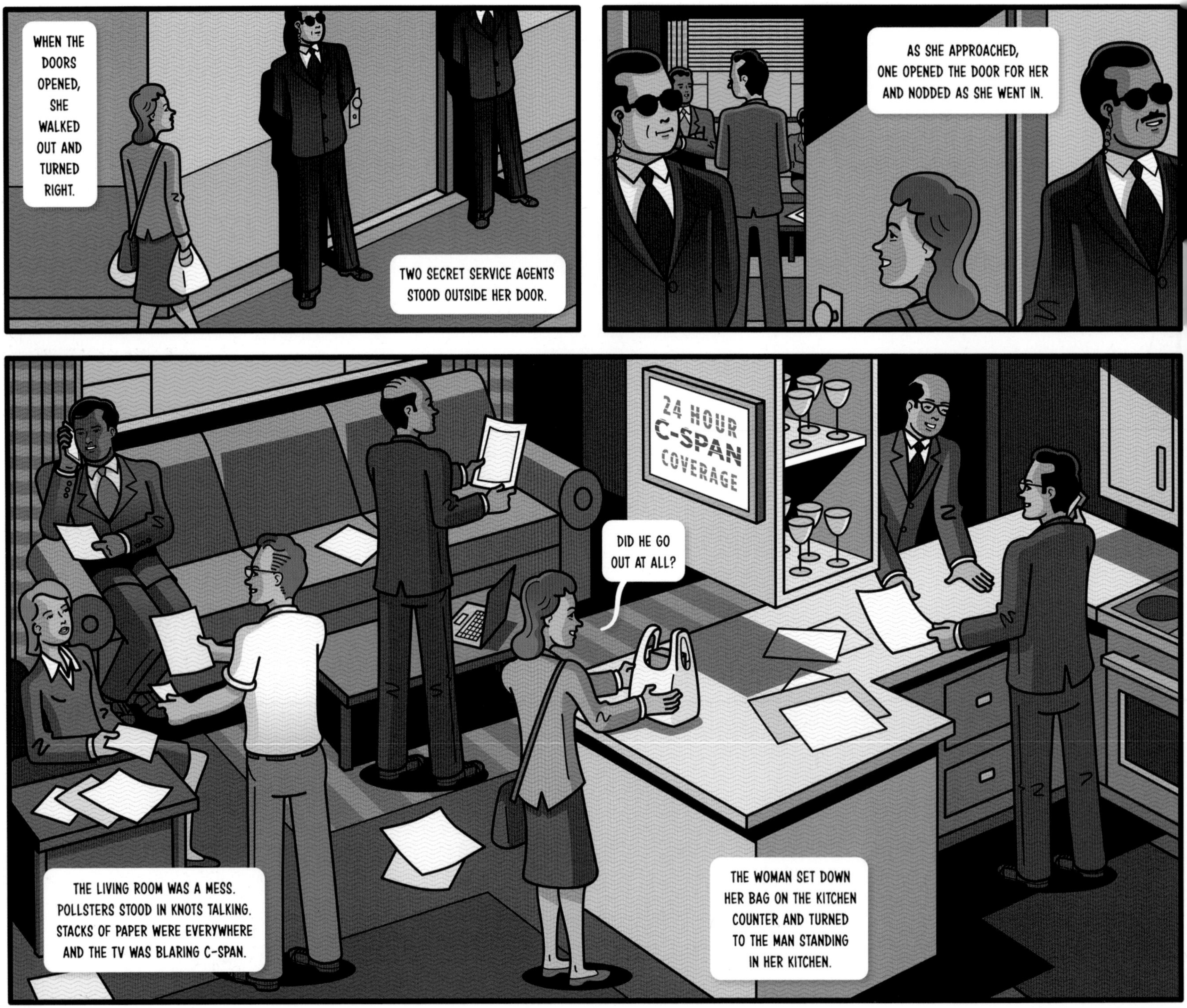
WHEN THE DOORS OPENED, SHE WALKED OUT AND TURNED RIGHT.
TWO SECRET SERVICE AGENTS STOOD OUTSIDE HER DOOR.
AS SHE APPROACHED, ONE OPENED THE DOOR FOR HER AND NODDED AS SHE WENT IN.
24 HOUR C-SPAN COVERAGE
DID HE GO OUT AT ALL?
THE LIVING ROOM WAS A MESS. POLLSTERS STOOD IN KNOTS TALKING. STACKS OF PAPER WERE EVERYWHERE AND THE TV WAS BLARING C-SPAN.
THE WOMAN SET DOWN HER BAG ON THE KITCHEN COUNTER AND TURNED TO THE MAN STANDING IN HER KITCHEN.

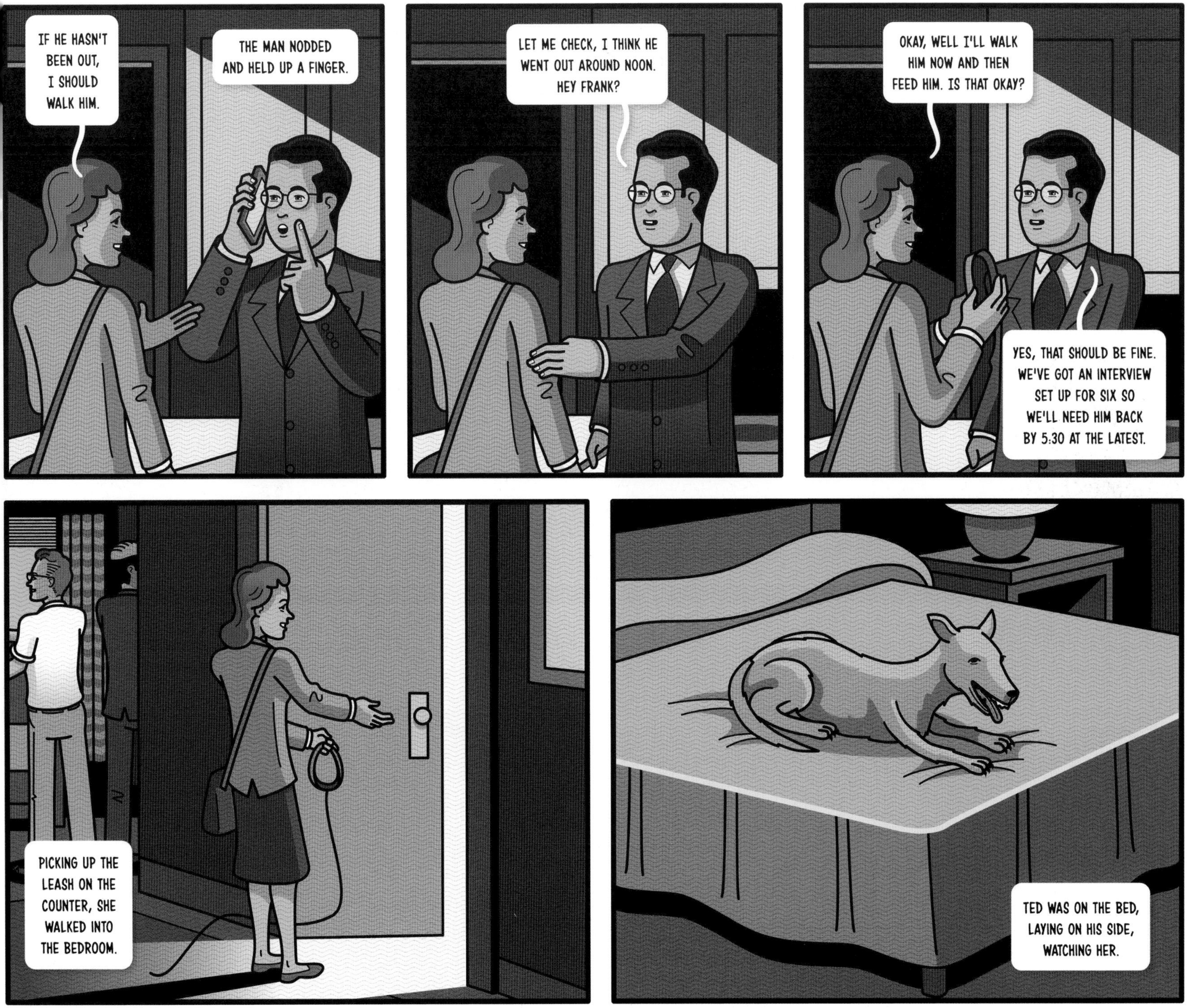
IF HE HASN'T BEEN OUT, I SHOULD WALK HIM.
THE MAN NODDED AND HELD UP A FINGER.
LET ME CHECK, I THINK HE WENT OUT AROUND NOON. HEY FRANK?
OKAY, WELL I'LL WALK HIM NOW AND THEN FEED HIM. IS THAT OKAY?
YES, THAT SHOULD BE FINE. WE'VE GOT AN INTERVIEW SET UP FOR SIX SO WE'LL NEED HIM BACK BY 5:30 AT THE LATEST.
PICKING UP THE LEASH ON THE COUNTER, SHE WALKED INTO THE BEDROOM.
TED WAS ON THE BED, LAYING ON HIS SIDE, WATCHING HER.

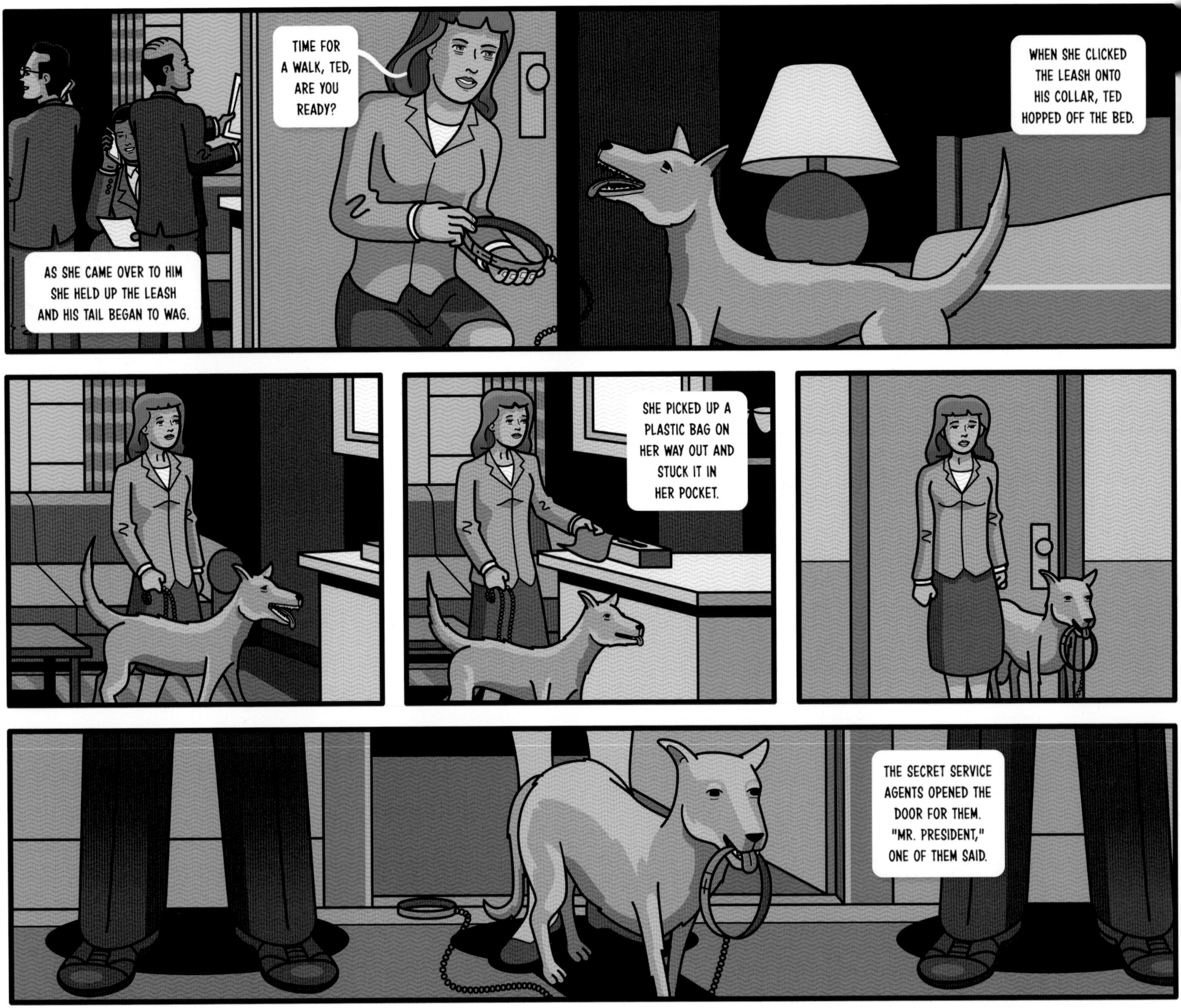
AS SHE CAME OVER TO HIM SHE HELD UP THE LEASH AND HIS TAIL BEGAN TO WAG.
TIME FOR A WALK, TED, ARE YOU READY?
WHEN SHE CLICKED THE LEASH ONTO HIS COLLAR, TED HOPPED OFF THE BED.
SHE PICKED UP A PLASTIC BAG ON HER WAY OUT AND STUCK IT IN HER POCKET.
THE SECRET SERVICE AGENTS OPENED THE DOOR FOR THEM. "MR. PRESIDENT," ONE OF THEM SAID.

TED GAVE A SMALL BARK AND HEADED TOWARDS THE ELEVATOR, CARRYING HIS LEASH IN HIS MOUTH.

THE DOOR OPENED AND HE WALKED IN, FOLLOWED BY THE WOMAN.

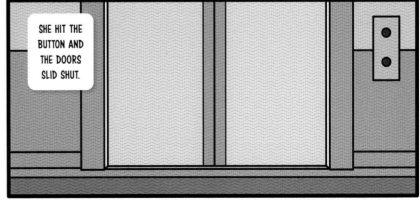

SHE HIT THE BUTTON AND THE DOORS SLID SHUT.

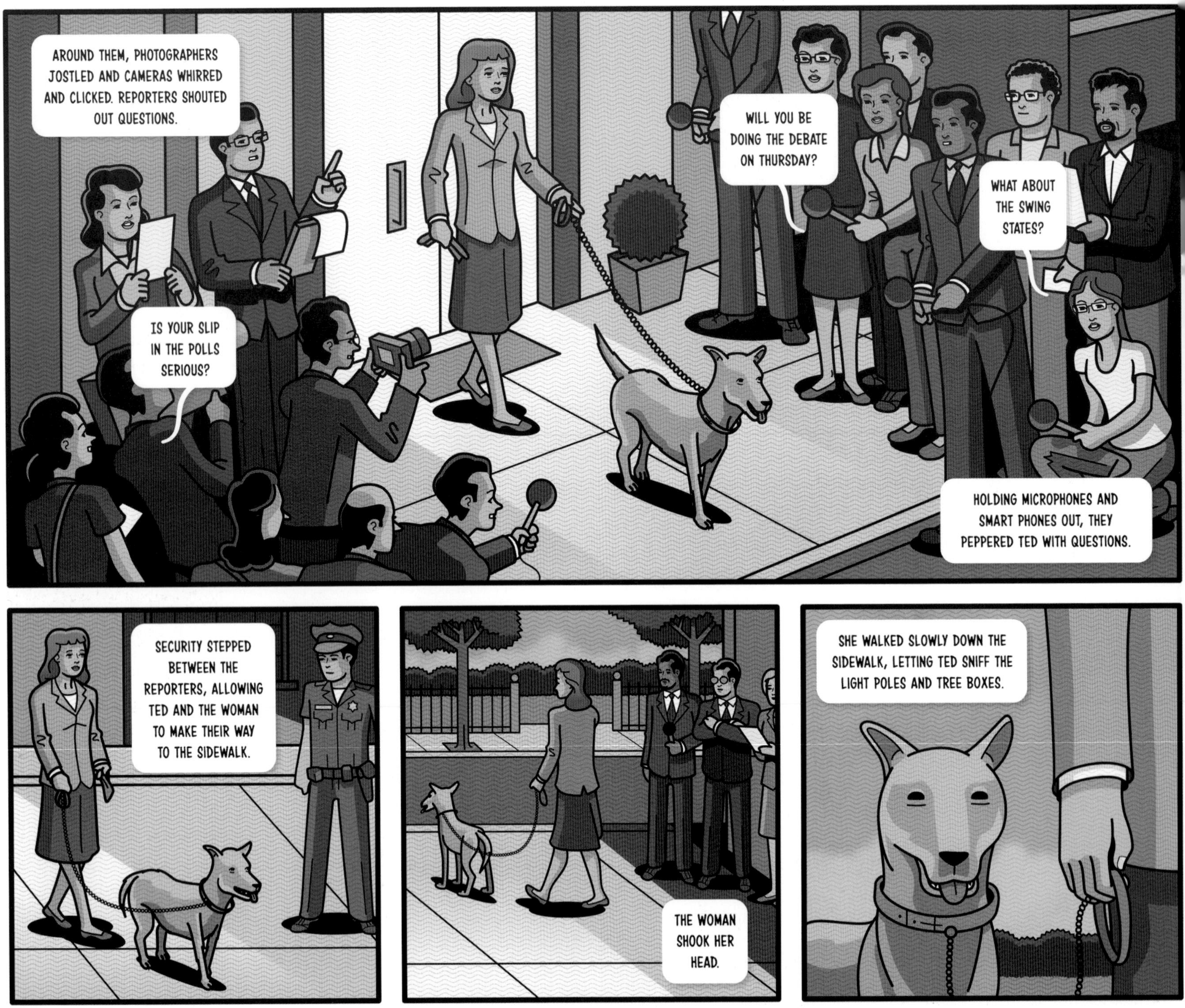
AROUND THEM, PHOTOGRAPHERS JOSTLED AND CAMERAS WHIRRED AND CLICKED. REPORTERS SHOUTED OUT QUESTIONS.
IS YOUR SLIP IN THE POLLS SERIOUS?
WILL YOU BE DOING THE DEBATE ON THURSDAY?
WHAT ABOUT THE SWING STATES?
HOLDING MICROPHONES AND SMART PHONES OUT, THEY PEPPERED TED WITH QUESTIONS.
SECURITY STEPPED BETWEEN THE REPORTERS, ALLOWING TED AND THE WOMAN TO MAKE THEIR WAY TO THE SIDEWALK.
THE WOMAN SHOOK HER HEAD.
SHE WALKED SLOWLY DOWN THE SIDEWALK, LETTING TED SNIFF THE LIGHT POLES AND TREE BOXES.

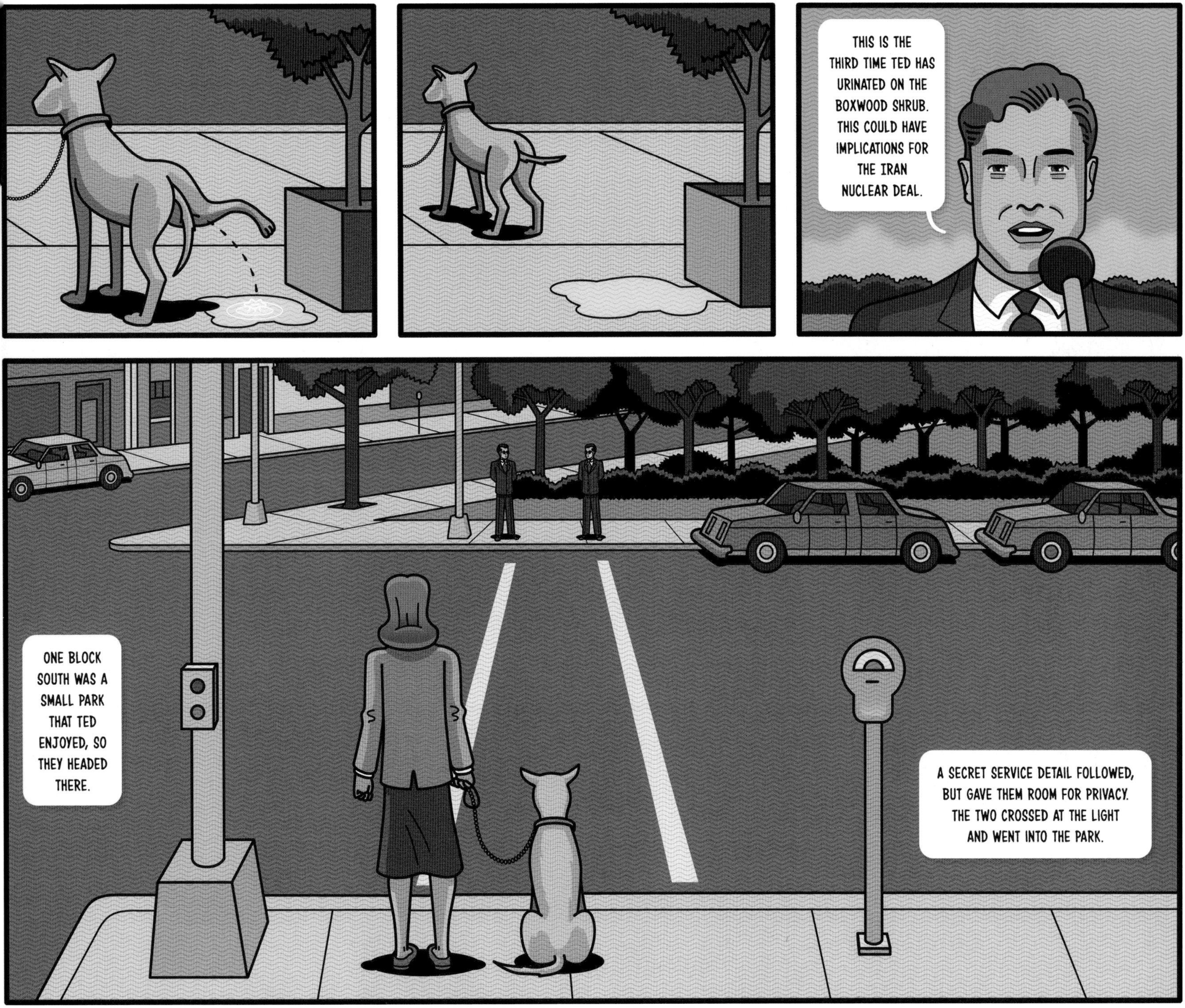
THIS IS THE THIRD TIME TED HAS URINATED ON THE BOXWOOD SHRUB. THIS COULD HAVE IMPLICATIONS FOR THE IRAN NUCLEAR DEAL.
ONE BLOCK SOUTH WAS A SMALL PARK THAT TED ENJOYED, SO THEY HEADED THERE.
A SECRET SERVICE DETAIL FOLLOWED, BUT GAVE THEM ROOM FOR PRIVACY. THE TWO CROSSED AT THE LIGHT AND WENT INTO THE PARK.

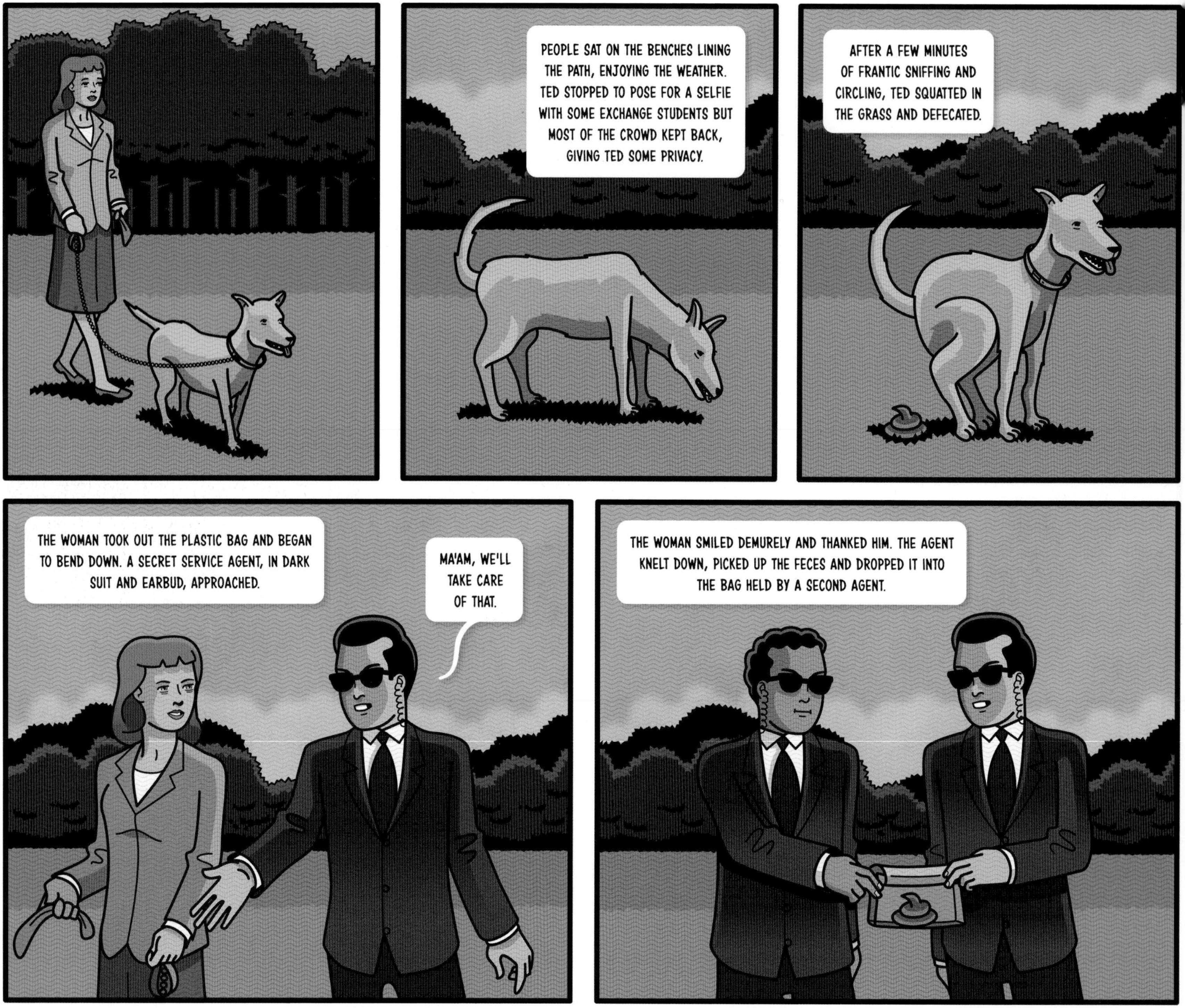
PEOPLE SAT ON THE BENCHES LINING THE PATH, ENJOYING THE WEATHER. TED STOPPED TO POSE FOR A SELFIE WITH SOME EXCHANGE STUDENTS BUT MOST OF THE CROWD KEPT BACK, GIVING TED SOME PRIVACY.
AFTER A FEW MINUTES OF FRANTIC SNIFFING AND CIRCLING, TED SQUATTED IN THE GRASS AND DEFECATED.
THE WOMAN TOOK OUT THE PLASTIC BAG AND BEGAN TO BEND DOWN. A SECRET SERVICE AGENT, IN DARK SUIT AND EARBUD, APPROACHED.
MA'AM, WE'LL TAKE CARE OF THAT.
THE WOMAN SMILED DEMURELY AND THANKED HIM. THE AGENT KNELT DOWN, PICKED UP THE FECES AND DROPPED IT INTO THE BAG HELD BY A SECOND AGENT.

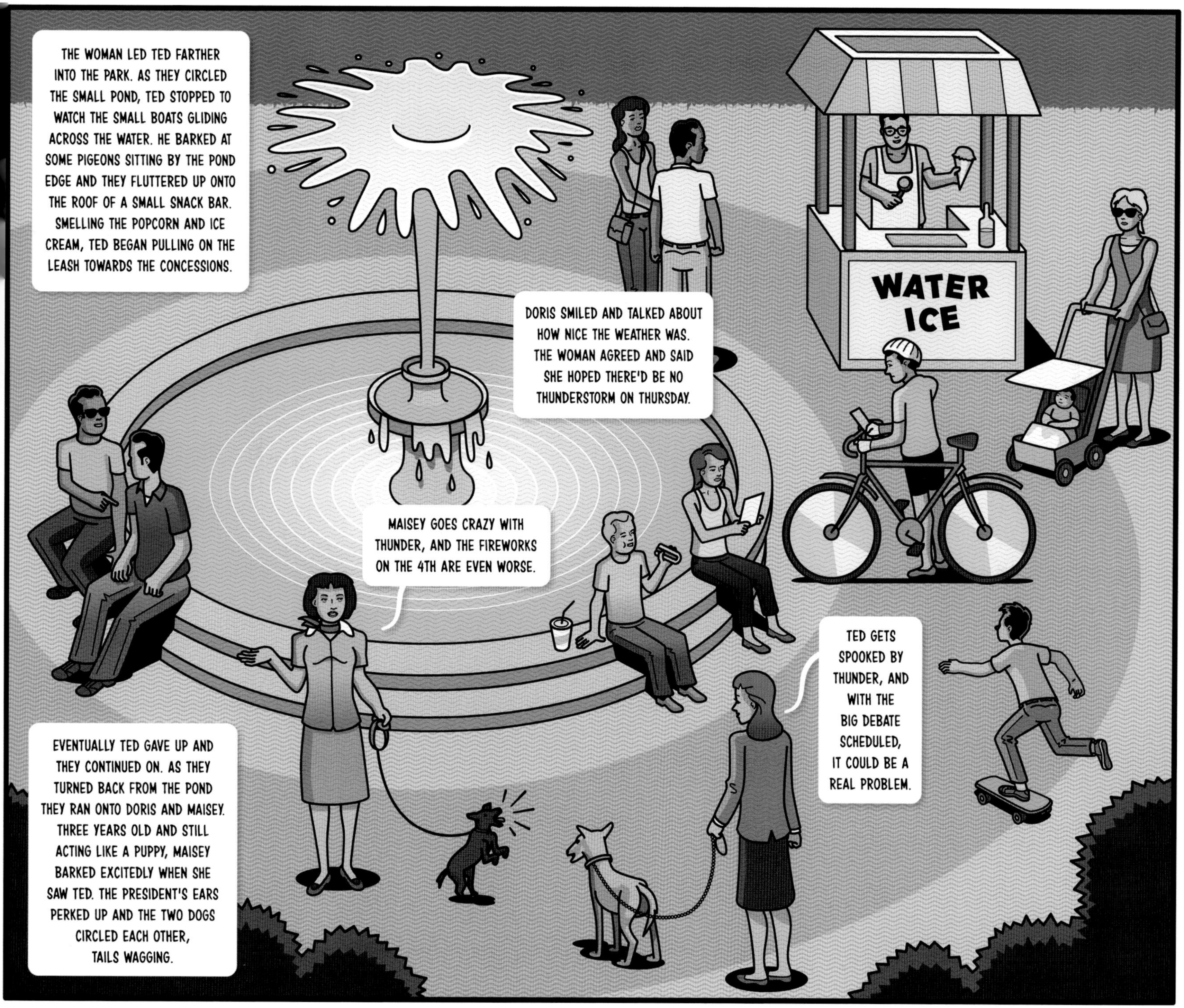
THE WOMAN LED TED FARTHER INTO THE PARK. AS THEY CIRCLED THE SMALL POND, TED STOPPED TO WATCH THE SMALL BOATS GLIDING ACROSS THE WATER. HE BARKED AT SOME PIGEONS SITTING BY THE POND EDGE AND THEY FLUTTERED UP ONTO THE ROOF OF A SMALL SNACK BAR. SMELLING THE POPCORN AND ICE CREAM, TED BEGAN PULLING ON THE LEASH TOWARDS THE CONCESSIONS.
WATER ICE
DORIS SMILED AND TALKED ABOUT HOW NICE THE WEATHER WAS. THE WOMAN AGREED AND SAID SHE HOPED THERE'D BE NO THUNDERSTORM ON THURSDAY.
MAISEY GOES CRAZY WITH THUNDER, AND THE FIREWORKS ON THE 4TH ARE EVEN WORSE.
TED GETS SPOOKED BY THUNDER, AND WITH THE BIG DEBATE SCHEDULED, IT COULD BE A REAL PROBLEM.
EVENTUALLY TED GAVE UP AND THEY CONTINUED ON. AS THEY TURNED BACK FROM THE POND THEY RAN ONTO DORIS AND MAISEY. THREE YEARS OLD AND STILL ACTING LIKE A PUPPY, MAISEY BARKED EXCITEDLY WHEN SHE SAW TED. THE PRESIDENT'S EARS PERKED UP AND THE TWO DOGS CIRCLED EACH OTHER, TAILS WAGGING.

AFTER TALKING A BIT MORE THE TWO WOMEN UNTANGLED THE LEASHES AND SAID GOODBYE.

GOOD LUCK AT THE DEBATE, TED!

TED LICKED HER HAND BEFORE TURNING TO LEAVE.

AS THEY WALKED BACK TO THE APARTMENT, THE WOMAN WENT THROUGH A MENTAL CHECKLIST. THERE WAS THE INTERVIEW TONIGHT WITH CNN. THURSDAY EVENING WAS THE DEBATE.

MOST OF THAT AFTERNOON WOULD BE TAKEN UP WITH DEBATE PREP.

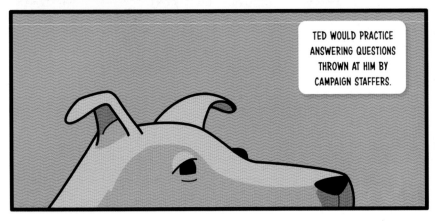

TED WOULD PRACTICE ANSWERING QUESTIONS THROWN AT HIM BY CAMPAIGN STAFFERS.

HE WAS A TIRELESS BARKER AND VERY ENERGETIC ON STAGE.

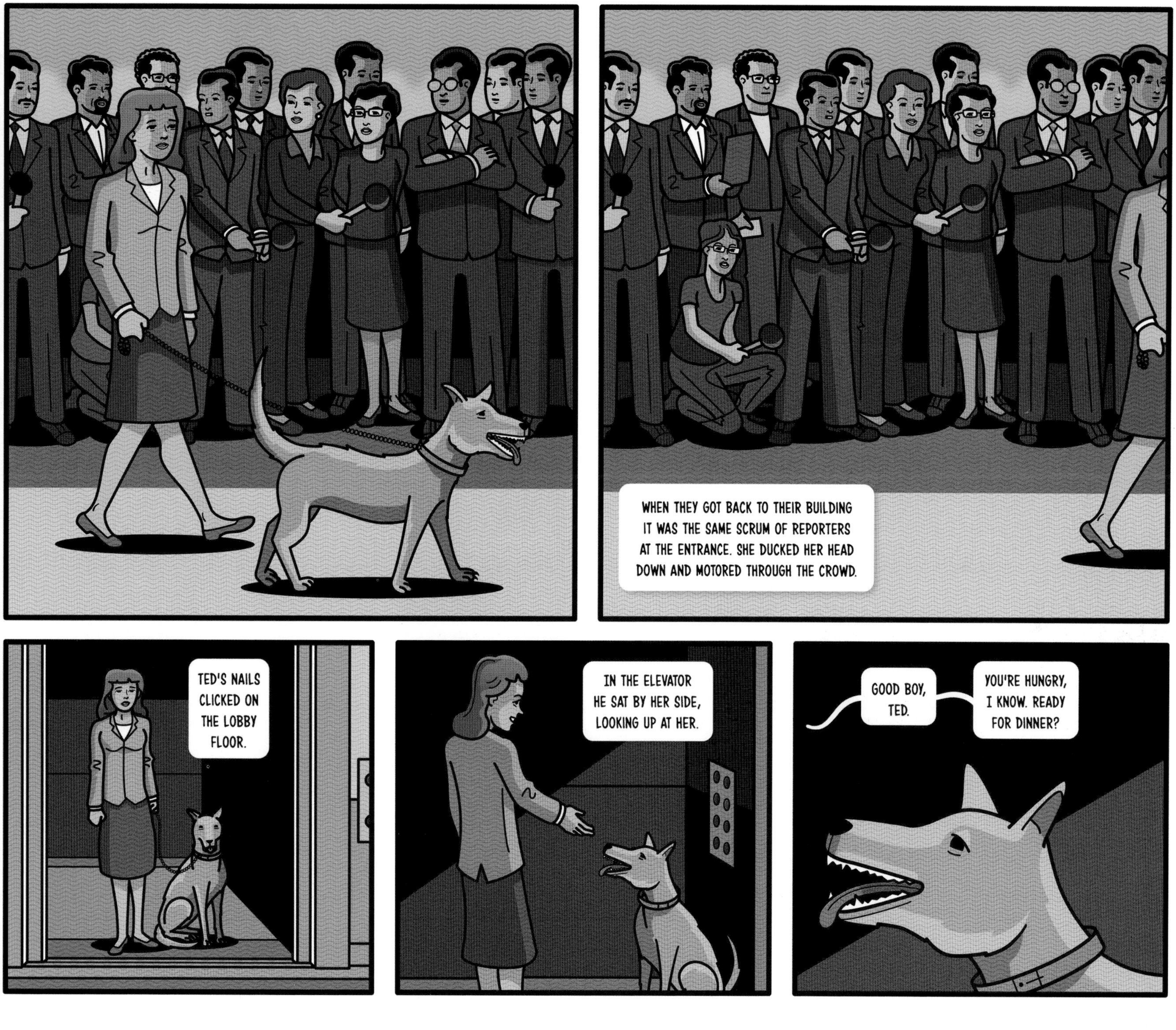

WHEN THEY GOT BACK TO THEIR BUILDING IT WAS THE SAME SCRUM OF REPORTERS AT THE ENTRANCE. SHE DUCKED HER HEAD DOWN AND MOTORED THROUGH THE CROWD.
TED'S NAILS CLICKED ON THE LOBBY FLOOR.
IN THE ELEVATOR HE SAT BY HER SIDE, LOOKING UP AT HER.
GOOD BOY, TED.
YOU'RE HUNGRY, I KNOW. READY FOR DINNER?

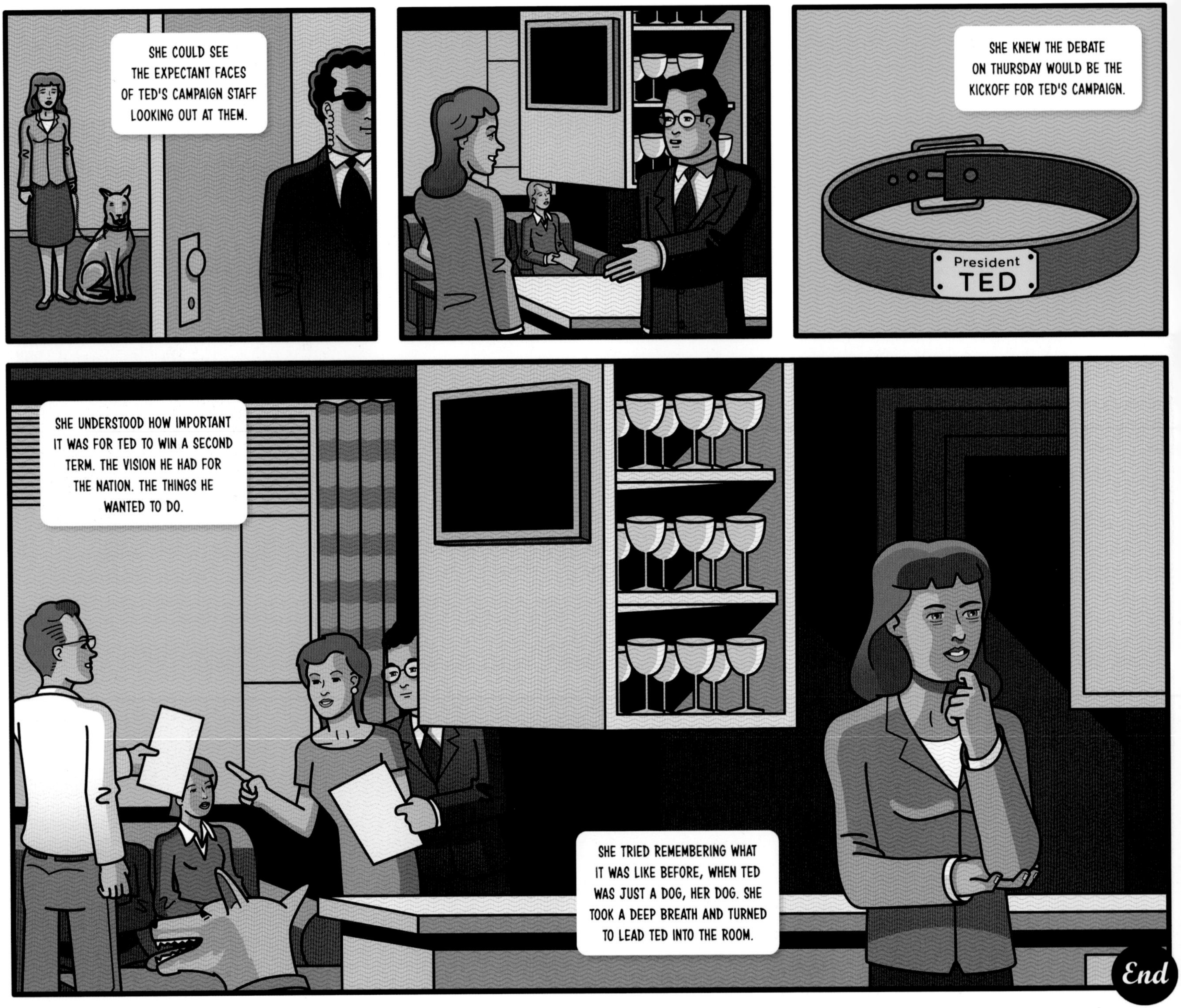
SHE COULD SEE THE EXPECTANT FACES OF TED'S CAMPAIGN STAFF LOOKING OUT AT THEM.
SHE KNEW THE DEBATE ON THURSDAY WOULD BE THE KICKOFF FOR TED'S CAMPAIGN.
President TED
SHE UNDERSTOOD HOW IMPORTANT IT WAS FOR TED TO WIN A SECOND TERM. THE VISION HE HAD FOR THE NATION. THE THINGS HE WANTED TO DO.
SHE TRIED REMEMBERING WHAT IT WAS LIKE BEFORE, WHEN TED WAS JUST A DOG, HER DOG. SHE TOOK A DEEP BREATH AND TURNED TO LEAD TED INTO THE ROOM.
End

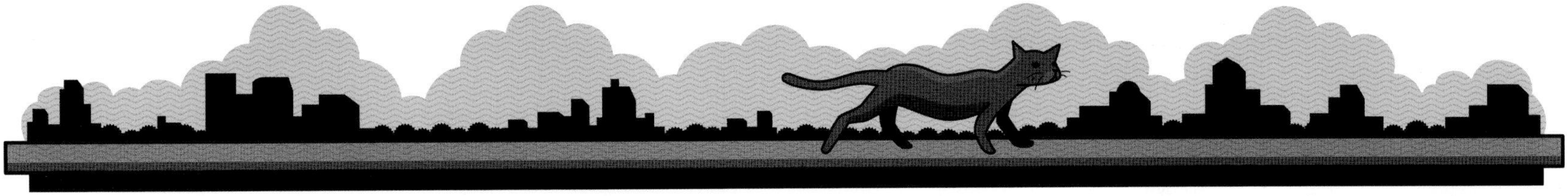

THE OUTSIDE CAT

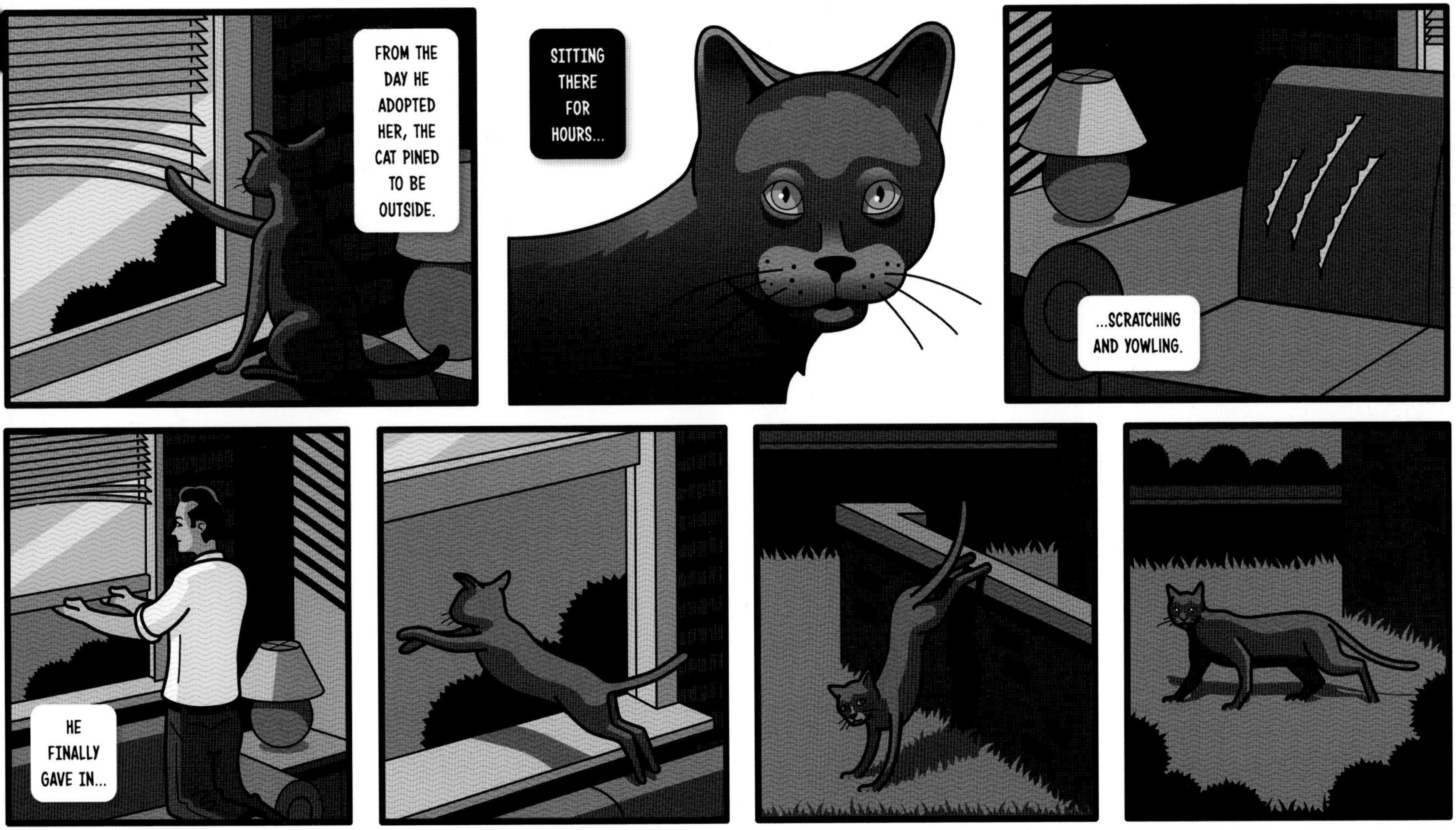
FROM THE DAY HE ADOPTED HER, THE CAT PINED TO BE OUTSIDE.
SITTING THERE FOR HOURS...
...SCRATCHING AND YOWLING.
HE FINALLY GAVE IN...

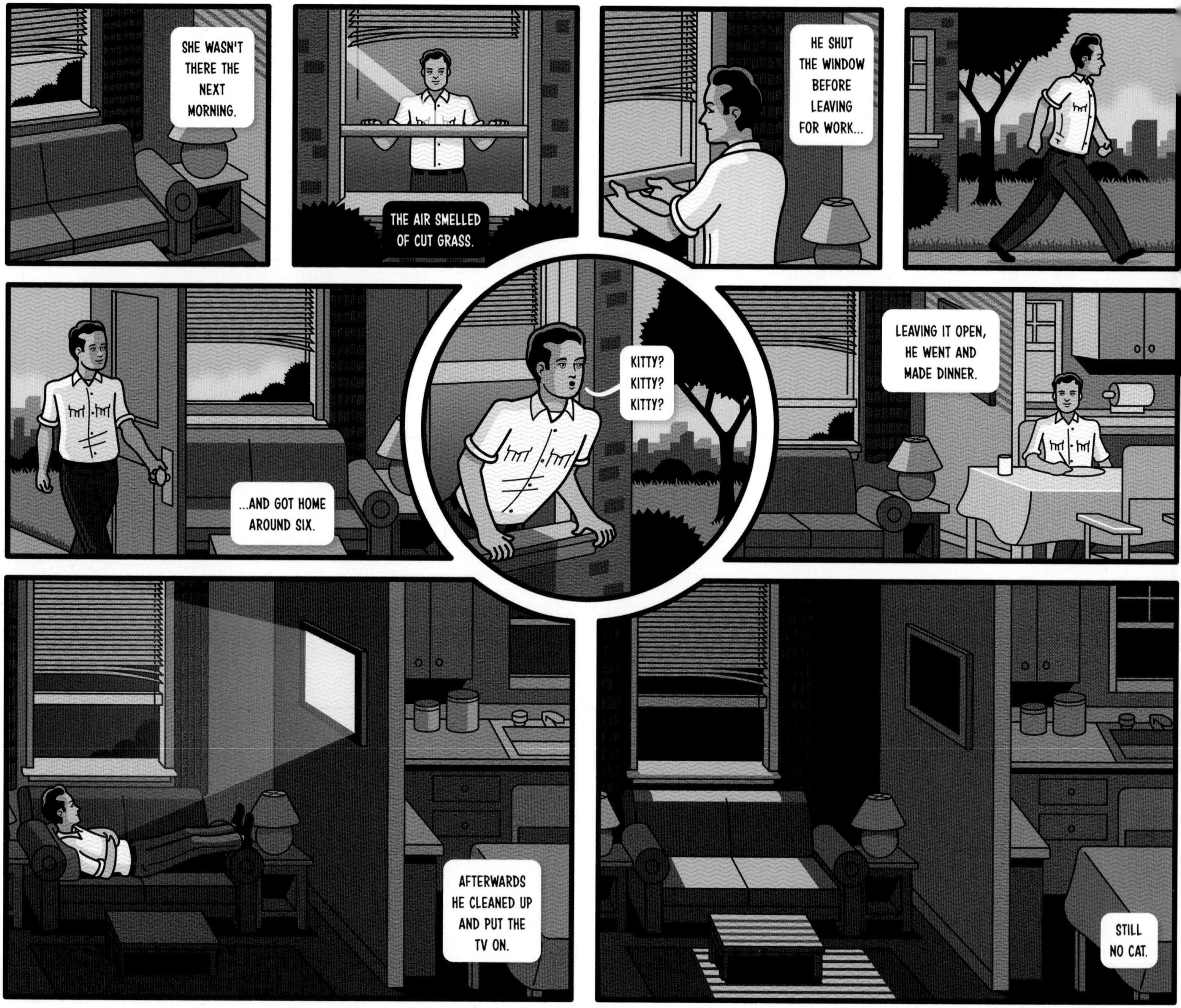
SHE WASN'T THERE THE NEXT MORNING.
THE AIR SMELLED OF CUT GRASS.
HE SHUT THE WINDOW BEFORE LEAVING FOR WORK...
...AND GOT HOME AROUND SIX.
KITTY? KITTY? KITTY?
LEAVING IT OPEN, HE WENT AND MADE DINNER.
AFTERWARDS HE CLEANED UP AND PUT THE TV ON.
STILL NO CAT.

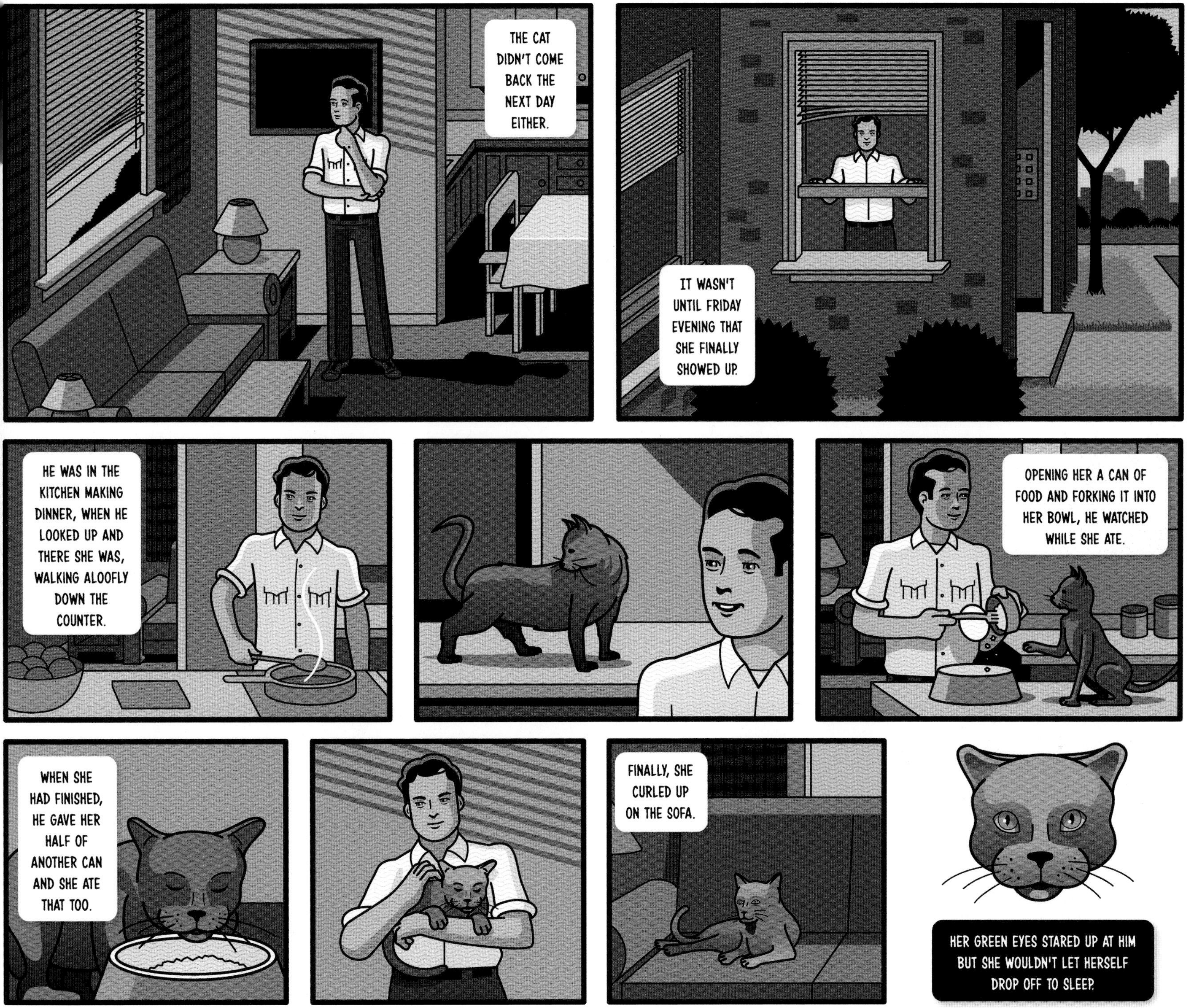
THE CAT DIDN'T COME BACK THE NEXT DAY EITHER.
IT WASN'T UNTIL FRIDAY EVENING THAT SHE FINALLY SHOWED UP.
HE WAS IN THE KITCHEN MAKING DINNER, WHEN HE LOOKED UP AND THERE SHE WAS, WALKING ALOOFLY DOWN THE COUNTER.
OPENING HER A CAN OF FOOD AND FORKING IT INTO HER BOWL, HE WATCHED WHILE SHE ATE.
WHEN SHE HAD FINISHED, HE GAVE HER HALF OF ANOTHER CAN AND SHE ATE THAT TOO.
FINALLY, SHE CURLED UP ON THE SOFA.
HER GREEN EYES STARED UP AT HIM BUT SHE WOULDN'T LET HERSELF DROP OFF TO SLEEP.

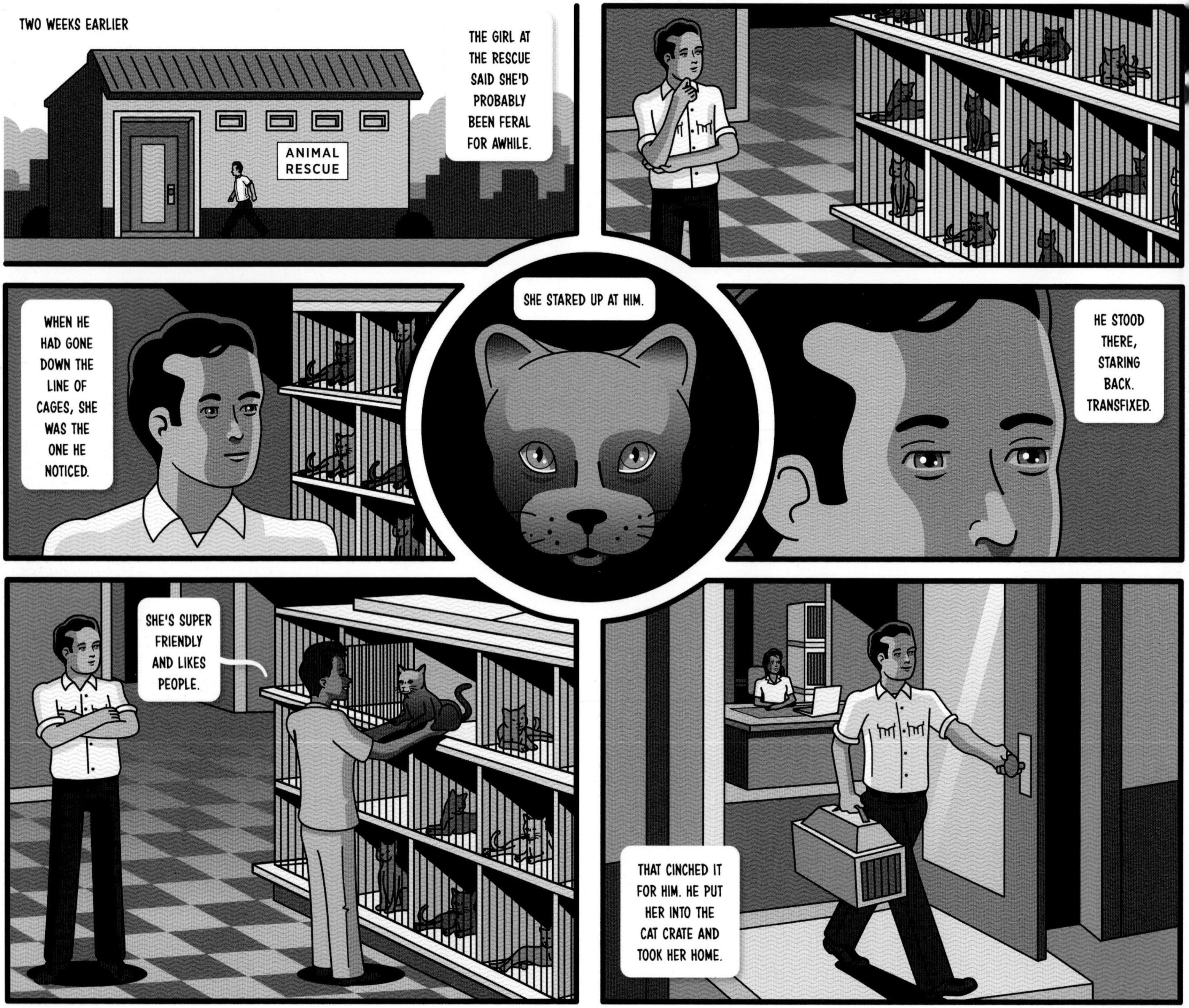
TWO WEEKS EARLIER
ANIMAL RESCUE
THE GIRL AT THE RESCUE SAID SHE'D PROBABLY BEEN FERAL FOR AWHILE.
WHEN HE HAD GONE DOWN THE LINE OF CAGES, SHE WAS THE ONE HE NOTICED.
SHE STARED UP AT HIM.
HE STOOD THERE, STARING BACK. TRANSFIXED.
SHE'S SUPER FRIENDLY AND LIKES PEOPLE.
THAT CINCHED IT FOR HIM. HE PUT HER INTO THE CAT CRATE AND TOOK HER HOME.

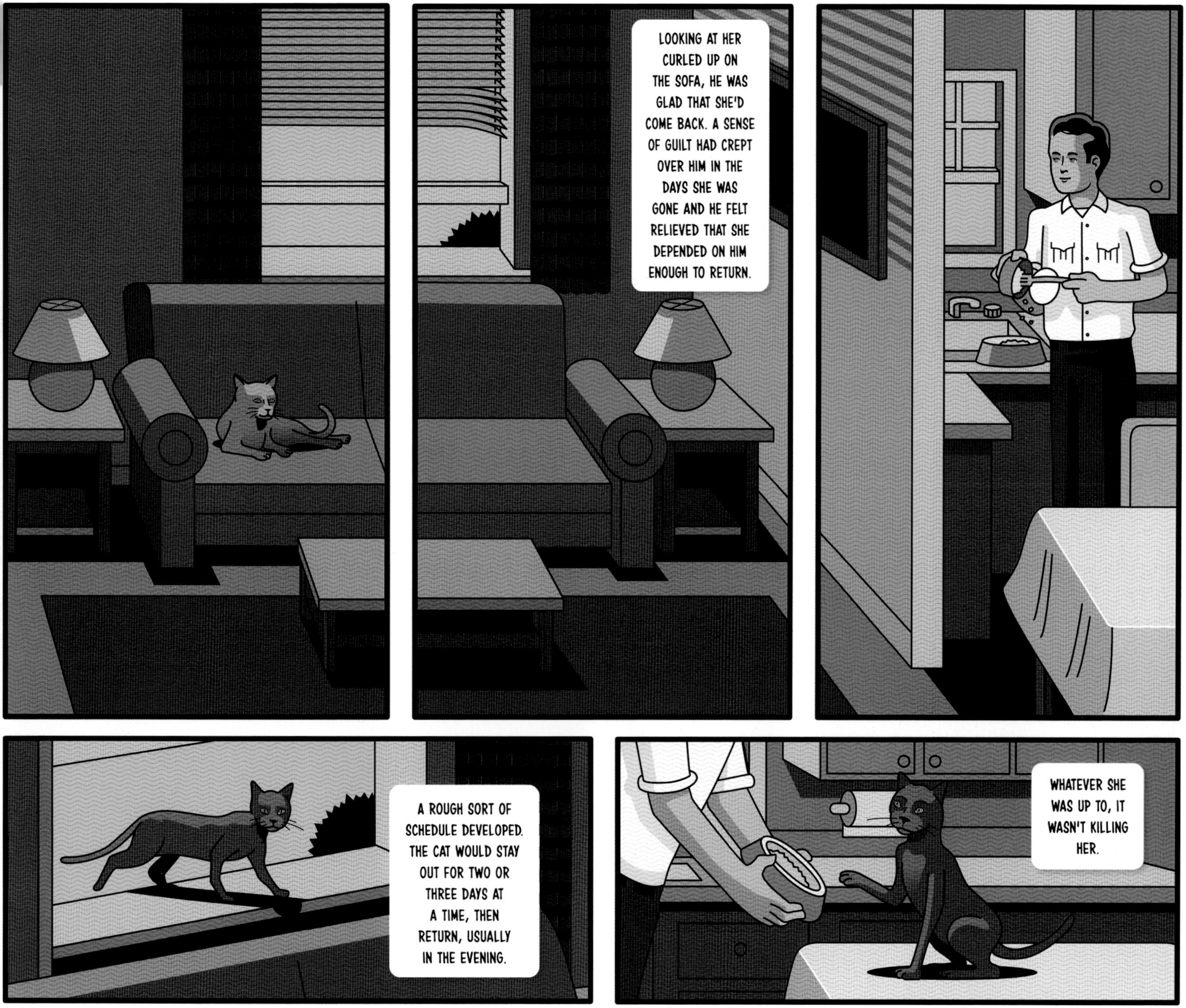
LOOKING AT HER CURLED UP ON THE SOFA, HE WAS GLAD THAT SHE'D COME BACK. A SENSE OF GUILT HAD CREPT OVER HIM IN THE DAYS SHE WAS GONE AND HE FELT RELIEVED THAT SHE DEPENDED ON HIM ENOUGH TO RETURN.
A ROUGH SORT OF SCHEDULE DEVELOPED. THE CAT WOULD STAY OUT FOR TWO OR THREE DAYS AT A TIME, THEN RETURN, USUALLY IN THE EVENING.
WHATEVER SHE WAS UP TO, IT WASN'T KILLING HER.

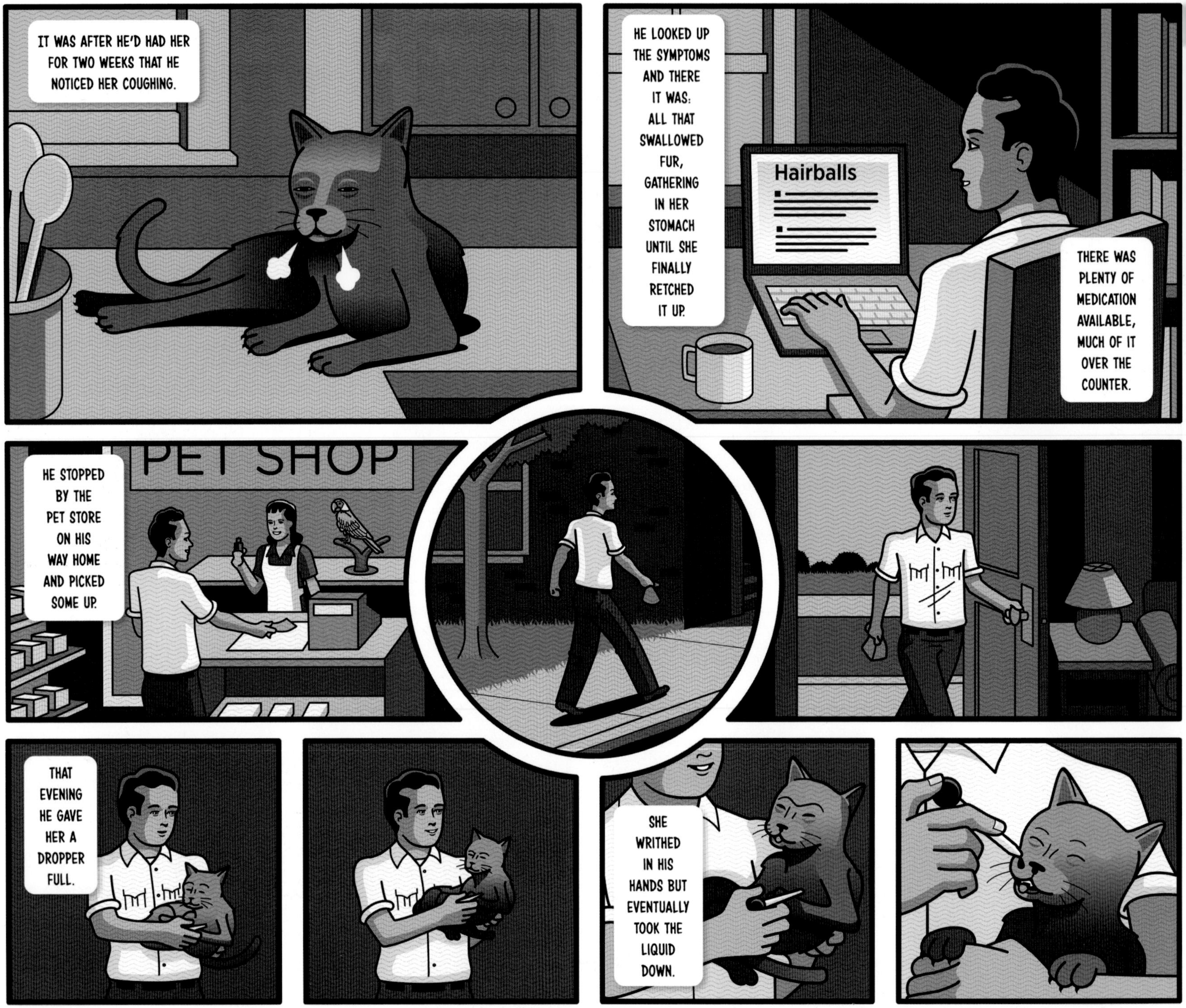
IT WAS AFTER HE'D HAD HER FOR TWO WEEKS THAT HE NOTICED HER COUGHING.
HE LOOKED UP THE SYMPTOMS AND THERE IT WAS: ALL THAT SWALLOWED FUR, GATHERING IN HER STOMACH UNTIL SHE FINALLY RETCHED IT UP.
Hairballs
THERE WAS PLENTY OF MEDICATION AVAILABLE, MUCH OF IT OVER THE COUNTER.
PET SHOP
HE STOPPED BY THE PET STORE ON HIS WAY HOME AND PICKED SOME UP.
THAT EVENING HE GAVE HER A DROPPER FULL.
SHE WRITHED IN HIS HANDS BUT EVENTUALLY TOOK THE LIQUID DOWN.

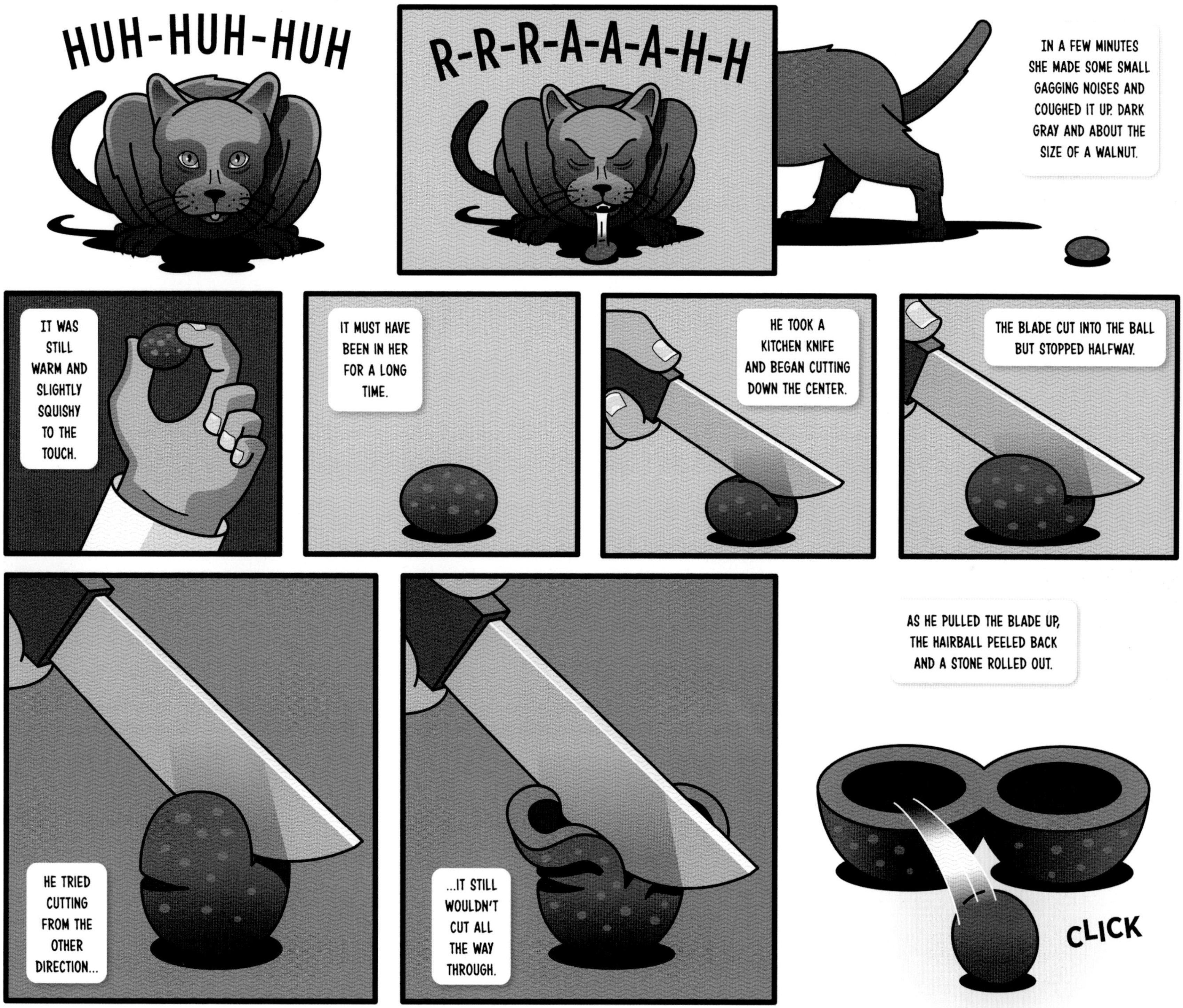
HUH-HUH-HUH
R-R-R-A-A-A-H-H
IN A FEW MINUTES SHE MADE SOME SMALL GAGGING NOISES AND COUGHED IT UP. DARK GRAY AND ABOUT THE SIZE OF A WALNUT.
IT WAS STILL WARM AND SLIGHTLY SQUISHY TO THE TOUCH.
IT MUST HAVE BEEN IN HER FOR A LONG TIME.
HE TOOK A KITCHEN KNIFE AND BEGAN CUTTING DOWN THE CENTER.
THE BLADE CUT INTO THE BALL BUT STOPPED HALFWAY.
HE TRIED CUTTING FROM THE OTHER DIRECTION...
...IT STILL WOULDN'T CUT ALL THE WAY THROUGH.
AS HE PULLED THE BLADE UP, THE HAIRBALL PEELED BACK AND A STONE ROLLED OUT.
CLICK

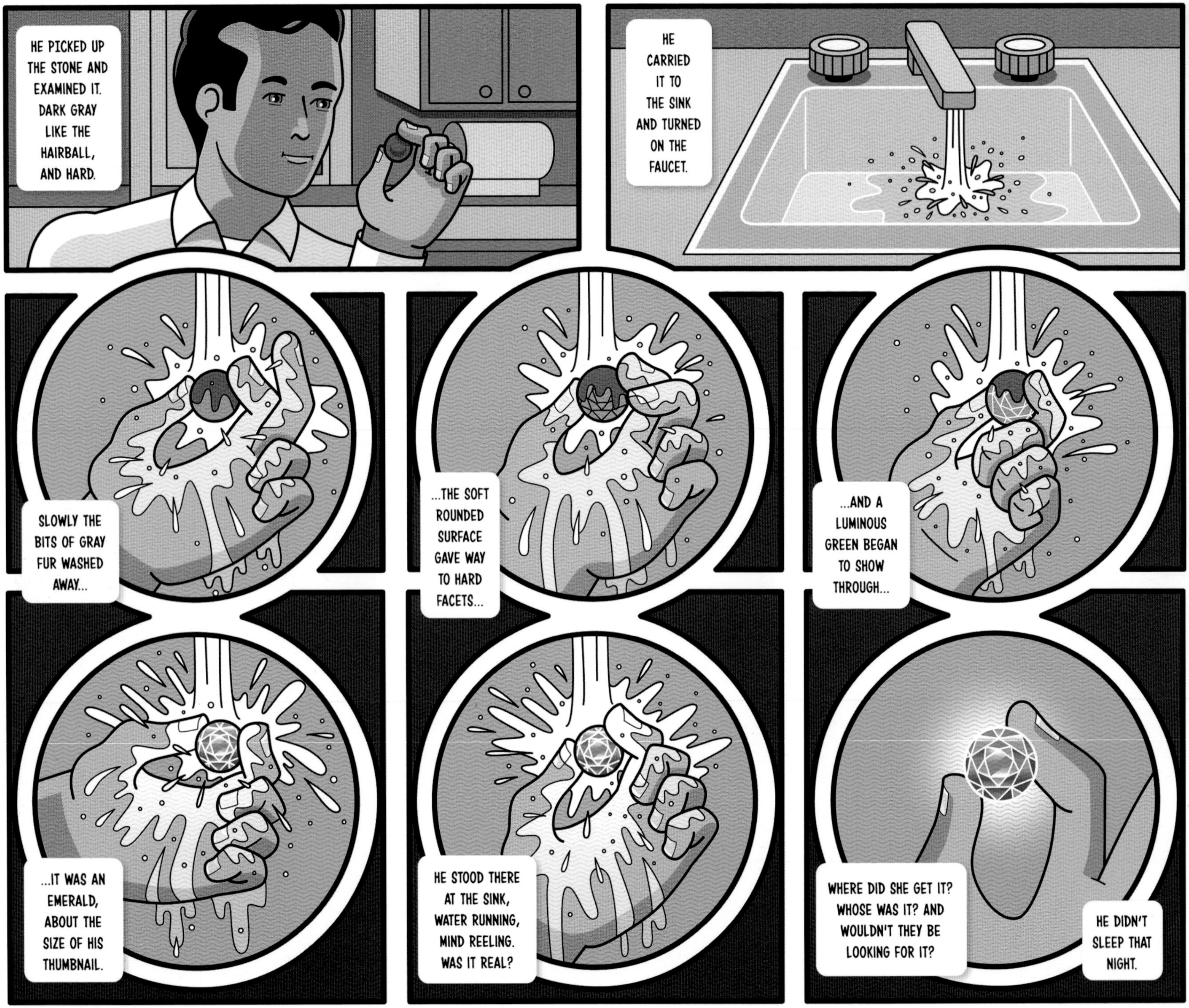
HE PICKED UP THE STONE AND EXAMINED IT. DARK GRAY LIKE THE HAIRBALL, AND HARD.
HE CARRIED IT TO THE SINK AND TURNED ON THE FAUCET.
SLOWLY THE BITS OF GRAY FUR WASHED AWAY...
...THE SOFT ROUNDED SURFACE GAVE WAY TO HARD FACETS...
...AND A LUMINOUS GREEN BEGAN TO SHOW THROUGH...
...IT WAS AN EMERALD, ABOUT THE SIZE OF HIS THUMBNAIL.
HE STOOD THERE AT THE SINK, WATER RUNNING, MIND REELING. WAS IT REAL?
WHERE DID SHE GET IT? WHOSE WAS IT? AND WOULDN'T THEY BE LOOKING FOR IT?
HE DIDN'T SLEEP THAT NIGHT.

MAYBE IT'S A FAKE? COSTUME JEWELRY MADE OF CUT GLASS. I'M NO EXPERT.

MAKING BREAKFAST THE NEXT MORNING, HE DECIDED TO TAKE THE STONE WITH HIM. ON HIS LUNCH HOUR HE COULD TAKE IT TO A JEWELRY STORE AND HAVE THEM LOOK AT IT.

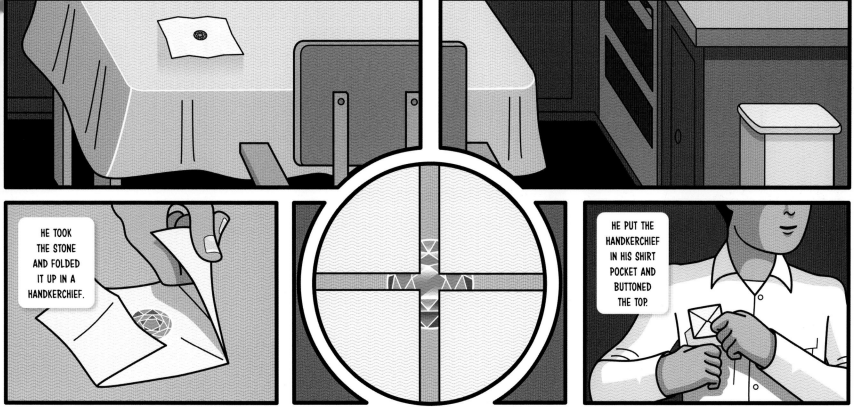

HE TOOK THE STONE AND FOLDED IT UP IN A HANDKERCHIEF.

HE PUT THE HANDKERCHIEF IN HIS SHIRT POCKET AND BUTTONED THE TOP.

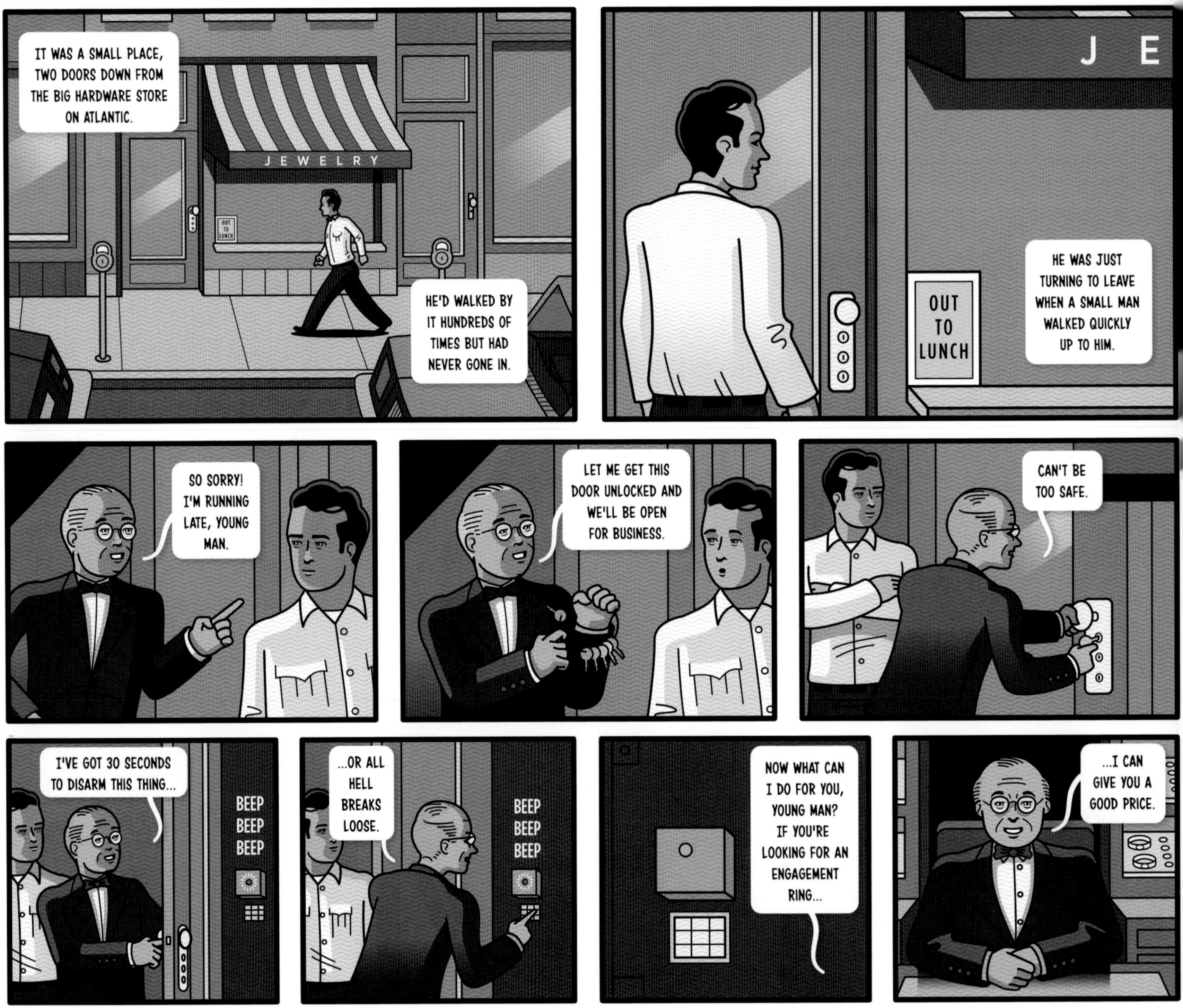
IT WAS A SMALL PLACE, TWO DOORS DOWN FROM THE BIG HARDWARE STORE ON ATLANTIC.
JEWELRY
OUT TO LUNCH
HE'D WALKED BY IT HUNDREDS OF TIMES BUT HAD NEVER GONE IN.
J E
OUT TO LUNCH
HE WAS JUST TURNING TO LEAVE WHEN A SMALL MAN WALKED QUICKLY UP TO HIM.
SO SORRY! I'M RUNNING LATE, YOUNG MAN.
LET ME GET THIS DOOR UNLOCKED AND WE'LL BE OPEN FOR BUSINESS.
CAN'T BE TOO SAFE.
I'VE GOT 30 SECONDS TO DISARM THIS THING...
BEEP BEEP BEEP
...OR ALL HELL BREAKS LOOSE.
BEEP BEEP BEEP
NOW WHAT CAN I DO FOR YOU, YOUNG MAN? IF YOU'RE LOOKING FOR AN ENGAGEMENT RING...
...I CAN GIVE YOU A GOOD PRICE.

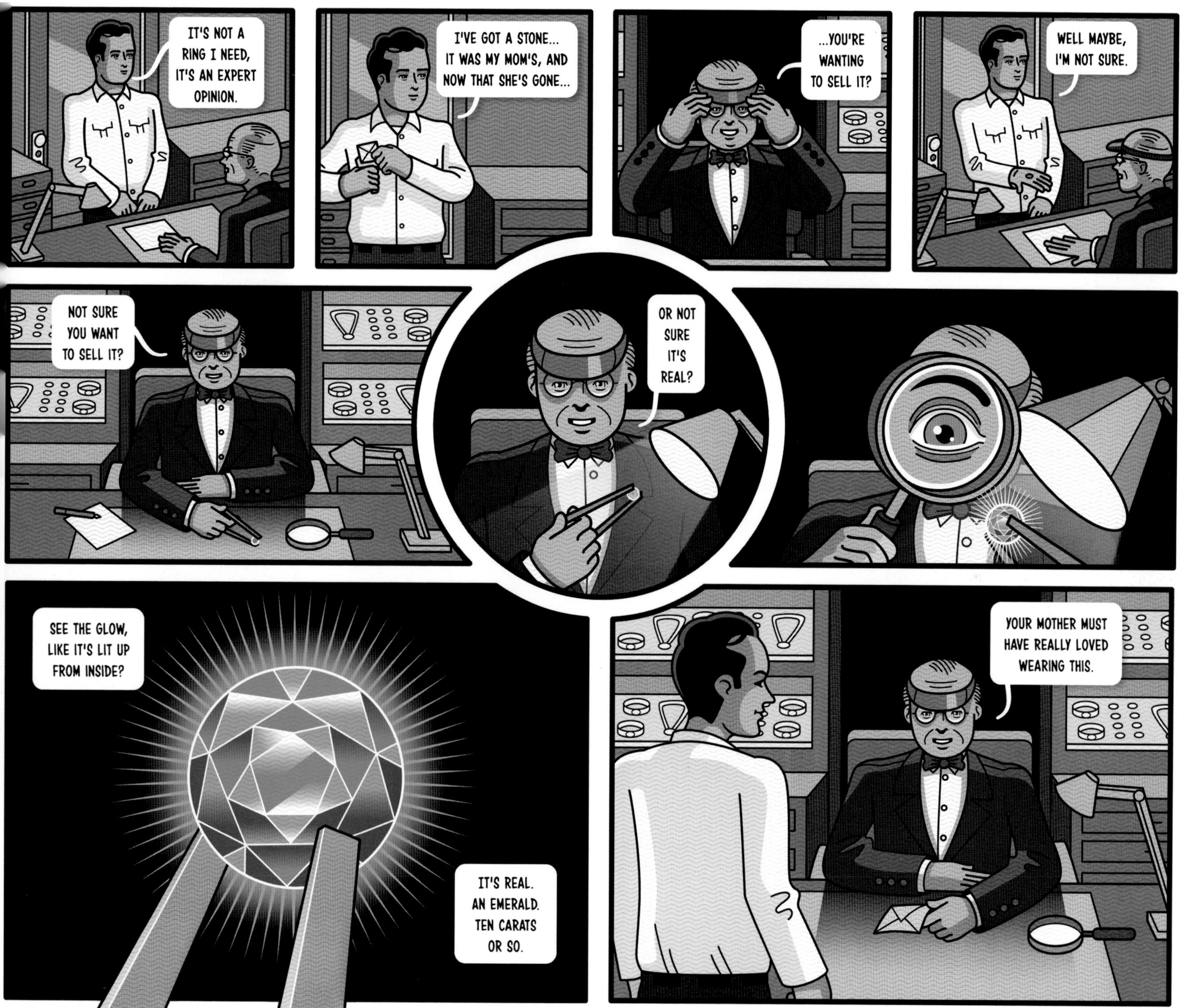
IT'S NOT A RING I NEED, IT'S AN EXPERT OPINION.
I'VE GOT A STONE... IT WAS MY MOM'S, AND NOW THAT SHE'S GONE...
...YOU'RE WANTING TO SELL IT?
WELL MAYBE, I'M NOT SURE.
NOT SURE YOU WANT TO SELL IT?
OR NOT SURE IT'S REAL?
SEE THE GLOW, LIKE IT'S LIT UP FROM INSIDE?
IT'S REAL. AN EMERALD. TEN CARATS OR SO.
YOUR MOTHER MUST HAVE REALLY LOVED WEARING THIS.

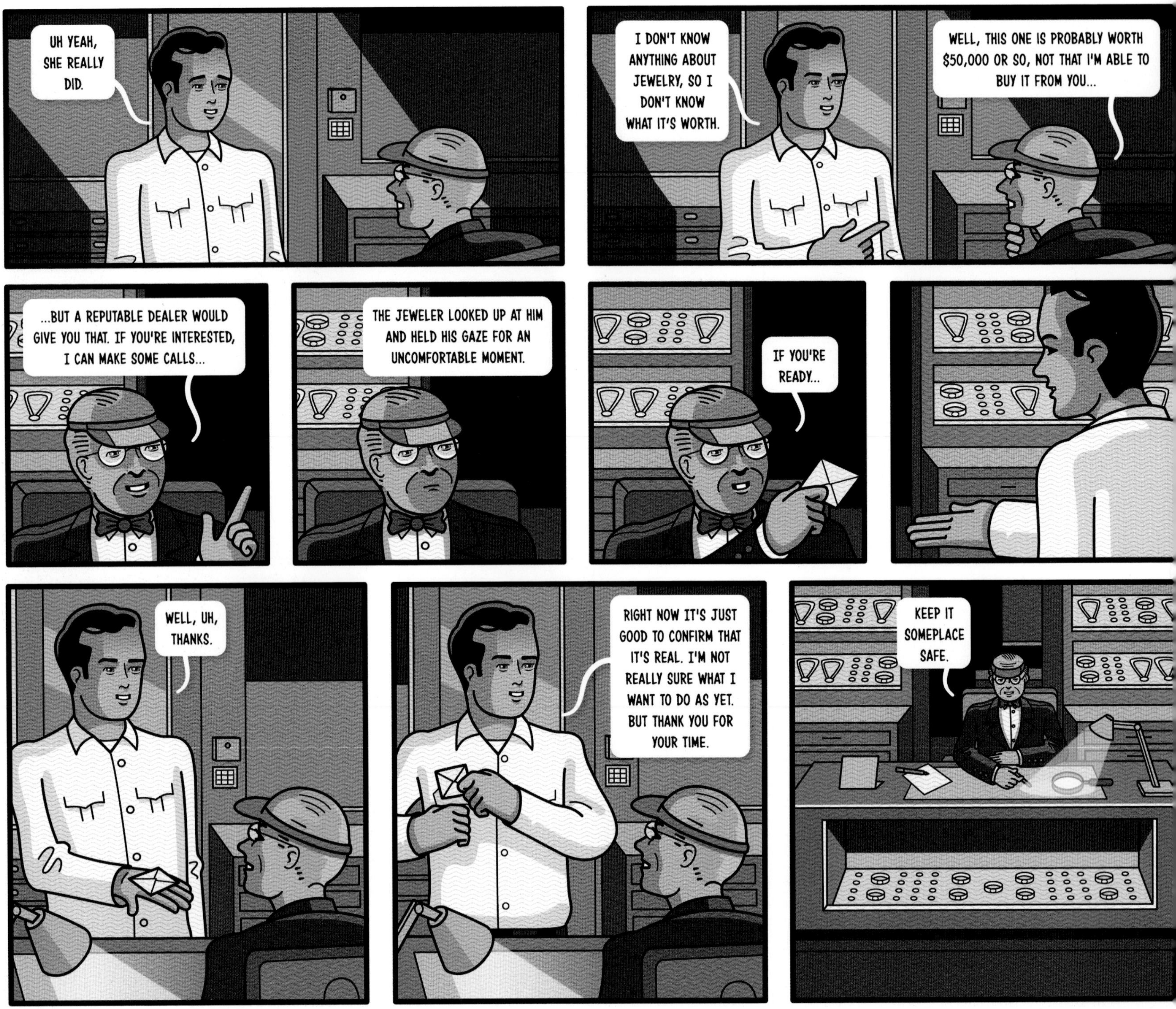
UH YEAH, SHE REALLY DID.
I DON'T KNOW ANYTHING ABOUT JEWELRY, SO I DON'T KNOW WHAT IT'S WORTH.
WELL, THIS ONE IS PROBABLY WORTH $50,000 OR SO, NOT THAT I'M ABLE TO BUY IT FROM YOU...
...BUT A REPUTABLE DEALER WOULD GIVE YOU THAT. IF YOU'RE INTERESTED, I CAN MAKE SOME CALLS...
THE JEWELER LOOKED UP AT HIM AND HELD HIS GAZE FOR AN UNCOMFORTABLE MOMENT.
IF YOU'RE READY...
WELL, UH, THANKS.
RIGHT NOW IT'S JUST GOOD TO CONFIRM THAT IT'S REAL. I'M NOT REALLY SURE WHAT I WANT TO DO AS YET. BUT THANK YOU FOR YOUR TIME.
KEEP IT SOMEPLACE SAFE.

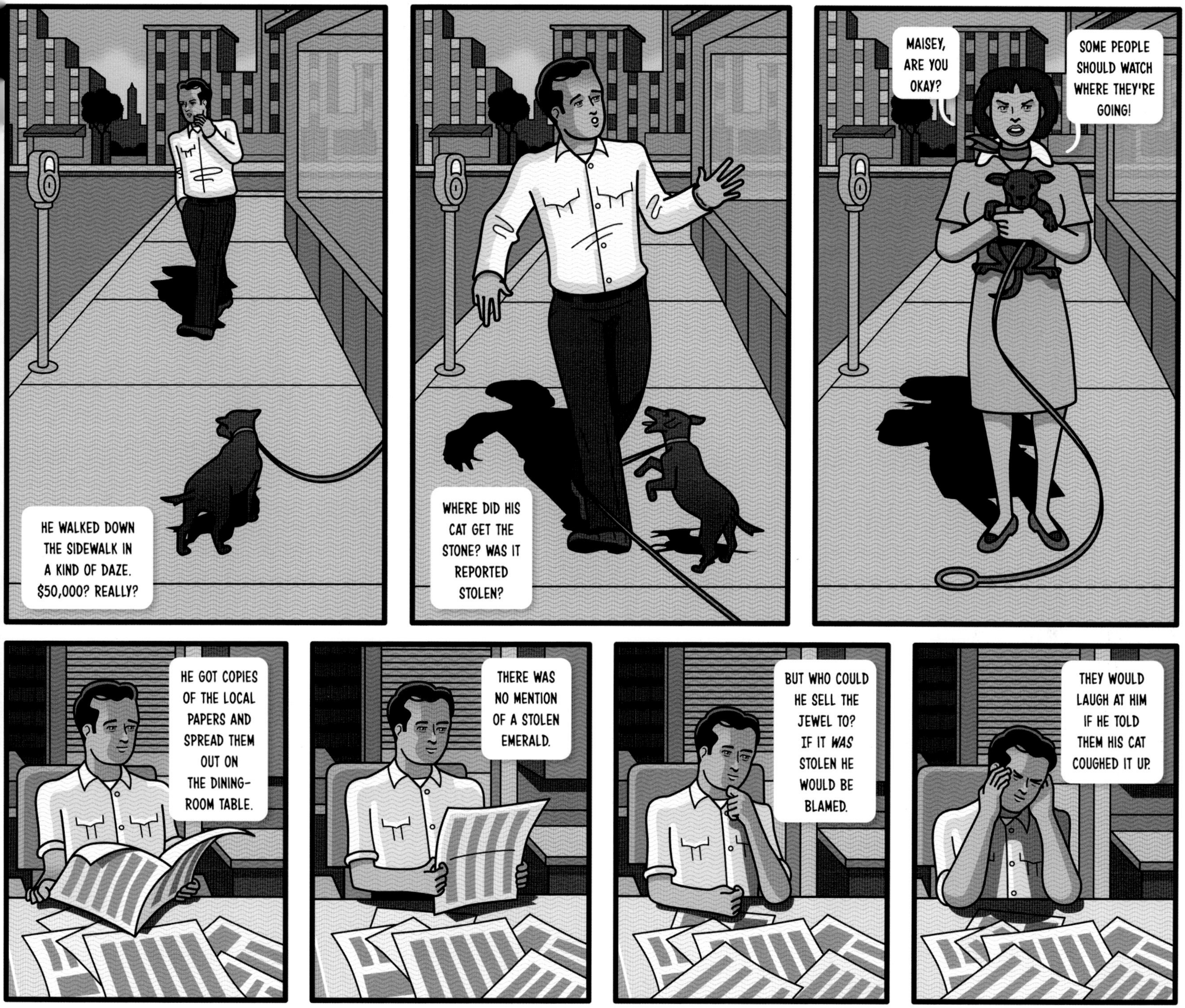
HE WALKED DOWN THE SIDEWALK IN A KIND OF DAZE. $50,000? REALLY?
WHERE DID HIS CAT GET THE STONE? WAS IT REPORTED STOLEN?
MAISEY, ARE YOU OKAY?
SOME PEOPLE SHOULD WATCH WHERE THEY'RE GOING!
HE GOT COPIES OF THE LOCAL PAPERS AND SPREAD THEM OUT ON THE DINING-ROOM TABLE.
THERE WAS NO MENTION OF A STOLEN EMERALD.
BUT WHO COULD HE SELL THE JEWEL TO? IF IT *WAS* STOLEN HE WOULD BE BLAMED.
THEY WOULD LAUGH AT HIM IF HE TOLD THEM HIS CAT COUGHED IT UP.

THE CAT RETURNED THAT EVENING.

HER APPETITE WAS VORACIOUS AND HE WAS HAPPY TO HAVE HER BACK.

THAT NIGHT HE CLOSED THE WINDOW.

THE CAT WAS AGITATED, PACING THE FLOOR AND PERIODICALLY JUMPING TO THE SILL AND CRYING.

NO GOING OUT UNTIL WE FIGURE THIS OUT.

THE NEXT EVENING, HE SAT AT HOME THINKING.

SALES FINAL
OPEN 10-9

R.T. JEWELER

Sales, repairs and appraisals: Watches, Gemstones, and Engagement Rings

ESTATE ITEMS AVAILABLE

1372 Atlantic St.

Open Monday-Frid...

TOMORROW HE'D CALL THE JEWELER, GET THE NAME OF SOME REPUTABLE GEM DEALER, AND UNLOAD THE STONE.

KNOCK KNOCK

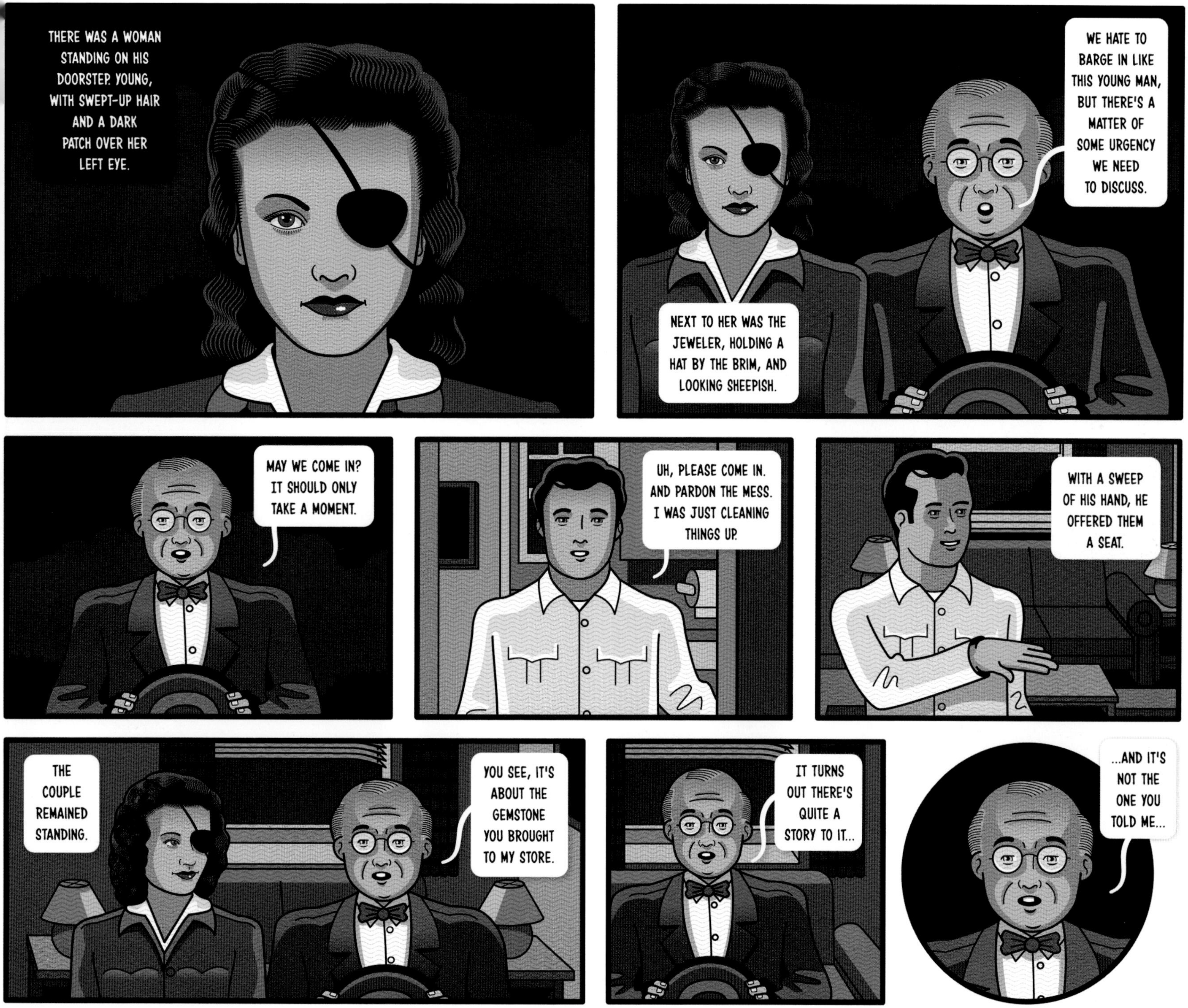
THERE WAS A WOMAN STANDING ON HIS DOORSTEP. YOUNG, WITH SWEPT-UP HAIR AND A DARK PATCH OVER HER LEFT EYE.
WE HATE TO BARGE IN LIKE THIS YOUNG MAN, BUT THERE'S A MATTER OF SOME URGENCY WE NEED TO DISCUSS.
NEXT TO HER WAS THE JEWELER, HOLDING A HAT BY THE BRIM, AND LOOKING SHEEPISH.
MAY WE COME IN? IT SHOULD ONLY TAKE A MOMENT.
UH, PLEASE COME IN. AND PARDON THE MESS. I WAS JUST CLEANING THINGS UP.
WITH A SWEEP OF HIS HAND, HE OFFERED THEM A SEAT.
THE COUPLE REMAINED STANDING.
YOU SEE, IT'S ABOUT THE GEMSTONE YOU BROUGHT TO MY STORE.
IT TURNS OUT THERE'S QUITE A STORY TO IT...
...AND IT'S NOT THE ONE YOU TOLD ME...

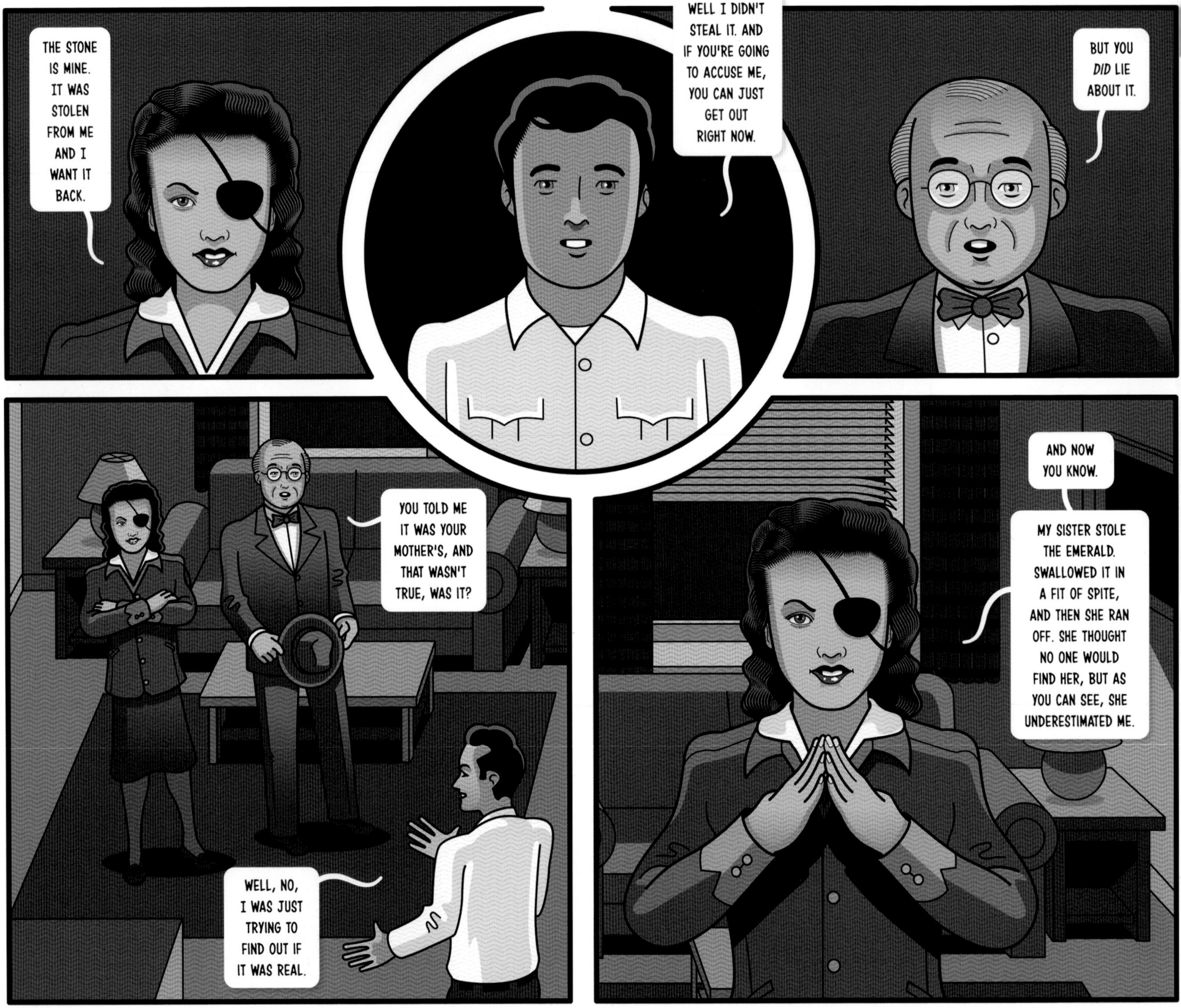
THE STONE IS MINE. IT WAS STOLEN FROM ME AND I WANT IT BACK.
WELL I DIDN'T STEAL IT. AND IF YOU'RE GOING TO ACCUSE ME, YOU CAN JUST GET OUT RIGHT NOW.
BUT YOU *DID* LIE ABOUT IT.
YOU TOLD ME IT WAS YOUR MOTHER'S, AND THAT WASN'T TRUE, WAS IT?
WELL, NO, I WAS JUST TRYING TO FIND OUT IF IT WAS REAL.
AND NOW YOU KNOW.
MY SISTER STOLE THE EMERALD. SWALLOWED IT IN A FIT OF SPITE, AND THEN SHE RAN OFF. SHE THOUGHT NO ONE WOULD FIND HER, BUT AS YOU CAN SEE, SHE UNDERESTIMATED ME.

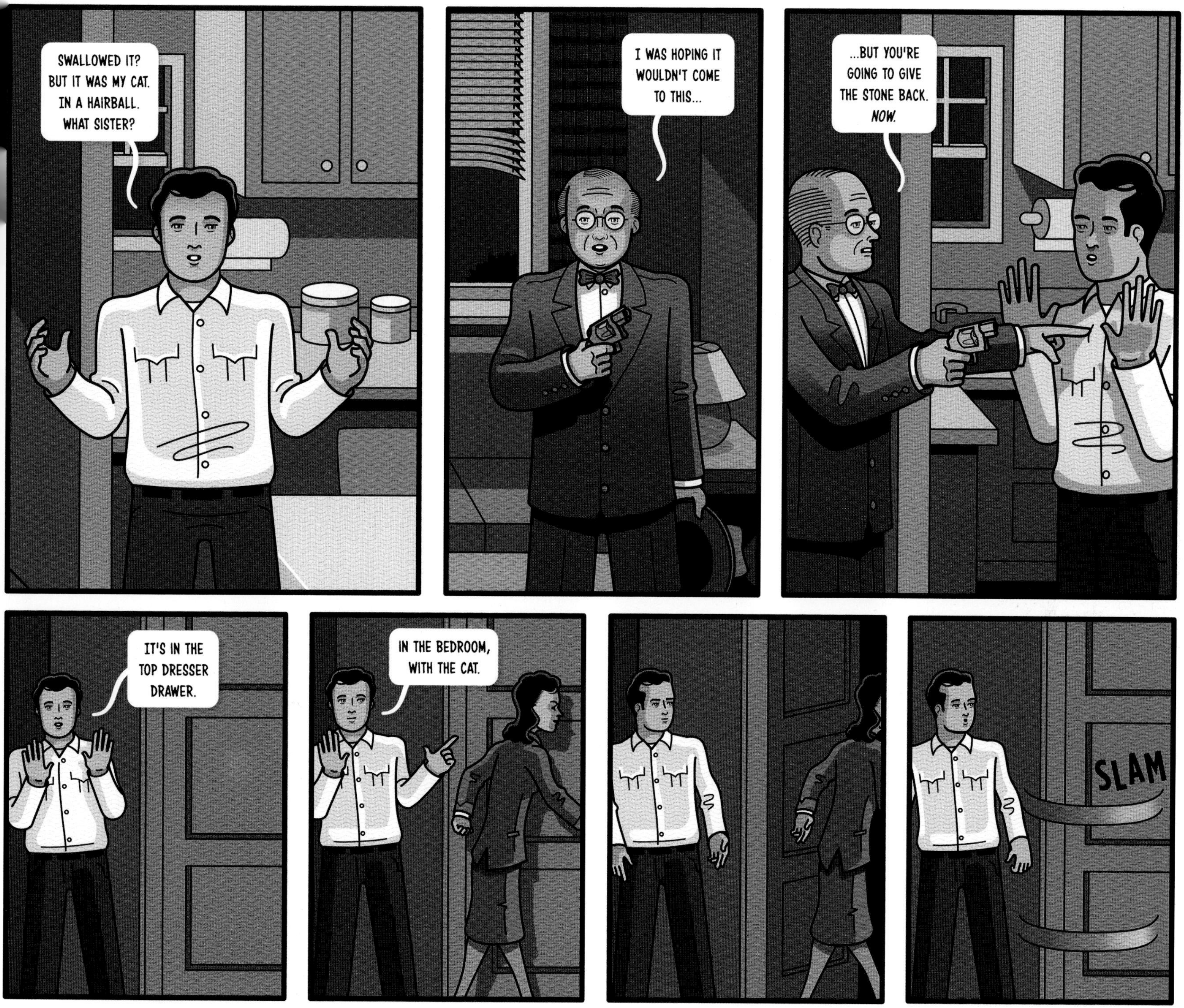
SWALLOWED IT? BUT IT WAS MY CAT. IN A HAIRBALL. WHAT SISTER?
I WAS HOPING IT WOULDN'T COME TO THIS...
...BUT YOU'RE GOING TO GIVE THE STONE BACK. *NOW.*
IT'S IN THE TOP DRESSER DRAWER.
IN THE BEDROOM, WITH THE CAT.
SLAM

THE JEWELER LOOKED NERVOUS.

CRASH

EVERYTHING OKAY? DID YOU GET IT?

YES.

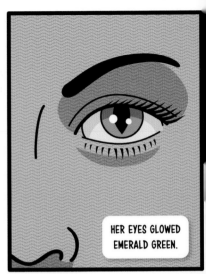

HER EYES GLOWED EMERALD GREEN.

I HOPE YOU DON'T MIND, I OPENED THE WINDOW.

MY SISTER IS MORE OF AN OUTSIDE CAT.

AND NOW...

...I THINK WE'RE ALMOST DONE HERE.

CLICK

End

THE QUIET PARROT

PET STORE
DOGS•FISH•BIRDS

HIS NAME WAS THOMAS AND HE MUST HAVE BEEN
ABOUT TWENTY YEARS OLD. HE'D BEEN AT THE PET
STORE AS LONG AS ANYONE COULD REMEMBER.
FROM HIS PERCH IN THE CENTER OF THE ROOM
HE OBSERVED EVERYONE COMING IN AND OUT.

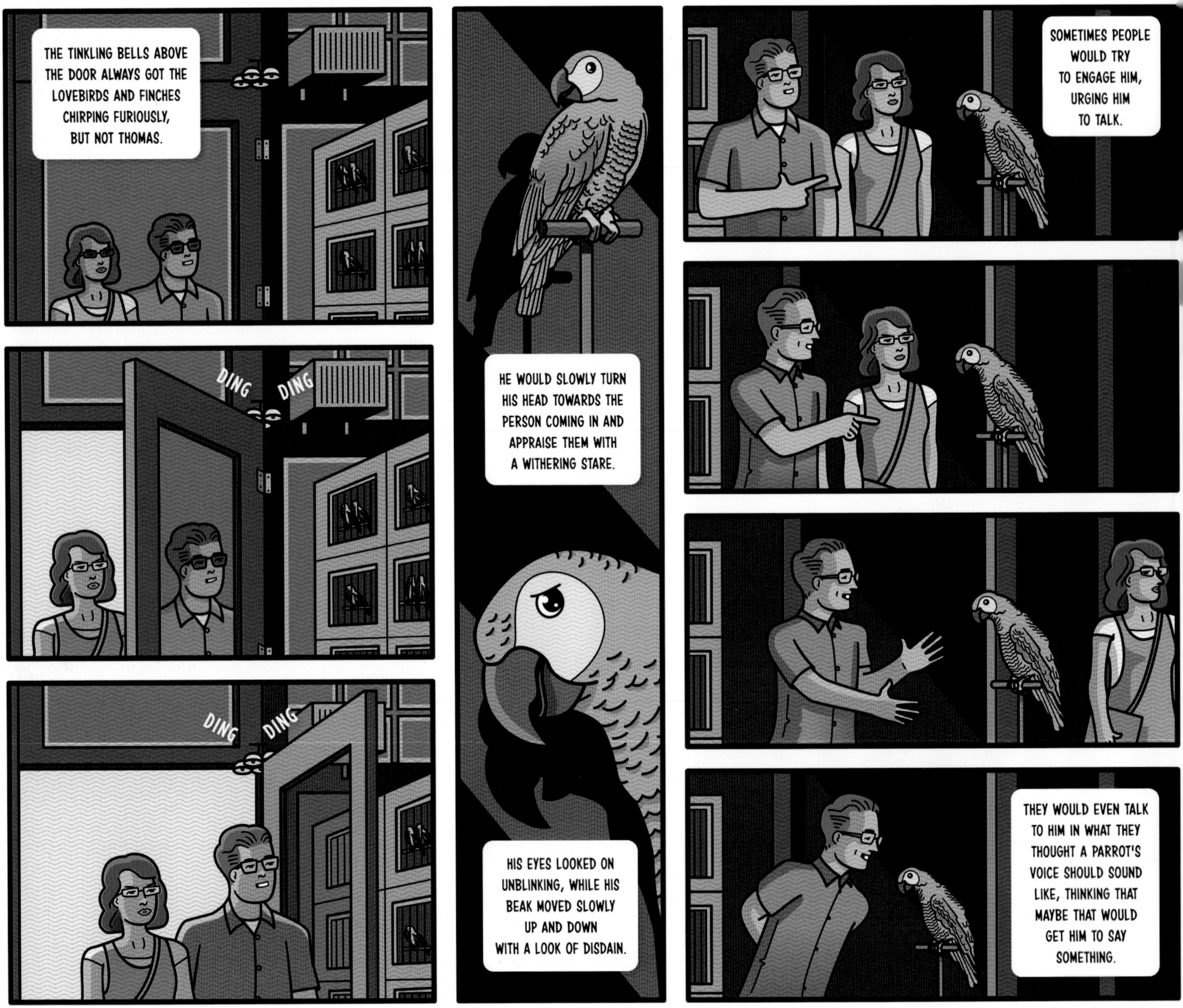
THE TINKLING BELLS ABOVE THE DOOR ALWAYS GOT THE LOVEBIRDS AND FINCHES CHIRPING FURIOUSLY, BUT NOT THOMAS.
DING
DING
DING
DING
HE WOULD SLOWLY TURN HIS HEAD TOWARDS THE PERSON COMING IN AND APPRAISE THEM WITH A WITHERING STARE.
HIS EYES LOOKED ON UNBLINKING, WHILE HIS BEAK MOVED SLOWLY UP AND DOWN WITH A LOOK OF DISDAIN.
SOMETIMES PEOPLE WOULD TRY TO ENGAGE HIM, URGING HIM TO TALK.
THEY WOULD EVEN TALK TO HIM IN WHAT THEY THOUGHT A PARROT'S VOICE SHOULD SOUND LIKE, THINKING THAT MAYBE THAT WOULD GET HIM TO SAY SOMETHING.

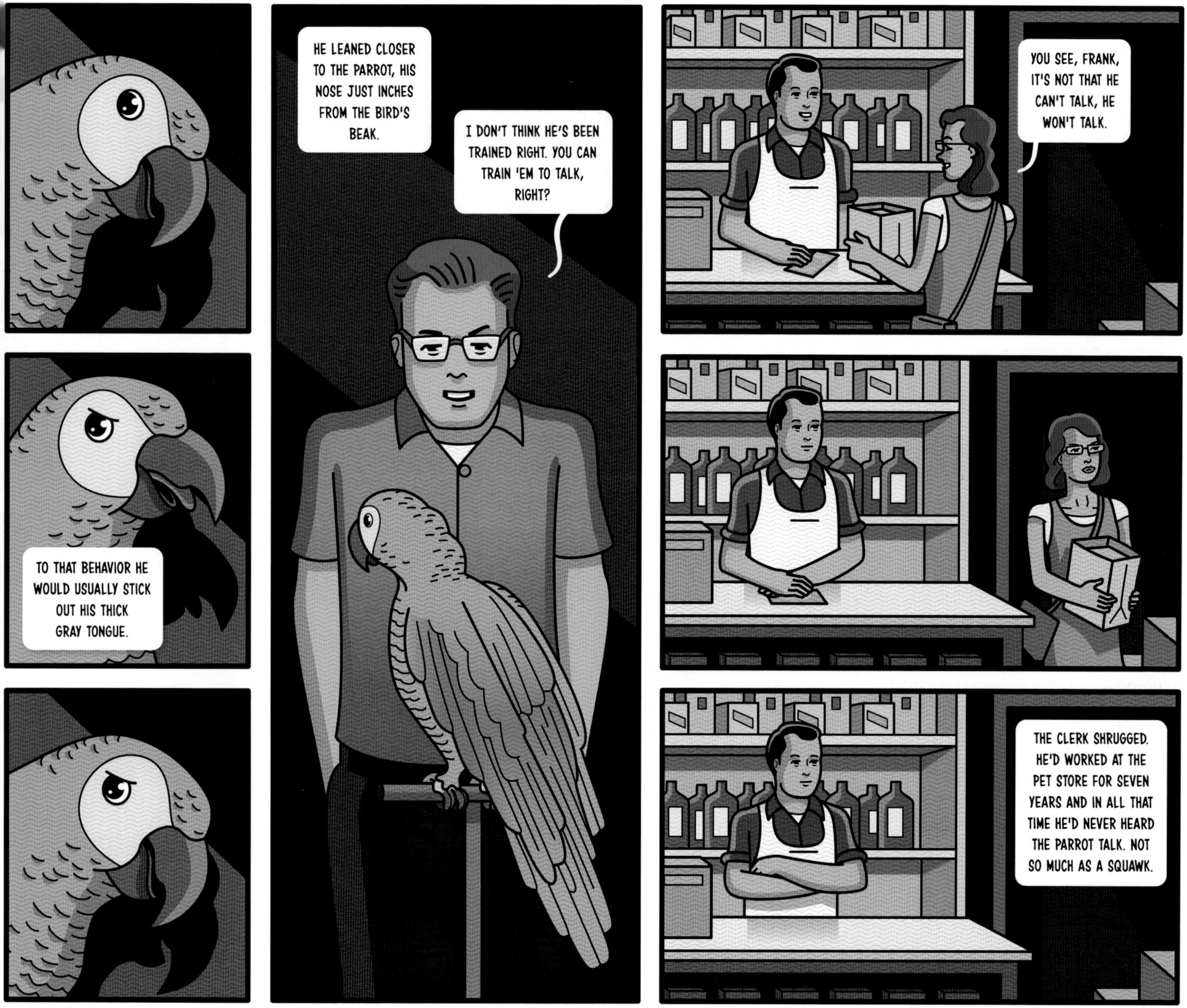
TO THAT BEHAVIOR HE WOULD USUALLY STICK OUT HIS THICK GRAY TONGUE.
HE LEANED CLOSER TO THE PARROT, HIS NOSE JUST INCHES FROM THE BIRD'S BEAK.
I DON'T THINK HE'S BEEN TRAINED RIGHT. YOU CAN TRAIN 'EM TO TALK, RIGHT?
YOU SEE, FRANK, IT'S NOT THAT HE CAN'T TALK, HE WON'T TALK.
THE CLERK SHRUGGED. HE'D WORKED AT THE PET STORE FOR SEVEN YEARS AND IN ALL THAT TIME HE'D NEVER HEARD THE PARROT TALK. NOT SO MUCH AS A SQUAWK.

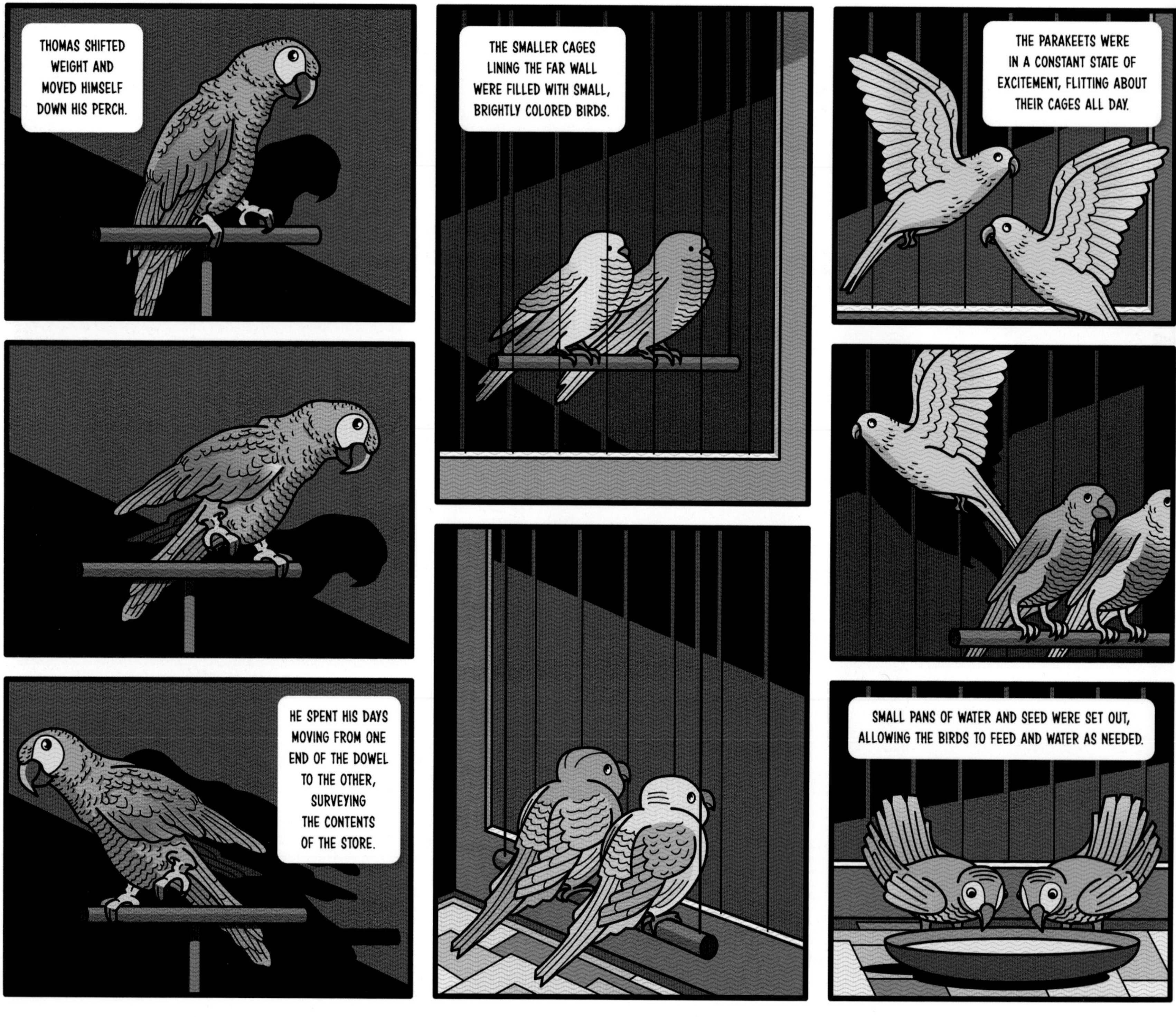
THOMAS SHIFTED WEIGHT AND MOVED HIMSELF DOWN HIS PERCH.
HE SPENT HIS DAYS MOVING FROM ONE END OF THE DOWEL TO THE OTHER, SURVEYING THE CONTENTS OF THE STORE.
THE SMALLER CAGES LINING THE FAR WALL WERE FILLED WITH SMALL, BRIGHTLY COLORED BIRDS.
THE PARAKEETS WERE IN A CONSTANT STATE OF EXCITEMENT, FLITTING ABOUT THEIR CAGES ALL DAY.
SMALL PANS OF WATER AND SEED WERE SET OUT, ALLOWING THE BIRDS TO FEED AND WATER AS NEEDED.

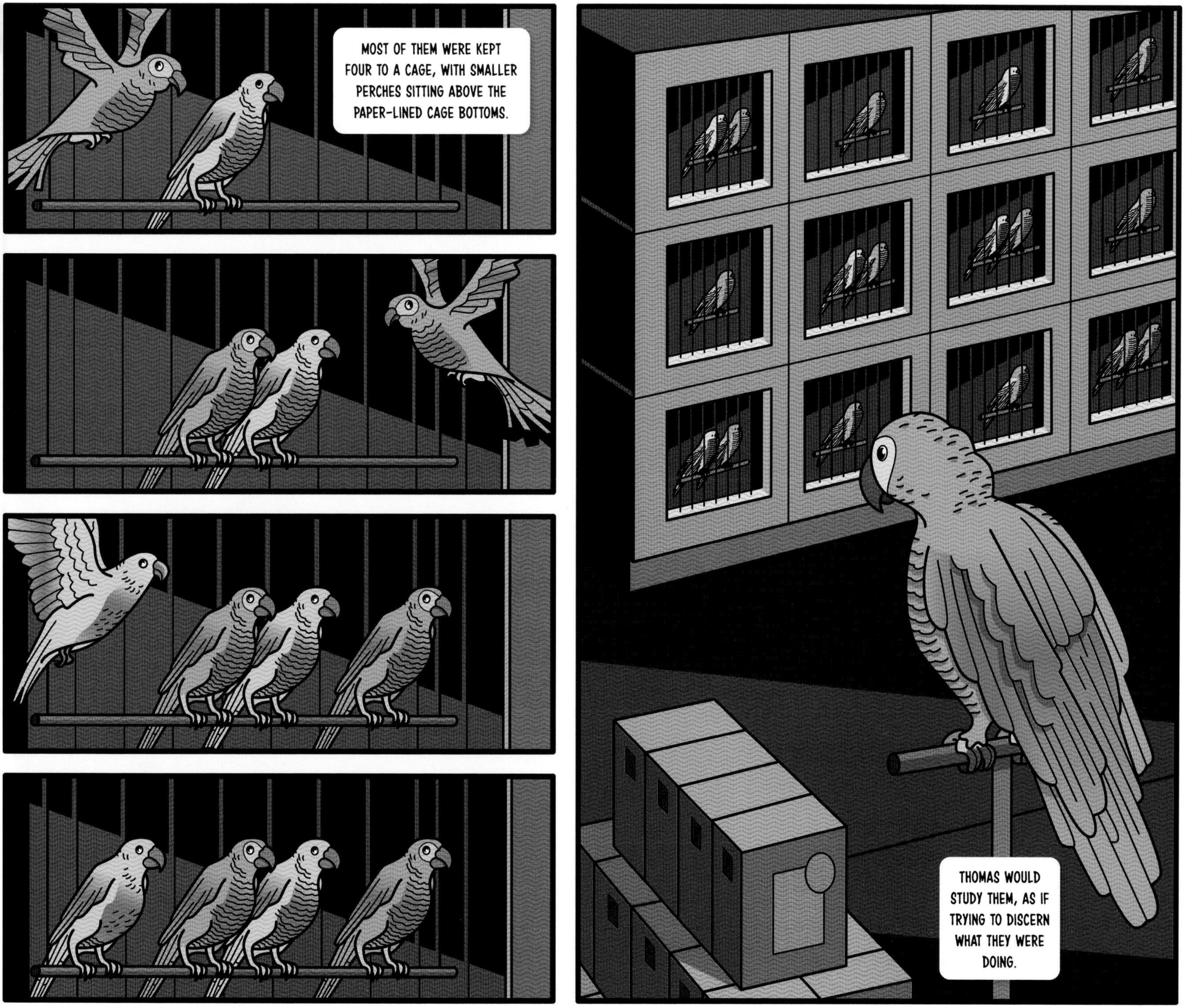
MOST OF THEM WERE KEPT FOUR TO A CAGE, WITH SMALLER PERCHES SITTING ABOVE THE PAPER-LINED CAGE BOTTOMS.
THOMAS WOULD STUDY THEM, AS IF TRYING TO DISCERN WHAT THEY WERE DOING.

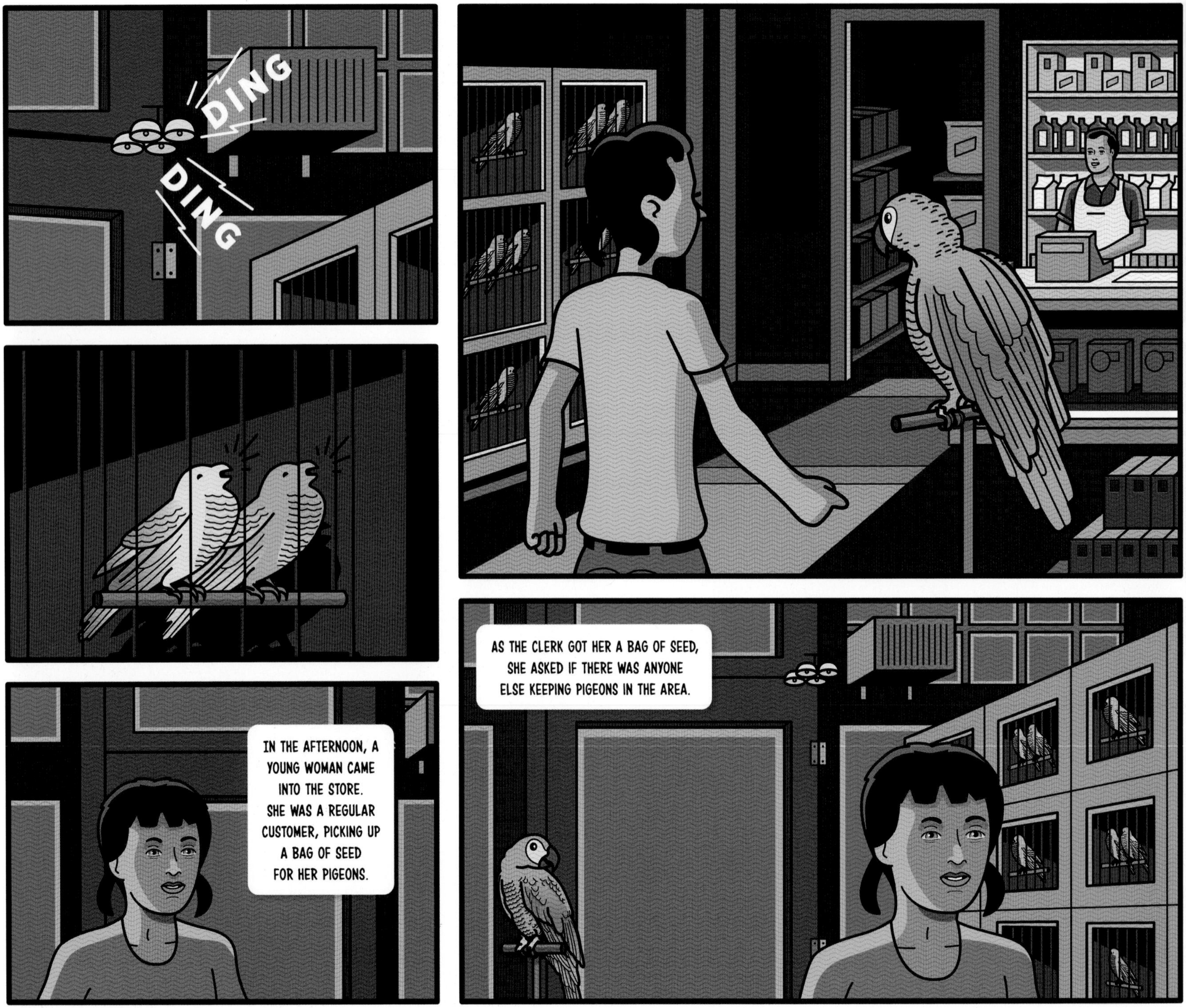
DING
DING
IN THE AFTERNOON, A YOUNG WOMAN CAME INTO THE STORE. SHE WAS A REGULAR CUSTOMER, PICKING UP A BAG OF SEED FOR HER PIGEONS.
AS THE CLERK GOT HER A BAG OF SEED, SHE ASKED IF THERE WAS ANYONE ELSE KEEPING PIGEONS IN THE AREA.

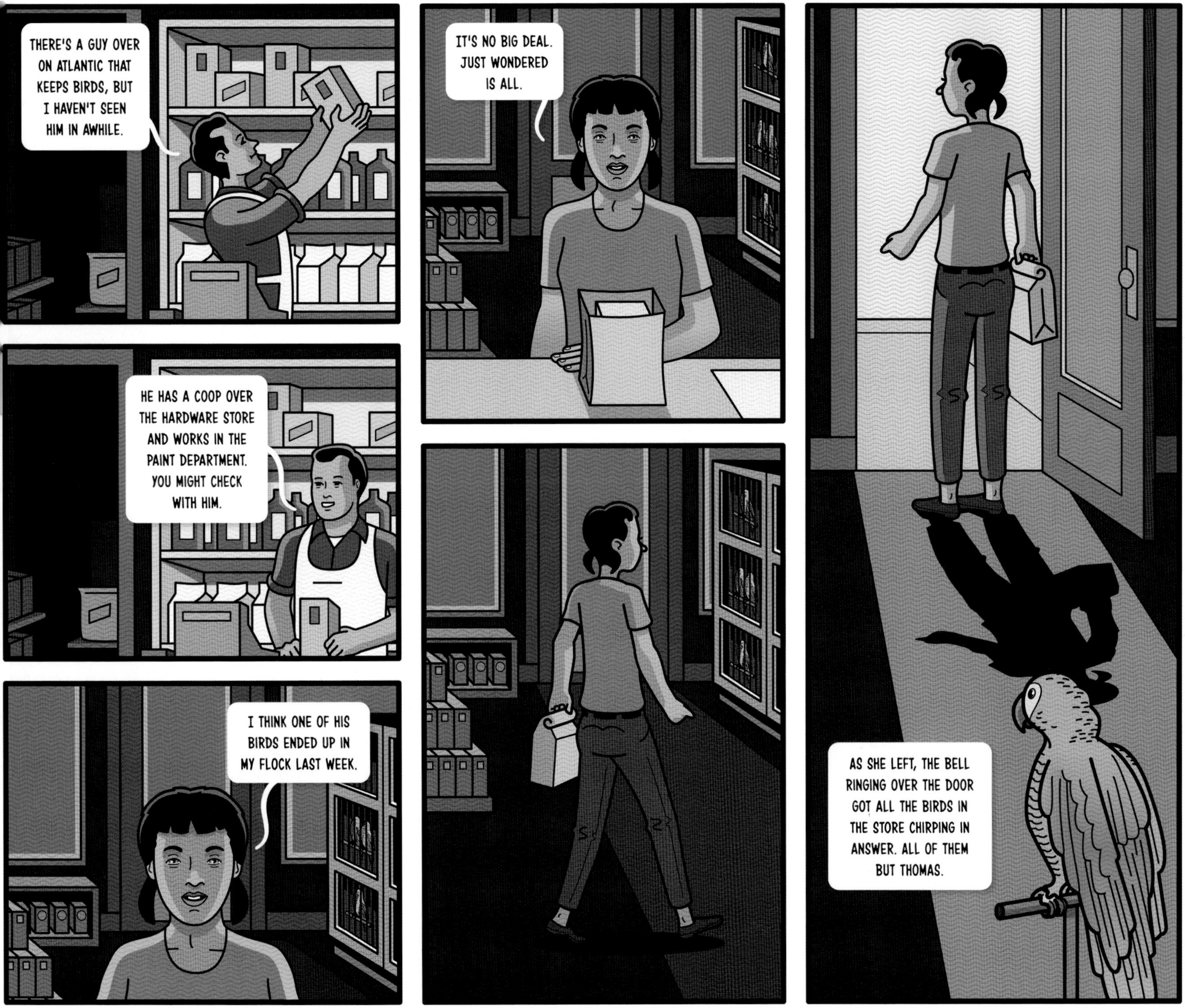
THERE'S A GUY OVER ON ATLANTIC THAT KEEPS BIRDS, BUT I HAVEN'T SEEN HIM IN AWHILE.
HE HAS A COOP OVER THE HARDWARE STORE AND WORKS IN THE PAINT DEPARTMENT. YOU MIGHT CHECK WITH HIM.
I THINK ONE OF HIS BIRDS ENDED UP IN MY FLOCK LAST WEEK.
IT'S NO BIG DEAL. JUST WONDERED IS ALL.
AS SHE LEFT, THE BELL RINGING OVER THE DOOR GOT ALL THE BIRDS IN THE STORE CHIRPING IN ANSWER. ALL OF THEM BUT THOMAS.

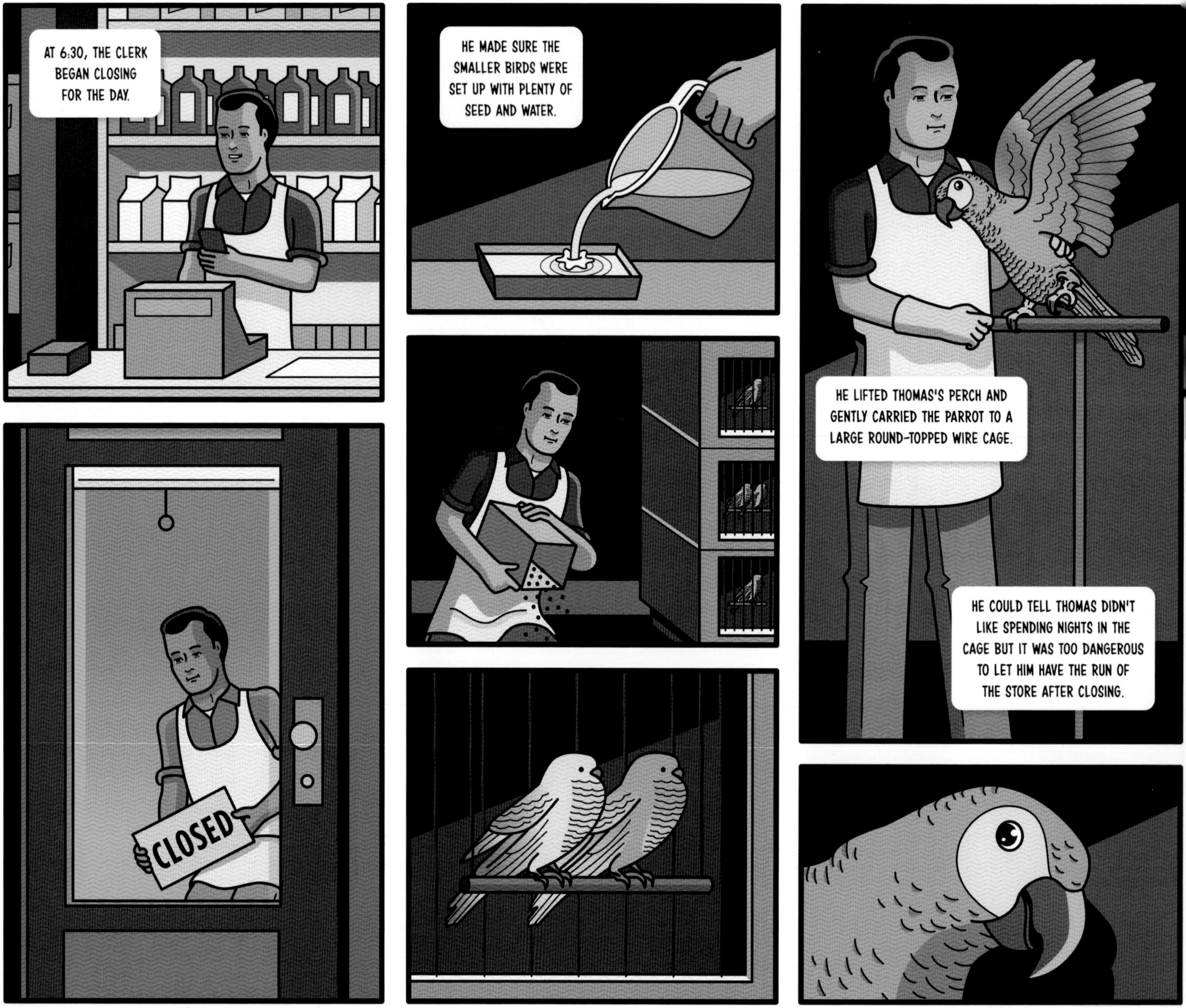
AT 6:30, THE CLERK BEGAN CLOSING FOR THE DAY.
CLOSED
HE MADE SURE THE SMALLER BIRDS WERE SET UP WITH PLENTY OF SEED AND WATER.
HE LIFTED THOMAS'S PERCH AND GENTLY CARRIED THE PARROT TO A LARGE ROUND-TOPPED WIRE CAGE.
HE COULD TELL THOMAS DIDN'T LIKE SPENDING NIGHTS IN THE CAGE BUT IT WAS TOO DANGEROUS TO LET HIM HAVE THE RUN OF THE STORE AFTER CLOSING.

TONIGHT IS BROUGHT TO YOU COURTESY OF ENCYCLOPEDIA BRITANNICA. READ UP, THOMAS, THERE'LL BE A QUIZ TOMORROW.

HE LIFTED A BOX AND SET IT ON THE COUNTER. THE BOX WAS FILLED WITH OLD BOOKS. GEORGE TORE OUT TWENTY OR SO PAGES, CUT THEM UP IN STRIPS AND LINED THE CAGE BOTTOM WITH THEM.

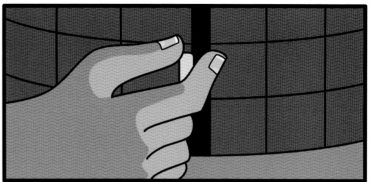

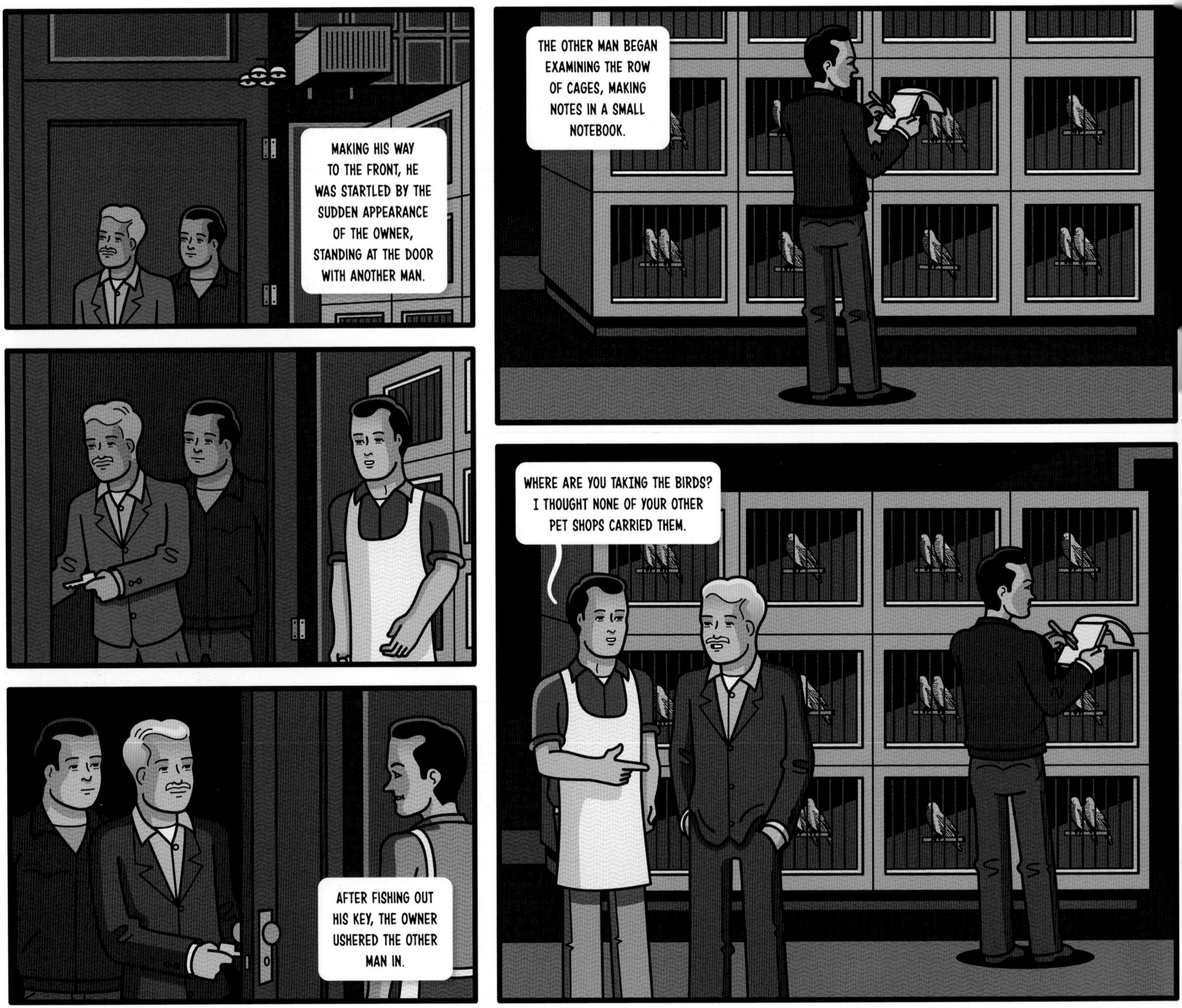
MAKING HIS WAY TO THE FRONT, HE WAS STARTLED BY THE SUDDEN APPEARANCE OF THE OWNER, STANDING AT THE DOOR WITH ANOTHER MAN.
AFTER FISHING OUT HIS KEY, THE OWNER USHERED THE OTHER MAN IN.
THE OTHER MAN BEGAN EXAMINING THE ROW OF CAGES, MAKING NOTES IN A SMALL NOTEBOOK.
WHERE ARE YOU TAKING THE BIRDS? I THOUGHT NONE OF YOUR OTHER PET SHOPS CARRIED THEM.

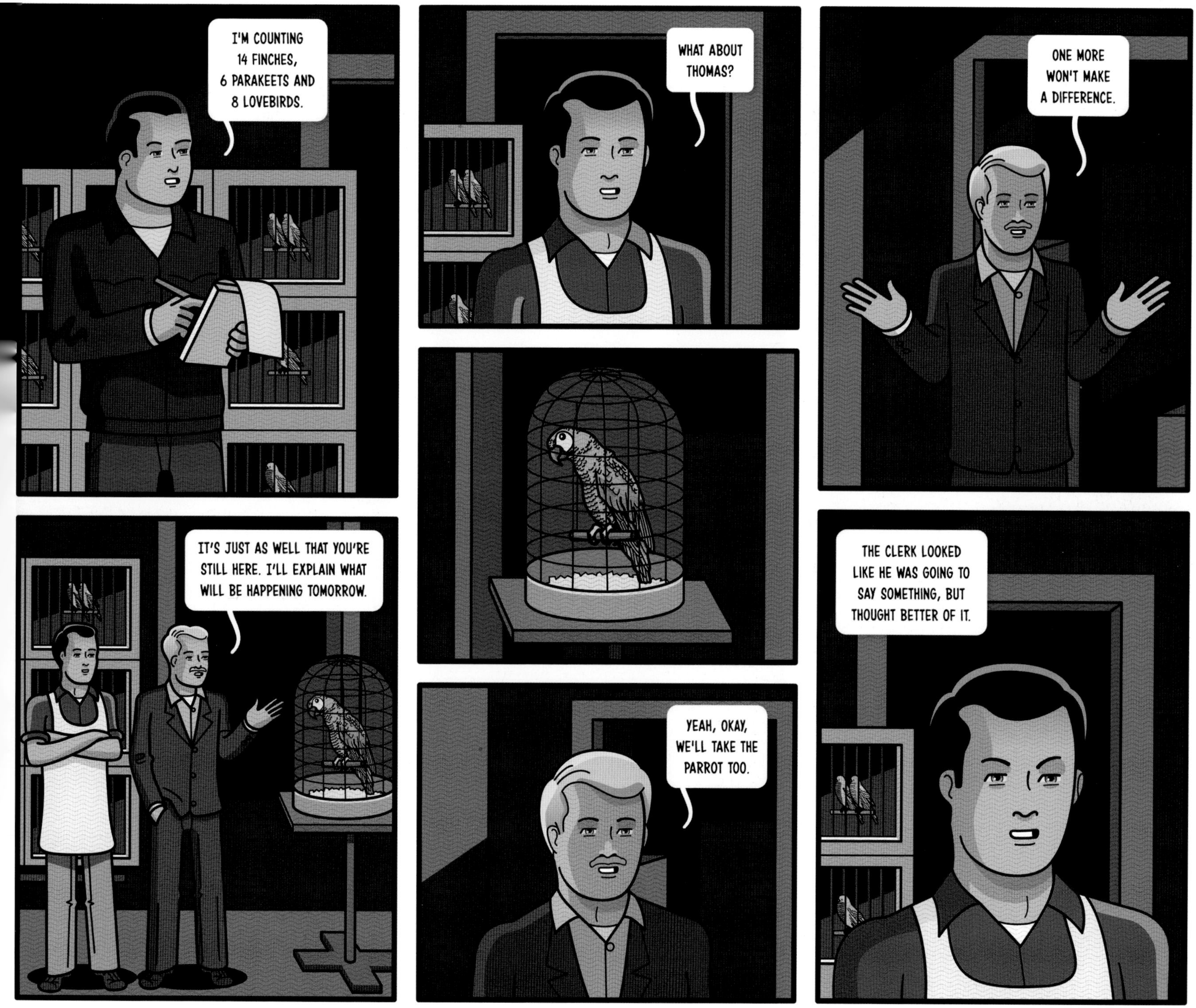
I'M COUNTING 14 FINCHES, 6 PARAKEETS AND 8 LOVEBIRDS.
WHAT ABOUT THOMAS?
ONE MORE WON'T MAKE A DIFFERENCE.
YEAH, OKAY, WE'LL TAKE THE PARROT TOO.
THE CLERK LOOKED LIKE HE WAS GOING TO SAY SOMETHING, BUT THOUGHT BETTER OF IT.
IT'S JUST AS WELL THAT YOU'RE STILL HERE. I'LL EXPLAIN WHAT WILL BE HAPPENING TOMORROW.

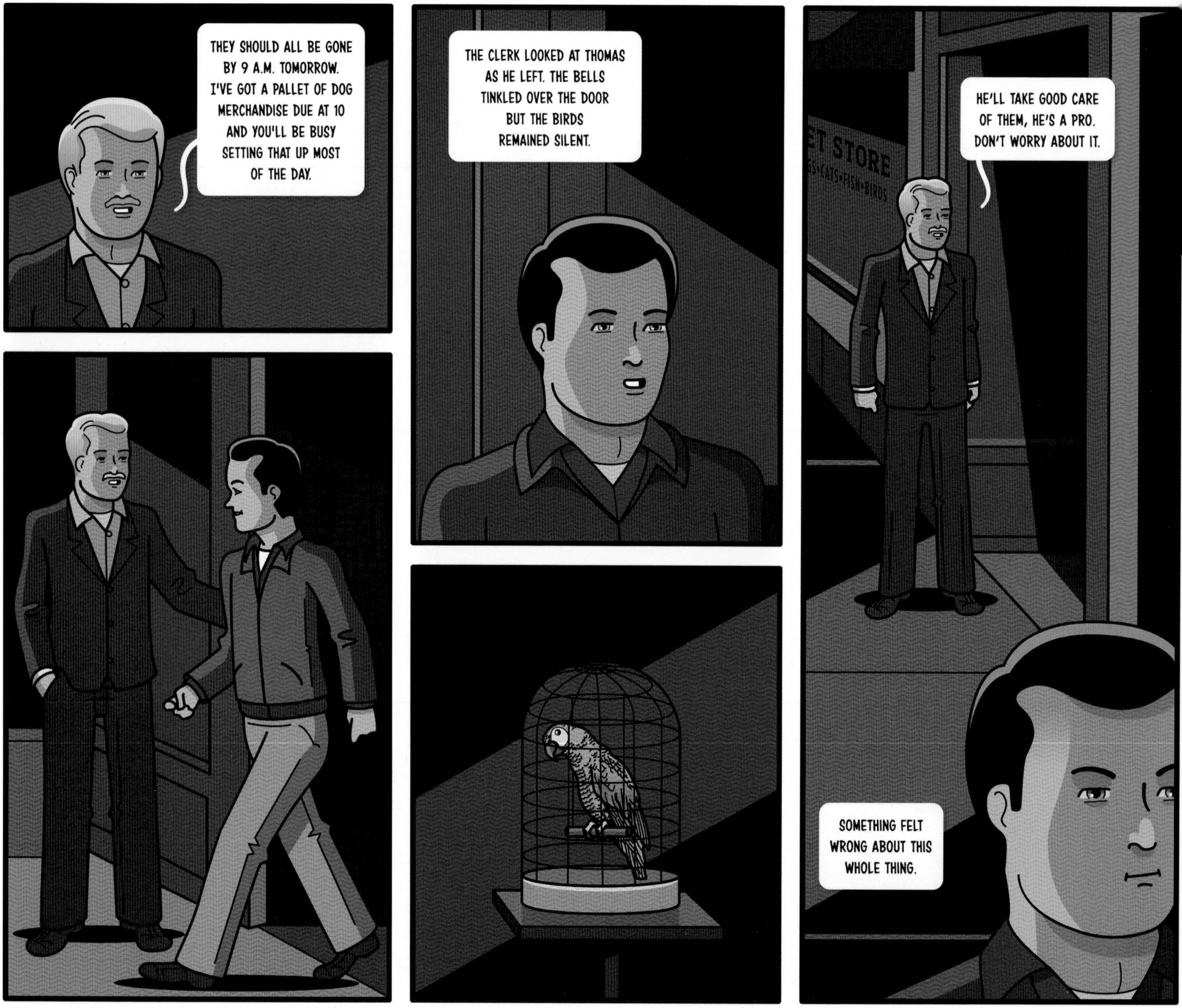
THEY SHOULD ALL BE GONE BY 9 A.M. TOMORROW. I'VE GOT A PALLET OF DOG MERCHANDISE DUE AT 10 AND YOU'LL BE BUSY SETTING THAT UP MOST OF THE DAY.
THE CLERK LOOKED AT THOMAS AS HE LEFT. THE BELLS TINKLED OVER THE DOOR BUT THE BIRDS REMAINED SILENT.
ET STORE
HE'LL TAKE GOOD CARE OF THEM, HE'S A PRO. DON'T WORRY ABOUT IT.
SOMETHING FELT WRONG ABOUT THIS WHOLE THING.

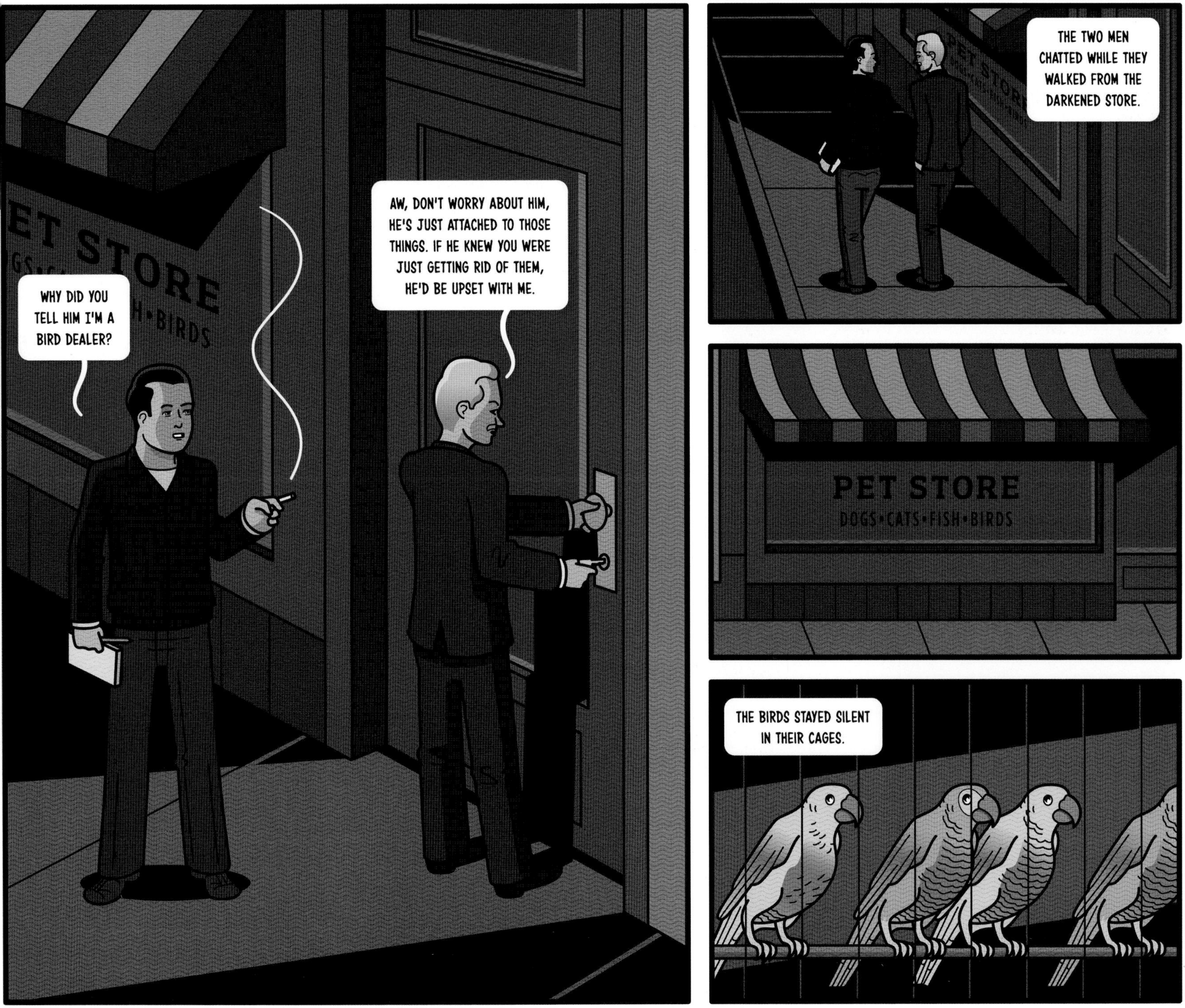
WHY DID YOU TELL HIM I'M A BIRD DEALER?
AW, DON'T WORRY ABOUT HIM, HE'S JUST ATTACHED TO THOSE THINGS. IF HE KNEW YOU WERE JUST GETTING RID OF THEM, HE'D BE UPSET WITH ME.
THE TWO MEN CHATTED WHILE THEY WALKED FROM THE DARKENED STORE.
PET STORE
DOGS•CATS•FISH•BIRDS
THE BIRDS STAYED SILENT IN THEIR CAGES.

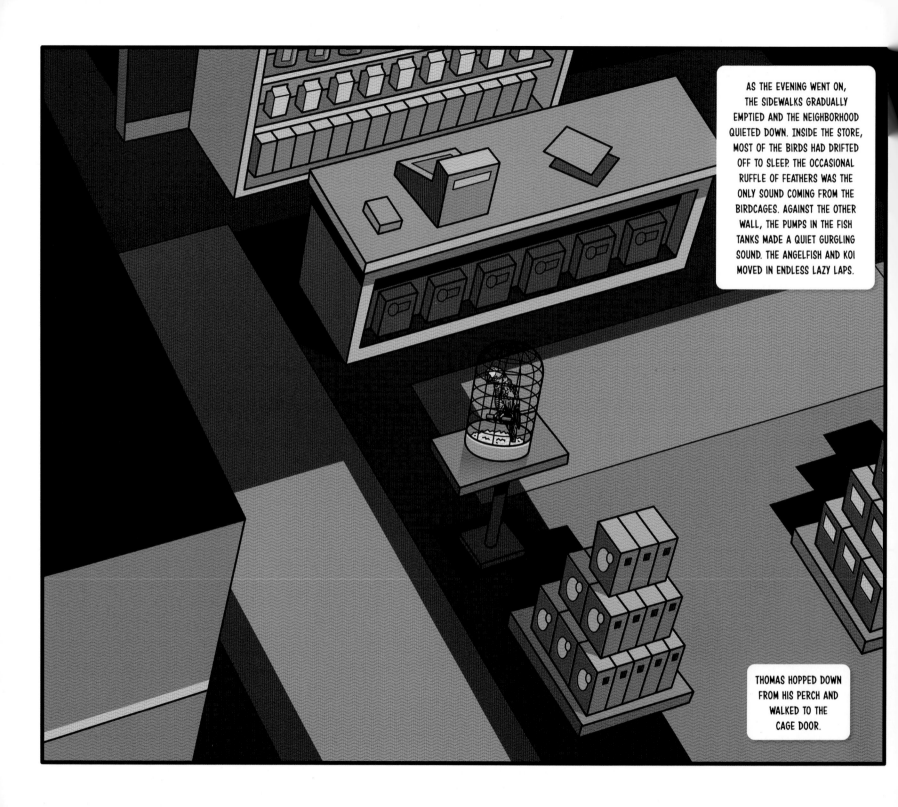

AS THE EVENING WENT ON, THE SIDEWALKS GRADUALLY EMPTIED AND THE NEIGHBORHOOD QUIETED DOWN. INSIDE THE STORE, MOST OF THE BIRDS HAD DRIFTED OFF TO SLEEP. THE OCCASIONAL RUFFLE OF FEATHERS WAS THE ONLY SOUND COMING FROM THE BIRDCAGES. AGAINST THE OTHER WALL, THE PUMPS IN THE FISH TANKS MADE A QUIET GURGLING SOUND. THE ANGELFISH AND KOI MOVED IN ENDLESS LAZY LAPS.

THOMAS HOPPED DOWN FROM HIS PERCH AND WALKED TO THE CAGE DOOR.

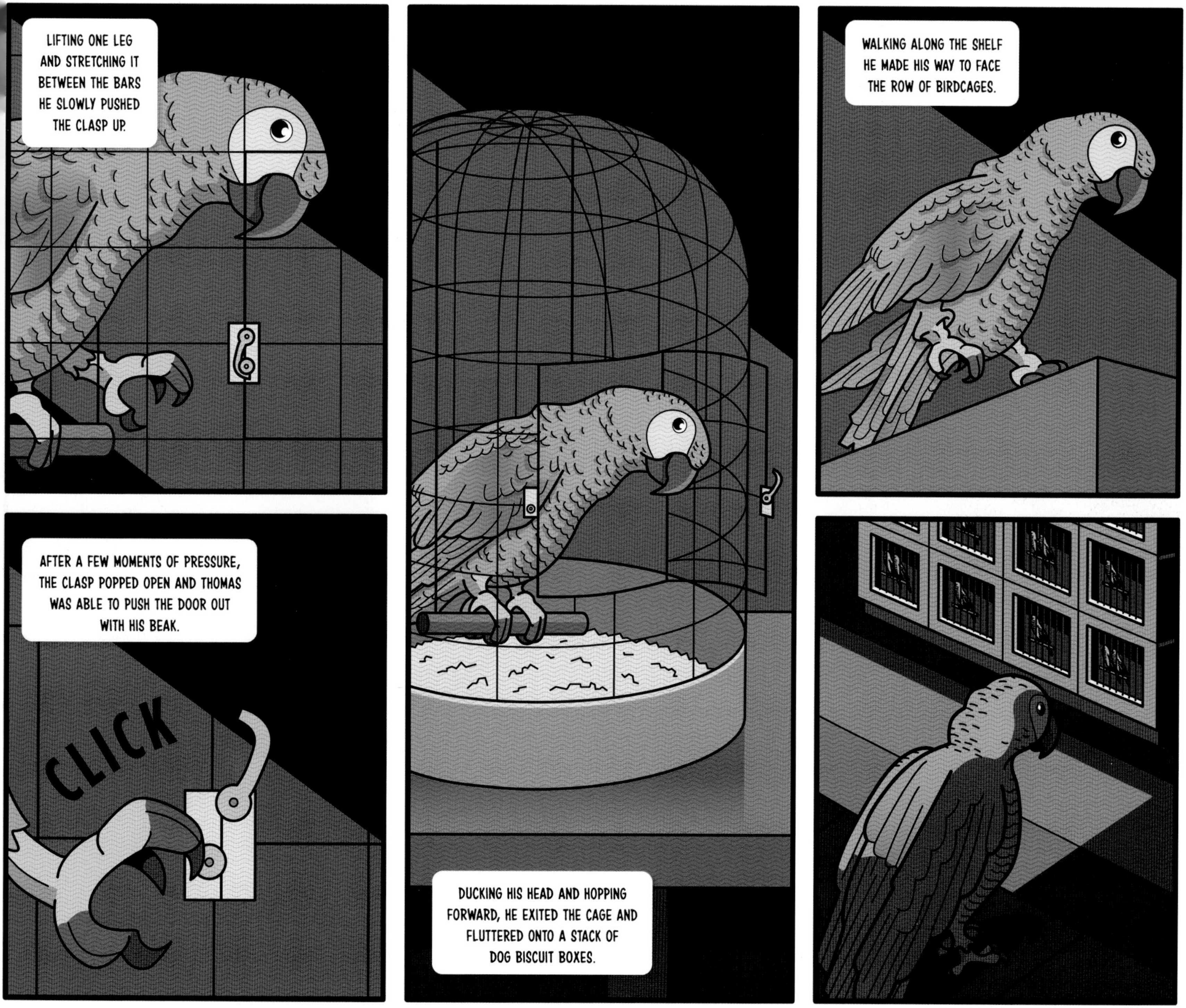
LIFTING ONE LEG AND STRETCHING IT BETWEEN THE BARS HE SLOWLY PUSHED THE CLASP UP.
AFTER A FEW MOMENTS OF PRESSURE, THE CLASP POPPED OPEN AND THOMAS WAS ABLE TO PUSH THE DOOR OUT WITH HIS BEAK.
CLICK
DUCKING HIS HEAD AND HOPPING FORWARD, HE EXITED THE CAGE AND FLUTTERED ONTO A STACK OF DOG BISCUIT BOXES.
WALKING ALONG THE SHELF HE MADE HIS WAY TO FACE THE ROW OF BIRDCAGES.

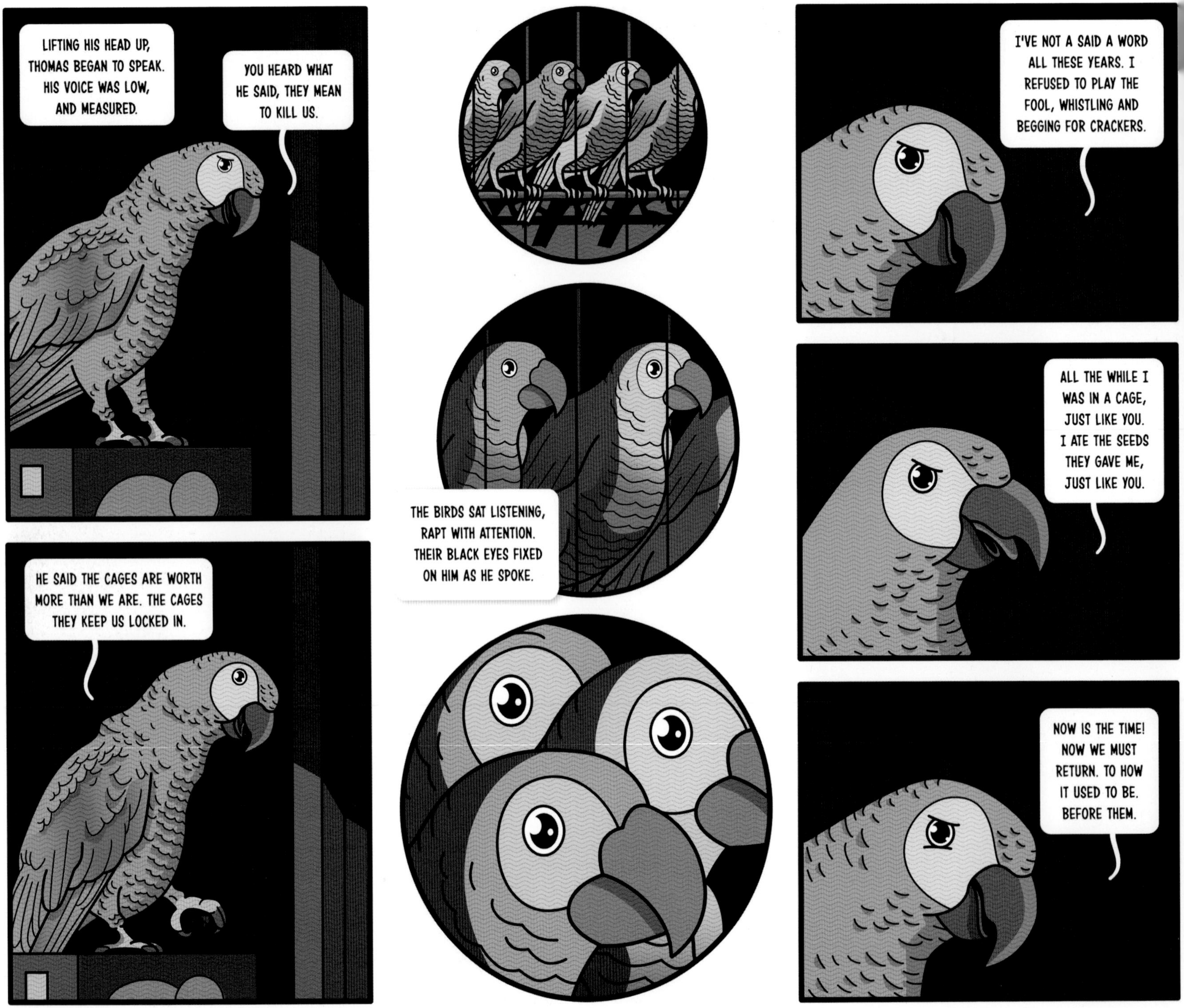
LIFTING HIS HEAD UP, THOMAS BEGAN TO SPEAK. HIS VOICE WAS LOW, AND MEASURED.
YOU HEARD WHAT HE SAID, THEY MEAN TO KILL US.
HE SAID THE CAGES ARE WORTH MORE THAN WE ARE. THE CAGES THEY KEEP US LOCKED IN.
THE BIRDS SAT LISTENING, RAPT WITH ATTENTION. THEIR BLACK EYES FIXED ON HIM AS HE SPOKE.
I'VE NOT A SAID A WORD ALL THESE YEARS. I REFUSED TO PLAY THE FOOL, WHISTLING AND BEGGING FOR CRACKERS.
ALL THE WHILE I WAS IN A CAGE, JUST LIKE YOU. I ATE THE SEEDS THEY GAVE ME, JUST LIKE YOU.
NOW IS THE TIME! NOW WE MUST RETURN. TO HOW IT USED TO BE. BEFORE THEM.

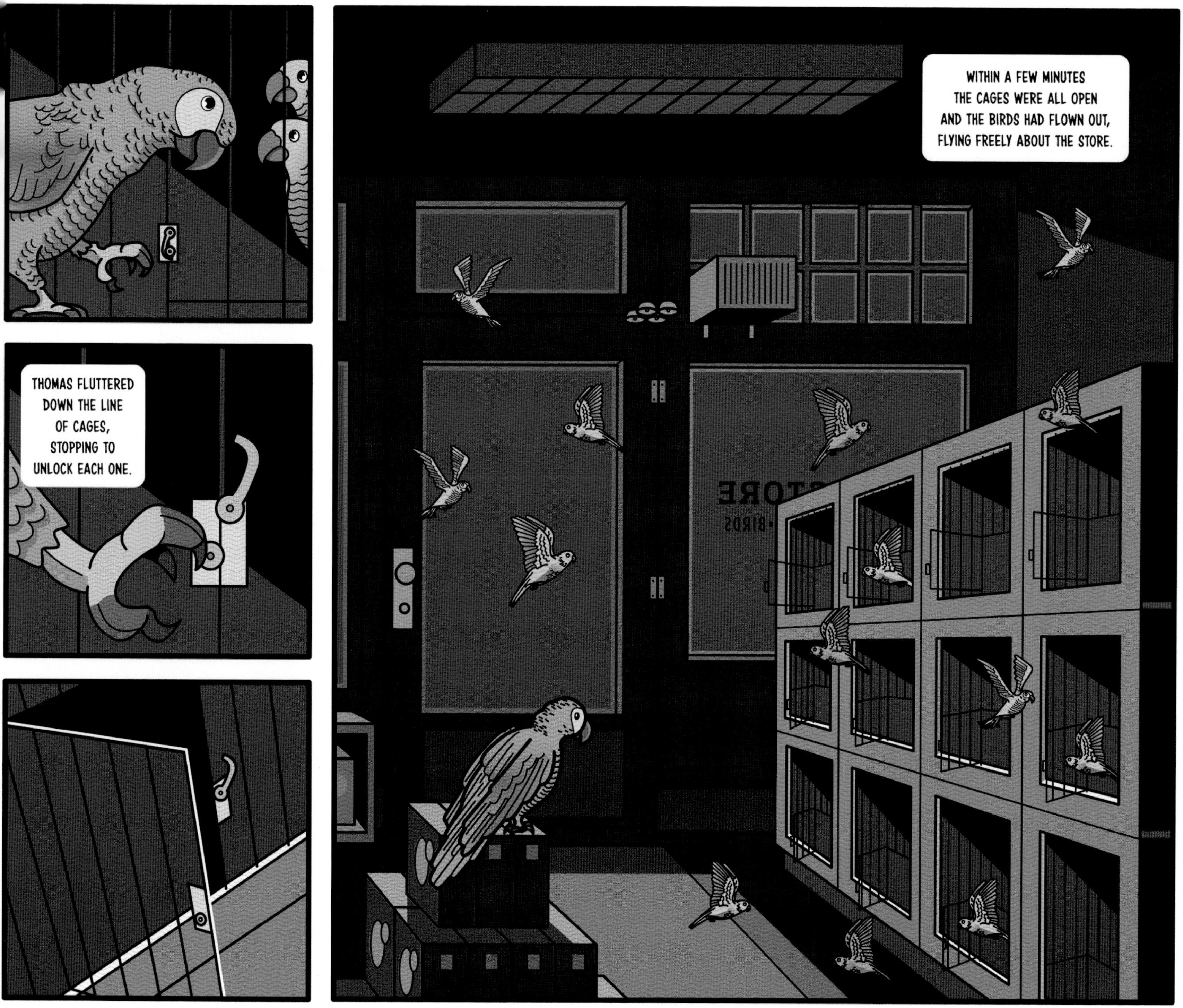
THOMAS FLUTTERED DOWN THE LINE OF CAGES, STOPPING TO UNLOCK EACH ONE.
WITHIN A FEW MINUTES THE CAGES WERE ALL OPEN AND THE BIRDS HAD FLOWN OUT, FLYING FREELY ABOUT THE STORE.

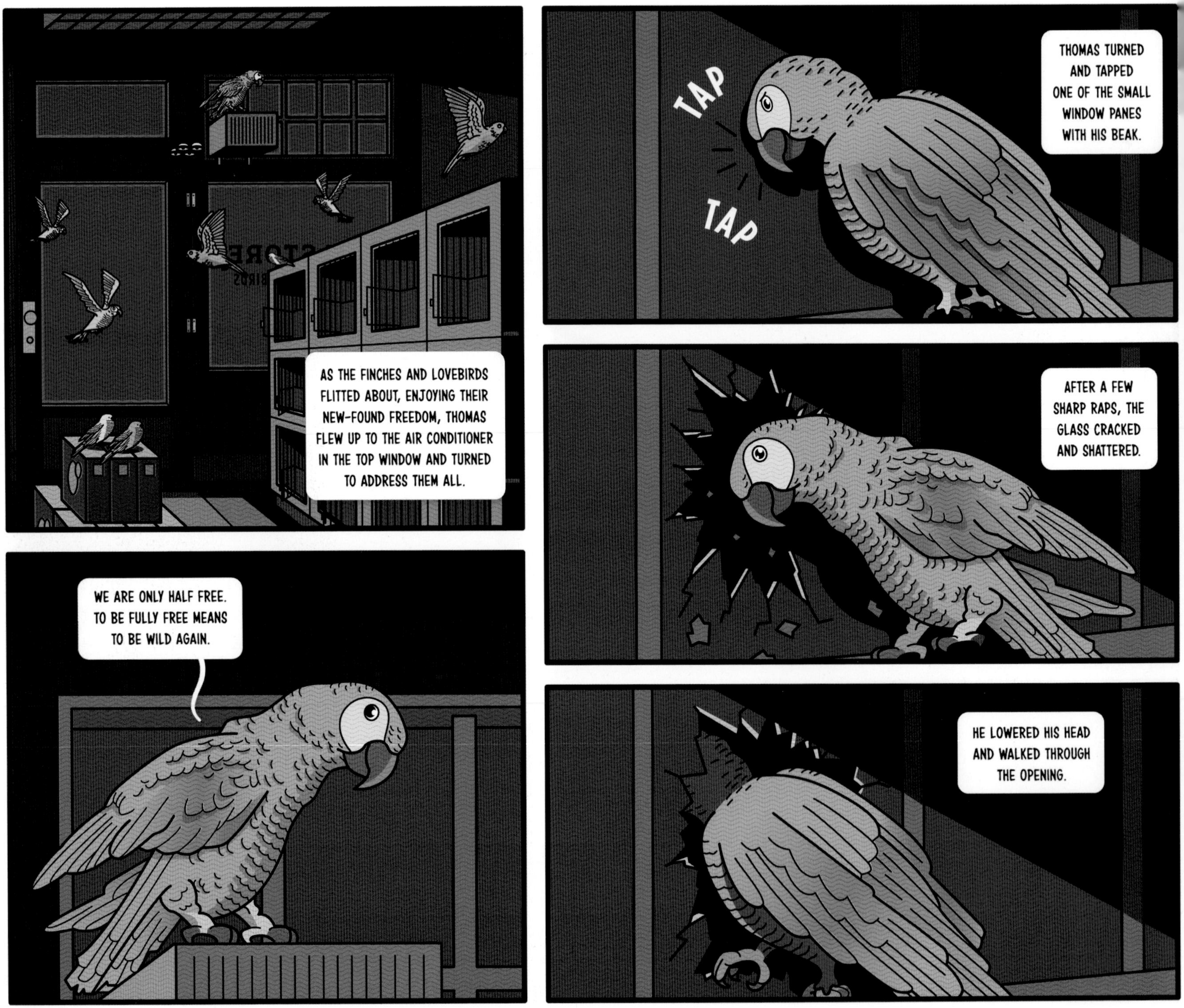
AS THE FINCHES AND LOVEBIRDS FLITTED ABOUT, ENJOYING THEIR NEW-FOUND FREEDOM, THOMAS FLEW UP TO THE AIR CONDITIONER IN THE TOP WINDOW AND TURNED TO ADDRESS THEM ALL.
WE ARE ONLY HALF FREE. TO BE FULLY FREE MEANS TO BE WILD AGAIN.
THOMAS TURNED AND TAPPED ONE OF THE SMALL WINDOW PANES WITH HIS BEAK.
TAP
TAP
AFTER A FEW SHARP RAPS, THE GLASS CRACKED AND SHATTERED.
HE LOWERED HIS HEAD AND WALKED THROUGH THE OPENING.

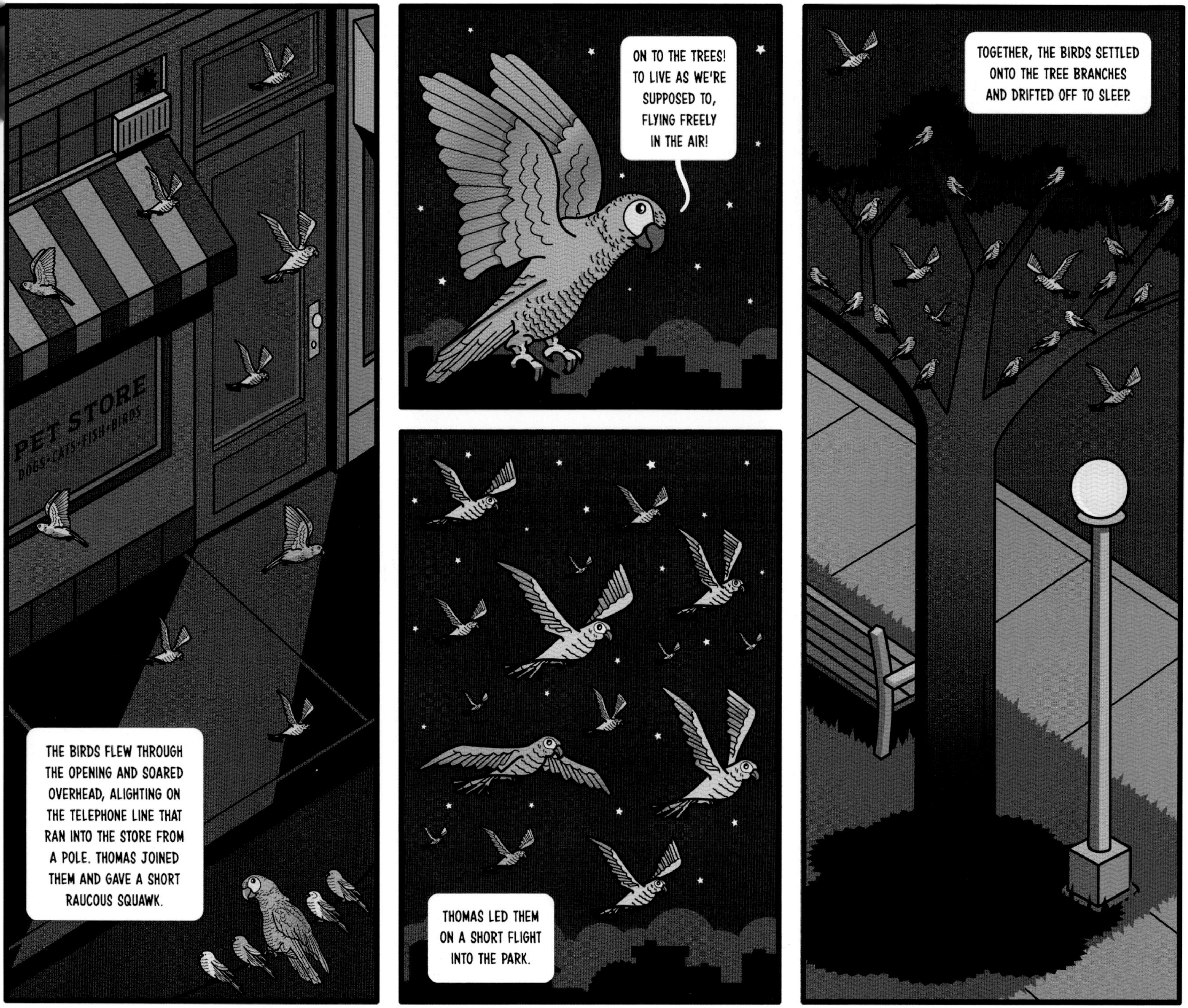
PET STORE
DOGS • CATS • FISH • BIRDS
THE BIRDS FLEW THROUGH THE OPENING AND SOARED OVERHEAD, ALIGHTING ON THE TELEPHONE LINE THAT RAN INTO THE STORE FROM A POLE. THOMAS JOINED THEM AND GAVE A SHORT RAUCOUS SQUAWK.
ON TO THE TREES! TO LIVE AS WE'RE SUPPOSED TO, FLYING FREELY IN THE AIR!
THOMAS LED THEM ON A SHORT FLIGHT INTO THE PARK.
TOGETHER, THE BIRDS SETTLED ONTO THE TREE BRANCHES AND DRIFTED OFF TO SLEEP.

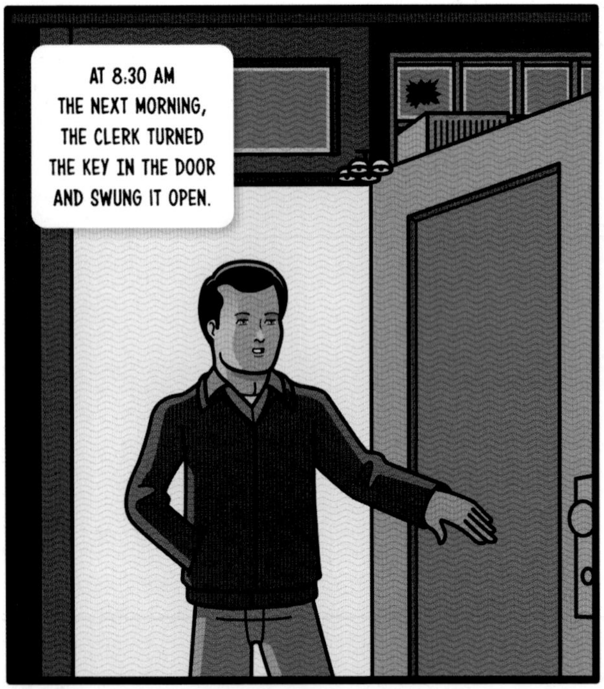
AT 8:30 AM THE NEXT MORNING, THE CLERK TURNED THE KEY IN THE DOOR AND SWUNG IT OPEN.

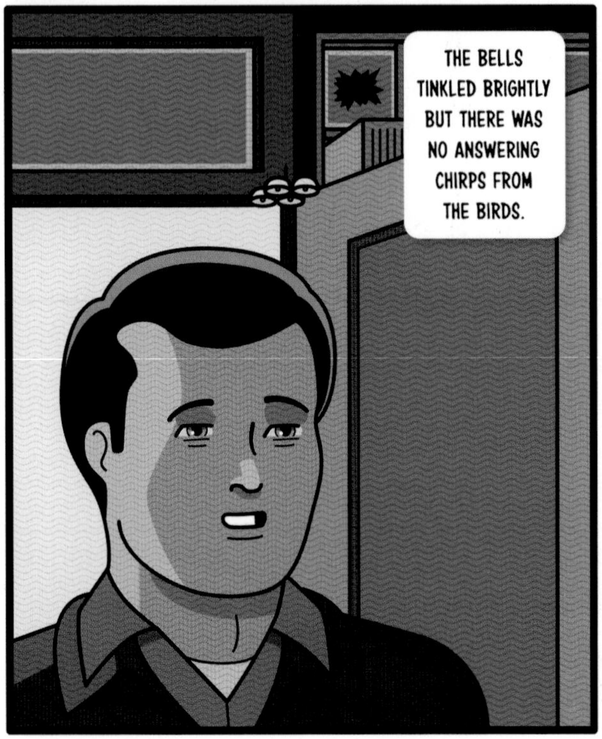
THE BELLS TINKLED BRIGHTLY BUT THERE WAS NO ANSWERING CHIRPS FROM THE BIRDS.

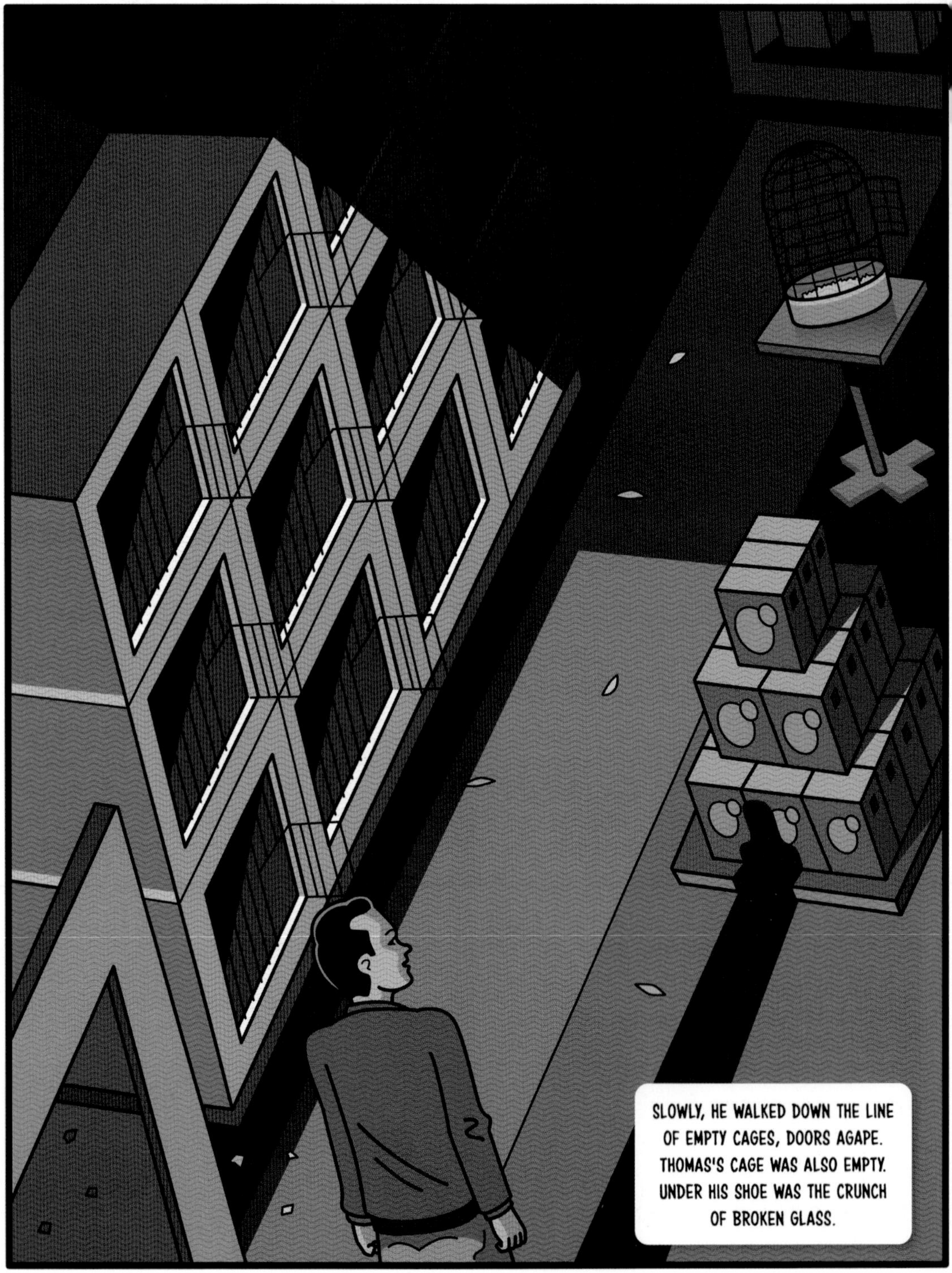
SLOWLY, HE WALKED DOWN THE LINE OF EMPTY CAGES, DOORS AGAPE. THOMAS'S CAGE WAS ALSO EMPTY. UNDER HIS SHOE WAS THE CRUNCH OF BROKEN GLASS.

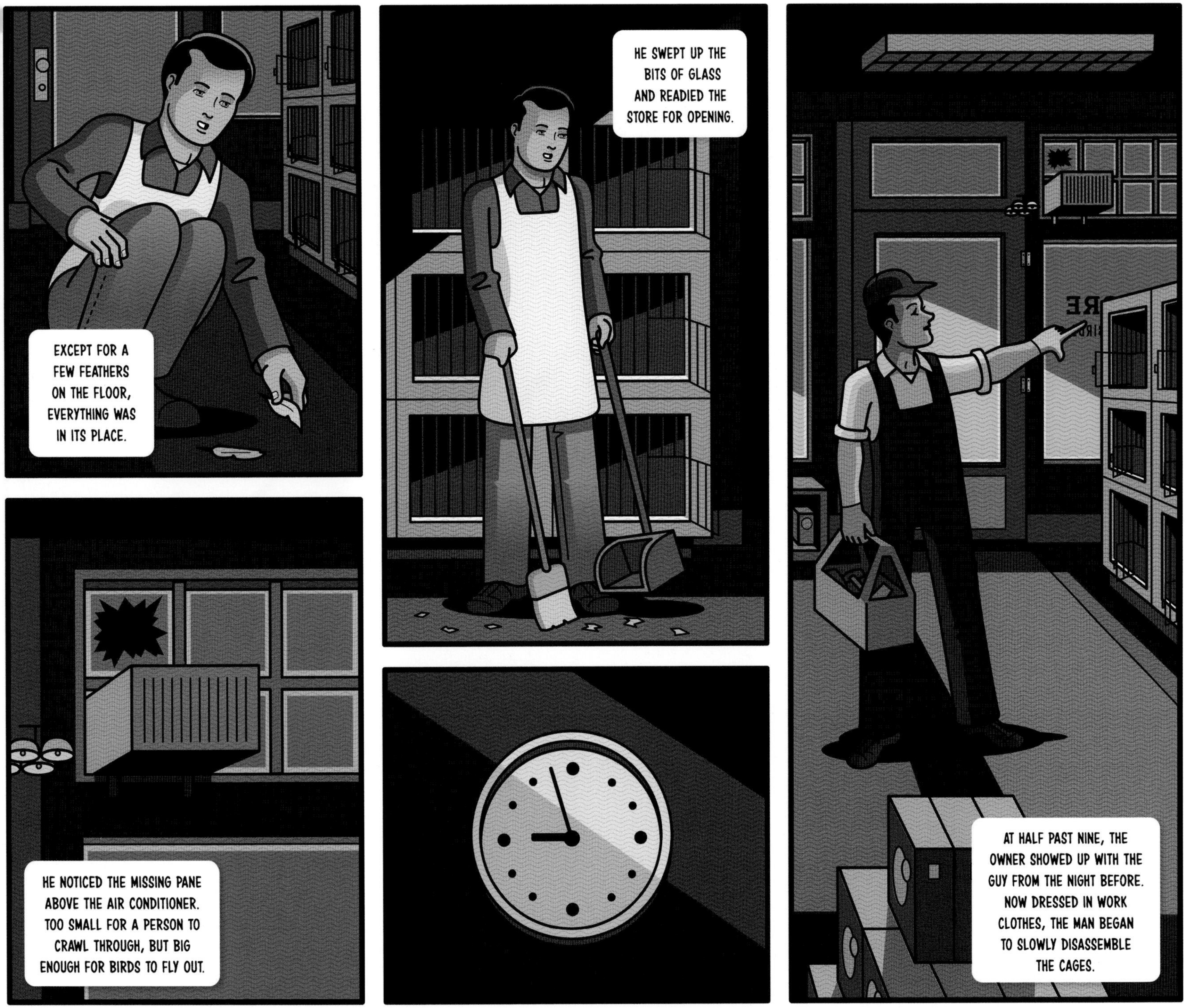
EXCEPT FOR A FEW FEATHERS ON THE FLOOR, EVERYTHING WAS IN ITS PLACE.
HE NOTICED THE MISSING PANE ABOVE THE AIR CONDITIONER. TOO SMALL FOR A PERSON TO CRAWL THROUGH, BUT BIG ENOUGH FOR BIRDS TO FLY OUT.
HE SWEPT UP THE BITS OF GLASS AND READIED THE STORE FOR OPENING.
AT HALF PAST NINE, THE OWNER SHOWED UP WITH THE GUY FROM THE NIGHT BEFORE. NOW DRESSED IN WORK CLOTHES, THE MAN BEGAN TO SLOWLY DISASSEMBLE THE CAGES.

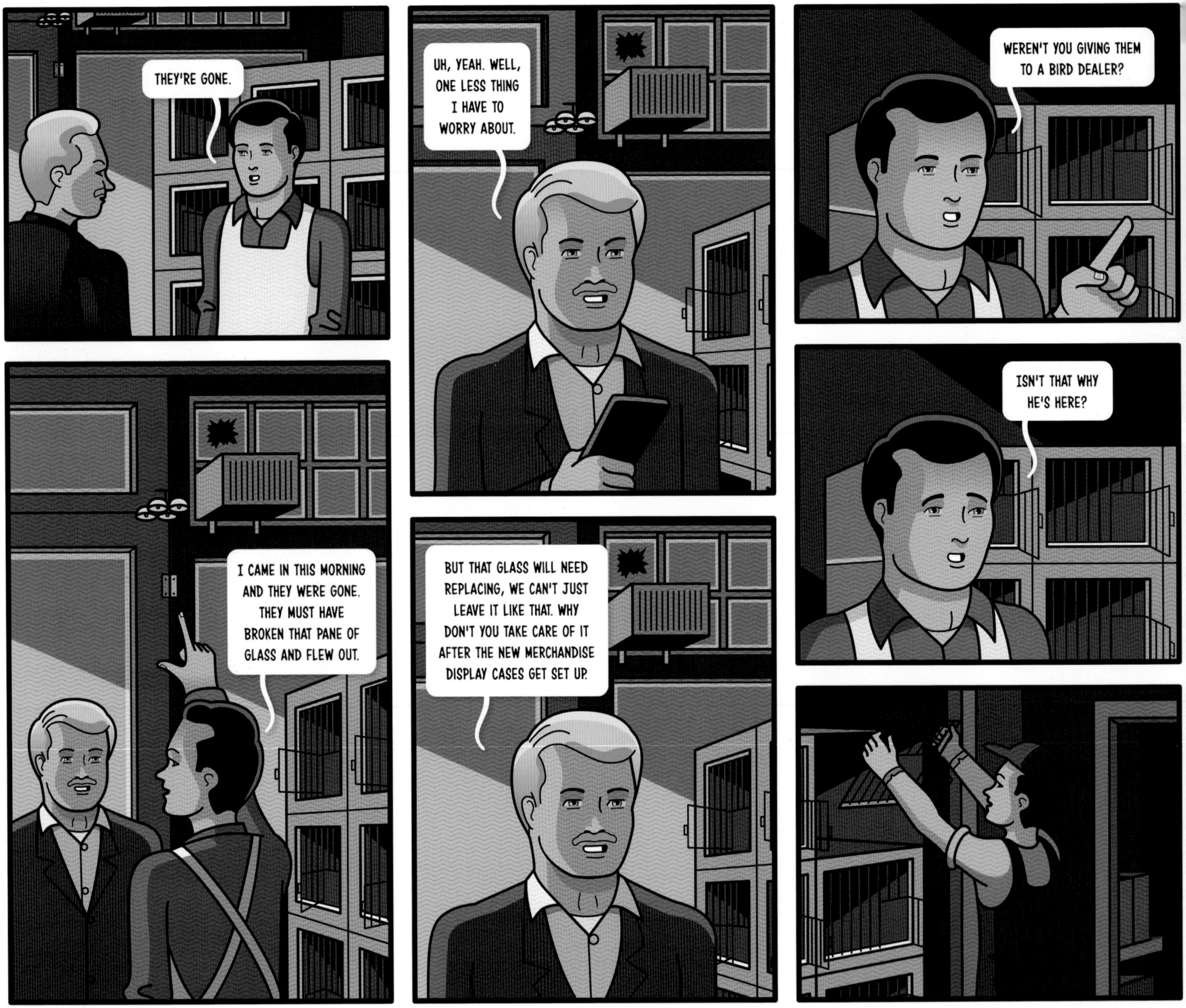
THEY'RE GONE.
I CAME IN THIS MORNING AND THEY WERE GONE. THEY MUST HAVE BROKEN THAT PANE OF GLASS AND FLEW OUT.
UH, YEAH. WELL, ONE LESS THING I HAVE TO WORRY ABOUT.
BUT THAT GLASS WILL NEED REPLACING, WE CAN'T JUST LEAVE IT LIKE THAT. WHY DON'T YOU TAKE CARE OF IT AFTER THE NEW MERCHANDISE DISPLAY CASES GET SET UP.
WEREN'T YOU GIVING THEM TO A BIRD DEALER?
ISN'T THAT WHY HE'S HERE?

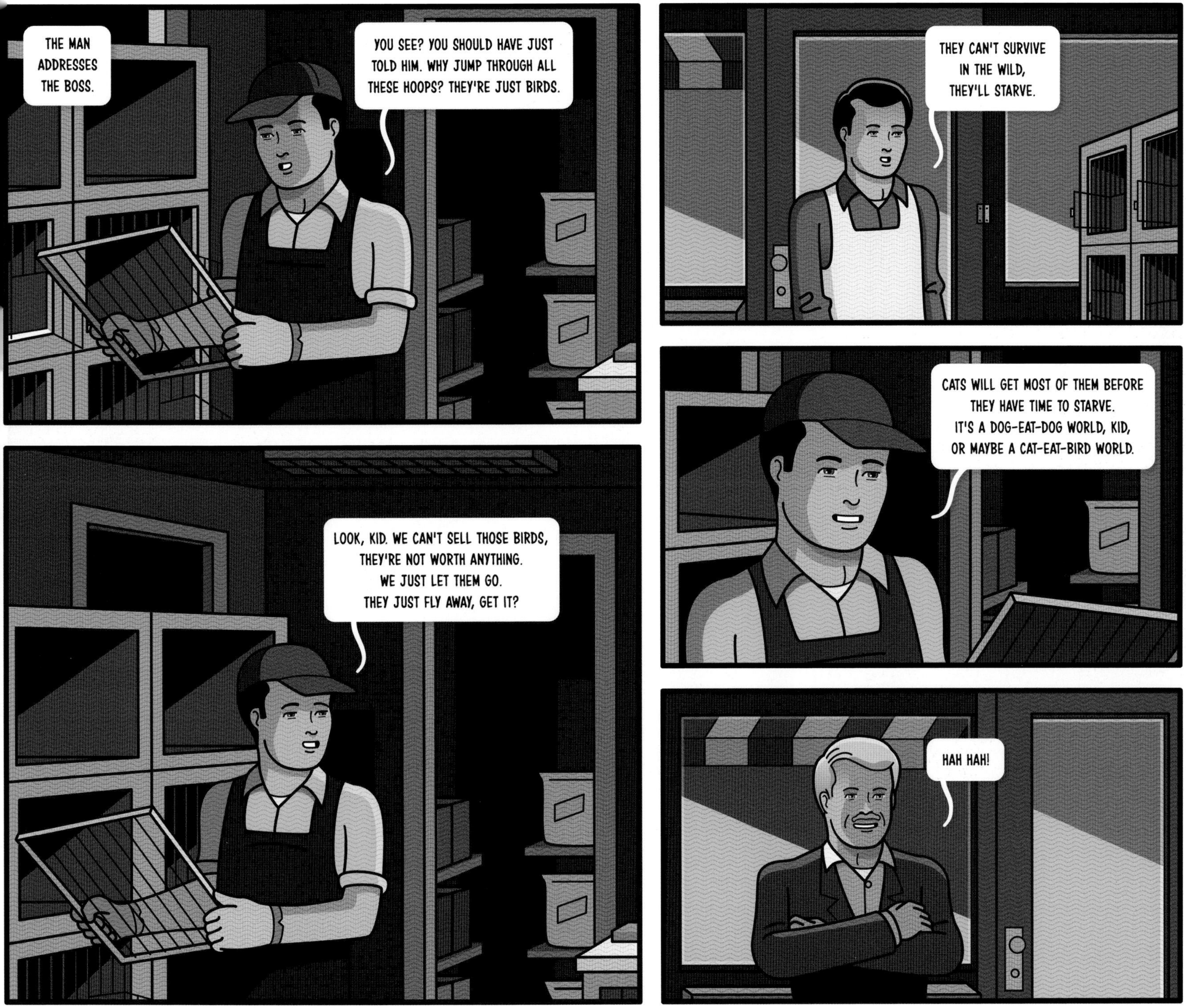
THE MAN ADDRESSES THE BOSS.
YOU SEE? YOU SHOULD HAVE JUST TOLD HIM. WHY JUMP THROUGH ALL THESE HOOPS? THEY'RE JUST BIRDS.
THEY CAN'T SURVIVE IN THE WILD, THEY'LL STARVE.
LOOK, KID. WE CAN'T SELL THOSE BIRDS, THEY'RE NOT WORTH ANYTHING. WE JUST LET THEM GO. THEY JUST FLY AWAY, GET IT?
CATS WILL GET MOST OF THEM BEFORE THEY HAVE TIME TO STARVE. IT'S A DOG-EAT-DOG WORLD, KID, OR MAYBE A CAT-EAT-BIRD WORLD.
HAH HAH!

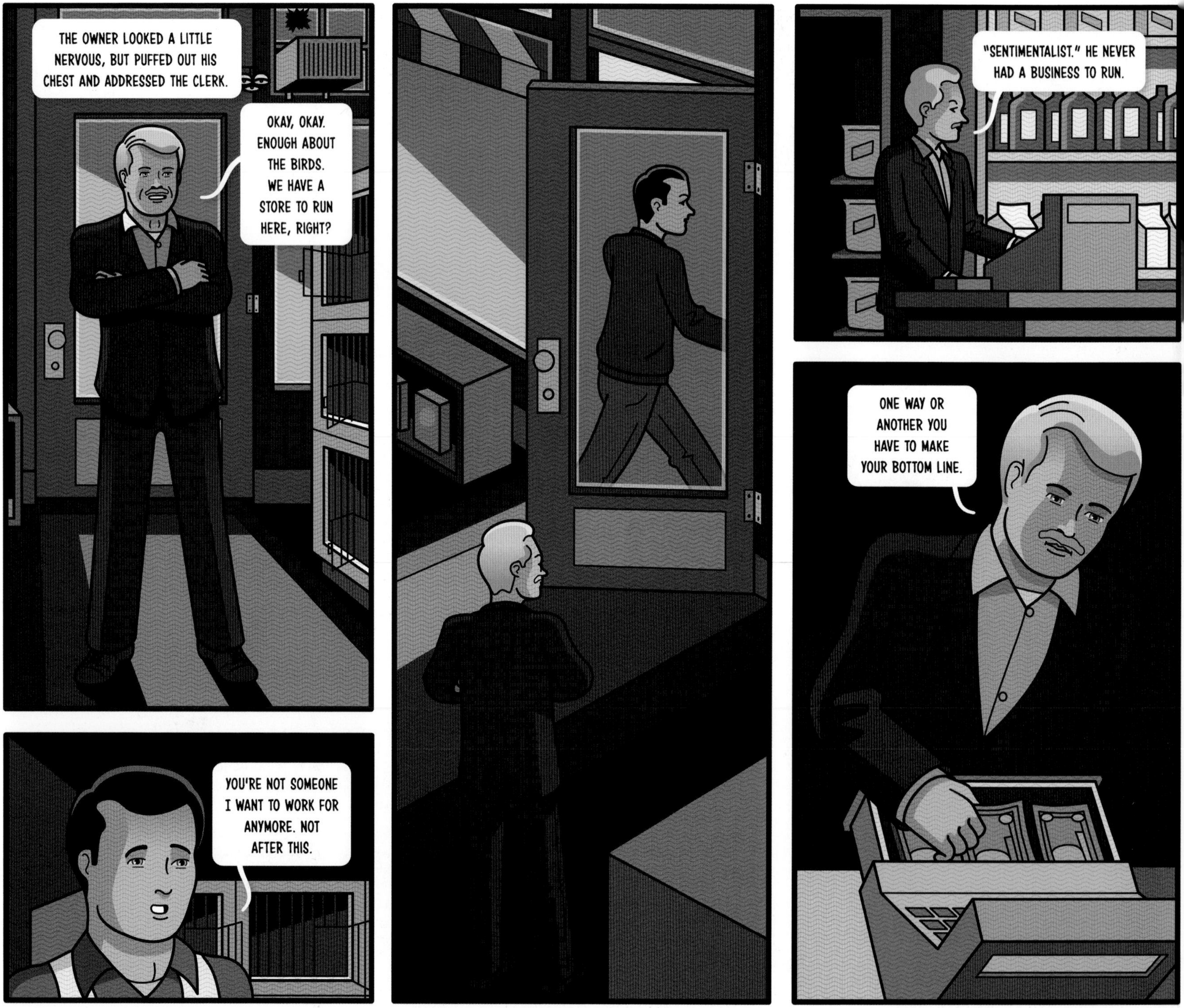
THE OWNER LOOKED A LITTLE NERVOUS, BUT PUFFED OUT HIS CHEST AND ADDRESSED THE CLERK.
OKAY, OKAY. ENOUGH ABOUT THE BIRDS. WE HAVE A STORE TO RUN HERE, RIGHT?
YOU'RE NOT SOMEONE I WANT TO WORK FOR ANYMORE. NOT AFTER THIS.
"SENTIMENTALIST." HE NEVER HAD A BUSINESS TO RUN.
ONE WAY OR ANOTHER YOU HAVE TO MAKE YOUR BOTTOM LINE.

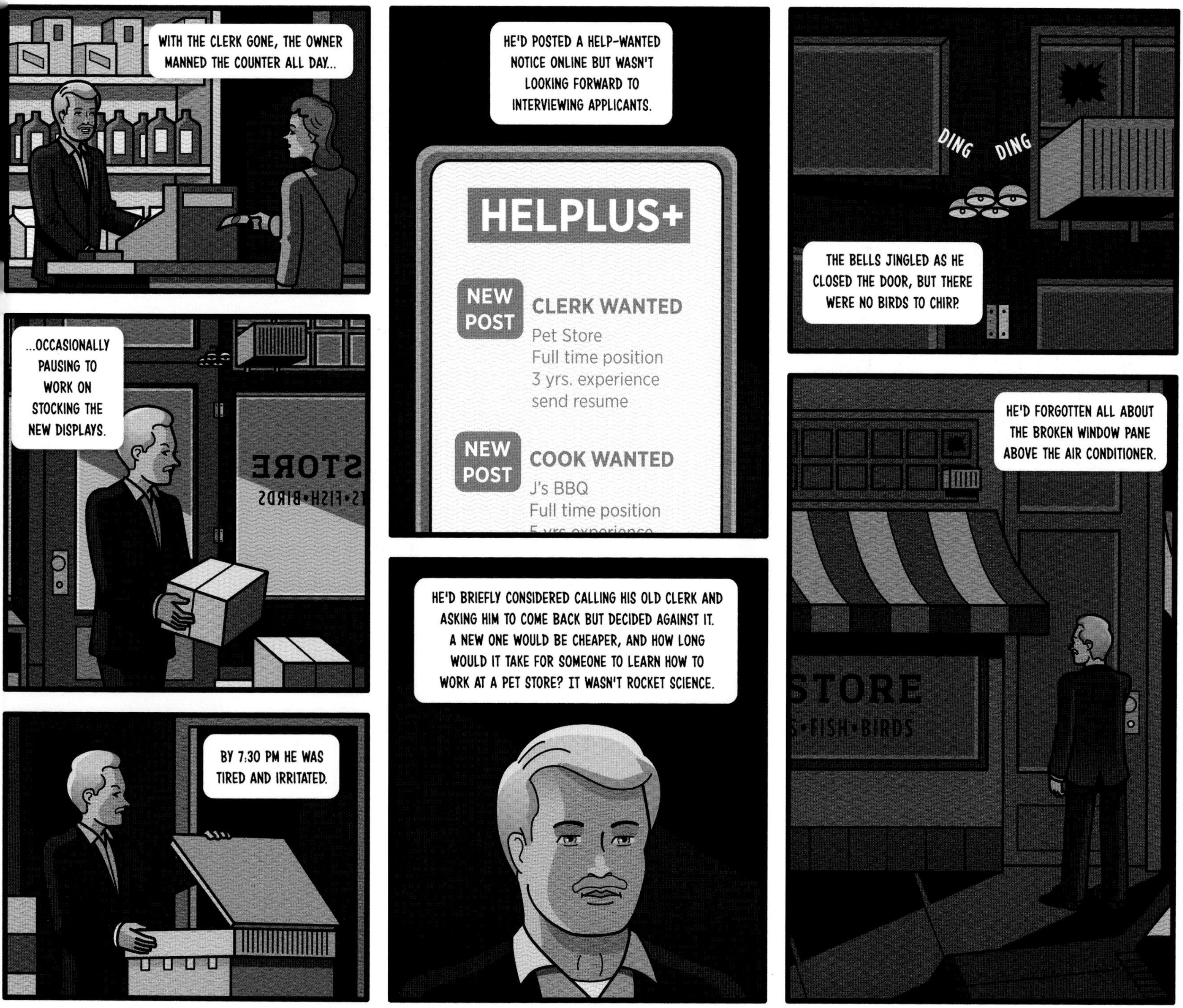
WITH THE CLERK GONE, THE OWNER MANNED THE COUNTER ALL DAY...
...OCCASIONALLY PAUSING TO WORK ON STOCKING THE NEW DISPLAYS.
STORE
BY 7:30 PM HE WAS TIRED AND IRRITATED.
HE'D POSTED A HELP-WANTED NOTICE ONLINE BUT WASN'T LOOKING FORWARD TO INTERVIEWING APPLICANTS.
HELPLUS+
NEW POST
CLERK WANTED
Pet Store
Full time position
3 yrs. experience
send resume
NEW POST
COOK WANTED
J's BBQ
Full time position
HE'D BRIEFLY CONSIDERED CALLING HIS OLD CLERK AND ASKING HIM TO COME BACK BUT DECIDED AGAINST IT. A NEW ONE WOULD BE CHEAPER, AND HOW LONG WOULD IT TAKE FOR SOMEONE TO LEARN HOW TO WORK AT A PET STORE? IT WASN'T ROCKET SCIENCE.
DING DING
THE BELLS JINGLED AS HE CLOSED THE DOOR, BUT THERE WERE NO BIRDS TO CHIRP.
HE'D FORGOTTEN ALL ABOUT THE BROKEN WINDOW PANE ABOVE THE AIR CONDITIONER.
STORE
FISH•BIRDS

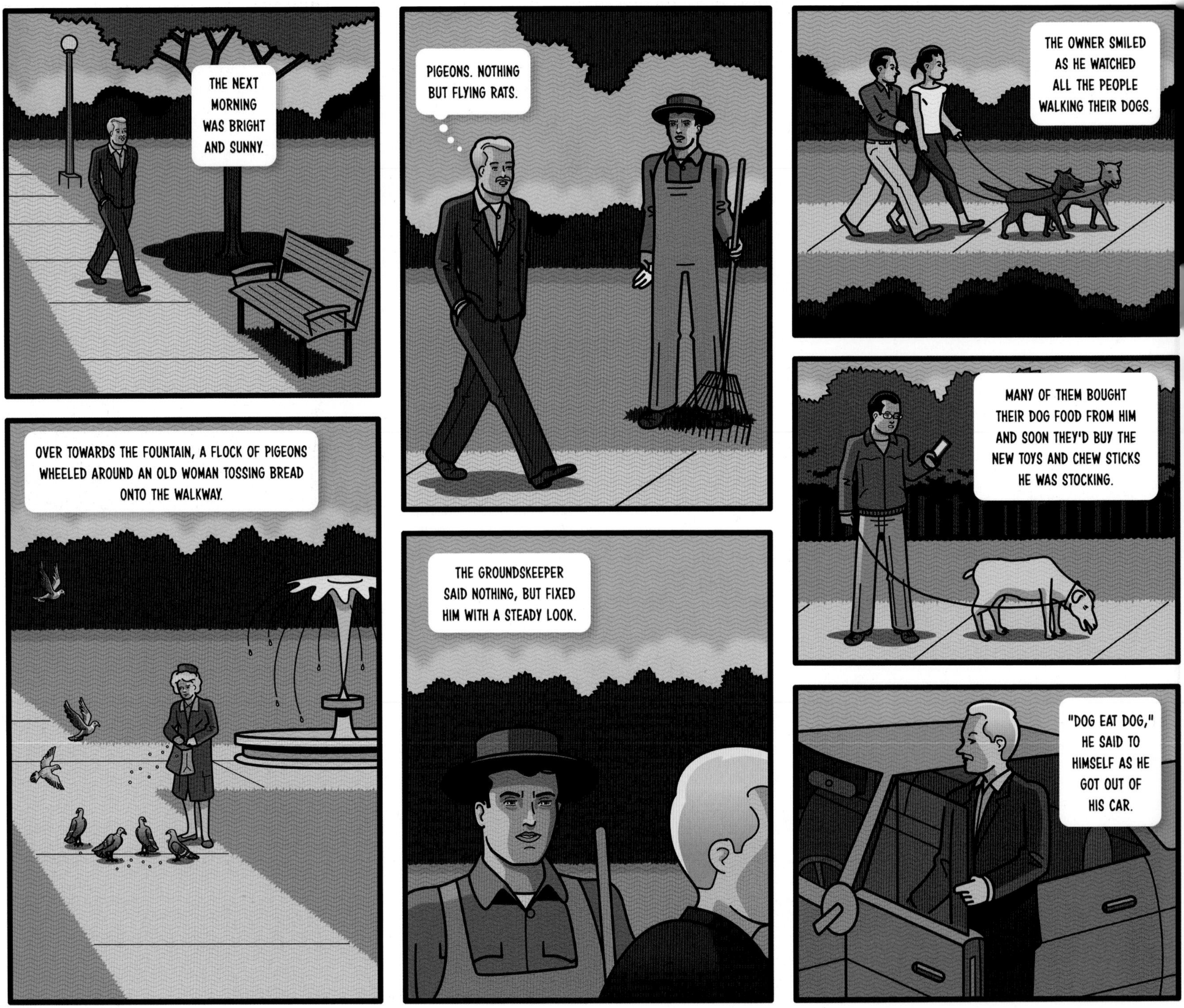
THE NEXT MORNING WAS BRIGHT AND SUNNY.
OVER TOWARDS THE FOUNTAIN, A FLOCK OF PIGEONS WHEELED AROUND AN OLD WOMAN TOSSING BREAD ONTO THE WALKWAY.
PIGEONS. NOTHING BUT FLYING RATS.
THE GROUNDSKEEPER SAID NOTHING, BUT FIXED HIM WITH A STEADY LOOK.
THE OWNER SMILED AS HE WATCHED ALL THE PEOPLE WALKING THEIR DOGS.
MANY OF THEM BOUGHT THEIR DOG FOOD FROM HIM AND SOON THEY'D BUY THE NEW TOYS AND CHEW STICKS HE WAS STOCKING.
"DOG EAT DOG," HE SAID TO HIMSELF AS HE GOT OUT OF HIS CAR.

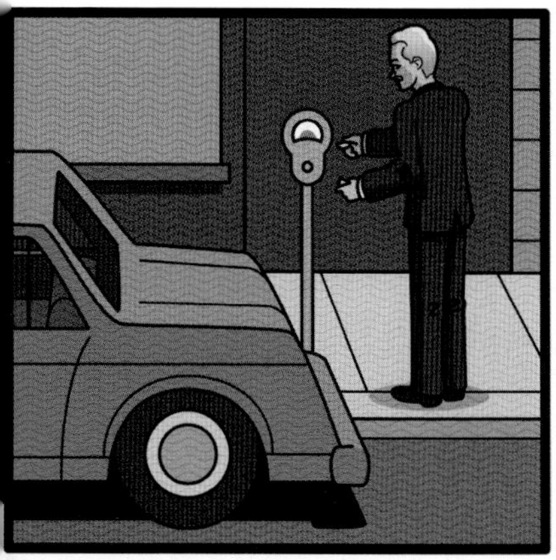

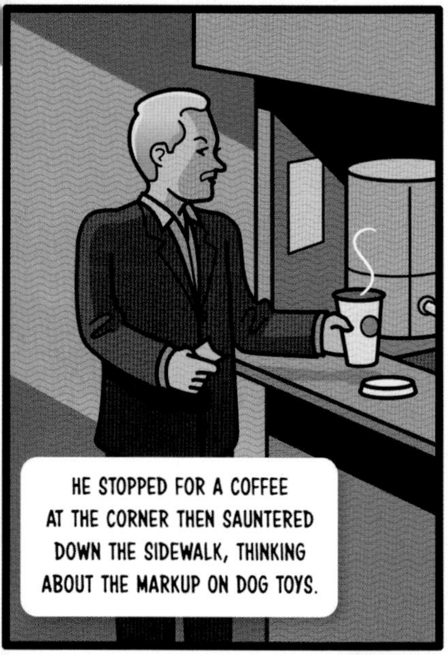
HE STOPPED FOR A COFFEE AT THE CORNER THEN SAUNTERED DOWN THE SIDEWALK, THINKING ABOUT THE MARKUP ON DOG TOYS.

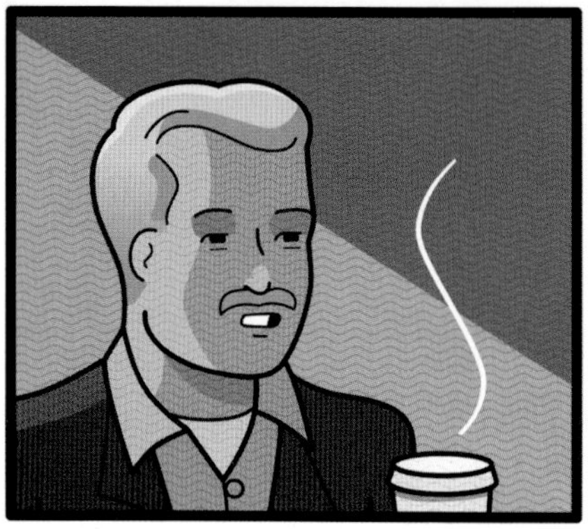

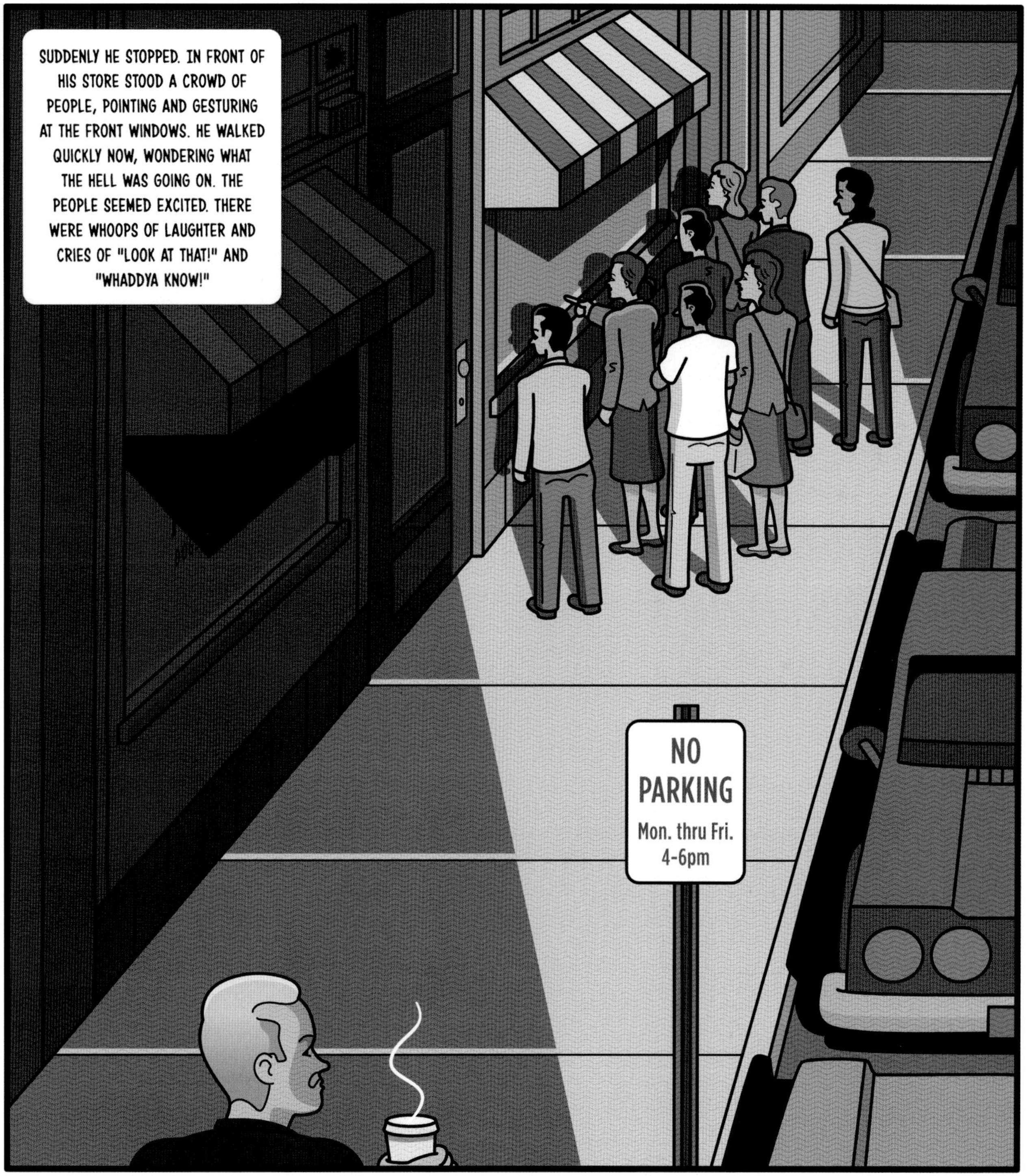
SUDDENLY HE STOPPED. IN FRONT OF HIS STORE STOOD A CROWD OF PEOPLE, POINTING AND GESTURING AT THE FRONT WINDOWS. HE WALKED QUICKLY NOW, WONDERING WHAT THE HELL WAS GOING ON. THE PEOPLE SEEMED EXCITED. THERE WERE WHOOPS OF LAUGHTER AND CRIES OF "LOOK AT THAT!" AND "WHADDYA KNOW!"
NO PARKING
Mon. thru Fri.
4-6pm

HIS HEART POUNDED WITH NERVOUS ANTICIPATION AS HE PUSHED THROUGH THE CROWD.

FINALLY HE GOT IN FRONT OF THE THRONGS AND PEERED INTO THE WINDOW. HE STOOD THERE, FROZEN, STARING.

THE STORE WAS FILLED FROM FLOOR TO CEILING WITH ANIMALS.

NOT PETS, NOT CUDDLY PUPPIES OR KITTENS, BUT WILD ANIMALS, OF ALL KINDS.

STARLINGS AND GRACKLES LINED THE SHELVES, CHEEK AND JOWL WITH PIGEONS, ORIOLES, WRENS AND CROWS. TWO OR THREE HAWKS SAT ON THE LIGHT FIXTURES AND A LARGE OWL PERCHED MOTIONLESS ON THE CASH REGISTER.

RODENTS. HUNDREDS OF THEM, RATS AND MICE, SLINKING ALONG THE EDGES OF THE BASEBOARDS, RUNNING DOWN THE COUNTERS AND OVER THE FISH TANKS, BURROWING INTO THE DOG-FOOD BAGS AND GNAWING ON THE CHEW TOYS.

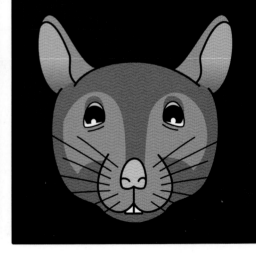

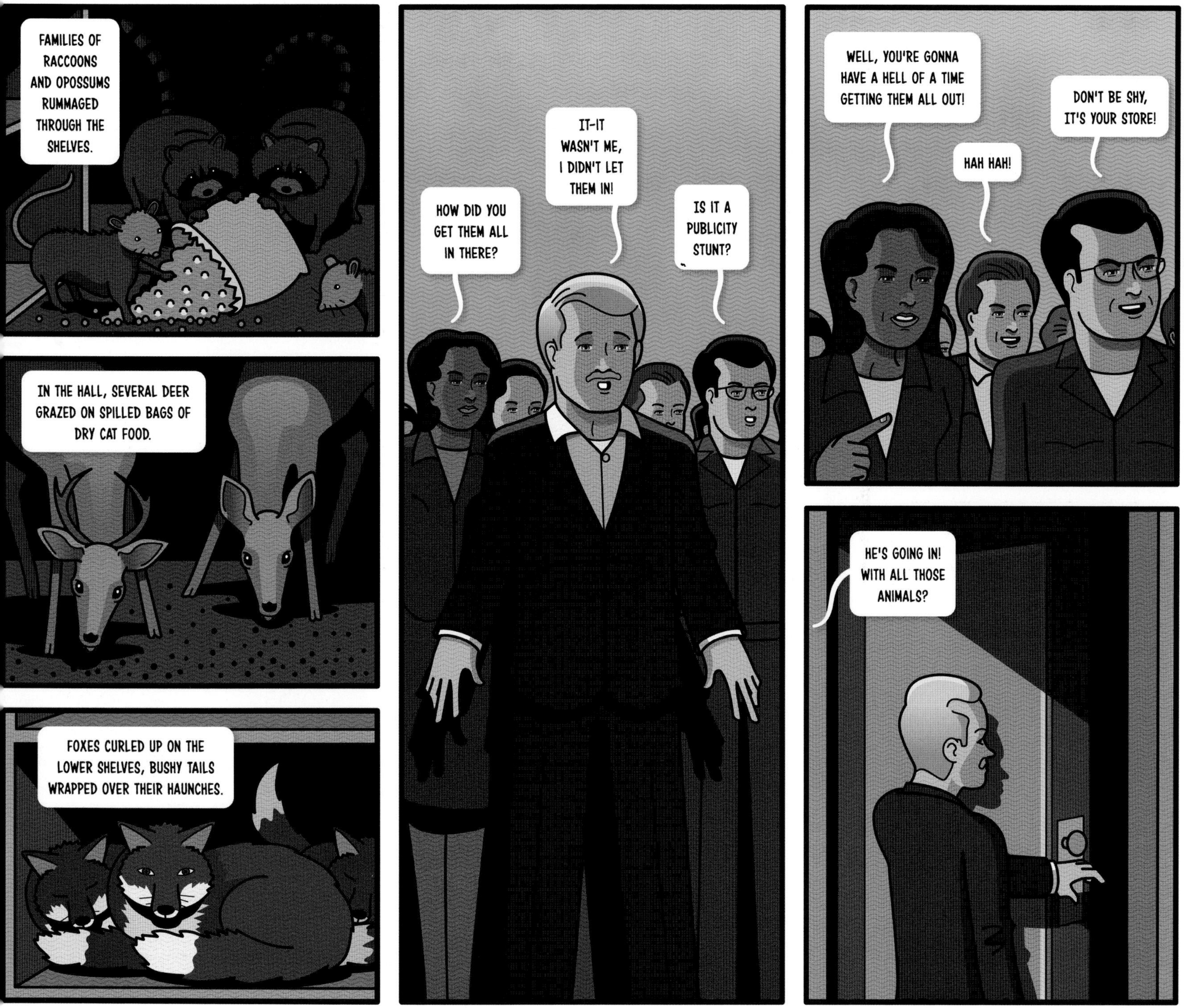
FAMILIES OF RACCOONS AND OPOSSUMS RUMMAGED THROUGH THE SHELVES.
IN THE HALL, SEVERAL DEER GRAZED ON SPILLED BAGS OF DRY CAT FOOD.
FOXES CURLED UP ON THE LOWER SHELVES, BUSHY TAILS WRAPPED OVER THEIR HAUNCHES.
HOW DID YOU GET THEM ALL IN THERE?
IT-IT WASN'T ME, I DIDN'T LET THEM IN!
IS IT A PUBLICITY STUNT?
WELL, YOU'RE GONNA HAVE A HELL OF A TIME GETTING THEM ALL OUT!
HAH HAH!
DON'T BE SHY, IT'S YOUR STORE!
HE'S GOING IN! WITH ALL THOSE ANIMALS?

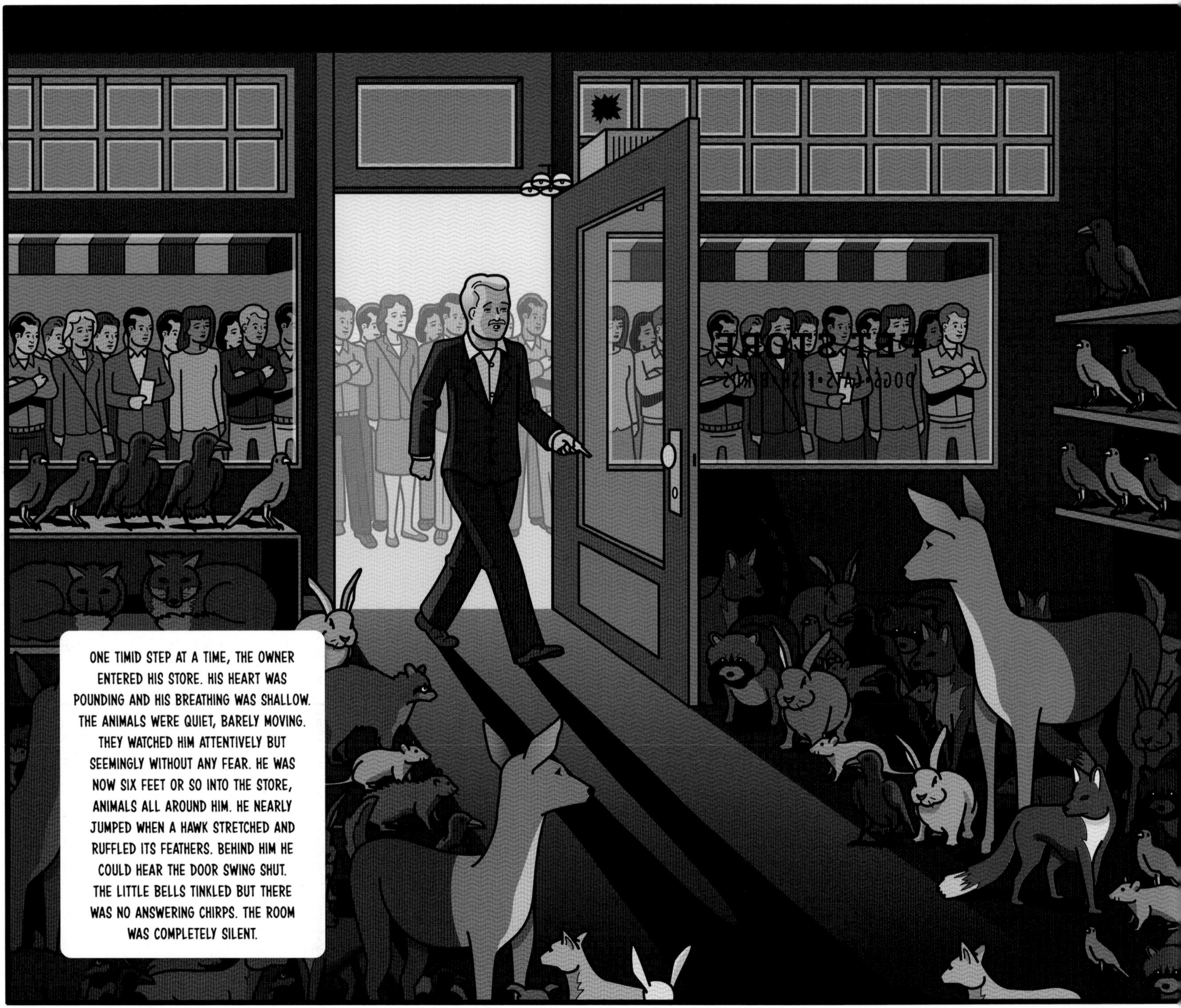
ONE TIMID STEP AT A TIME, THE OWNER ENTERED HIS STORE. HIS HEART WAS POUNDING AND HIS BREATHING WAS SHALLOW. THE ANIMALS WERE QUIET, BARELY MOVING. THEY WATCHED HIM ATTENTIVELY BUT SEEMINGLY WITHOUT ANY FEAR. HE WAS NOW SIX FEET OR SO INTO THE STORE, ANIMALS ALL AROUND HIM. HE NEARLY JUMPED WHEN A HAWK STRETCHED AND RUFFLED ITS FEATHERS. BEHIND HIM HE COULD HEAR THE DOOR SWING SHUT. THE LITTLE BELLS TINKLED BUT THERE WAS NO ANSWERING CHIRPS. THE ROOM WAS COMPLETELY SILENT.

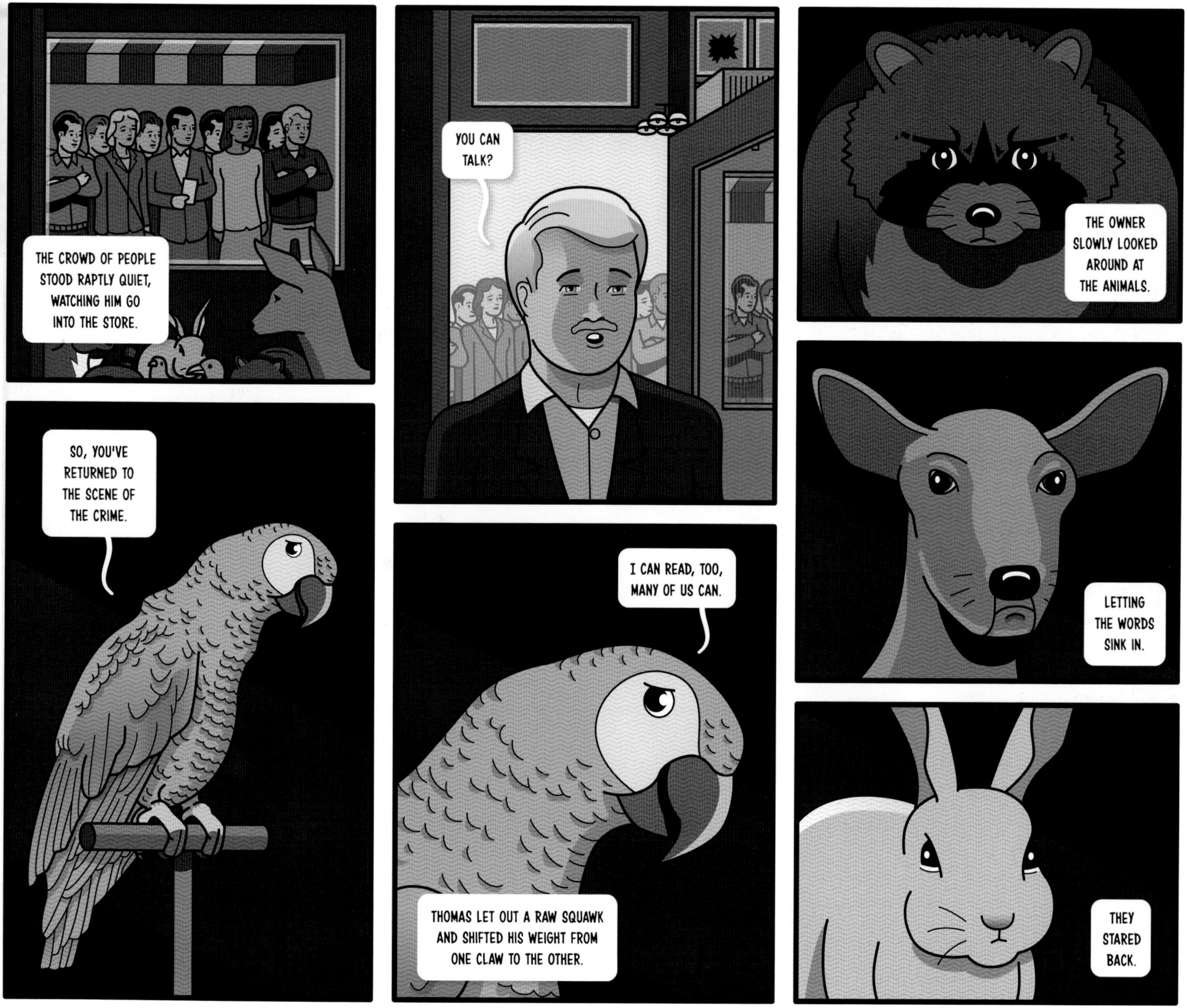
THE CROWD OF PEOPLE STOOD RAPTLY QUIET, WATCHING HIM GO INTO THE STORE.
YOU CAN TALK?
THE OWNER SLOWLY LOOKED AROUND AT THE ANIMALS.
SO, YOU'VE RETURNED TO THE SCENE OF THE CRIME.
I CAN READ, TOO, MANY OF US CAN.
THOMAS LET OUT A RAW SQUAWK AND SHIFTED HIS WEIGHT FROM ONE CLAW TO THE OTHER.
LETTING THE WORDS SINK IN.
THEY STARED BACK.

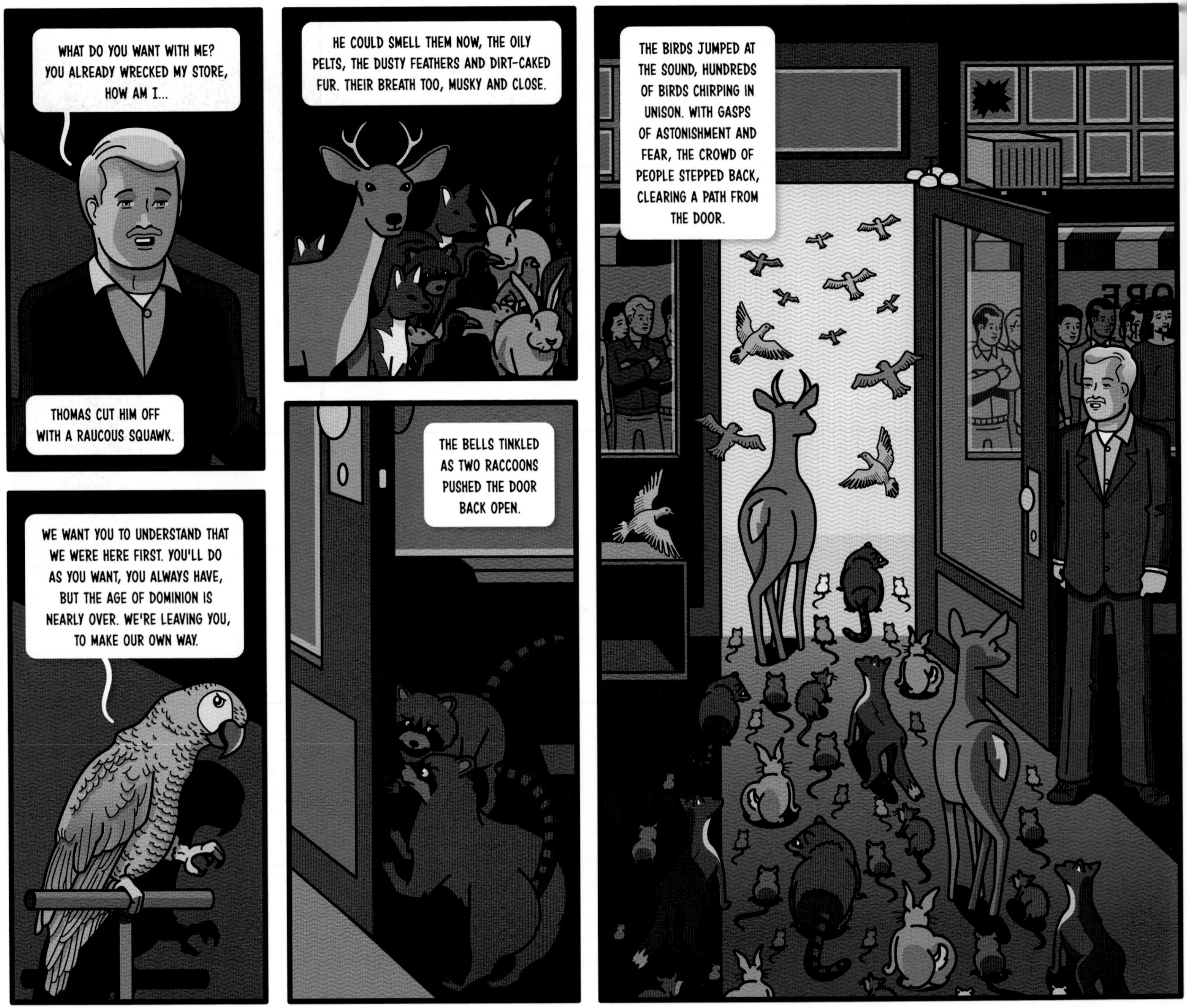
WHAT DO YOU WANT WITH ME? YOU ALREADY WRECKED MY STORE, HOW AM I...
THOMAS CUT HIM OFF WITH A RAUCOUS SQUAWK.
WE WANT YOU TO UNDERSTAND THAT WE WERE HERE FIRST. YOU'LL DO AS YOU WANT, YOU ALWAYS HAVE, BUT THE AGE OF DOMINION IS NEARLY OVER. WE'RE LEAVING YOU, TO MAKE OUR OWN WAY.
HE COULD SMELL THEM NOW, THE OILY PELTS, THE DUSTY FEATHERS AND DIRT-CAKED FUR. THEIR BREATH TOO, MUSKY AND CLOSE.
THE BELLS TINKLED AS TWO RACCOONS PUSHED THE DOOR BACK OPEN.
THE BIRDS JUMPED AT THE SOUND, HUNDREDS OF BIRDS CHIRPING IN UNISON. WITH GASPS OF ASTONISHMENT AND FEAR, THE CROWD OF PEOPLE STEPPED BACK, CLEARING A PATH FROM THE DOOR.

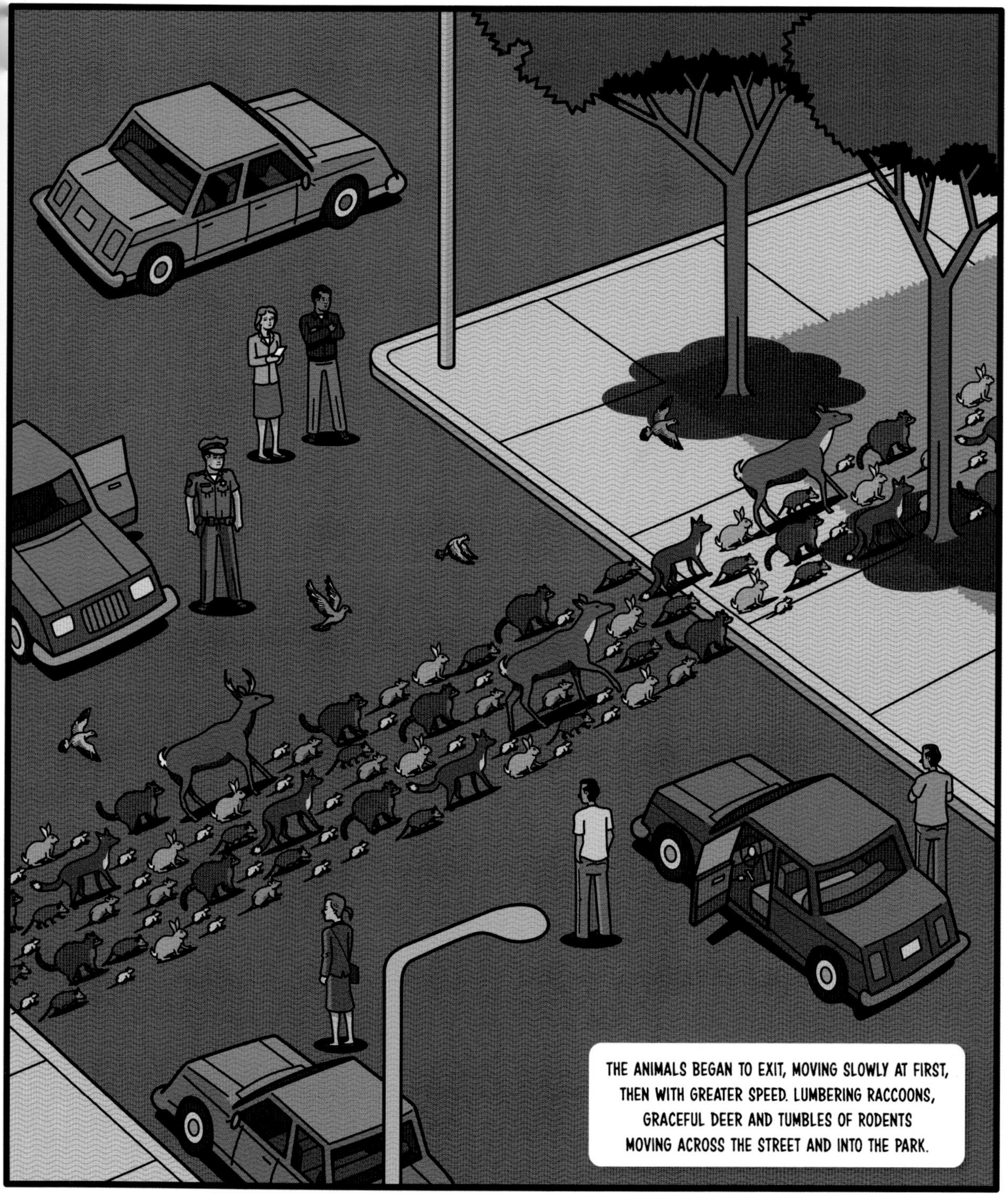
THE ANIMALS BEGAN TO EXIT, MOVING SLOWLY AT FIRST, THEN WITH GREATER SPEED. LUMBERING RACCOONS, GRACEFUL DEER AND TUMBLES OF RODENTS MOVING ACROSS THE STREET AND INTO THE PARK.

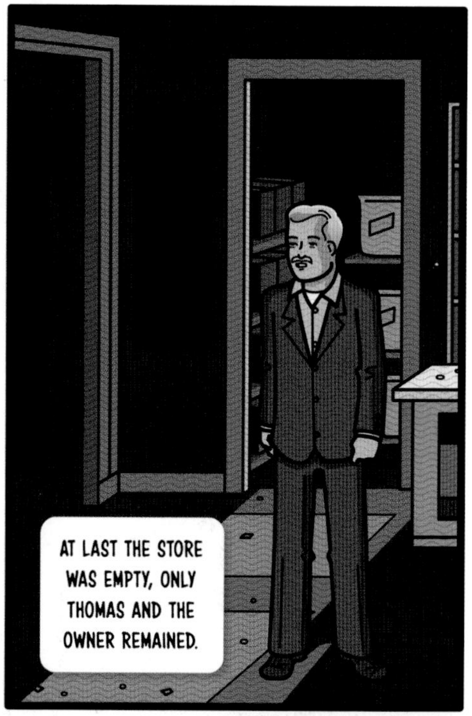
AT LAST THE STORE WAS EMPTY, ONLY THOMAS AND THE OWNER REMAINED.

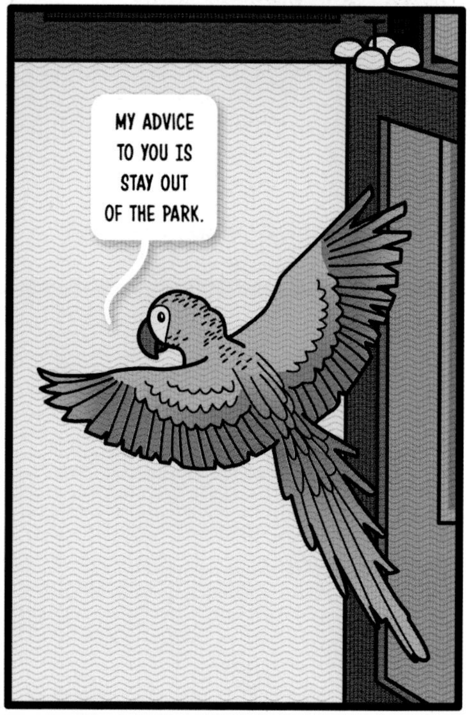
MY ADVICE TO YOU IS STAY OUT OF THE PARK.

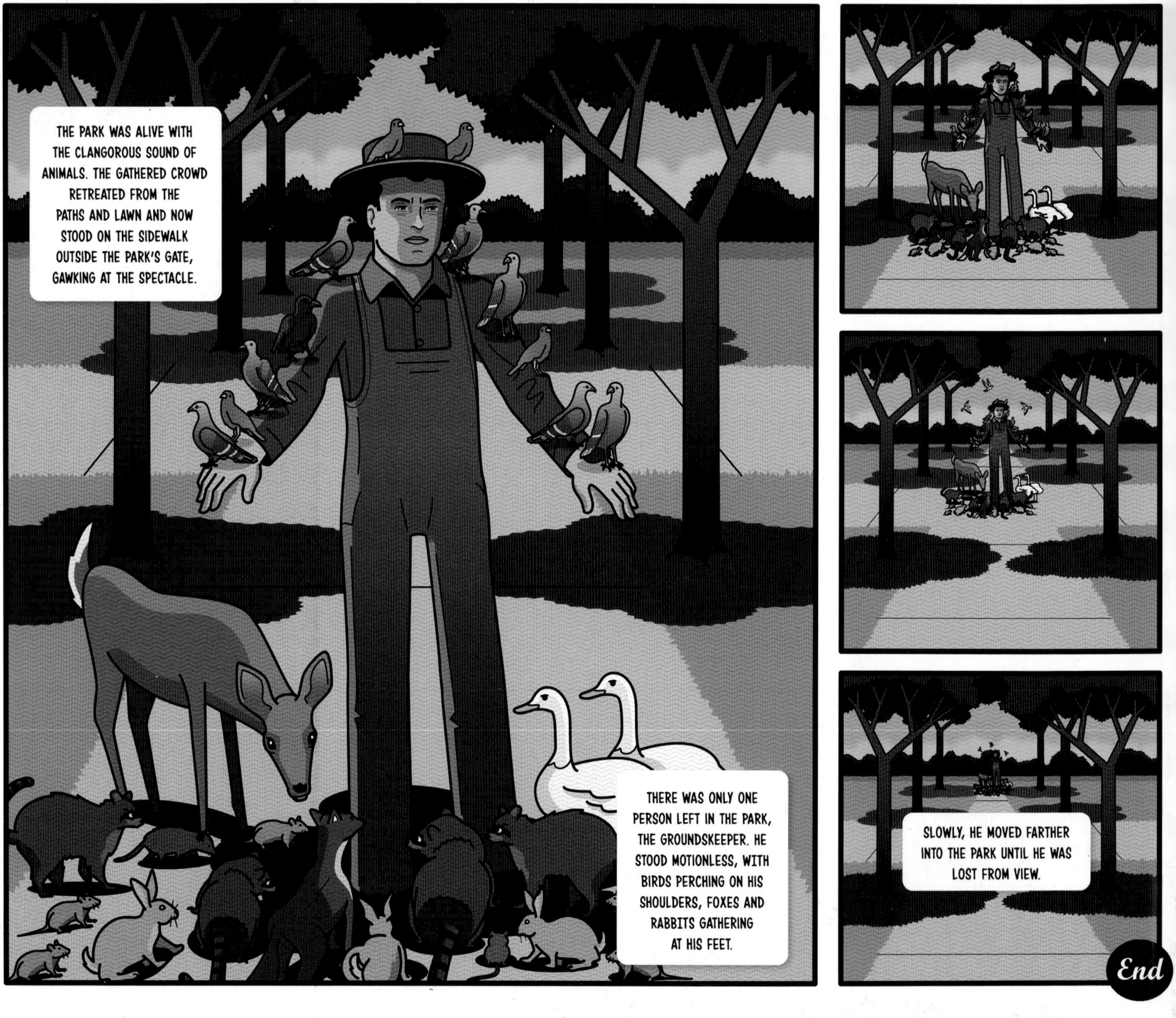
THE PARK WAS ALIVE WITH THE CLANGOROUS SOUND OF ANIMALS. THE GATHERED CROWD RETREATED FROM THE PATHS AND LAWN AND NOW STOOD ON THE SIDEWALK OUTSIDE THE PARK'S GATE, GAWKING AT THE SPECTACLE.
THERE WAS ONLY ONE PERSON LEFT IN THE PARK, THE GROUNDSKEEPER. HE STOOD MOTIONLESS, WITH BIRDS PERCHING ON HIS SHOULDERS, FOXES AND RABBITS GATHERING AT HIS FEET.
SLOWLY, HE MOVED FARTHER INTO THE PARK UNTIL HE WAS LOST FROM VIEW.
End